BREAK ME

ALSO BY TIFFANY SNOW

BREAK ME

A CORRUPTED HEARTS NOVEL

TIFFANY SNOW

Montlake
Romance

Published by Montlake Romance, Seattle
www.apub.com

Amazon, the Amazon logo, and Montlake Romance are trademarks of Amazon.com, Inc., or its affiliates.

ISBN-13: 9781503943681
ISBN-10: 1503943682

Cover design by Eileen Carey

Printed in the United States of America

For Jessica Poore.
You make Montlake a family.

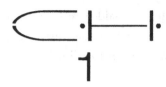

1

O. M. G.

I turned slowly in front of the full-length mirror.

I looked *fantastic!*

I smoothed the fitted bodice of my high-neck halter dress. Black satin wrapped around my neck, flowing into black-on-black horizontal stripes that ended just under my breasts. The fabric changed to a shimmery gold with vertical black stripes extending down the skirt. It was sleeveless and fit perfectly. The designer off Etsy who'd made it had done an incredible job. The light glinted off the subtle gold tones and the skirt flared in a perfect bell to my ankles.

The doorbell rang and I nervously adjusted my hat, turning it slightly until it was just right. Tugging on silver gloves that went past my elbow and halfway up my arm, I then slipped on a pair of matching gold ballet slipper flats and hurried through the living room to the front door, swinging it open just as the bell rang again.

"Happy Hallo—" My voice trailed away in dismay. "What are you wearing?" I blurted.

Jackson Cooper—my erstwhile boss and current boyfriend—stood in my doorway, eyeing me with the same look of shock that I was sure was on my face.

"I'm wearing a tux," he said, gesturing to his attire—a gorgeous black tuxedo with a blindingly white shirt, perfectly tied bow tie, and black shoes that shone even in the dim light. "What the hell are *you* wearing?"

"A dress," I said, maybe a little defensively. Okay, a lot defensively. I was starting to be a bit concerned that I'd misinterpreted what Jackson had meant when I'd asked what kind of party we were going to on Halloween. "I'm a dalek."

"I can see that," he said, gesturing to my hat, a gold dome complete with knobs and eye stalk. "But *why* are you dressed as a dalek?"

"It's a Halloween party, isn't it? I asked you and you said, 'Yes, it'll be fancy, so dress up.' That's what I did."

"China . . ."

That's me. China Mack. Well, sort of. Mack was a shortened version of my middle name—Mackenzie—not my real last name, which was so long it had proven unpronounceable by 99 percent of the people who tried. In school, I'd never been able to fit my whole name in those little bubbles on standardized tests. Not that I'd had to take many of those. Once my IQ was measured at one hundred seventy-five—genius range—I'd never taken another one of those tests. Instead, I'd been fast-tracked and had graduated MIT at the age of nineteen with two undergrad degrees in computer science and biological engineering plus a master's in engineering. That was four years ago.

Jackson passed a hand over his eyes while I bit my lip, awkwardly switching the wire whisk I was holding to the other hand. The gold, palm-sized, half-moon-shaped balls attached up and down the length of my skirt banged against the door as I stepped back. The noise made me wince, as did Jackson's sigh.

"You do that a lot," I said.

"I do what a lot?"

"Sigh." He said nothing, so I continued. "I mean, it's perfectly natural. Your body even requires sighing. When a person needs a breathing machine, sighs have to be programmed into the ventilator or the patient will suffer from oxygen deprivation."

His lips twitched. "Is that so?"

I nodded . . . and my hat slid off. Jackson caught it neatly before it hit the floor. "Thanks," I said, taking it from him. The two little knobs on the side looked a little like Shrek to me, but it went with the costume. "I guess I should go change."

"Probably a good idea."

"This'll make a great cosplay costume for ComicCon, though," I said, turning my back to him. "Unzip me?"

"Mmmm . . . yes, please . . ." This was followed by the slow lowering of my zipper and the touch of Jackson's lips to the back of my neck. Suddenly I wasn't sorry at all that I needed to change.

Twenty minutes later, Jackson was buttoning his shirt and tucking the tails back into his slacks while I stood in front of my closet clad in my favorite Victoria's Secret Dream Angels panty and bra set in dove-gray lace with white trim. Hands on hips, I surveyed my clothing.

"I have a problem."

"Just one?"

I wasn't the best at inferring whether someone was joking or not—one of my many social inadequacies—so I turned to glance at Jackson. He was grinning at me and looking too sexy for a man who'd just given me three orgasms in a row. But the smile meant he was teasing.

"Yes, just one at the moment, but it's a big one." I gestured to my clothes. "I don't have anything to wear."

"Surely you have a dress, a skirt, something," he said.

I shook my head. "I own a TARDIS dress, a *Star Trek*—the Original Series—Uhura minidress, and Princess Éowyn's wedding gown from *Return of the King*."

"If you own Princess Leia's metal bikini, we're skipping the party."

"That chafes," I said absently, turning around to poke through my closet again. Did I have anything in the back that I'd forgotten?

"We'll revisit that later," he said. "What about Mia?"

"She's out at a friend's house," I replied. "What about her?" I failed to see how my niece's presence would alleviate my problem.

"I meant, what about her clothes?" Jackson asked. "You two are about the same size. She probably has something you can wear."

I gave Jackson a look. "She wears like a size two. Besides, I can't just go wear someone else's clothes. Not only is it rude, it's unsanitary."

"I'm sure she washes her clothes," he said, reaching for my hand.

"But she washes her yoga pants with her fleece," I protested, obediently letting him lead me to my niece's bedroom, which used to be my storage room before she moved in a couple of months ago.

"So?"

"So . . . everyone knows that if you wash fleece with something stretchy, lint becomes forever embedded in the stretchy fabric. She should wash her yoga pants with other stretchy workout wear, though why she wears workout clothes just to sit on the couch and watch television is beyond me."

Jackson opened Mia's closet and began searching through it. Selecting a garment, he pulled it out and held it up in front of me. "That should work."

I looked down. "But it's really short . . ." As in miniskirt short.

"Yes."

"It's October. I'll freeze."

"No, you won't. I'll keep you warm."

I opened my mouth to tell him he couldn't physically fulfill such a promise, but the look in his eye and the set of his jaw told me his patience might be wearing thin. I took the dress.

"Okay." I unzipped it, stepped in, and pulled the black fabric up my legs, shimmying to get it over my hips. "She shouldn't even own a dress like this. She's only fifteen."

"Kids nowadays," Jackson said, and I was glad to see him smiling slightly again.

I pushed my arms through the holes and turned around so he could zip me. "It barely covers my . . . tush."

"Your *tush*?" he teased with a laugh.

"Well, what else are you supposed to call it? *Butt* sounds vulgar. *Ass* is worse. *Rear* sounds like I'm a granny." I looked over my shoulder at him. "What do *you* call it?"

His hand settled on the body part in question and squeezed. "I call it awesome," he said softly, his lips by my ear.

Though he hadn't really answered my question, I wasn't dumb enough not to appreciate a heartfelt compliment on my . . . "Posterior?" I tested out. Jackson just laughed.

"That's even worse. Come on. Let's go."

I had to change my shoes and ended up wearing black Converse sneakers because I didn't own anything other than tennis shoes. I'd shopped specially for the gold flats for my dalek dress, which I didn't think went with the black dress I was now wearing. I wasn't a fashion maven, but it made sense that my shoe color should match my dress.

Jackson looked me up and down, making me do a twofer of my nervous tics: push my glasses up my nose and tighten my ponytail. My hair was so thick and long that I almost always wore it up just to keep it out of my way.

"Well? Will this do?" I asked, though since he'd picked out the dress, he had only himself to blame if I still wasn't dressed appropriately.

The corner of his mouth lifted in a half smile. "It's perfect."

"I still think it's pointless to have a Halloween party that you can't dress in costume for," I grumbled, pulling my coat out of the closet.

"I'll take that under advisement."

The house where he took me was too huge to be called a mere home. Three stories with towering columns in front, it hearkened back to the days of Southern belles and mint juleps, elaborate even by Raleigh, North Carolina standards. A valet greeted us when we pulled up and took the car keys from Jackson.

"Whose house is this again?" I asked as we ascended the stairs to the front door. Lights sparkled at the windows and I could hear music inside as well as voices, talking and laughing.

"My erstwhile business partner," he said, taking my hand. "Philip Jacobs. He was the principal investor for my first company, SocialSpeak."

SocialSpeak, the social networking website and app that Jackson had built. Two years after it had become common parlance and boasted a user base of nearly a billion people, he'd sold it for a cool $2.1 billion.

"So you have a lot to thank him for," I said.

"It goes both ways. He was rich before and he's even richer now, because of me."

Something in Jackson's voice was different and I frowned as I glanced up at him. His lips were pressed together and his jaw was set in a grim line. "He wasn't happy you made him richer?" I asked.

"He didn't want to sell. I did and I had controlling interest. I wanted to get the capital for Cysnet. SocialSpeak was never anything more to me than a way to make money. Philip saw it as a lot more than that."

"If there's bad blood between you two, then why are we going to his party?" I asked as we stopped in front of the door.

"Because it was just business. He's a businessman, first and foremost. We're still friends, despite our differences."

I was distracted from asking anything more about Philip because the door swung open to reveal a butler. Looming over us, he had to be more than six five, his square head twice the size of mine. His eyes were deep set with thick black eyebrows, and his salt-and-pepper hair was combed straight down over his forehead.

"Good evening, Mr. Cooper," he intoned, his voice resonating through the foyer. He didn't smile. I wasn't sure he even knew how. "Please come in."

I stared up at him, openmouthed, my feet rooted to the floor.

"Thank you, Ruskin," Jackson replied, dragging me past the butler. I craned my neck around Jackson to keep my eyes on the giant.

"You said it wasn't a costume party," I hissed to Jackson.

"He always looks like that," he replied.

"He always looks like Lurch?"

"Yep."

And people said *I* was weird.

The mansion had its own ballroom and I was again reminded of antebellum balls as an orchestra played while dancers swirled around the polished marble floor. I felt immediately underdressed as I took in the long gowns and high heels adorning the women who passed. Their hairdos were upswept and they wore more than a handful of diamonds and other glittering gems.

"How long do we have to stay?" I asked, tugging at the hem of my dress. Crowds weren't my thing. People weren't either, generally speaking. Computers were so much easier.

"We just got here. You want to leave already? I thought you'd enjoy going out for a change." Taking my hand, he threaded my arm through his and led me toward the bar set up in one corner.

"I like staying in. Friday night is old movie night." I was a creature of habit—deeply ingrained habits—that kept me feeling in control even when so much was beyond my control. I liked knowing what to expect. Surprises weren't in my vocabulary.

"Lots of people go out on Halloween," he replied. "Think of it as an expected societal convention. Either this . . . or stay at home and hand out candy to strangers all night."

I frowned. He had a point, damn it. Those little shits hit up my neighborhood *hard*, too.

"A glass of chardonnay and a Glenfiddich 15 on the rocks," he told the bartender. He handed me the wine. "Time to put on a smile and pretend to have fun."

I obediently stretched my lips into my best fake smile, which wasn't very good. Jackson grimaced.

"We've got to work on that," he teased. I stuck my tongue out at him, which I should've thought better of because his eyes immediately darkened and I knew his thoughts had jumped straight into the gutter.

I pointed a finger at him. "I'm not having sex with you in a closet here."

"Their bathrooms are really spacious."

"Eww. No." I sipped my wine, enjoying our banter. Jackson was so easy to talk to. He "got" me, all my weird hang-ups and quirks included. It also didn't hurt that the sex was fantastic. I once had told him we must have what was referred to in common parlance as *chemistry*.

"We've got chemistry, physics, and fucking biology," he'd replied before kissing me.

Although I'd wanted to correct him, I'd realized in the nick of time that he'd been giving me a hyperbolic compliment, plus an endearment. So I'd concentrated on the kissing rather than grammatical interpretations of physical attraction.

Just then, Jackson reached out and tugged me toward him, turning me and sliding his arm behind my back, nestling me into his side. A flash went off, blinding me, then three more in rapid succession.

"Thank you, Mr. Cooper." Two photographers with cameras that looked more complex than necessary for this day and age moved on, talking to one another and scanning the crowd for what I assumed were more famous faces.

"What the heck was that?" I blurted, blinking to get the black spots out of my vision.

"Just the press, society pages, that sort of thing," he said. "It happens sometimes."

Oh yeah. Jackson's multiyear achievement of gracing *Forbes* Ten Most Eligible Billionaires list meant people liked to see what fortune-hunter model he was currently dating. Except I fell into neither the "fortune hunter" nor "model" categories.

"No one's taken our picture before," I said.

"We've yet to be somewhere very public."

"We eat Thai every Wednesday."

"Carryout."

I had no retort, so I took another sip of wine. Okay, maybe more of a gulp than a delicate sip. I'd seen the women Jackson had been with before: Victoria's Secret Angel, a tennis pro, a Hollywood starlet.

"What are the papers going to say about me?" I asked quietly, watching the couples swirl past us. The music floated through the air, the chandeliers were down low . . . aesthetically speaking, it was very romantic in the cliché popularized version of the term. But I also found that I liked it. And I liked being there with Jackson. His arm was warm and solid against my back.

"It doesn't matter what they say. They always vilify whoever I'm with. Just ignore them."

Awesome. "I thought I'd left public ridicule behind with high school."

"Society pages are *Mean Girls* on steroids."

Ruskin-the-scary-butler approached before I could note how impressive it was that Jackson had seen the chick flick *Mean Girls*. "Mr. Cooper," he said with grave importance. "Mr. Jacobs would like to speak to you in the library. Will you follow me?"

"Of course."

Ruskin's dark eyes slid to me. "Privately," he added.

Jackson glanced down at me. "You'll be all right on your own for a few minutes?"

Immediate panic set in at being left by myself in a ballroom full of strangers, but I forced my fake smile. "You bet!" I said, way too chipper. He and I both winced, then he brushed a kiss to my lips.

"I'll be quick. Finish your wine."

I watched him follow Ruskin until they were swallowed by people. I looked around, shifting my weight self-consciously from one foot to another, and pushed my glasses up my nose. I felt as though my life preserver had just deflated and left me adrift in a cold, apathetic ocean.

Wine helps, though, as I'd come to learn. Why hadn't I drunk more often before now? I finished the glass in two large gulps, then got a refill from the bartender.

"You can top that off," I said when he stopped pouring at half a glass. He eyed me, but added more of the golden liquid. "Thanks." If I finished this off, chances were Jackson could drop me in the middle of Times Square on New Year's Eve and I wouldn't care.

"Excuse me, aren't you accompanying Jackson Cooper this evening?"

The voice came from right behind me, startling me so much that I dribbled down my dress and choked. I turned around, coughing. "Uh-huh," I managed, patting my dress with a little cocktail napkin the bartender had given me. "Who are you?"

The woman was petite and had glasses, too, which immediately made me feel a kindred spirit with her. Then I saw the nametag and "Press." Oh no.

"Oh, um, I mean—" I began.

"Because that's awesome." She looked me up and down and started jotting on a little notepad, though where she'd produced it from, I had no idea. Her dress was tiny and tight, like mine. "What's your name?"

I had the feeling I was doing something wrong, but didn't know how to refuse a direct question with an obvious answer. "Um . . . China. China Mack."

"China . . . Mack . . ." she said, drawing out the syllables as she wrote. "And you're Jackson's date tonight?"

"He's my boyfriend," I corrected her. Her eyebrows flew up.

"Really? How long have you been dating?"

"A couple of months." I looked around, trying to think of a way to politely extricate myself from the conversation.

"And what do you do, China?"

Okay, that was a tougher question. It wasn't like I could say, *"I work for a secret government agency called Vigilance, created by the president himself with software I helped write. We keep profiles of every person in the United States and our software assigns values and probability as to whether they are or will potentially become a terrorist. I'm 1984 come to life and taken to the nth degree. And if you tell anyone this, you're likely to wind up missing-presumed-dead."*

"I write software," I said. I was desperate to get away, so before she could ask any more questions, I said, "Sorry. Gotta go."

Weaving my way through the crowd, I made my way to a doorway and sidled through it, hoping I wasn't going somewhere I shouldn't, though at the moment, I hardly cared. So many people around and it felt as if they were all looking at me. It was stifling, like I couldn't breathe.

The hallway was dark and quiet, and I immediately felt better. I let the tall door swing softly shut behind me. Maybe I'd just walk around and hang out for a while, then text Jackson and see if he was finished with his meeting.

The hallway seemed endless, with periodic sconces giving it a dim glow. No doubt Lurch felt right at home here, especially on All Hallows' Eve . . . not that I was suspicious or anything. Historically, tonight was merely the night before All Saints' Day, which, as I wasn't Catholic, I didn't observe anyway. Neither was I Irish, where I'd celebrate the Celtic tradition of Samhain. Yet all those thoughts didn't stop the goose bumps erupting on my skin or the shiver that ran down my back.

I drifted farther from the party, the sound of music and voices fading more with each step I took. I passed several doors, all closed and rather forbidding, but again—probably just my imagination. Then I crossed by one that was open a scant inch and I heard voices.

Stopping to listen was tacky and rude, and if I hadn't heard Jackson's name, I would've passed right by.

". . . Cooper's not going to go down without a fight. I have my people in place, but his resources are vast and formidable."

Another man's voice responded. "It doesn't matter. I have an excellent source that will ensure he won't be able to touch us, though he may expend considerable effort to do so."

None of that sounded good. I sidled closer to the door, hoping to get a look inside and see who was talking.

"He won't heed your warning."

"Then we'll have to make him listen another way."

My heart was pounding as I stood outside the door. The men didn't sound friendly and they probably wouldn't take kindly to my eavesdropping.

"Have you found the asset?"

"Not yet. But soon. My source assures me it will be soon."

A heavy hand fell onto my shoulder and I jumped about a foot.

"Guests are not allowed here."

I spun around to see Lurch towering over me, the light behind him casting his face into shadow. Fear flooded me, irrational as it may have been.

"I-I was just . . . looking for the bathroom," I squeaked, then cleared my throat and pushed my glasses up my nose. "Is it not this way?"

Lurch didn't speak, merely lifted a ponderous hand and pointed back the direction from which I'd come.

I ducked beneath his arm and slipped away down the hall as fast as I could without running. I glanced back once to see he'd moved on and that someone else stood in the shadows outside the door, but I couldn't make out their features.

Unnerved, I scurried back to the ballroom, scanning the crowds for Jackson until I spotted him nursing a drink and likewise eyeing the crowd for me. I hurried to his side.

"What was the meeting with Philip about?" I asked once I'd reached him. He looked relieved to see me.

"Tell you in the car."

I perked up. "Does that mean we can leave?" The encounter in the hallway and conversation I'd overheard had me shaken and I was anxious to tell Jackson about it.

He pulled me into his arms. "Not without a dance."

The orchestra was playing "Sing, Sing, Sing" and the casual dancers had departed the floor to leave it to those more expert in the activity.

"I've never danced before," I protested. "I don't know how."

"That's the easy part about being a girl," he said. "You don't have to know. Just follow."

He spun me in a circle, catching me and pulling me back in. It took a few more times, but I caught the hang of it, and we were spinning with the rest of them in no time. I laughed, relaxing a little and enjoying the sense of freedom it gave me to dance like this, even amongst strangers.

"See? You're a natural," Jackson said as the strains of "Come Fly with Me" filled the air, the singer's voice a low baritone that slid inside my ears like warm honey. I was breathless as he pulled me close into a slowly revolving circle.

"Or maybe it's because I have a good partner."

His eyes were warm, their dark depths gazing into my own, and a smile played about his lips. I never thought I'd be one of those girls who felt at home in a man's arms, but we fit so well together. It made me feel . . . not alone . . . which was a big deal. I'd felt alone and been alone for a lot of my life. Loneliness was just part of my daily existence. To not be lonely . . . was incredibly pleasing. And addicting.

Flashbulbs broke the mood and I stumbled. Jackson caught me, turning our backs to the photographers and quickly leading me from the floor.

"They're really persistent," I said when we'd found a quiet alcove and left the cameras behind.

"I've gotten used to it," he said with a shrug. "I should've warned you. Philip's daughter plans this event and she likes to make the society pages."

"This is definitely different than what I'm used to," I said, which was an understatement.

"I'm glad you came tonight," he said, slotting our fingers together. "I want everyone to see that I'm officially off the market." Lifting our joined hands, he pressed a kiss to my knuckles. It should've been romantic, but his words were ricocheting inside my head.

"Off the market?" I repeated. "What do you mean?"

He gave me a strange look. "You and me is what I mean. I really don't want to be on *Forbes* billionaire bachelor list three years in a row."

I stared. "You don't mean . . . surely you're not talking marriage yet . . . are you? I mean yeah, I consider you my boyfriend, but we've only been together for six weeks and three days."

"I'm certainly too old to be dating for fun, China," he said. "If you're not serious about us, then you should tell me now." The relaxed smile on his face had faded to a shuttered expression, the warmth in his eyes turning chilly.

"I didn't know I'd have to decide something like that so soon," I protested, trying not to panic at the thought of *commitment* and *forever* and *I love yous*.

"I know what I feel," he insisted. "We're perfect for each other. And I can finally trust that the woman by my side is there for me and not for my money or fame or any of that bullshit."

I shook my head, trying to think clearly. The music and the press of the people had made me anxious earlier. Now I was trying to fight off a panic attack and still concentrate on what Jackson was saying.

"I don't know," I said. "I don't know if we're 'perfect for each other.' I've never even *had* a boyfriend before. It would seem unwise to settle on the first one—"

"Settle?" he interrupted. "Did you seriously just say that you'd be *settling* for me?"

Okay, that hadn't come out right and now things were going horribly wrong. "No, of course not. I didn't mean—"

"Maybe you should go," he said stiffly. "Go find your next boyfriend so you can have a better pool of candidates for whom you can *settle.*"

Even I—social-cue misfit—could tell that he was hurt and angry, and that now wasn't the time or place to finish this conversation.

"I'll have my car take you home," he said.

"I can get home on my own," I replied, swallowing the sudden lump in my throat. I hated confrontation. Had never had a fight with a boyfriend. What was I supposed to do? The nuances of hurt feelings and anger battling with manners made the conversational undertones indecipherable to me. I wanted to fix things, but didn't know how. What I *did* know was that I wanted to be alone. Now. And not in Jackson's car.

I spun away from his grip on my elbow and stepped into the crush of people.

"China, wait—"

One of the few good things about being short was the ability to get easily lost in a crowd. Though I didn't know if Jackson had followed me or not—part of me hoped he had—I was quickly swallowed into the morass of bodies, which seemed to have expanded exponentially since we'd arrived. By the time I got to the front door, the Uber I'd ordered from the app on my phone was waiting. Unfortunately, so was someone else.

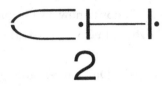

2

"What, no costume?" Clark asked, holding open the passenger door of his black Porsche.

Clark Slattery—and I'd only found out his last name after we'd been forced into a working partnership together—used to be military intelligence turned freelance intelligence. Now he was the brawn behind my brains at Vigilance.

"What are you doing here?" I asked, pushing aside my dismay at what had occurred between Jackson and me. Whatever had brought Clark to the party, it couldn't be good. He and I had begun our "friendship" on the false pretense that he was romantically interested in me after he'd moved in next door. But in the end, he'd just been using me for information, a fact I hadn't taken kindly to. Two months into our new partnership the awkwardness had eased, but he was far from my favorite person . . . even if he did look like Superman on Red Kryptonite (a black-leather-jacket-wearing, bad-boy version of the caped hero I'd always secretly had the hots for).

"Happy Halloween to you, too, Mack," he said. "Always such the pleasant and friendly coworker."

"I'm not paid to be pleasant and friendly," I retorted.

"And you do it so well," he shot back. "Now get in the car. We have a situation."

"But I'm on a date," I protested. Which was true . . . sort of.

"Yeah? Where is he?"

I glanced around, hoping Jackson had come after me when I'd made my dramatic exit. That's how it always happened in the movies. Yet again, I was reminded that real life is a far cry from Hollywood's version. Jackson was nowhere in sight. I swallowed my disappointment.

"Fine." I got in the car. Clark slid behind the wheel and we took off.

Downtown Raleigh on Halloween night was busy, especially since it was on a Friday. Traffic slowed us down as Clark drove toward our headquarters.

"So are you going to tell me what's going on?" I asked.

"When we're in a secure location, yes." He glanced at me, the pure blue of his eyes making him appear more angelic than he was. There wasn't an angelic or holy bone in his body.

I sighed. The night had begun so well. I'd been so excited about my costume—which I'd spent a fortune on—and going to a fancy party with my dreamy boyfriend . . . Now I was stuck with Clark, going to work on a Friday night, wearing my niece's skin-tight dress. I tugged again at the hem, but it wouldn't budge past midthigh.

"So what are you supposed to be? Buffy the Vampire Slayer?"

I shot Clark a look. "I'm a brunette, not blonde, and Buffy doesn't wear glasses."

"My mistake. So where's the boy toy?"

Clark never called Jackson by name. And since anything I said about it only made Clark reach for more nicknames, I didn't even comment on it.

"I left him inside."

"Problems in paradise?"

I shrugged. "I don't really want to talk about it." Turning away, I gazed out the window. I had never had any kind of boyfriend-girlfriend relationship before. Jackson and I had never argued until tonight and I was at a loss as to how or if I should attempt to repair things. He seemed to be at a higher emotional commitment level than I was, which, while gratifying, also left us at loose ends.

"Good." I glanced at Clark in surprise. His lips twisted. "I didn't really want to listen."

Asshat. Mia's pet name for Clark, which I heartily agreed with. If he wasn't so damn good at what he did, I'd lobby that either he or I had to go.

We arrived at headquarters a few minutes later. Back in the fifties, the city fathers of Raleigh had decided to build a bomb shelter underneath the city, which had been a good idea until the wall fell and the USSR broke up. Then it just became an empty space. There'd been a brief revival of the acres underground in the seventies and eighties, with restaurants and a thriving music scene, but even that had fallen by the wayside. The businesses had closed up, one by one, until the area had all but been forgotten, the entrances boarded up and built over. Until now.

Though a far cry from Research Triangle or the posh setting downtown where Cysnet resided, the subterranean labyrinth underneath Cameron Village was more than adequate for our needs. All but forgotten by everyone except the most senior of residents, it held the most advanced electronic surveillance software in the world. Better than the NSA. More secret than the CIA.

We parked in the garage, underneath which stretched a data labyrinth of servers spanning more than three football fields. Housed in concrete and surrounded with a state-of-the-art water cooling system, it was undetectable, even if you knew it was there.

Clark typed a code into the numeric pad by the entrance, then placed his palm on the reader. It scanned, turned blue, and the door slid open. I walked in front of Clark.

The corridor was really a scanning tube, mapping us both as we walked. Even after passing the code and palm print, software compared our strides and bodies to those on file. If I wasn't recognized by the system, the floor would instantly electrify with just enough charge to knock me unconscious. It freaked me out and I never relaxed until I reached the other side and open air.

It allowed me to pass and I let out my breath in relief. An elevator awaited, taking us down three levels. A metal walkway led to the brain of Vigilance. The servers were the heart but here—where dozens of screens lined the walls and four arced rows of multilevel workstations faced them—this was the eyes, ears, and the brain.

A skeleton crew was working tonight, a holiday and weekend, and the manager in charge saw me right away. Setting aside the tablet he was holding, he hurried over to where Clark and I stood.

"Hey, boss," he said. "Sorry to interrupt your evening."

"It's fine, Derrick. What's going on?"

"Someone hacked us."

It took me a moment to process that statement because the likelihood of that event actually occurring was about the same as getting struck by lightning . . . twice.

"Show me." I didn't ask if he was sure. I'd had free rein to hire my staff and I'd only chosen the very best. I'd even poached a few from Cysnet. Derrick knew his stuff. If he said we'd been hacked, then we had.

He used the nearest workstation to toggle one of the screens and I read the network traffic log displayed. Shit.

"It took them a while," I said. "Why didn't any of our penetration sensing alerts go off?"

"He disabled them."

Holy shit. "Scroll." Derrick obediently scrolled the screen so I could follow the trail.

Clark sidled up next to me. "You can read that?" he asked.

I gave him a look. "Of course." I pointed. "See the lines in red? Those are denials."

"There are lots of those."

"Yes, because he was testing for weaknesses." I turned to Derrick. "I'm assuming the IP trace led nowhere."

He nodded. "Bounced around through a dozen countries before we hit a dead end."

"How long was he in?"

"Four minutes before we blocked him."

"And you've addressed the weakness he exploited?"

"Yes. He won't get in that way again."

"What did he do while he was in?" I knew a hacker didn't need a lot of time to plant a back door so they could come back later. Or a bot that would send data to him via our network.

"Looked around, basically. We've run file checks and he left nothing behind. It was like he was curious and that was all."

Hmm. "Okay, well it looks like you've done everything I would have done. Good job. But it can't happen again."

"I've called in Mazie to harden the perimeter firewalls."

I nodded. Mazie was head of network security. She was going to be royally pissed that someone had hacked her firewall.

"Let's work again on tracing that IP," I said. "Put Roscoe on it. He can sniff out IP trails better than anyone. Even if we didn't get him live, chances are he probably uses the same pattern when he's online. We might get lucky. And by Monday, I want to know everything that the hacker saw."

"Will do." Derrick hurried away, pulling out his cell to make the call.

I turned to Clark. "Give me a ride home?"

"Sure."

Back in the car, I asked, "So how did you find out?"

"I was working in my office when Derrick and his minions suddenly started going apeshit, running around and chattering in technese—" Clark's term for when he couldn't understand what we were saying "—so I asked him if I should bring you in."

"He could've just called me."

"It wasn't a big deal. Got me out of doing paperwork for a while."

Clark liked to be in the field. Having to do the administrative part of his job drove him batty. And made him cranky.

"Want to grab some food?" he asked. "I'm starving."

My initial response was to say no—spending time with Clark outside of work wasn't high on my To Do list—but I was hungry and I didn't really want to go home yet. Now that the work emergency was out of the way, my confusion and vague unease about Jackson had returned. I didn't want to think about that. Not yet, anyway.

"Sure."

"Any preference on food?"

I glanced at the clock on the dash. "It's getting late, so anything spicy would be bad for digestion, which rules out Thai, Indian, and Mexican. Most traditional restaurants are probably going to be closed except for a pub or bar-and-grill. As it's Halloween, there's a high probability that the number of holiday revelers imbibing will be significantly more than usual."

"Got it. Greasy burger dive coming right up."

That hadn't been what I'd suggested, but it sounded good, so I didn't argue. Ten minutes later, we were parking in the lot of a diner so old it looked like it had grown out of the concrete and the rest of the city block had been built around it.

"Best burgers in the city," Clark declared, beeping the car locked and leading the way inside. The handwritten sign on the window proclaimed the shop open twenty-four hours.

There didn't appear to be a hostess to seat us, but Clark seemed to know where he was going, heading into the rear and sliding into the last booth with his back to the wall. I sat opposite him. A peppy waitress with black-and-purple hair approached us.

"Happy Halloween," she said brightly. "What can I get you?" The fluorescent lights glinted off her nose piercing.

"Two double-patty-bacon-burger specials, with everything. Extra fries, two Cokes, two chocolate shakes," Clark ordered.

She jotted it down on a little pad of paper. "Got it. I'll be right back with those Cokes."

"You ordered for me," I said, surprised. "Why would you do that? What if I'd wanted something else?"

"Trust me. I got the best thing on the menu. It's not like you want to eat a salad in this place. And the spaghetti is nothing but mush. I made that mistake once."

When our Cokes came, I sipped mine, staring glumly at the worn tabletop. Would Jackson call me? He hadn't texted, though I'd checked a dozen times. Even as I thought it, I checked my phone again.

"Spill," Clark abruptly ordered. "What happened?"

My eyes narrowed. "Why should I tell you?"

He shrugged. "Maybe I can help."

"Why would you want to help?"

"Because, Mack, as smart as you are—and I can't believe some of the shit you can do—your social skills are lacking, to put it nicely. Plus, I'm a guy, so I can give you a guy's perspective."

He did make sense. And yet . . . "You'll just laugh and make fun of me."

"I won't." He drew an *X* on his chest. "Cross my heart and pinky swear."

I considered, then decided I'd chance it. "Okay. We were at this fancy party and basically, he said that he's off the market and that if I'm not seeing our relationship as serious, then we shouldn't bother continuing to date."

Clark let out a low whistle. "Wow, that's harsh. He really said that?"

That didn't sound good. "Yeah. I told him I didn't know, that it seemed unwise to . . . settle . . . on the first man I dated." I waited to see what Clark's reaction would be to my word choice. Maybe it was just Jackson who was offended. Alas, Clark's eyebrows flew upward.

"That's what you said? That you shouldn't settle on the first guy you dated?" He laughed out loud. "I bet that went over like a shit ton of bricks."

I grimaced. "Yes, apparently that was the prevailing opinion."

"And you hadn't discussed your relationship status before?" he asked.

I shook my head. "We've been sleeping together and I'd just assumed we'd take it slow—"

"Classic rookie mistake," Clark interrupted. "Jackson's ready to settle down and get married. The minute a man hits that point, it'll be with the next woman he dates."

That didn't sound good. "It's not that I'm opposed to settling down," I lied. "I guess I was just . . . surprised . . . at the high level of commitment and weight he'd given to our relationship. Marriage is a big step." *Surprised* was putting it mildly. *Dismayed* was more like it, but I didn't want to reveal how shocked I'd been at the idea of marriage.

"You've been together . . . what . . . almost two months?" I nodded. "That's usually a make-or-break time frame, so he wasn't totally out of line by wanting you to put up or shut up."

That was a lot of idioms back to back. I shook my head in confusion. "What?"

"I mean . . . after two months of dating, you should be able to tell him whether you're thinking along the lines of a serious, monogamous let's-see-where-this-goes or if it's just a fling."

"Oh." Good to know.

"What do *you* want?"

My eyes met Clark's. "I don't want to lose him. But I'm not ready for talk of marriage. So . . . I don't know."

We had to stop talking for a moment as our food arrived. The plates were laden with fries fresh from the fryer and massive burgers dripping with cheese and bacon. The chocolate shakes were proportionally gargantuan-sized, topped with whipped cream and a cherry.

"Wow," I breathed. My mouth was already watering.

Clark laughed. "Your eyes are about as big as these plates," he said, still smiling. When he smiled—which wasn't often—a dimple appeared in his cheek. With looks rivaling the best Superman Hollywood had offered and a physique to match, Clark didn't exactly blend in.

"It looks amazing . . . and extremely unhealthy." I picked up a fry and popped it in my mouth. My eyes slid shut. Pure heaven.

"Everyone who eats carrots dies," he quipped, picking up his cheeseburger and taking a large bite. I cut mine in half before attempting to get my mouth around it. "I'd rather eat cheeseburgers."

I didn't want to discuss Jackson and me anymore, so I fell back on my trick of asking questions when I didn't want to worry about having to talk. "You used to be intelligence," I said. Clark nodded, eating three fries at once. "Wasn't that difficult, given your physical appearance?"

"What do you mean?"

"Intelligence officers should be able to blend in, not be memorable. You don't."

Clark's eyebrows lifted. "Did you just give me a compliment?"

I felt my cheeks warm. "Don't flatter yourself. I'm merely hypothesizing that you aren't considered average in appearance and that it would have complicated your job, perhaps even complicates your current job, which affects me."

"So you're doubting my ability to do my job?" His eyes narrowed and the smile was gone.

"No, I'm not—"

"Because you really shouldn't go there. By all appearances, you shouldn't be able to do what you do, either."

That gave me pause. "What's that supposed to mean? Because I'm a girl?"

"Yes. And because you're young—twenty-three, right? You barely top five feet, I could bench-press you, and God help the person who changes your schedule."

I sucked down a long swallow of chocolate shake. "For your information, I'm five foot two and three-quarters. And I've been very flexible lately with my schedule." Which had irritated me no end, but I wasn't about to tell him that.

"Oh really? So did you go crazy and order pizza on Thursday instead of Monday?"

Asshat. "No, but I did order extra cheese," I retorted.

He burst out laughing again. I watched him, then it tickled me, too, and I couldn't help a laugh. It broke the tension I'd been sensing and I relaxed, eating more of my burger.

"Okay, so here's some free advice," he said. "Despite his wanting to 'put a ring on it,' men like the chase, so you did the right thing, holding him at arm's length, especially if you're not ready. Give him a few days to think it over, see that you're not being unreasonable, and he'll come crawling back."

"That shouldn't be a problem because he has yet to call or text me," I said, glumly holding up my still-silent phone.

"He will. Trust me."

"So what do I do then?"

"If you want to stay together, that's up to you. But if you need time, tell him that. He shouldn't rush you. Nothing worth having ever came easy."

That made sense, but still . . . "It feels like playing a psychological game. Why can't we just agree to date for a predetermined time agreeable to us both, then decide at the conclusion whether or not we're suited for matrimony?"

"Because it *is* a game. The kind of game men and women play and if you want to win, you gotta learn how to play."

"But if both sides know that they're playing a game, how is it effective?" It didn't make sense. My burger and fries were gone so I drank my shake, my gaze on Clark as I sucked the ice cream.

"People are human," he said, using a napkin to wipe the grease from his fingers. "They're more than logic. They're the accumulation of millennia of urges and instincts and survival of the fittest. They're emotion and feelings and all the messiness that implies."

My shake was gone and I sat back, turning this over in my head. "It's sound advice," I said. "Thank you."

"No problem." He glanced at my empty plate and shook his head. "I don't know where you put it."

"I have a really high metabolism."

A full stomach and the late hour combined to make me sleepy. By the time Clark had dropped me off and I was unlocking my door, I was more than ready to climb into my Endor Star Wars pajamas (my autumn nightwear) and go to bed. Especially since it was over two hours past my usual bedtime of ten thirty.

But I came wide awake when I saw the man sitting on my couch. It took me two frantic heartbeats to recognize him.

"What the hell, Jackson? Why are you sitting in my living room? In the dark?" I flipped on the nearest lamp.

"Isn't it obvious?"

I gave him a look. Nothing was ever "obvious" to me when it came to social cues. I would guess and hope that he was here to apologize, but I'd read enough *Cosmo* articles to know that the only thing harder for a man to say than "I love you" was "I'm sorry."

"You were angry with me. I took you by surprise," he said, "and I thought we should talk."

"I'm not sure what to say. I think we're at different places in our lives." Clark's words came back to me. "I don't know if I'm ready for a ring and marriage yet."

"I understand that, now. I should've realized it sooner. You're new to relationships and then I start talking love, marriage, and a baby carriage. It's no wonder you got spooked."

I supposed *getting spooked* was one way to put it, though that felt slightly demoralizing. As if he were putting me on the same level as an animal with no cognitive capabilities.

"I don't want to end our relationship," I said. "But I do need to take it slow, without the pressure of knowing you're in a rush to get married. When I marry, I want it to be forever." I wanted the kind of love my parents had.

"You're right. I'm sorry," he said. "I don't want to lose you, either. I can go slow. I just hope you eventually feel the same about me as I do you."

That was pressure, too, but I let it pass. It was amazing and frightening how much better I felt at his words, a realization of how much power I'd given Jackson—power to make me happy . . . and the power to hurt me. It had a sobering effect on the relief and gladness surging through me. I'd been hurt before, but not by a boyfriend and lover. The feeling was different, an acute pain somewhere deep inside at the thought of him not being in my life.

"I'm glad we can make up," I said, "and I accept your apology. I'm wondering, though, why you seem so sure of this relationship, when you haven't yet been in a relationship that *hasn't* ended."

"You and I are cut from the same cloth," he said with a sigh. "I've never been with someone that I can relate to as much as you and I connect. Not just on an intellectual level, but on an emotional level. Do you understand?" I nodded. He was right. I felt it, too. Jackson was the first person since my mother who seemed to understand and accept me for who I was—not who he wanted me to be.

He nuzzled my neck, kissing the sensitive skin underneath my ear. "Now we can have make-up sex."

My eyes slid shut at his touch. "Is make-up sex better than regular sex?"

"Absolutely." He slid my glasses off and carefully set them aside, then returned to kissing my neck.

I didn't care what he called it. Since Jackson had introduced me to sex, I liked it all. I didn't know if we were particularly well suited, or if he was just inordinately talented, but we had a really good time together in bed.

His hand slid up my thigh and underneath the hem of my borrowed dress, pushing it out of the way. Hooking my leg underneath my knee, he rearranged me so I was straddling him, and my skirt was up to my hips.

I pushed at his tuxedo jacket, shoving it down his arms and off, then tugged at his bow tie. He began kissing me, which was distracting, but worth it. Jackson was a good kisser. I could get lost in the softness of his lips, the heat of his tongue, the gentle pressure that gradually grew more demanding.

I managed to get the bow tie off and three buttons undone before his hand slid between my thighs. The matching dove-gray lace-trim hipkini panties I wore didn't stop him, his fingers slipping underneath the satin to touch me.

For a computer programmer, Jackson had talented fingers, silencing my thoughts as he stroked me, leaving only instinct and senses. I moaned into his mouth when he pushed one, then two fingers inside me, slowly moving in the way he knew drove me crazy.

Reaching down, I grabbed the hem of my dress, tugging it up over my head.

"Ow ow ow ow!"

I couldn't see a thing. The damn dress was half on and half off.

"What happened? What's wrong?" Jackson asked.

"The damn zipper caught in my ponytail," I explained, wincing as it pulled at my hair. My cheeks were burning as I sat half undressed on his lap.

Jackson gave a low chuckle. "Hold on."

I felt him reaching behind me, then a little tug, and I was loose. The dress floated free and I could see again.

"Now where were we?" he murmured against my lips.

"You were showing me how much better make-up sex is."

He stood, lifting me with him like I weighed nothing. He did that a lot, ever since I'd nearly broken both our necks on his staircase a month ago when he was trying to help me up it. Now he said it was just safer if he carried me, especially when stairs were involved.

We made it up the stairs with my legs firmly latched around his waist and my lips attached to his neck. The cologne Jackson wore was subtle and expensive, and when added to the scent of his skin, was completely addicting.

Jackson set me on the bed and I grabbed his shirt, pulling him down with me when he would have stood. I kissed him just like my granny's Harlequins had taught me to, and I could tell he appreciated it by the press of the hard length of him between my thighs. Which reminded me . . .

I pushed on his shoulders and he broke off our kiss. "Turn over," I said. Jackson was a particular fan of blow jobs. Though really, from a man's perspective, what wasn't to like? I'd been tentative at first and there was a mishap involving teeth, but I'd gotten much better. I was ambivalent about the act itself, but what it did to Jackson was a huge turn-on, so . . . practice made perfect.

Jackson lay on his back, me between his spread legs, and watched as I undid the rest of the buttons on his shirt, then started on his belt.

"I like that set a lot," he said, referring to my matching bra and panties. He rarely saw any set twice, given my obsessive search for The Perfect Bra, and of course I couldn't get a bra without matching panties . . . which is why I had drawers overflowing with lace and satin (which I say metaphorically because in reality they were all arranged by color and various degrees of coverage, separated by lift style).

"Thanks. It's new." I got the belt and worked my way down to the zipper.

"Thought so. Why don't I just buy you a shareholder's seat for Victoria's Secret? At least then you'd get a discount."

I paused in tugging at his slacks. "You can do that?" He just smiled. I rolled my eyes. "Tease."

"Look who's talking," he said, motioning to where I had his pants half on and half off.

Oh yeah.

A naked Jackson was a sight to behold and I took a minute to appreciate the extraordinary view of his body. He was not just in shape, but muscled and firm. He didn't manscape, but didn't need to. His chest had a smattering of hair across his pecs, then a thin trail from his navel down, which, in my opinion, was perfect. His back was completely devoid of hair and smooth to the touch.

Folding his arms behind his head, he smirked at me. "Enjoying the view?"

I particularly enjoyed when he did that because it made his biceps bulge. I gave a happy sigh. "You know I do." My gaze drifted slowly from his eyes down his neck to his shoulders and arms, then down his chest to his stomach, then further . . .

Mr. Happy—my designation for what the Harlequins often referred to as his "member"—was standing at attention and twitched as I watched. I glanced back at Jackson's face. His smirk was gone and his eyes were so dark they were nearly black as he watched me look at him.

"I love it when you get that look in your eye," he said.

"What look?" I asked, settling between his thighs and placing a kiss on the tip of Mr. Happy.

"That look that says you want me."

"I do want you." I took him in my mouth and his jaw set. I kept my eyes on his as I took him deeper. It didn't take long before he'd given up the silence and was gasping my name, in between *holy fuck* and *God yes*.

The thing about being small and having a large boyfriend was that he could pretty much switch positions and put me where he wanted me quicker than I could fathom if he tried to tell me. The first time he'd wanted to put his tongue between my legs while I was sucking him, it had taken almost ninety seconds of explanation and hand motions before he'd just said, "Fuck it," and flipped me around himself.

Tonight was no exception because before I knew it, he'd pulled me up and flipped me around, settling me on top of Mr. Happy. My eyes clamped shut as he slid home.

"I believe . . . this is called . . . the Reverse Cowgirl," I said, my voice breathless.

"Are you checking off a list?" he asked.

I had the feeling he might think it was odd if I said *Yes*. "Of course not. That would be weird."

"You are, aren't you."

Pause pause.

"Maybe."

His chuckle was lost in the midst of my moaning. His hands gripped my hips, lifting me off him for a brief moment. He liked to say that his only speed was Warp Three, but I certainly wasn't complaining. Some women reportedly had a problem achieving orgasm with penetration alone. I wasn't one of them. And I was loud.

"Oh God, oh yes . . . don't stop . . . yeah, right there . . . oh Jackson . . . yeah yeah yeah . . ." etc. etc. It wasn't as though I recorded myself, just was viscerally aware of words pouring from my mouth as my orgasm crashed over me. Jackson waited until I was through, then continued, bringing me to orgasm again before allowing himself to "explode in ecstasy," as Harlequin would say.

I collapsed next to him in the bed, both of us sweating and breathing hard.

"That was make-up sex," he said.

"I'm a fan."

His hand found mine between us, lacing our fingers and pressing our palms together. It was sweet and I turned my head to look up at him. He smiled and squeezed my hand.

"I'm a fan of *you*."

The last little bit of unease inside melted away, replaced by a warm glow that made me feel like I'd finally found that perfect bra.

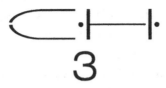

3

I was towel-drying my hair when I walked into the kitchen in the morning. Jackson was already there, drinking a cup of coffee and reading the paper.

See? I thought, remembering how Clark had given me a hard time about being inflexible in my routine. Not only had I let Jackson brew the coffee (after I'd taught him properly, of course), but didn't even freak out when he read the paper first and disordered the sections.

"So where did you run off to last night?" Jackson asked as I poured a steaming mug of coffee. "I got here pretty quick but you took a while."

"Oh, a work thing," I said, noncommittal. Part of my employment agreement was that when working for a super-secret government agency, you couldn't exactly put it on your resume.

"The new job you won't tell me about?"

While my job wasn't exactly a sore spot between us, Jackson wasn't pleased that I'd quit working at Cysnet for what I'd explained was a once-in-a-lifetime opportunity that I really couldn't tell him about due to nondisclosure reasons. It had helped that dating the boss would've made working at Cysnet very awkward, so the new job had come along at a good time.

"That's a rhetorical question," I replied, adding cream to my coffee.

I heard the paper rustle as Jackson turned pages and I hoped he'd let it drop. Sitting down opposite him at the table, I smiled to see he'd put my favorite section—Life & Entertainment—at my place.

Jackson Cooper didn't do the Walk of Shame, so he kept a few changes of clothes at my place. It wouldn't do to leave my house wearing his tuxedo from last night. Today he was in jeans that fit very well in all the right places and a long-sleeved polo in a deep gray that complemented his eyes. I sighed a little into my coffee. The view was very nice indeed.

"So what did your ex-business partner want?" I asked, flipping through the newspaper.

"To warn me."

I abruptly put the paper down. "Warn you about what?"

"That the government wants Cysnet."

"The government? But . . . that's ridiculous. Why?"

"I'm guessing it's because they saw the problems that could happen by using an outside contractor like Wyndemere. It's not solely under their control. If they own Cysnet, then they own all its proprietary technology. Not only could they get their projects done cheaper, they could make money off any patents they register."

"But it's not as though you're going to sell the business." The very idea was absurd. Cysnet was Jackson's baby.

"I don't think they're looking to buy," he said dryly. "The government has other means at their disposal to get what they want."

Which reminded me. "That must be what they were talking about."

Jackson frowned. "Who?"

"I don't know who, but I overheard two men talking about you," I said, relating to him the conversation. "But what could the government possibly do to take away your company?"

"Cysnet is publicly traded. Though I'm CEO and on the Board of Directors, all it would take would be a vote of no confidence by the Board to oust me."

"But Cysnet *is* you," I argued. "It would be like Apple without Steve Jobs."

"Apple survived," he said grimly.

"But it's not as good. Everyone knows that." I took a breath. "So . . . what are you going to do?"

"There's nothing I *can* do," he said. "I have to wait and see what their next move is."

I suddenly realized what I was staring at and I snatched up the paper again. "Oh my God! It's me! I mean, it's us!"

There, on page six, were two photos of Jackson and me dancing at the party last night. We were gazing at each other and smiling. Another photo had been taken when we'd first arrived. His arm was around my waist as we walked side by side.

I'd never seen photos of us together before. I looked young—really young—standing next to him. And apparently the columnist thought so, too, because the headline read TECH MOGUL ROBS THE CRADLE.

I read the story aloud. "Jackson Cooper was spotted at his ex-partner's Halloween bash last night, this time sporting a new companion. China Mack, dressed in a stylish and flattering LBD, added Geek Chic touches that we love—glasses, ponytail, and sneakers. We think Cooper may just have met his match in this girl techie who can keep him on his toes on the dance floor, and behind the computer monitor. Our eyes and ears are open for more word on this new binary couple." Huh.

"Binary couple?" Jackson echoed.

I shrugged. "I do look kinda young. It must be the ponytail."

Jackson snorted. "Please. You look like you're about seventeen. I'm surprised someone didn't try to arrest me for statutory rape."

I stuck my tongue out at him. "I can't help it I'm aging more gracefully than you," I said archly.

"I've got a few years before you roll out the walker," he retorted.

The front door suddenly flew open and Mia came bounding in. "Aunt Chi! OMG, you're not going to believe this!" She glanced at Jackson in surprise. "What are you doing here?"

That was weird. Mia knew we were dating. "He stayed over," I said. We'd had to have a conversation about Jackson spending the night because I was worried about setting a bad example, but when I'd mentioned that to Mia, she'd just rolled her eyes and told me she'd grown up watching *Gossip Girl*.

"But . . . I thought you broke up."

Now it was my turn to be surprised. "How did you know that?"

"Because you're trending on Twitter."

I choked on my coffee. By the time I'd stopped coughing and mopped up the spilled coffee, Jackson already had his phone out.

"#YouGoGirl," Mia said.

"YouGoGirl?" I sputtered.

"#ChinaMack, too. And #CooperDumped. TMZ started that last one."

"What's on TMZ?"

"Someone videoed you telling Jackson off and storming out. I even have a gif of it. See?" She flipped her phone around and I watched myself silently berating Jackson, then turning on my heel with a flip of my ponytail.

"So are they hating on me?" I winced, not wanting to imagine being the target of the online social community's wrath.

"Nooooo," Jackson answered instead of Mia. "Not exactly."

"What do you mean 'not exactly?'" Mia snorted. "They *love* her. She's a new hero. She's even a verb."

"Excuse me?" I interrupted.

"Yeah. When girls tweet about dumping their crappy boyfriends, they say they 'China Macked' them."

I couldn't process what was going on and pulled up Twitter on my own phone. "Oh wow . . . I've got over a million new followers!" Quite the improvement over the six hundred I'd had before. "My tweets during *Supernatural* are going to be epic . . ."

"I'm going to go print off some screenshots," Mia said. "This is so cool." She took off, her steps thumping rapidly up the stairs.

"You can't just tweet whatever you want," Jackson said. "Not anymore."

"Don't be ridiculous," I said, scanning through the trending topic of me. So weird. "The first thing I need to correct is the assertion that we're no longer dating." Jackson snatched the phone out of my hand. "Hey!"

"You can't just do and say whatever you want," Jackson repeated more forcefully. "You never know what can backfire."

"So I'm not supposed to use social media anymore?" I was crestfallen. "Not even to correct the erroneous assumption that we're no longer in a romantic relationship?"

"I'll put out a statement or something," he said.

"That doesn't sound good. Are you angry?" It hadn't been my fault that someone had videoed our conversation. If anything, it was Jackson's fault for being famous.

"Of course not," he said. "But maybe you should have some help with any . . . online communication."

I gave him a look. "I've been tweeting and posting and Instagramming for quite a while without adult supervision."

"But it's different now. One wrong tweet, one bad joke, and it can destroy your life. And let's face it, China, it's not as though nuances of communication are one of your strengths."

That was an observation I couldn't deny, as much as I disliked my shortcomings being pointed out to me, especially by my boyfriend.

"Come on now, don't pout," Jackson cajoled, a smile playing about his lips.

"Don't be ridiculous. I don't pout." I purposefully rearranged my face into what I hoped was a pleasant expression.

My phone rang. It was my best friend, Bonnie. "Gee, I wonder what she wants," I joked. "Hello?"

"Oh my God! You're on TMZ!"

I laughed, glancing at Jackson as he stood and mouthed that he was going. I nodded. He gave me a quick kiss and whispered, "I'll call you."

Bonnie was still rattling off about my newfound fame as Jackson left. "So tell me everything!" she said, finally taking a breath.

So I did, including what the news didn't know, that Jackson and I had made up.

"Wait a minute," she said. "He told you he wants a serious relationship? As in commitment? And you told him you weren't ready?"

When she said it like that, it sounded kind of bad. "Um, yeah. I guess. I mean, I've never been in a relationship before, so we should take it slow, right?"

"Taking it slow is fine. I'm just stunned that you found that rare and elusive creature: the non-commitment-phobic man."

"I didn't know they're rare."

"Honey, if I had a dollar for every relationship I had that ended because the man couldn't commit . . . well, I wouldn't be rich, but I could have a helluva night out."

That got a laugh out of me.

"So when are you seeing him again?" she asked.

"Not sure. He left earlier, said he'd call later."

She snorted. "Typical man. Doesn't plan ahead, just assumes you'll be at home waiting for him on a Saturday night."

"Maybe," I agreed. "But it's not a big deal to me. I mean, it's not as though I have an overwhelmingly active social life." My schedule was etched in stone, as Clark had so gently reminded me.

"You have other plans tonight, remember?"

Searching my brain, I came up empty. "I do?"

Bonnie made a noise of frustration. "Yes, you do. You promised me you'd be my plus-one at Mike's graduation party, remember?"

That jogged my memory. Mike was a classmate of Bonnie's at the culinary school. By all rights, she should have graduated by now, too. Unfortunately, Bonnie was constantly having to repeat classes. Though her dream was to be a chef, she had difficulty pulling off even some of the most basic tasks. Like not burning things. Luckily for her, she came from a wealthy family and indulgent parents. Unluckily for me, I was her favorite guinea pig for practicing her culinary skills.

"Yeah, yeah, I remember now. Do I really have to go? All those strangers . . ."

"Don't you dare ditch me, China," she warned. "You know Mike and I hooked up a couple of times. I do *not* want to show up alone and looking all pathetic."

"So showing up with a girl isn't pathetic?"

"It's better than alone," she retorted. "Besides, you promised."

"I was under duress," I said. "You were going to make me eat kale again." I hated kale. As far as I was concerned, that food fad needed to go the way of the grapefruit diet.

"Kale is a very versatile and healthy vegetable—" she began.

"Fine, fine, I'll go," I interrupted, before she could really get going on all the wondrous benefits of the bitter, leafy weed.

"Awesome! Okay. I'll pick you up at seven."

"But I do laundry at seven," I said, but she'd already ended the call. I had the feeling Bonnie knew I did laundry from seven until ten p.m. and just hadn't wanted to argue with me about it. Now I'd have to do laundry this afternoon, which meant I needed to leave soon if I wanted to stop by Retread.

Having to change my schedule made me uncomfortable, like having an itch you couldn't scratch. And I was cranky until I got to Retread.

It was my favorite store. It had vintage everything, from old records—the real, vinyl ones—to ancient Harlequins, Chia Pets, Star Wars action figures, comic books, posters of Farrah Fawcett and Rick Springfield back in their heyday, you name it.

"Hey, Buddy," I called out as I entered. The familiar musty smell of old things and dust assailed me. "It's me." I didn't need to explain further. Although Retread was *my* favorite retail shopping experience, it wasn't even a blip on most people's radar. I'd rarely seen any other customers and had no idea how he stayed in business.

A curly-haired, bespectacled head popped up from behind the counter which was overflowing with a hodgepodge of . . . stuff.

"You're early," Buddy said, standing up and brushing dust off his T-shirt and jeans. He was also well aware of my Set In Stone Schedule that wasn't so Set In Stone anymore, sadly.

"I know. Have plans tonight, but wanted to stop by and see if there's anything new." I was already rummaging through a stack that hadn't been here last week.

"Well actually," Buddy said, reaching underneath the counter. "I do have a little something special for you." He brandished an album.

"*5150!*" I squealed, snatching the vintage record from him. "That's so awesome! How'd you find it?"

"Just got dropped off today. I held it for you. I know you've been looking for it a while now."

"Aww, thank you!" I had the unusual impulse to hug him, but I knew he wouldn't appreciate it, so I didn't. "Any new Harlequins?"

"Always."

Buddy knew I was always on the lookout for old Harlequins for my grandma. I almost always sent them to her in Florida . . . just as soon as I finished reading them. I was currently in the middle of *A Highlander's Wicked Ways*.

I had a sack full of musty paperbacks and my precious Van Halen album when I stepped outside. A man loitering by the curb and wielding a camera that had to weigh ten pounds hurried up to me and began snapping photos.

"Who are you? What are you doing?" I asked, instinctively trying to shield my face.

"I'm Ralph," the guy said, face still behind the camera. "Nice to meet you."

That was one question down. "And what are you doing?" He followed me as I headed for my car.

"You're China Mack," he said.

"Yes, but that doesn't explain why you're following me and taking nonstop photos of me," I complained, unlocking my car. He was in the way as I tried to load the bag into my trunk.

"You're the latest thing. There's a bounty out for photos of you. Ten grand."

I shut my trunk with a thud, staring at Ralph. "You're joking. Someone wants to pay ten thousand dollars for a photograph of me? Just a random photo?" How bizarre.

"You're trending, you know. Gotta strike while the iron's hot." He snapped more photos.

I stood there, uncertain what to do. Should I smile? I was finished shopping, so I wanted to get in my car and go home, but it seemed rude to just leave.

"Um, well, it's been nice meeting you, Ralph," I said. "But I have to go now. I hope you get your ten thousand dollars."

"You bet," he said, snapping more photos as I got into my car. "Sweet ride."

Now that was a compliment I could appreciate. My Ford Mustang was my pride and joy. Shaking my head at the bizarre events of today and the fickleness of popularity, I drove home, where Mia was waiting.

"Oh my God, Katy Perry totally tweeted you," she said the minute I walked in the door.

"The singer with that horrendous stage show like an adult preschool horror film?" I asked, depositing my treasures on the kitchen counter.

"I liked that show!" she protested. "Anyway, that doesn't matter. She tweeted you and said, 'Go, girlfriend. #GirlsRuleBoysDrool.'"

"So it was a tweet supporting me," I said, getting a can of Red Bull from the fridge.

"Yes and it was favorited over six thousand times and retweeted three thousand times."

Wow. That *was* impressive. "Have you been on Twitter all day?" I asked.

"No. I've been on Instagram and Facebook, too. You're trending on Facebook, by the way."

It was as though I'd stepped into an episode of *The Twilight Zone*. "Do they hate me?"

Mia gave me an exasperated look. "No. I told you that. It's like tons of massive love for dumping him."

"So what's going to happen when they find out I didn't dump him?" Ah, the double-edged sword of public opinion.

"Yeah, about that. Maybe you should keep a lid on that for a few days," she said, grabbing a bag of chips from the cupboard. "Like, he has to grovel to get back in your good graces or something."

I couldn't imagine Jackson groveling to anyone, even me, though he *had* apologized, which was Close Enough in my book. "Bonnie thinks I'm lucky to have found a guy who wants a serious relationship and is thinking about marriage."

"True," Mia said. "He can date anyone he wants to, but you—" She cut herself off, her cheeks flushing. "I'm sorry. I didn't mean that the way it sounded."

"No, you're right," I said. "I'm not often exposed to situations where dating options are . . . abundant." Painful, but true. Bonnie had been after me for ages to get out more and date, but it was just too stressful and littered with pitfalls if I said or did the wrong thing, which in those kinds of social situations, happened way too often.

"I'm going with Bonnie tonight to a party," I said, struck with an idea. "Will you do my makeup and hair again? Like you did before?" The first time I'd had dinner with Clark—back before I realized he was just playing a part—Mia had worked her magic to make me look all girly and pretty. It wasn't something I'd been able to replicate.

"Absolutely," she said. "And I have the perfect dress for you to wear."

The perfect dress turned out to be a floaty little something with a floral print, spaghetti straps, and a skirt that barely brushed midthigh.

"How do you wear dresses this short?" I complained, futilely trying to tug the hem lower. "If I bend over, everyone's going to see my . . . well, everything."

"First, don't bend over," she said, running a brush through my hair. "You crouch down if you need something. Second, you're short, so this hemline looks super cute on you. You've got great legs."

I looked down. They looked the same as always to me. Pale and spindly. Mia had wanted me to wear a pair of high-heeled sandals, but I put my foot down. Literally. I'd break my neck. Instead, I was adopting the same look as last night with a pair of pink Converse.

"I'm going to do a loose French braid," Mia said. "With a lot of body on top. Kind of like that girl in *Frozen*."

"What's *Frozen*?" I asked, at a complete loss.

Mia stopped and stared at me. "Please tell me you've seen *Frozen*." I shook my head. "It's only the best Disney movie of all time," she exclaimed.

That presumption had to be stopped right then and there. "No, you're wrong. The best Disney movie by any measurement was *The Lion King*. But as with most young people, your concept of history begins at your birth, so I understand if you've neglected to take prior films under consideration."

"I actually have seen *Lion King*," Mia retorted, pulling perhaps a bit too tightly on my hair as she braided. "It was cute and all, but nothing compares to Elsa's signature song 'Let It Go.'"

"One song does not a movie make," I argued. "The soundtrack to *The Lion King* holds the record for most copies ever sold for an animated movie at over seven million."

"*Frozen* is the highest-grossing animated movie of all time," she shot back.

"Oh yeah?" I combed my brain. "Well, Pumbaa was the first Disney character to pass gas."

Silence. The tugging on my hair stopped, too. "I don't have a comeback for that," she said at last. We both laughed.

"Okay, time for makeup," she said, gathering her many supplies and making me sit on the toilet lid.

I'd gotten better at not blinking so much, but putting on mascara was still a trial and she muttered a few times under her breath when it smeared and she had to clean the marks with a Q-tip.

"There," she pronounced after about ten minutes. "All done." She handed me my glasses.

Standing, I took a look in the mirror, then shook my head in amazement.

"How do you make me look like this?" I asked. The girl staring back at me looked sweet and pretty, with hair carelessly braided to appear as though it was about to fall down any second. The makeup was subtle but accentuated the blue of my eyes and instead of my skin merely looking pale, it looked smooth and soft.

"You're pretty, Aunt Chi," she said. "I just make you stunning."

She hugged me then, which always took me aback. Mia was so touchy-feely, it had been hard to get used to. Her view that I was "stunning" was a bit farfetched, but it was sweet of her to view me that way, so I awkwardly patted her back. "What are you doing tonight?" I asked once she let me go. It was Saturday night, after all.

"Michelle was going to come over, if that's okay," she said. "We were going to order pizza and watch a movie."

"Yeah, that's fine. Money for pizza is in the cookie jar."

"I know."

Just then my cell buzzed. I glanced at the caller ID. Jackson.

"Remember, you have plans with Bonnie tonight," Mia admonished, pointing a finger at me. "Friends don't ditch friends for boyfriends."

I waved her away as I walked back into my bedroom and answered the phone.

"I'm on my way to pick you up," Jackson said. "Thought we'd grab some Thai food and stay at my place tonight."

My conscience twinged. He knew that Saturday night was Thai night for me, so he was talking my love language. And staying at his place was infinitely better because there were no teenagers to worry about overhearing . . . things. But what Bonnie had said stuck with me and I took a deep breath. I didn't want him to take me for granted, right?

"It's a little late in the evening, isn't it?" I asked. "I didn't hear from you all day, so I've already made plans."

Nothing for a full five seconds. "I didn't realize I was on a time limit," he said, his voice frosty.

I fidgeted, twisting the length of my braid around my finger. "You aren't," I said hastily, then winced. "I mean, it's just that Bonnie had asked me to go to this party a few weeks ago and I said I would." Which was true.

"You hate parties."

"I know, but I love Bonnie, so I said I'd go. I did just attend a party with you as well, so it's not unprecedented behavior."

"Does this have to do with your newfound fame?" he asked.

That conversational twist left me at a loss. Had the phone line cut out? Had I missed something? "I'm not following you. How does Bonnie's party have anything to do with us?"

"I mean that I've seen what's on Twitter and posted on the Internet. I'd hate to see you take relationship advice from strangers with attention spans the length of a gnat's."

"Of course not," I said. "I doubt anyone who's posted their opinion on our relationship is actually qualified to make a judgment or give advice, at least not without a psychology degree and interviewing us. And you know I don't put any stock in the pseudosciences of psychology or sociology anyway." Especially the latter. Vague, sweeping pronouncements and sketchy "science" does not a discipline make.

There was silence.

"Hello? Jackson? Are you still there?" Had we been disconnected?

There was a low chuckle. "Yeah, I'm here. I just forget sometimes."

"Forget what?" Now I was totally lost.

"That you're not like everyone else."

Hmm. "Is that a good thing or a bad thing?" Just to be clear.

"It's a good thing, China," he said. "Trust me. It's a very good thing."

I wasn't sure what exactly had just happened. He'd been fine, then upset, now was fine again. And people said women were the emotional ones.

"Follow my Twitter feed," I said. "They're supposed to release a trailer for the next *Star Wars* movie tonight. I'm going to sneak-watch it when Bonnie isn't looking." The doorbell rang before Jackson could answer. "That's Bonnie. She's picking me up. Gotta go."

"Be careful. Text me when you get home. Have fun."

"I'll try," I said. Yeah because me and parties went together like spinach and applesauce. "Text you later."

"Be careful what you tweet," he warned just before I ended the call.

I still didn't understand how my tweets would be an issue, but was glad that Jackson was again in a good mood. I just hoped it lasted.

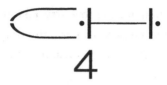

4

Bonnie gave a wolf whistle when I stepped into the living room. "Wow, girl! Mia did her thing, didn't she? You look fantastic."

That made me smile. It was a novel thing for me, to look pretty and girly. My wardrobe consisted of dozens of pairs of jeans, three times as many T-shirts of varying fandoms, plus the little button-down shirts I wore over them to keep me warm because I was perpetually cold.

"Thank you," I said, doing a little pirouette. "Mia could make a silk purse from a sow's ear," I said, quoting my granny. Bonnie just looked at me with a confused expression on her face. "It's an idiom," I explained. "It means that . . . oh, never mind." It wasn't important. And usually *I* was the one left confused by idioms.

"Let's go then," she said.

"I'm leaving," I hollered upstairs to Mia. She poked her head around the corner. "Be good. Don't let Michelle play with my stuff." By which I meant my office, loaded to the max with everything from a life-size Iron Man Mark 42 replica to a Harry Potter alcove, a TARDIS, and a thousand other collectibles that most people probably viewed as "toys."

"I know better," Mia said. "Don't worry and have fun."

It was pointless telling me not to worry. I'd found that ever since my niece had moved in and I'd become her temporary guardian, worrying for her well-being and safety was a constant thing. No wonder parents looked tired all the time.

"You're the second person to tell me to have fun," I said. "The fact that I'm going to a socially acceptable form of entertainment and have to be told to be amused means that parties are not fun for all involved." I'd only been to a few parties and had yet to have "fun." But it would be a revelation if others also didn't enjoy the gatherings.

"Honey, half the people are probably not having fun. They're just faking it."

Huh.

Bonnie and I had barely stepped outside when we were blinded by a flash of light. I blinked, trying to get the black spots from my vision, and recognized the cameraman.

"Ralph! What are you doing at my house?" Sure enough, it was the same guy that had found me today at Retread.

"Girls' night out, eh?" he asked, ignoring my question. "Who's your friend?" He snapped more photos, getting right up in Bonnie's face.

"Ugh." She pushed him away in disgust and got in the car.

I had to bypass Ralph, too, as I went to the passenger side. "You're trespassing, you know," I informed him. "This is private property."

"By the time the cops get here, I'll be gone," he said with a shrug. He was snapping continuously now as I got in the car. I was mindful of my short skirt and kept my knees together.

"You should find another occupation," I said. "You're highly dependent on my comings and goings for your income. It must be a stressful job."

"You're feeling sorry for him?" Bonnie hissed, starting the car.

"I'm just pointing out a fact," I said. She shook her head, sighing as we backed out of the driveway and took off.

She took me to downtown Raleigh and parked the car, then we walked a block and a half to our destination. I was a little concerned as we descended a staircase to under the street level.

"This is a safe place, right?" I asked.

"Of course! It's a great, really fun bar. You're going to love it."

I didn't know about "great" or "really fun," but it certainly was crowded. I followed Bonnie toward the back where there was a big group of people standing and sitting in an area with a couple of couches and several eclectic and uncomfortable-looking armchairs. My nerves went taut as Bonnie greeted several people.

". . . and this is my best friend, China," she said, tugging me forward.

I pulled my lips back from my teeth in my best imitation smile and thrust my hand out. "Nice to meet you."

The man she was introducing to me seemed a little surprised, but smiled and shook my hand. "Mike. Nice to meet you, too, China."

"Mike's the man of the hour," Bonnie explained. "He's even landed a job at a four-star Michelin restaurant in DC."

"That's really impressive," I said. "There are only two jobs per one thousand applicants for cooks and chef positions in the District of Columbia. Though the hourly wage is one of the highest in the nation. Congratulations."

"Um, yeah," he said with a quick glance to Bonnie. "Right place at the right time, I guess."

Someone else latched on to Mike and tugged him away, then Bonnie was introducing me to more people in a whirlwind of faces and names. They all smiled and said polite things, as did I, and I finally found a moment to slip away from Bonnie's clutches.

Standing alone at the bar, I took a deep breath. Social situations like this were very difficult for me and stressful. I often needed a few minutes alone to get my bearings back whereas Bonnie seemed to become even more energetic with each added person.

"What can I get you?" the bartender asked.

"Um, I'm not sure," I said. "Something sweet, tangy, and strong?"

He smiled. "Got it."

I watched him make a drink the way I'd never seen it done before. He used gin, fresh lemon juice, muddled a sprig of rosemary with sugar, added a couple of other ingredients I couldn't name, then shook it all with ice and strained the resulting liquid into a little, old-fashioned champagne cocktail glass. He added a lemon twist and sprig of rosemary before setting the drink in front of me with a flourish.

"Cheers," he said, then waited.

I took a cautious sip. My eyes widened and I took another. "Wow. This is really good. What is it?"

"It doesn't have a name," he said. "I custom-made it just for you." He winked, then wandered off to take another order, leaving me to my unnamed but delicious cocktail.

"Excuse me." I glanced over my shoulder and saw a man trying to edge in to the bar to place an order.

"Oh, sorry." I picked up my drink and moved aside.

"Hey, wait," he said. I stopped. "Are you . . . is your name China?"

I gave the guy a once-over, nearly 100 percent certain I'd never met him before in my life. "Who are you?" I asked.

He smiled, and it was a nice smile. He looked older than me by about five years or more, with dirty-blonde hair and warm brown eyes. Taller than me, he wasn't tall by most standards, I'd say five ten. "You probably don't remember me, but we went to the same high school together. Briefly."

High school? That had been Marian High School. I'd attended there for two semesters before graduating. But I certainly hadn't had any friends there, especially boys.

"Um, I was really young . . ." I began, but he interrupted.

"Oh yeah, I know. You were the girl genius that no one knew what to do with."

I didn't know what to say to that, so I took another sip of my drink. I tried not to remember those early years in my life that had been so painful and awkward, especially after my mom had died.

"I'm sorry, that came out wrong," he said with a grimace. "I just meant . . . I remember you." He held out his hand. "Let's start over. I'm Chad."

"Nice to see you again, Chad," I said, shaking his hand.

"We were in Advanced Calculus together," he said. "For a short time, anyway."

I remembered the class. I'd found it incredibly dull and remedial. The other kids had hated me, the twelve-year-old usurper in their high school. They'd glued my locker shut and locked me in the janitor's closet. Not exactly The Best Years of My Life.

"So what are you up to now?" he asked, accepting his drink from the bartender. Something clear in a short glass.

I dearly wanted to say, *"I head up a secret government agency that uses cutting-edge software to predict criminal and terrorist behavior."* But that would be blowing my security clearance and employment contract to smithereens.

"I develop software," I said, which was generic enough for people to get the gist that I did-something-with-computers. "What about you?"

"Insurance," he replied. "I'm in town for a convention and came a few days early to spend time with a buddy of mine from college." He motioned to where a man stood chatting animatedly with two women. "He lives here."

My skill level at small talk was somewhere around the region of my skill level at softball. I knew the basic mechanics and what was supposed to happen, but I never could get it quite right. Nonetheless, I tried.

"So . . . insurance," I said. "Not exactly rocket science, right?" I gave a little laugh and he grimaced. Uh-oh. That hadn't been right then. "I meant, it must be nice to have an occupation that isn't cognitively demanding." By the look on his face, I'd just made it worse. Crap. I took a big gulp of my drink. Damn small talk. I hated it.

"I'm sure I deserved that," Chad said with a half smile. "We weren't exactly kind to you the short time you attended Marian."

I shrugged. "It's in the past. Children can be cruel."

"Well," he said, "for all the shitty things that people did to you at Marian, let me formally apologize for myself and on behalf of everyone else who isn't as fortunate to run into you as I am."

Chad had a sheepish smile, but his eyes were sincere. It wasn't often in life when an apology was forthcoming from someone who'd wronged you years before, and I appreciated it.

"Thank you," I said. "I accept."

"Can I buy you a drink to seal our newfound acquaintance?"

I realized my drink was gone. I must've sucked it down while trying to figure out small talk. "Yes. That would be nice."

The bartender made another of the sweet-tangy drinks for me. I was feeling much more relaxed now, which had the unexpected effect of enhancing my efforts at making small talk. It helped that Chad was easier to talk to than many people I encountered.

"You really turned out . . . just gorgeous," Chad said with a smile. "Wow."

That was surprising to hear and I couldn't stop the grin on my face. It was a new thing for me, compliments on my physical appearance. Jackson didn't say much about how I looked usually, unless I was dressed inappropriately, like last night. Not that I was vain enough to need that—my sense of self-worth was just fine, thank you very much—but the part of me that had Mia fix my hair and makeup tonight purred like a kitten.

"Hey, can I take a picture with you?" he asked. "I saw you're seeing Jackson Cooper, so not only are you successful and beautiful, you're famous." He was grinning when he said it, which I took to mean he was teasing me.

"Oh, I'm not famous," I said hastily, but he was already holding up his phone for a selfie. He slung his arm over my shoulders and I had time for my quick show-my-teeth grimace as he snapped a photo.

"There you are!" Bonnie had come to rescue me, thank God. She tugged on my arm. "C'mon. I have to go to the bathroom."

"Bye, Chad," I tossed over my shoulder.

"I'll tag you," he called back as Bonnie hauled us both through the crowd to the ladies' room.

Bonnie disappeared into a stall and I pulled out my phone. It was still ten minutes until midnight, but it didn't hurt to check the website. They might've released the trailer early.

"Are you having a good time?" Bonnie asked when she came out. She adjusted her skirt and washed her hands.

"Sure," I automatically replied, knowing that was the expected response that would please her. The website was taking forever to come up. I really hoped the server wouldn't overload. I was looking forward to seeing the trailer the second it was released. I opened Twitter and started searching. *Jackpot.* Someone had gotten ahold of the trailer early. It was already trending.

"China!"

"Just a sec," I muttered, clicking links until I got to the trailer. It popped up and began playing. I squealed in excitement. "Come see!"

She hurried over to me. "Is that *Star*—"

"Shhhh!"

We watched in rapt silence. Well, *my* silence was rapt. Bonnie was just quiet, watching over my shoulder until it finished.

"The new trailer," she said. "You should be happy, right?"

I shook my head, disappointed. "I'm surprisingly let down. I find the continued trend of a female as the main protagonist with a male sidekick extremely irritating."

"You're a woman. You should be glad they're giving a girl the starring role in saving the universe."

"I'm not opposed to a female hero. I'm opposed to there being a female hero just for the sake of wanting to make her female. What does it contribute to the story?" I was busily tweeting as I talked. "If current mores and societal values, i.e., political correctness is allowed to influence the story being told, then it's not really part of the *Star Wars* universe. It's merely a reflection of ourselves. It wasn't just Luke and the story of the Empire and the Jedi that made *Star Wars* such an epic tale, but the romance between Princess Leia and Han, and his story of redemption."

After an uncharacteristically long silence, I glanced up from my phone to see Bonnie surveying me, hands on her hips. "What?"

"Can we get back to your Real Life problem, please? If you're not sure you want to get serious with the first guy you have ever dated, then what's the logical thing to do?"

I frowned. "I don't want to break up with him."

"I know, that's not what I meant," she said. "The only way to know if he's The One is to expand the pool of candidates, right?"

I considered it. The reasoning was sound, but . . . "I don't know if Jackson would like—"

"Jackson's not here," she interrupted. "I'm not saying you have to sleep with a slew of other men. Just . . . shop around."

I frowned. "'Slew' is an indeterminate number." And sounded like a lot. More than a dozen? A baker's dozen?

She rolled her eyes. "C'mon. Let's go expand your pool."

I would much rather have stayed hidden in the bathroom and tweeted more about the *Star Wars* trailer, but Bonnie was having none of it. She snatched my phone from me as we left the bathroom.

"And I'll hold on to this so you can devote your full attention to your experiment," she said.

"You're being highly manipulative and bossy tonight," I informed her. She stopped walking and gave me a kiss on the cheek.

"I know I am, but it's just because I love you." She slung an arm around my shoulders and squeezed, quickly letting go. She knew I got uncomfortable with displays of affection. She'd even tried to psychoanalyze it with me one time, but when she realized that I'd developed the aversion to physical affection about the same time as when my mother died, she dropped the subject.

I was glad that same aversion didn't preclude romantic, sexual touching, because that would be extremely inconvenient. I'd decided that my antipathy for touch only included platonic relationships, which I had no doubt a psychologist would make hay from, not that I'd subject myself to psychoanalysis anytime soon. It always went back to the mother, right?

Bonnie thrust a drink into my hand and set about introducing me to and chatting with no less than fifteen men. I counted. John, Mark, Lewis, Ron, Stephen (with a *ph*, I was told), Brian, Bryan, Camden, Harrison, David, Daniel, Tom and Thomas (not the same guy), Juan, and Bradley. Their occupations ranged from accountant to bartender, lawyer to artist ("My medium is whatever moves me at that moment."), sales director to luxury car salesman. There was even a sous chef and arm model thrown in there somewhere. Bonnie put dibs on the arm model, but I just thought longingly of Jackson's biceps and quads. And none of them interested me for more than a few passing minutes.

I toughed it out for another hour. By then, I'd reached my limit on social interaction with strangers, "expanding my pool" or not. Fighting my way through the crowd to where Bonnie was, I hollered in her ear, "I'm going home now."

"Don't go yet," she implored, grabbing my arm. "It's barely after one."

"I'm exhausted," I said, which was true, but I was more mentally and emotionally tired than physically. I just wanted to curl up in my *Star Wars* pajamas and eat my Fig Newtons. "I'll catch a cab and call you tomorrow."

She tried again to make me stay but I remained adamant until finally she handed over my phone and I trudged up the stairs back to the street, sucking in a lungful of fresh air. The drinks had made me sleepy, too, so that I was yawning by the time I reached the top . . . and stepped into a horde of people.

Flashes went off from multiple areas, blinding me. Voices erupted in a cacophony as I was hemmed in from all sides.

"China! Oh my God, it's you! Will you take a selfie with me?"

"China! I love you!"

". . . say hi to us, China . . ."

". . . autograph, just a quick one . . ."

"China!" "China!"

My name, called over and over. There had to be at least three dozen people all crowding around me, touching me, tugging at my hair and my dress.

"Stop it!" I started to panic. I couldn't move forward or back, I was stuck in one spot as they closed in, and the flashes documented it all. "Stop! Move back!" But no one listened. I didn't even think they could hear me.

Someone jostled me and an elbow flew up, knocking me in the face and my glasses to the ground. I saw stars, then nothing but dark blurs. My hair was pulled again and someone shoved into me, knocking me to the ground. I screamed in alarm, but there was so much noise. A foot landed in my gut, cutting me off midscream. I curled into as small a ball as I could, pulling my feet and arms in close and burying my head, hoping to not get hurt any worse.

A waft of air and space cleared around me. I heard people yelling and the scuffle of feet against concrete. Suddenly, I was scooped in a man's arms and lifted up. I didn't know who my unlikely savior was, but I clung to his neck, feeling him striding away from the crowd. He slid me into the backseat of a car and followed me in. The slam of the door abruptly muffled the sounds from outside.

My hair was a mess and all over. I couldn't see more than a foot in front of my face without my glasses and at the moment, I was crying too hard to see even that. Tears streamed down my cheeks and I was shaking. One strap of my dress had torn and I held the bodice up with one hand to preserve what little modesty I had left.

"Shh, it's okay. You're okay." Jackson's voice soothed me, his hand stroking my hair. He moved slightly, then I felt him spread his suit jacket over my shoulders and tug it closed in front.

It took several minutes before I could get my tears under control. I wiped my cheeks with the back of my hand before he gave me his pocket square. Using that instead, it came away streaked in black. Lovely. So not only had I lost my glasses and torn my dress, between the tangled hair and smeared makeup, I probably looked like a hysterical raccoon.

"How did you find me?" I asked, my voice rough from crying.

"Twitter," he said. "Wil Wheaton retweeted you and then everything blew up. The *Star Wars* fanboys are having a war about what you tweeted. #BringBackHanAndLuke is trending. And all the female fans are hating on you and calling you antifeminist."

"But I didn't post my location."

"You didn't have to. Some guy posted a pic and tagged you, checking in here. I knew you were with Bonnie, but started to worry when his tweet started being retweeted. Then with all the *Star Wars* furor, I wanted to make sure you were okay, so I had Lance drive me over."

"A guy tagged me? Who?" Then I remembered. "Oh. Oh yeah. Chad."

Jackson's brows raised. "Who's Chad?"

"A guy I went to high school with," I said with a sigh. I hadn't thought a thing about it when he said he'd tag me. But giving away my exact location and a close-up photo of me had proven to have disastrous consequences.

Jackson winced when he saw my face, taking the cloth from me and dabbing at my chin. The cloth came away with red stains. I hadn't even realized I was bleeding. "I underestimated the public's interest in you," he said. "I'm sorry, China. I should've taken better care."

I was upset. My emotions were overtaking my logic at the moment, the panic of the sudden crowd love-attack still had me shaking. I was grateful Jackson had saved me, but anger bloomed that this situation had even happened. Logic said I shouldn't be as angry as I was, but I couldn't seem to help it. Since I had no other outlet for my anger and fear, I took it out on Jackson.

"I could've been killed, you know," I snapped, tears tightening my throat. "Or seriously hurt. I had no idea what I was walking into."

"I know—"

"You *don't* know," I interrupted. "I'm not that big, Jackson. They knocked off my glasses. They tore my clothes."

"China, I'm sorry—"

It was all suddenly too much. Too many people. Too much change. Nothing felt right or normal or comfortable. I was more anxious and stressed than I had been in years and I wanted nothing more than to be in my house, by myself, doing what I always did.

"Take me home," I interrupted him.

"My house is closer."

"I don't want to be in your house. I want to go home."

Lance was driving and I saw him glance in the rearview mirror at this. Jackson gave a stiff nod and Lance took the next left turn, heading west now instead of north.

We rode in stilted silence for a few miles before Jackson spoke. "I know you want to get home, but I'd like to take you to the hospital to get checked out."

I was shaking my head before he was even through speaking. "I'm not going to the hospital. I'm fine."

"China—" he began.

"One in twenty-five patients ends up with a hospital-acquired illness. Over one hundred thousand people die a year from infections contracted in hospitals or health care facilities. That's more than car accidents and homicides combined." I rattled off the statistics. "I'm fine. Just banged up a little."

My stomach ached where I'd been kicked and I hurt in various spots on my legs and arms from scrapes against the pavement. My head throbbed from hitting the ground and the pressure behind my eyes said I'd be feeling the loss of my glasses soon. But nothing was permanently damaged and last I'd heard, hospitals didn't treat OCD.

We pulled up to my townhouse and I was struggling to get out of the car before it had even stopped moving. Tomorrow I was going to hurt all over, I could tell already. Jackson was out and around before I'd succeeded, though, and took my arm to help me.

"Who's here?" he asked, distracting me from his touch.

A car I knew very well sat in my driveway and I inwardly groaned. Why oh why did he have to keep bothering me outside of work? As if it wasn't enough that I had to put up with him there, he couldn't even give me the weekend without inflicting his presence on me. Twice.

"Somebody I work with," I hedged. I hadn't told Jackson that Clark and I were now working together. He knew Clark was black-op-for-hire and ex-Army intelligence. God only knew what he'd think my new job was if he found out about Clark being a part of it. "I'm fine. I can take it from here." He needed to leave before Clark decided to make his presence known.

As if my thoughts had conjured him, my front door flew open and Clark stepped out.

One of my shoes was untied and I tripped when I took a step. I would have fallen flat on my face if Jackson hadn't caught me. His jacket slipped off and I was left clutching my dress to my chest.

"What the fuck happened?" Clark was on his way double-time, making it to my side in three seconds flat.

"You," Jackson said, in a tone that was anything but welcoming. "What are you doing here? And why were you in China's house?"

Well, shit.

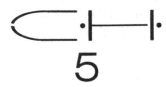

5

"Good to see you, too, dickhead. Now answer my question. What the fuck happened to Mack?"

I decided then and there that in my next employee review of Clark, I was going to recommend he attend a class on anger management. And I was definitely going to fail him on *Gets Along Well With Others.*

"I got caught in the middle of a crowd," I said, leaving it at that and forestalling whatever counter-insult Jackson was getting ready to hurl.

Clark's steel-blue gaze raked me from head to foot and I swallowed. My thin dress I clutched to my chest suddenly seemed inadequate armor. I shivered in the cold and Clark's jaw went tight.

"Come on, let's get you inside," Jackson said, moving me toward the front door.

I put on the brakes. "I need some space, Jackson," I said. Between last night's party, Ralph the photographer following me around, and tonight's fiasco, I was at the end of my tolerance for the changes to my life. "This is just . . . it's too much right now."

"You're upset," he said, lowering his voice. Probably in the vain hope that Clark wouldn't hear. "You aren't thinking clearly."

"I'm not thinking clearly," I repeated, stung. He'd just implied I was too emotional for rational thought, which was incredibly insulting. Next he'd be saying that I must be premenstrual. I shrugged off his jacket and handed it to him. "I'll talk to you later, Jackson."

I turned away but he grabbed my arm, pulling me back around to him.

"Don't leave it like this," he said, an urgency in his voice that surprised me.

Tugging my arm, I tried to free myself from his hold. "Let go of me."

"China—"

Suddenly, Clark was there. "The lady said to let her go." His tone was as smooth and cold as a glacial lake. It sent a shiver down my spine, and not in a good way.

"Stay out of this," Jackson shot back, the anger in his voice sounding warning bells in my head. The last thing I needed was these two getting in a fight.

"Maybe six weeks with your arm in a cast would teach you some manners," Clark said.

"Enough," I interrupted, anxious to avoid anyone ending up in a germ-infested hospital. "I just want to go home."

His hold loosened and I was able to pull free. "I can't just leave you here with him," he said to me. "He broke into your apartment. We should call the police and have him arrested."

Yeah, *that* would be a shit ton of giggles.

"Don't make threats you can't keep," Clark said, his lips twisting into a dangerous smirk.

"It's fine," I said hurriedly. "Just go. Please. I'll call you."

Jackson's gaze swung from Clark to me. After a long moment, he nodded, then turned and got back in the car. Lance drove him away.

I released a pent-up breath. One problem down, one more to go. I faced off with Clark. "Why *are* you here?" I asked. "Surely n-not another hack?" My teeth clacked together, chattering from the cold. I wanted my pajamas and my bed badly.

He shook his head, shrugging out of his leather jacket and swinging it over my shoulders. "Not a hack, no. Let's get you inside before you freeze to death."

I was too tired, too cold, and hurting too much to argue. He slid his arm behind my back and I leaned on him more than I wanted to as we went inside.

"Where's your med kit?" he asked, settling me onto the couch.

I waved toward the kitchen. "Far cabinet on the right. Middle shelf."

He returned quickly enough, carrying the clear plastic container I'd stocked myself. Crouching in front of me, he tore open some antiseptic wipes and began dabbing my chin.

"So what happened?" he asked.

I winced at the burn of the alcohol and his touch gentled even further.

"This guy at the party Bonnie took me to posted a photo on Twitter and tagged me," I said. "Apparently my current popularity resulted in a flash mob outside the bar, where they wanted to love me to death." I tried to sound casual, but my hands were still shaking.

"Are you okay?" he asked, resuming the dabbing.

I nodded. "Oh yeah. Totally. I'm fi—" My voice broke. I cleared my throat and tried again. "I'm fine." I hoped Clark would drop it, and he did.

"Well, it definitely looks like you lost a bar fight," he said, dabbing at the shredded skin on my knees. "Don't you know any self-defense moves?"

"Self-defense wouldn't have helped me tonight. I was caught in the middle of a feeding frenzy." I shuddered at the memory of being so helpless.

"I'm impressed that you used the old 'I need space' line on Coop," he said, taking my hand in his. He turned it palm up and used a new wipe to clean the scrapes there.

I frowned. "'I need space' line? It wasn't a line. I feel . . . crowded. And . . . unsettled. Like nothing is under control." I shook my head. It was difficult to explain the feeling of the ground spinning under my feet and me clinging to the edges. "He dragged me to a party last night and, well, you know how that went. Then tonight. And that Ralph guy following me around and taking pictures—"

"Wait," he interrupted. "Who's Ralph?"

"My paparazzi guy," I explained. "He followed me to Retread and he was taking photos of Bonnie and me when we left tonight."

"The paparazzi was here?" he asked. "You know his name?"

I shrugged. "Well, he was outside Buddy's store earlier, taking pictures, and I thought it would be rude not to be formally introduced. He seemed all right."

"Of course you'd be nice," Clark said, placing a tiny Band-Aid on my forehead. He sighed the way my mother used to when she had to explain jokes to me.

"I've found it benefits me more to be nice than not to be." *Treat others how you want to be treated* was the Golden Rule, after all.

Clark's gaze was on me again and this time I made the mistake of looking at him. His eyes were such a clear, deep blue—it amazed me anew. If you didn't know he was a ruthless hired gun with a talent for getting information out of people—whether they liked it or not—you could easily mistake him for one of the various Hollywood iterations of the Man of Steel. Black hair, square jaw, carved cheekbones, and a chiseled body that would make women drool completed the picture.

"People are basically shitty," he complained, ruining the image completely. Everyone knew Superman didn't cuss. "You should remember that."

"Why are you here again?" I asked, wanting to change the subject. I didn't need more reminders of how bad I was at reading people. After all, I'd once thought Clark was a sales guy who wanted to date me. And I *didn't* ask how he'd gotten into my apartment. I knew a locked door was merely a ten-second pause for Clark, if that.

"They found out what the hacker did while he was in the network," Clark said, putting another Band-Aid on my skinned knee. "I thought you'd want to know."

"You were at work? Again? Don't you have a life?" I hadn't meant it to sound the way it came out, but I was surprised. Clark was incredibly good-looking, seemed to have plenty of money, but was at work on both Friday and Saturday nights.

"Not until we find out who the leak in the NSA is," Clark replied.

That sobered me. One of the reasons Vigilance was top secret was because the president feared there was a spy within the National Security Agency. Someone with enough clearance to know things that could put American lives in danger.

"So what did he do?"

"He only accessed one set of files." Clark glanced up at me. "Yours."

I let out a deep sigh and stood.

"Where are you going?" he asked.

"I need cookies." My usual bedtime snack of Fig Newtons, I ate two every night. Tonight, I grabbed the entire package and brought it back to the living room. I bit into one and was immediately transported back to Granny's house when I was little. She'd doled them out like they were gold when I'd go visit her. I offered the package to Clark. "Want one?"

He looked at me as though I'd offered him a dead rabbit. "Those aren't real cookies. They're disguised laxatives."

I nearly choked on my cookie, laughing. He had a point, I suppose, based on my own digestive experience. But it wasn't enough to make me stop eating them. It did, however, make me feel as though I could handle the news Clark had just given me.

"It's not that strange, I guess, if he was looking for the head honcho," I said. "I'm sure he also knew he had a limited time frame."

"You're not worried?"

"There's nothing I can do about it now. If we track him down, we can arrest him. Until then, everything that can be done, *is* being done. Worrying about it won't change the facts or anyone's behavior."

Clark's lips twisted. "Logic instead of emotion. So refreshing, coming from a woman."

"Remind me to add 'sexist' to your personnel review," I said without heat. I was too tired to get angry. "Thanks for the information. And the doctoring."

Clark grabbed his jacket. "Chalk up playing doctor as one of the things I never thought we'd do together, Mack." He shot me one of his grins that told me I needed to Google *what does playing doctor mean*, then headed out the door.

I woke in the morning to a phone call from Bonnie.

"Holy crap, girl! You sure know how to make a headline," she began our conversation.

I rubbed sleep from my eyes and sat up, stifling a groan. I'd been right. I ached all over today. Thank God it was Sunday.

"What are you talking about?"

"Pull up Page Six."

I reached for my iPad and went to the website. My own image greeted me.

"Oh. Oh wow." An understatement. The picture was of Jackson carrying me from the crowd last night. My head was buried between his neck and shoulder and you could see my bleeding knees. Jackson's face looked carved in stone. The headline read "Knight in Silicone Armor Saves His Damsel."

"I guess things are all patched up between you two now?" Bonnie asked.

I sighed. "Actually, no. I kind of broke up with him last night. I think."

"Really? *You* broke up with *him*?"

Grimacing, I said, "Don't sound so surprised."

"No, no, it's not that. I think it's great that you dumped him. I doubt he's ever been dumped in his life. Playing hard to get is a great approach."

"I'm not *playing* anything," I said. "I just need space. So much has changed so quickly and I feel like I'm a square peg trying to fit into the round hole of his life."

"Doesn't he know that you don't do sudden change?" She sounded irritated. "I thought he understood you." I didn't point out that Bonnie thought she "understood" me, too, yet had dragged me to a party last night.

"I thought so, too. I said I'd call him, but I don't know. I need some time." Too much change too fast, problems with work, and a whirlwind of social activities. I was tired of the whole thing. "I'm just going to do my normal routine today." Which sounded blissful.

"Good luck with that," Bonnie said with a snort. "With this kind of publicity, I doubt you'll be able to step outside your door."

And she was right. When Mia and I peeked out the window later, it was to see not only Ralph, but three other cars holding men with cameras set up across the street.

"Glad I went to Retread yesterday," I muttered. I glanced at Mia. "Fall break is coming up next week. Why don't you go home early and stay a couple of weeks? I'm sure your teachers will give you the home-work." I didn't want Mia to have paparazzi following her around, too. "By then, this will have blown over."

"I hate to leave you to deal with this alone," she said with a frown.

My heart twisted. I loved my family, but I wasn't particularly close to them. Mia was the closest thing I had to a sister, even with our eight-year age difference. To hear her say that she wanted to support me hit me "right in the feels," as Dean, my *Supernatural* boyfriend, would say.

"I know, and I really love you for that," I said. "But I need to protect you right now. And that means shipping you home for a bit. Plus, I know Oslo and Heather miss you." My brother was a good father and Heather really was a good stepmom, even if they sometimes didn't understand Mia.

Mia considered, studying me. Finally, she sighed. "All right. I'll go. But I'm still totally going to follow the saga on Twitter."

"Saga?"

She nodded. "Didn't you see? After that picture hit this morning, #ChinaJack started trending. Everybody loves Jackson again and how romantic it was that he saved you."

Last night had felt anything but romantic, but I didn't bother trying to explain that.

"Go pack," I said. "I'll book your ticket and call your dad."

Getting Mia to the airport proved to be more complicated than I thought, and I ended up ordering her a taxi just so we wouldn't have the cameras following us to the airport.

"Text me," I said, hugging her tightly. Her long blonde hair was up in a ponytail that bounced and swung in perfect boppity fashion when she walked. She was as into fashion and makeup as I was into *Doctor Who*. "I'll try to remember how you did my makeup."

She hugged me back. "Just remember, contour first, then powder."

When we broke apart, I was surprised to see tears in her eyes as she picked up her pink Hello Kitty suitcase.

"I'm going to miss you, Aunt Chi," she said.

I forced a smile for her benefit, even though my gut ached. This must be how parents felt when kids went off to college, and she wasn't even my kid. "You'll be back before you know it," I assured her.

Waving her out the door, I watched as she climbed into the taxi. Once it had driven away, I closed the door. The silence of my apartment suddenly felt oppressive. Shit. I missed her already.

To take my mind off it, I called my grandma. "How's tricks?" I greeted her.

"Aw honey, your granny still has it," she said. "I won twenty bucks at the poker game last night."

"I thought they said you couldn't gamble anymore?" Grandma lived in a retirement community down in Florida and they'd recently been chastised by the police for running a poker game, citing it was against the state gambling laws.

"We've gone underground," she said. "We switch the location of the game every week, and you can only get in with a password. If it hadn't been for that sore loser Helen, we wouldn't have to go to the trouble. Though honestly, it's put a bit of spark in it, knowing we're breaking the law."

I laughed. My grandma was an incorrigible force of nature who'd decided when she turned seventy that she was too old for rules or embarrassment. I loved every crazy story she told me, wishing I was as carefree as she was. Maybe when I was seventy, I would be.

"So what was the password?" I asked.

"This week it was Clark Gable," she said. "Next week I think I'll make it Lana Turner."

"Movie stars?"

"*Real* movie stars," she said. "Not like the ridiculous celebrities you have nowadays, where a woman has to only flash her hoo-ha and suddenly she's famous."

"Speaking of hoo-has," I said. "Did you get the batch of Harlequins I sent?"

I was glad Grandma didn't keep up with celebrity gossip as she didn't mention my back-to-back appearances in the paper. We chatted for a while—she was really looking forward to Viagra Wednesday this week, which I *didn't* need to know but she insisted on telling me—before we signed off. Then it was cleaning, ironing, and in bed by ten thirty.

I glanced at my phone as I lay in bed. It hadn't rung today. Though I had thought about calling Jackson a few times, it had been a relief not to speak to a soul all afternoon. I felt more in control. I'd had my pre-bedtime Fig Newtons—only two tonight—was in the right pajamas with the sheets tucked under my arms just so. The paparazzi had left the front of the house a couple of hours ago and things felt normal. Would calling Jackson and continuing a relationship with him spin my life out of control yet again? Could I handle that? Even for him?

I fell asleep with the questions unanswered inside my head.

Something woke me in the middle of the night. I lay in bed, staring at the ceiling, and listening.

It sounded like metal clanking, and it was coming from my office.

Goose bumps erupted on my skin. I knew I was alone in the house—or really, I *should* be alone. But something was making that noise, like machinery whirring.

What I wanted to do was pull the covers over my head and pretend I hadn't heard anything. But I knew that wasn't an option. Maybe it was just that something had fallen over. Goodness knows I had a ton of fandom memorabilia in my office. Mia could've moved something before she'd left, or one of her friends. My office was like a magnet for her friends, especially the Harry Potter alcove.

Even as I told myself it was nothing, I fumbled with putting on the spare set of glasses I'd dug out earlier. Looking around my bedroom, I grabbed the nearest thing I had to a weapon, which happened to be a replica of Narsil, the sword from *Lord of the Rings*. Its edges were blunt, but it was better than no weapon at all.

I crept down the hall, closer to the sounds that still hadn't ceased. A cold sweat broke out on my skin. My eyes were adjusted to the dark, so I didn't have trouble seeing. But what I saw when I peeked through the open doorway made me question my prescription lenses.

My Iron Man replica was staring at me, light glowing behind his eyes. And he'd moved, by several feet, toward the door. As I watched, his arm moved, the sound effects of metal against metal that I'd programmed myself into the replica made it seem more real than the movie, especially in the dark.

I was in such shock, I couldn't move, my mouth hanging open. His hand opened, palm facing me, and the sound effect of the repulsor beam blaster powering up filled the room. Rooted to the floor, I emitted a squeal of fear when it went off, my imagination expecting something to happen to me. But nothing did.

Iron Man and I stood in a standoff, his glowing eyes and chest eerie and menacing as he towered a foot over me.

Logic finally asserted itself and I ran behind the now-mobile suit and ripped off the rechargeable power pack. It immediately went dark, the arm dropping back to its side. My knees were shaking and I sank to the floor, unable to stand. The adrenaline rush had gone, leaving me weak and trembling.

The suit was one I'd bought and customized myself, adding networking capability and programming some basic movements and sound effects. What I *hadn't* programmed was for it to wake up on its own. Which meant someone else had accessed my network, found the suit, and decided to have a little fun at my expense. Considering the strength of my firewall, it was a very talented someone, which basically meant one person—the same guy who'd hacked Vigilance.

Going back to sleep was out of the question—I was too rattled. I put on my *Saving People. Hunting Things. The Family Business* T-shirt, jeans, and tennis shoes. After washing my face, brushing my teeth, and pulling my hair back in a ponytail, I was ready.

Getting in to work at five o'clock in the morning on a Monday guaranteed a few raised eyebrows, especially since they knew I usually arrive at seven o'clock on the dot. I ignored the looks cast my way from the skeleton staff and unlocked my office.

It was nice having my own office and it was rather large by most standards. One wall was glass that overlooked the crew floor and the wall of screens. Being back at work calmed my still-frayed nerves. After all, it wasn't every day that I got attacked by Iron Man.

Derrick was still there and I pinged him a message, asking for an update. Sixty seconds later, he was in my office.

"This is what we have so far," he began, handing me a folder before taking a seat opposite my desk. "Roscoe got further than I did with the IP trace and has set up tripwires that'll spring and let us know if he comes out that way again."

"So where did he originate?" I asked, skimming through the papers in the file.

"Roscoe thinks he's near the DC area."

I glanced up in surprise. Derrick's expression was grim. "Not another government agency, do you think?" I asked.

"I don't know. Roscoe's still working on it. We'll keep you updated."

I nodded. "And apparently the only thing he accessed was my records."

"Yes. It's as if he knew what to look for."

Yes, it did seem that way. Then he'd hacked my home network . . . for fun? To scare me? Just to see if he could? Or had he been looking for something else?

I didn't mention to Derrick I'd been hacked. If word got out that I was too incompetent to protect my own home, how could I be trusted to protect Vigilance? It was embarrassing.

"Okay. Thank you, Derrick." I dismissed him.

An hour later, I got an unexpected call. "Mr. Gammin," I said. "I haven't heard from you in a while." Stewart Gammin was the president's chief of staff and our method of communication to the executive branch. I'd never met the president himself, not that I was in a big hurry to do so. "What can I do for you?"

Gammin was as cunning a politician as they came and twice as dangerous, because *he* didn't need to worry about reelection. His was the hidden hand behind what the cameras saw, and power was his currency.

"We have a situation," he said by way of greeting.

My lungs froze. Surely he didn't know about the hack? I wasn't prepared to tell him until we knew more. "What is it?"

"An unexpected visit from a Chinese billionaire," he said. "Simon Lu. I'm sending you everything we have on him now."

A second later, an encrypted email popped up on my screen. I ran decryption and unzipped the attachment. "Got it."

"Go over it with Slattery," he said. "I'll be by in a couple of hours to detail what I need done." He signed off without so much as a "Have a nice day."

"And people say *my* social skills are lacking," I muttered, sending an email to Clark to let him know we needed to meet in my office ASAP, then printing two sets of what Gammin had sent. He arrived before the papers had even finished collating.

"So I hear you were in early today," Clark said, flopping down in a chair, knees spread as he leaned back.

It was difficult to concentrate when he did stuff like that, his body lovingly encased in a black polo, his biceps straining the elasticity of the garment's sleeves. Jeans were his favorite attire as well and he wore the nice ones that clung to his narrow hips and made his . . . backside . . . look hard enough to bounce a quarter off of.

I swallowed, jerking my eyes away before he noticed my staring. At some point, Clark's looks wouldn't affect me—they'd become ordinary—but today wasn't that day, damn it.

"Couldn't sleep," I said vaguely.

"Your scrapes look better," he observed.

Absently, I touched the scab on my chin that I'd not bothered to cover with makeup. "Gammin's going to be here soon to go over this." I handed him his set of documents.

"Simon Lu," Clark read aloud. "I've heard of him."

My eyebrows climbed. "You have?"

He nodded. "Ruthless fucker. Started one of the biggest Internet companies in China, thanks to corporate espionage and tech stolen from US companies."

"Why would he be coming here?"

"No idea. But somehow I doubt it's an acknowledged visit." At my questioning look, he clarified. "Back channel communication, wheeling and dealing."

Ah.

We were quiet for a few minutes, perusing the file at our own speed. Iron Man was nagging at me. I couldn't tell the staff what had happened, but somehow I thought it might be safe to tell Clark. Somebody ought to know, just in case I disappeared inside my TARDIS tonight and didn't return.

"Um, you know that hacker?" I asked, still pretending to read the file on Lu.

"Yeah."

"I think . . . he . . . ah . . . hacked my home network last night."

No response. I carefully glanced up through my lashes to see Clark frowning at me.

"What do you mean?" he asked.

So I explained about Iron Man's attack. "I'd programmed him myself, trying to make it more lifelike, like the movies," I said. "He hacked my network, activated it, and took control."

"That's not good," Clark said, his lips pressed in a grim line.

"I don't really want to . . . tell anyone," I said. "My credibility will drop to nothing. And if I'm a weak link in this project, I could be fired. Or worse." I'd known from the moment Gammin had first approached me about running Vigilance that bowing out of the project would be the equivalent of signing my death warrant.

"So do you think the hacker was just screwing around? Playing with your toys?"

"I don't know." A sentence I despised saying under any circumstances.

My intercom dinged, announcing Gammin's arrival.

"Don't say anything to him," I said to Clark, who nodded just as Gammin rapped sharply on my door and stepped inside.

"Good morning," he said, taking the chair next to Clark. He was tall with dirty-blonde hair and pleasant but forgettable features. I'd pegged him to be around forty-five years old. "I take it you've had time to go over the file?"

"Lu seems like quite the businessman," I said. The guy was worth over three billion.

"Yes, he's a saint," Gammin replied. "Which is why we need to know all we can about him. He's coming here to discuss the upcoming trade bill. Some high-profile tech companies are making noises about bringing manufacturing back to the mainland, and their senators are listening to them. If the rumored tax breaks are put into the trade bill, it may incentivize them to remove millions of jobs from China. The visit is being kept under wraps, very low profile."

"So what do you want us to do?" I asked.

"He wants us to listen in," Clark answered.

Gammin gave a little smile. "Exactly."

"Isn't spying more of a job for the CIA?" I asked.

"Usually, yes. But the president wants his team on it, which means you."

"Lu isn't going to come here alone," Clark said. "He'll have a full security detail. Do we have any assets with him?"

"Negative. But we do know he's going to be attending a VIP dinner tonight at the hotel where he's staying. The setting should be ideal. Do what you need to do, but I want his communications monitored for the duration of his stay. I trust you have the ability to do that?"

That question was directed at me and I nodded. "But if it's a VIP dinner, how are we supposed to get in?" I asked.

"Wait a second, it's not *we*," Clark interrupted.

"Failure isn't an option so I want both of you to go," Gammin said. "You'll get her in and out." He glanced at Clark, who was clearly displeased by this information. "She may need to work on the fly," he explained. "No one else on your team has the tech know-how to do it. She's the best, so she'll do it."

Gammin reached into the inside pocket of his jacket and withdrew a thick vellum envelope, which he handed to me. I slit it open as he talked. "We don't have the list of attendees, but have set up a cover for you two."

"Which is?"

"You're a couple. Been together for about six months. Clark's a rich playboy whose family is in the tech business. You," he looked at me, "are young and dumb. Just a bit on the side for Lothario here."

I laughed outright. "So I'm supposed to be his arm candy? You're joking."

"Gotta go with her on this one," Clark said.

I shot him a dirty look. "The only thing *more* unbelievable is that you're in the tech business."

"I'm sure you two can figure something out," Gammin interrupted. He looked slightly pained as he gave us a once-over. "Try not to kill each other, okay?"

Sure. No problem.

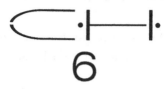

6

"You can't wear jeans and a T-shirt tonight," Clark said once Gammin had left.

"No kidding."

"Which means a tux for me and a cocktail dress for you."

I grimaced. Twice within three days I had to put on a dress? Most women probably enjoyed getting the opportunity to dress up. Not me. And now Mia was gone, so who'd do my hair and makeup?

"Do you own a cocktail dress?" he persisted.

My cheeks warmed but I answered honestly, shaking my head.

Clark sighed. "That's what I thought. C'mon. Let's go shopping." He stood.

"Don't be ridiculous," I sputtered. "I have to work, not go shopping."

"It *is* for work," he said. "Now quit stalling and let's go."

I didn't see any way around it, so I reluctantly followed him out to the parking garage.

"We'll take my car," he said, pulling open the passenger door for me.

I balked. "I can just follow you," I said, putting on the brakes.

"And have you get lost because you have no idea where to find a cocktail dress?" he countered. I didn't reply. "I bet dollars to donuts that you do all your shopping online."

Damn. "Not all of it," I muttered. As many times as I'd tried, shopping for shoes online was trial and error because not every size seven was an actual size seven.

"In you go," he said, giving me a little push. I got in the car but also shot him a dirty look, which he didn't see because he was already shutting the door.

"So did you and the boy wonder patch things up?" he asked as he drove.

I hesitated, my stomach doing a guilty flip-flop. "I didn't call him. I said I would, but I didn't."

"Why not?"

I turned toward him. "Is it always like this?" I asked.

He looked blankly at me. "Like what?"

I waved my hand vaguely. "That your whole life has to change to accommodate a romantic relationship." It seemed unfair to me.

"Well . . . yeah," he said with a shrug.

I was afraid he'd say that. "But what if it ends? Then you have to change back to what it was before. It seems like a lot of trouble to go through."

"It can be," he said. "But you have to weigh that against what you get out of the relationship."

"So . . . like a Pros versus Cons list?" I could do lists. Neat little precise orders of items to be weighed in a logical fashion. My fingers practically itched to grab a pen and notebook.

"Um, well, yeah, I guess, though that's being a little mercenary about it."

I was already digging in my backpack. "Don't be ridiculous. It's not mercenary. It's perfectly logical, and I'm disappointed I didn't think of it myself." Unearthing a notebook and a pen, I flipped to a pristine page and began writing. *Jackson—Pros vs. Cons*, I wrote at the top, then neatly made two columns and labeled those as well.

"These never end well," Clark said, looking dubiously at my notebook. "Haven't you ever watched *Friends*?"

"It was before my time and I never saw what was funny about it."

"Really?"

"So . . . Pros," I began, thinking. "Well, there's the obvious."

"That he's rich?"

That had a tone to it, but I didn't know what it meant, so I just took the comment at face value. "Yes, that's a pro because the alternative— his being poor—would most decidedly make a relationship difficult, introducing strain and even awkwardness. Especially when a woman is financially more successful than a man. So yes, Jackson being wealthy is a pro." I wrote in one column. "Not to mention that intellectually, he's quite stimulating." Dumb was boring. I wrote some more. "Though his wealth wasn't the obvious thing I was referring to. I meant the sex was obvious."

"How is that obvious?" Clark asked. "He could be bad in bed for all I know. Or for all you know either."

I snickered. "Please. I would know if Jackson was bad in bed."

"How?" Clark countered. "You were a virgin, right? So you have nothing to compare against. He could be an awful partner for all you know."

I felt the need to defend my ability to judge Jackson's sexual prowess. "I may not have a comparison, but I do know that I am sexually fulfilled by his level of passion and experience."

"Why? Because you have an orgasm?"

My face flooded with heat, but I answered just as bluntly. "Of course. That is the yardstick by which sexual fulfillment is measured, correct?"

Clark parked the car in the lot of a little boutique, turned, and looked at me. "If you think sexual fulfillment is just having an orgasm, then I'd definitely put Jackson's technique in the Cons column."

He was out of the car before I could think of a proper comeback, a not-uncommon event around Clark. With a sigh, I followed him to the door and inside the store, glancing around curiously at the muted rose carpet and the antique chandeliers dotting the ceiling. Full-length mirrors were placed strategically around while mannequins showcased different dresses and outfits.

"May I help you?" A woman had hustled forward, addressing her heavily accented question to Clark.

"Oui," he replied, then rattled off rapid-fire French. She responded just as quickly, looking pleased at someone speaking her native tongue.

Of course, I couldn't follow anything they were saying. Languages weren't my thing. There wasn't enough structure to them and they were constantly changing. I did notice when he gestured to me and the woman looked my way, too. Shifting my weigh uneasily from one foot to the other, I pushed my glasses up my nose.

The woman frowned, eyeing me up and down. "Elle est très petite, non?"

Okay, I knew enough basic French to understand that. "Yes, I know I'm the size and stature of your average fifth-grader," I groused.

Clark snorted, then tried to cover it with a cough. I gave him the stink eye.

"Bien, mademoiselle," the woman said. "Zee have plenty of beautiful dresses zat will suit you."

"But I just need one." She latched on to my elbow and tugged. "You are surprisingly strong," I muttered, having no choice but to follow her. Glancing over my shoulder, I saw Clark wink, then settle into an overstuffed armchair.

If I'd had claims to modesty, they were brushed aside with a Gallic shrug and wave as I was stripped to my underwear and various garments pulled over my head and up my legs. Most of them I didn't even get to see before the woman who'd introduced herself as Marie shook her head and tugged them back off. I felt like a human mannequin as she studied me.

"I have just zee thing," she said, popping out of the dressing room. She was back in moments, carrying a cherry red dress.

"Oh no," I said, backing away. "I don't wear red." Red was eye-catching. People paid attention to those who wore red. You had to have a certain charisma and panache to pull off red and be subject to all those staring sets of eyeballs.

Getting away from Marie in the confines of the dressing room proved impossible. I didn't think a lady her age could be so quick or adept, but before I knew it, she was zipping me into the dress. Reaching up, she tugged my hair tie out.

"Hey! What are you doing?" But she was already fluffing my considerable length of hair.

"Beautiful," she pronounced, then spun me around to face the mirror.

Oh. Oh wow. I'd thought the dalek dress was awesome, but this one was even better.

It was tight but stretchy, wrapping around my body and ending right above the knee. It was off the shoulder, exposing a lot of skin at my neck and chest. I'd always thought my collarbone protuberances were ugly, but in this dress they looked feminine and fragile. My sun-deprived skin looked the perfect shade of pale ivory against the red fabric and my dark hair contrasted both. It even made my blue eyes stand out.

"You like?" she asked.

I nodded, still staring in the mirror. "Yes. Yes, I do."

"Let's show zee gentleman." Then she was tugging me out again.

I could've gone without a stamp of approval from Clark, but it wasn't up to me, and quick as a flash, I was standing before him as though asking permission to buy the dress I wanted for prom.

His head was bent over his phone. He glanced up, then back down at the phone, then back up at me, where his gaze remained. I wasn't very good at reading facial expressions, so I decided he either looked shocked or frightened. Since I knew very few things frightened Clark—and I wouldn't even make the top hundred—I decided on shocked.

"Well?" I said impatiently, after waiting for what felt like an eon for him to say something. "This will work, right? This is what you had in mind?"

Clark's gaze went from my head all the way to my bare toes and back up. Goose bumps broke out on my skin as if he'd touched me, which was disconcerting.

"It'll do," he said, returning his attention to his phone.

My chest constricted and I drew in a breath at the prick of pain and embarrassment his easy dismissal had caused. Marie looked as though he'd just told her France was a third-world country with cuisine to match.

Spinning on my heel, I hightailed it back to the dressing room. That was the problem with trying to look like a girl. When I failed utterly, it was demoralizing. I'd rather be in my T-shirt and jeans and meet low expectations for my looks rather than trying to be the hottie that I so wasn't.

Marie took the dress from me without a word while I jerked my hair back up into a ponytail and shoved my feet back into my Converse. I took a deep breath. I was the boss. Clark worked for me, not the other way around.

I didn't bother speaking to Clark as I walked by him toward the register. I certainly didn't need him to assuage my bruised ego. I was smart. That was my "thing." Some girls were athletic, others were funny, and some were beautiful. The only box I checked was "Wickedly Smart." And that was okay.

"I'll take the dress," I told Marie, digging out my credit card.

"Do you need shoes?" she asked.

I ran inventory of my shoes, remembering a pair of candy-apple red Converse in the back of my closet. I saved them to wear around Christmas.

"No, I have shoes."

I felt Clark's presence behind me as I signed the receipt and accepted the garment bag from Marie. Before I could protest, Clark had slipped his finger under the hanger and taken it from me.

"I can carry it," I said as he slung the dress over his back.

"I know you can. Let's go."

Irritation edged out my hurt as I followed him out the door and to his car. Now he wanted to play at chivalry after he'd just insulted me to my face?

I shouldn't let it bother me. I shouldn't let it bother me, I repeated over and over inside my head. Clark and I had a professional working relationship. Not a personal one. I had to remember that.

Clark cleared his throat a couple of times and I glanced at him, waiting. "Were you going to say something?" I finally asked, my voice frosty.

"Yeah." He cleared his throat again and I waited. "The dress—"

I stiffened. "They don't accept returns," I interrupted.

"No, it's not that." He glanced at me, then back to the road. "It looked amazing. I guess I was just . . . not expecting that. You're always in . . ." He waved a hand toward my jeans and T-shirts. "Anyway, I just thought you should know. It was a good choice."

I wasn't sure what to say, so I settled for a quiet, "Thank you," then decided the silence was awkward. I reached forward and turned on the radio, rolling the dial until I hit a news station. That was the thing about my job—I could no longer be oblivious to the news of what was happening in the world.

". . . Tong Enterprises, an international telecommunications company based in Shanghai, is filing a case with the State Department, citing evidence of corporate espionage and attempted theft."

That caught my attention. Tong Enterprises was Lu's company. I turned up the volume.

"Sources at the State Department say that one of the companies cited in the suit is American corporation Wyndemere, which was just involved a few months ago in an attempted terrorist infiltration. The Department of Justice is still tracing ties Wyndemere had with both international and domestic corporations, searching for any further terrorist connections. One of the companies rumored to be under investigation is Cysnet, run by billionaire tech entrepreneur Jackson Cooper. In other news . . ."

And I stopped listening. I stared straight ahead, seeing nothing. The DoJ was investigating Cysnet? I should've known things had been too quiet after the fallout from the near-loss of Vigilance. Wyndemere had declared bankruptcy soon afterward and I thought Jackson's lawyers had severed all ties between the two companies.

"Coop's not having a good week," Clark mused. "Gets dumped by his girlfriend, now the DoJ is after his company."

"I didn't dump him," I said sharply. "I should call him, see if there's anything I can do."

Clark slanted a look at me, then back to the road. "He's already dragged you too far into his life. The paparazzi is one thing. The DoJ is another. Cooper is toxic right now."

"I thought that was when friends were supposed to stick by each other," I persisted. "When things get rough. It's easy to be someone's friend when things are good."

Clark snorted with disdain. "If you think Coop wants to be friend-zoned, then you're delusional."

I bristled. "What's that supposed to mean? You don't think he'd want anything to do with me unless we're in a romantic relationship?"

"It means you still believe in friendship, true love, rainbows, and unicorn farts." His blue-eyed gaze caught mine for a moment. "It's sweet and all, but you need to wise up. Fast. The only person you can depend on is yourself. Eventually, you'll lose everyone close to you or they'll turn on you and betray you. I'm sure Cooper's already learned that life lesson."

"That's not true," I said. "There's a place for cynicism, yes, because people are human. But it's just as wrong to expect the very worst."

"Very rarely does anyone's lack of faith and loyalty surprise me," he said. "I've been around too long."

An unwanted twinge of sympathy struck me at not just his words, but the way he said them. Clark suddenly looked tired and I wondered just who had disappointed him so badly that the scars still remained.

I didn't know what words to use, how to express the pang of sympathy inside. "I . . . wish you didn't feel that way," I finally said. "It's sad."

Clark gave me a sharp look, the moment of vulnerability gone like a shadow. "Don't even think of feeling sorry for me."

So much for trying to read social cues. Pressing my lips together, I turned to stare out the window. Clark reminded me of a tiger, beautiful but deadly, with sharp teeth and claws that remained hidden until they were embedded in your skin.

We pulled into the parking garage and Clark maneuvered to where I'd parked. I got out, removing the garment bag from the back seat, and when I turned around, Jackson was leaning against my car.

It felt like a sucker punch in my gut and I froze. Jackson shouldn't be here on many levels—not least of which was that I hadn't called when I said I would—but most importantly, how the hell had he found out where I worked and gotten into the garage?

Before I could decide on my next course of action, Clark was striding toward him. Jackson pushed himself away from my car and stood his ground, his eyes darkening as he focused on Clark's rapid approach.

"You need a lesson in when your presence isn't wanted, Coop," Clark sneered. "You're violating several laws just by being on this property. I'm debating arresting you or shooting you and, gotta say, I'm leaning toward the latter."

"What the hell are you doing with my girlfriend?" Jackson snapped, completely ignoring Clark's threats.

"None of your business. And maybe you'd better rethink your relationship status." His smile was slow and sent a chill down my back. "I hear she unfriended you, which, in non-tech terms, means to go fuck yourself."

Their antipathy for each other made me wince and for a long moment, I watched them trading barbs. But when Jackson's jaw tightened and he took a step toward Clark, I realized I needed to intervene.

"Enough!" My voice wasn't terribly loud, but it did echo in the garage, enough at least to make them both pause and glance my way. I hurried forward while I had the chance. "What is with you two? Clark, I'll take care of this. Jackson, what are you doing here?"

Clark crossed his arms over his considerable chest, his blue eyes focused like lasers on Jackson. "He's trespassing. Let's just shoot him and dump the body."

"Clark!" I hissed in exasperation.

"No one will miss him. I bet some people would even thank us."

I took hold of Clark's shoulders and turned him away, then gave him a shove that moved his body maybe half an inch. He was a big guy. "Just go inside," I ordered. "I'll handle this." Jackson looked ready to spring at Clark and rip him apart, piece by piece. I honestly didn't know who'd win in a fight like that, and I had no desire to find out.

Clark's gaze fell on me and I couldn't decipher what I saw in his eyes. I did know that whatever it was made me feel unsure, as though I was disappointing him somehow. But that didn't make any sense so it must just be my stunted social-cue barometer misreading things again.

When Clark had disappeared inside, I turned back to Jackson. He was closely watching where Clark had entered the building, his brow furrowed in thought.

"Why are you here?" I asked, drawing his attention back to me.

"I needed to see you, and I can't trust anything other than face-to-face communication right now," he said.

Nausea roiled my stomach. "Is that because of the DoJ?" I asked.

He nodded. "I think it's in retaliation for the pressure I've been putting on some politicians to do something about the hacking coming out of China and Korea. It's relentless and they deny it all the time. I've had friends' entire businesses get hijacked because of theft by the Chinese. They need to be stopped. But someone's pushing back and using the DoJ to do it."

"Tong Enterprises?" I asked, thinking about Simon Lu and his trip to the States to meet with undisclosed officials behind closed doors.

"Yes, I think so. And if they can trump up some kind of evidence that Cysnet knew that ISIS had infiltrated Wyndemere, then they can levy fines against me. Enough to effectively put us out of business."

Dismayed, I said, "But Cysnet is your life. You built it from the ground up. We had no idea Wyndemere had been compromised."

"I know. I'm working on it. It's just going to take some time."

Okay, he had a plan. That was good. "Is there something I can do to help?" Which was why I assumed he was here. Though I was at a loss as to what exactly I could do in this particular situation.

But he shook his head. "It's my problem, not yours. I just wanted to see you, explain why you may not hear from me for a few days."

Ouch. He hadn't said it out loud, but my guilt reared its head. "I'm sorry I didn't call," I blurted.

His gaze remained steady. "You said you needed space. I was giving it to you."

"Truly, Jackson, it's not you. I'm just—"

"Please don't use the *It's not you, it's me* speech," he interrupted. "I get it. I was moving too fast." He moved closer, pinning me against the car. Lifting a hand, the back of his fingers brushed my cheek. "I don't want to scare you off."

Bending his head, his lips caught mine, soft and coaxing, making me forget all the reasons why I hadn't called him. His taste was sweet— not in the sugary sense—but in familiarity and intimacy. It unsettled me. I didn't want to depend on Jackson for normalcy. What if I changed everything for him and we broke up?

"I . . . I gotta go," I said, breaking off the kiss and sliding out from between Jackson and the car. He snagged my arm, pulling me to a halt.

"Are you going to tell me about Clark?" he asked. "Why you're working with him?"

Jackson wasn't dumb. He'd figured that part out and I didn't doubt that sooner or later, he'd figure the rest out. But it didn't have to come from me and it didn't have to be today.

"You know I can't tell you," I said. "But you do need to leave. How'd you find me here, anyway?"

His eyes shuttered. "You're not the only one with secrets, China. And secrets are poison to a relationship." He paused, his lips thinning. "I don't like you working with Clark."

"It wasn't my decision."

"I don't trust him."

I frowned. "You don't need to. You're not the one working with him. I am."

"I meant, I don't trust him with you."

I backpedaled, my thoughts spinning. "You mean . . . you're jealous?" The idea was absurd. No man had been jealous about me. Ever.

"Men like Clark chew women up and spit them out," he said, sliding a finger along my jaw. "Just make sure things stay professional between you two."

"Jackson, isn't that like the pot calling the kettle black? You've dated so many women, Google has a search term for you." Yes, I'd found it while torturing myself looking at photos of him and all his past girlfriends.

My cell buzzed and I pulled it out of my pocket. It was a text from Roscoe. He'd gotten a hit on our hacker.

"I gotta go," I said to Jackson. "When will I see you again?"

"As soon as I can arrange it."

He cupped my jaw and went in for another kiss.

"I've gotta go," I said, turning my head. His lips skated along my jaw. It took an incredible amount of willpower to slide out of his reach. I hurried to the entrance, only glancing back once to see him watching me.

Shoving Jackson and our extremely confusing relationship from my mind, I tracked down Roscoe. "What have we got?" I asked.

Roscoe was about a decade older than me and had the same hangdog expression you'd expect to see on a basset hound. He was a perpetual hypochondriac and squirted antibacterial gel on his hands constantly. You never asked Roscoe the typical "How are you?" question unless you wanted a detailed account of his diet, body temperature, and bowel movements.

Clark had made that mistake once and I'd had a hard time keeping a straight face as Roscoe went through his current cruciferous vegetable diet and the havoc it had wreaked on his digestive system. The look of boredom that gradually turned to horrified disgust on Clark's face as Roscoe droned on had been hilarious to watch.

Currently, Roscoe was on a strict regimen of protein smoothies and pork—a diet choice I hadn't quite figured out but didn't particularly want to ask—and he was chewing on a strip of bacon as he bent over the massive printout he'd spread on the table.

"Hey, boss," he said, glancing up at me. Roscoe spoke mainly in a monotone and rarely saw the need to get worked up over anything. "Want some?" He held out the half-eaten bacon.

I forced a smile. "Thanks, but I've eaten."

He shrugged, returning his attention to the printout. "Our guy popped up again last night," he said. "He tripped an alert I'd set on a router in Austria."

I didn't ask how he'd done that or how many laws he'd broken by doing so. I was more interested in results than analyzing the ethics and legalities of the How.

"Could you trace him?"

Roscoe nodded. "Better than we have before. It got us to a metro area before he realized he'd been made and pulled the plug."

"So where was he?"

"Well, he bounced around Eastern Europe for a while, then over to China and Bangladesh. A router in Switzerland, another in Turkey, before finally returning home to the States."

"I don't need a roadmap, Roscoe," I said.

He looked balefully at me. "But I want you to know how hard I worked."

I pressed my lips together. "Point taken," I said. "Continue."

With a long-suffering sigh, he turned back to the printout, his finger moving along the lines of traffic and IP addresses scattered across the map. "He ended up there." He pointed.

"Boston?"

"Yeah."

"Could you tell what he was doing when you tracked him?"

Roscoe nodded again. "Trying to poke around a home network. Here."

He handed me a scrap of paper with an IP address scrawled on it. My network's IP address.

Crap.

"Okay, thanks."

Roscoe left and I returned to my work, only getting buzzed on my cell a few times that afternoon. One text was from Mia, telling me about being back at home with her parents and how she was watching Twitter for updates about Jackson and me, but there'd been nothing since Saturday night. I told her there wasn't really anything to tell.

OMG, she texted. *Are you two on a break?*

I thought about it. *I guess so.*

Like Ross and Rachel. They were on a break, too. It didn't end well.

Another *Friends* reference. I sighed. I'd have to try watching that show again. Apparently Rachel and Ross had had quite the turbulent romance.

How are things with your dad and Heather? I texted. Heather was Oslo's second wife and though they'd been together for several years, Mia had always had issues with her stepmom.

It's okay. They want me to move back home.

I felt a twinge of panic at that, which was strange. I should want her to go back home with her parents, but I'd also gotten really used to not coming home to an empty house. At first, Mia had really rocked my routine all out of whack, but now she was a part of it. Without her, I'd have to forgo the dumplings on Chinese night because there were too many for me to eat alone and they were never good the next day.

What do you want to do? I texted. I should tell her they were right and she should stay home . . . but I couldn't.

I dunno. It's nice to be home, but I miss it there, too.

Okay, well she hadn't ruled either option out. I supposed this was a wait-and-see thing.

Whatever you decide, I'll support you, I texted.

Thanks.

Gotta go. Have a date. Not really—it was work—but it made me sound slightly less pathetic to say I had a date.

With who?

Asshat. I smiled as I typed in her pet name for Clark. Mia liked to think my dating life was more interesting than it really was. Might as well try to live up to it.

No way! Okay, well remember, you and Jackson are on a break! ☺

I took that to mean I should be guilt-free for whatever I chose to do . . . not that anything would happen. I signed off with a promise to *tell all* to her later—I'd have to make something up—and went to get ready for my non-date with Clark the Asshat.

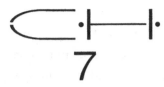

7

I'd taken my network offline before I'd left for work, so I wasn't worried that the hacker had gotten in again. But it was annoying that he was still trying. Apparently, he'd found my files and network to be too much fun to leave alone. At least I hoped that's all it was, though since he'd traced me from Vigilance's system, he was more worrying than your everyday teenage social misfit hacker wanting to show off. His taking over of my Iron Man was a direct insult and throwdown to me, and he was going to be sorry he started this fishing expedition.

I was turning the problem over in my head as I dressed for the "mission" tonight. I'd had to raid Mia's closet for a purse because all I had were backpacks and I needed something to carry my equipment in. I was supposed to compromise any and all electronic devices of Lu's that I could. I was counting on him having at least a smartphone and watch that would be vulnerable, a twofer that would be tricky to hack, but once I had one, I had them both.

The dress looked even better on me at home than it had in the store and I took a moment to admire the effect. I'd brushed my hair to a gleaming shine, the ebony waves falling past my shoulders. Makeup wasn't my thing, but I knew enough to use a little powder, blush, and mascara. I dared not attempt eye shadow or eyeliner. "Smoky eye" would probably turn out more like "black eye" in my less-than-capable hands.

Glasses were a must, though I thought with the mascara, they kind of amplified my blue eyes, so I didn't mind them. A squirt of perfume that I'd "borrowed" from Mia and I was ready to go.

Clark was supposed to pick me up, which made it feel almost too much like a date, but I shook off the feeling. He'd been crystal clear that he viewed me as a rather irritating coworker he was forced to work with, despite his preference for working alone. I didn't mind. We'd found a truce of sorts in our dealings with one another and when he wasn't trying to be an ass, he could be clever and even funny. While still not in my Top Ten Buddies to hang out with, I could appreciate his dedication to the job and his expertise. In that, we were alike.

The doorbell rang as I slung the heavy purse over my shoulder and I hurried to get it. Clark stood on the stoop and I had to blink a few times.

He wore black pants and a black shirt with a deep blue jacket—all colors that set off his hair and eyes. Two buttons were undone on his shirt, showing a triangle expanse of bronzed skin that drew my gaze. Clark's physique was perfection—wide shoulders, deep chest, narrow waist and hips. And when he smiled, a girl's knees went weak.

Not mine, of course. I knew what he was really like.

His gaze dragged from my head to my feet and stopped. "You can't wear those," he said.

I glanced down at my Converse. "Why not? They're comfortable and they match my dress."

"Normal women don't wear tennis shoes with a cocktail dress. You're working undercover. You need heels."

"I'll kill myself in heels," I argued. "Plus, I don't have any."

"You don't have a single pair of dress shoes? Seriously?"

"Asked and answered," I replied, crossing my arms over my chest. "Can we go now?"

He heaved a sigh and said, "C'mon. I'll improvise."

Clark *improvising* turned out to be hauling me into Nordstrom and straight to the shoe department. He zeroed in on a pair of sparkly silver shoes with a four-inch heel.

"No way," I said. "I'll fall."

"Just try them," he said, handing them to the salesman. "Size seven, right?"

I nodded, too anxious at the thought of having to wear the shoes to consider how he knew my shoe size. The salesman returned quickly, opening a box and handing me the shoes.

I put them on, admiring them. They were really pretty and dainty. Princess shoes.

"Looks like they fit," Clark said.

"Yes, but I haven't *stood* in them yet," I retorted. I got to my feet and as I expected, felt as if I was going to topple over any second. I took a cautious step, surprised when I didn't immediately twist an ankle.

"See, Mack?" Clark said. "I knew you could do it." He turned to the salesman and handed him a credit card. "We'll take them."

I took a tour of the shoe department, walking carefully. A woman eyed me as I passed by her twice. On the third time, she said, "It might be easier if you think of them as just any other shoe. Walk heel-toe, not flat-footed."

"Thanks," I said. Taking her advice to heart, I practiced some more, getting more confident with each trip around.

"Ready?" Clark asked, pocketing the receipt as he came up to me. His gaze lingered on my feet and legs, then he cleared his throat.

"Ready as I'm going to be," I replied, taking a deep breath.

Clark headed for the car and I followed, walking carefully. Asphalt wasn't as easy as carpet and linoleum was downright nerve-racking.

"Stick to the plan," he said. "You're a terrible liar and a worse actress. Keep your mouth shut as much as possible."

I was about to retort in outrage at his judgment of my thespian skills, but he'd already gotten in the car. He hadn't even opened my door for me. "What a gentleman," I groused, climbing into the passenger side.

"I know you don't want me doing this with you," I said. "But you could at least pretend."

"I'm not a big believer in hiding my feelings."

No shit. I was uncomfortable around people in the best of circumstances, but rarely had I come across someone in my adult life who could be as openly hostile toward me as Clark, or as dismissive. I'd been demanding respect for my intellect and talents for years, commanding hundreds of millions of dollars in R&D projects, then on real-life scenarios where the entire future of a business rested in my hands. I was unaccustomed to being treated as the inept ingénue, and I didn't like it.

I could probably try to pull rank and tell him to watch his attitude, but I didn't see how that would help me. Not really. Whatever Clark's problem, me being a hardnose bitch about protocol wasn't going to make it any better. I just had to ignore it the best I could and do the job.

The VIP dinner was located in an exclusive hotel downtown. Clark gave the valet his keys and reached for my hand. I instinctively drew back.

"We're supposed to be madly infatuated, remember?"

I felt like the misbehaving toddler forced to hold Daddy's hand as we entered the hotel. Not that his hand wasn't nice. It was. Clark's hand was rough, but holding it wasn't an unpleasant feeling. It still swallowed mine, and helped steady me on the slippery floor.

Clark led me toward a set of stairs guarded by two men. They looked over our invitation carefully, then let us pass. Clark let me go in front of him and I tried not to be self-conscious with him inches behind me on the narrow staircase. I needed to focus so we could do our job.

Clark already thought I would be incompetent at undercover work. I certainly didn't want to confirm his low opinion.

I was met by a man at the top of the stairs, though "Hulk" would've been more apt. He had to be at least six five and three hundred pounds. At some point, it didn't matter if it was muscle or fat—it was just bulk that you didn't want propelled in your direction. His head was shaved, his eyes were beady, and I wouldn't have been surprised to see him crack his knuckles.

"Your bag," he said, holding out a meaty hand.

I handed him my purse. He looked me up and down, then unzipped the purse and glanced inside. I'd considered this possibility, so I'd tossed a handful of tampons on top of my things, hoping for the instinctual male reaction. I wasn't disappointed. As soon as he saw the little white wrappers, he couldn't get rid of it fast enough.

"Turn around," he said to Clark, who got the full pat down. The guy was very thorough.

"You could at least buy me dinner first," Clark wisecracked.

Hulk wasn't amused. "Your turn," he said to me, and Clark's smirk disappeared. Apparently, he wanted to retaliate for having come within inches of touching feminine hygiene products because I'd had less invasive pat downs from the TSA. When his hand touched the inside of my knee and scooted upward, Clark was suddenly there.

In a move that was too fast for me to see exactly how he'd done it, Clark had the guy against the wall and his arm twisted up behind his back. "You're about to lose some fingers," he snarled.

I watched, eyes wide and holding my breath. Clark was a big guy, but the beefy security guard topped him by a few inches and about a hundred pounds.

After a long pause, Clark let go of him, then took my elbow and pulled me in front of him and through the doorway, his hands on my bare shoulders. The guard didn't try to stop us.

"What was that for?" I asked, once we were out of earshot. "You could've gotten us thrown out."

"You'd have preferred a cavity search?"

My cheeks flushed. "Of course not." Even though we were through the doorway, his hands remained on my shoulders, sending unwelcome flutters through my stomach.

"Then don't worry about it. It's not my first rodeo, sweetheart."

I stopped in my tracks and rounded on him. Enough was enough. "Sweetheart?" My frustration and irritation with him was reaching its limits.

His eyes flickered down toward my cleavage, then back up to my eyes. "Relax. It's a part. You getting all pissy with me isn't in the playbook."

I stepped closer, right into his personal space. I had to tip my head back a good ways to look him in the eye. "It may be a *part*," I said, "but just remember to watch the hands, and the *sweethearts*."

Clark's eyes narrowed, his jaw tightening in a way that nearly made me take a step back. Leaning down, he set his lips by my ear. "I'm in charge of keeping you alive tonight. If I were you, I wouldn't piss me off."

I swallowed hard, looking into his eyes, inches from mine. Clark played by a different set of rules—his own. I didn't know the exact reason why he'd given up his autonomy to work at Vigilance. He'd never said and I hadn't asked. But I did know from the little Gammin had let me view of Clark's file that a) he was dangerous and b) he was smart. Clark was very valuable to people who knew of his existence—and that number was precious few—and I had little doubt that his value didn't lie in his conversational skills.

"Champagne?"

We both turned to see a waiter holding a tray full of champagne flutes. He waited patiently as Clark took two glasses and handed one to me.

"Let's focus on the job and get the hell out of here," he said.

I wholeheartedly agreed.

Champagne probably wasn't the best idea, but I downed half the glass anyway, glancing around the room as I did so. There were about twenty people there, maybe a few more—mostly men but a handful of women. I spotted Lu talking to a man in the far corner. I couldn't tell who the man was, not with his back to us, but he looked familiar, which was weird. I shouldn't know anyone here.

I had a small device I'd helped Yash design that could clone a cell phone's SIM card in seconds—a procedure that would usually require the IMSI number on the card and its authentication code. Since the authentication code had to be achieved electronically—it couldn't just be read off the SIM, and obtaining it could sometimes brick the phone—I'd had to ask Yash for assistance. Telephony and all things cellular expert that he was, all I had to do was remove the SIM in Lu's cell phone and replace it with the clone that was already programmed to both transmit any communications to Vigilance and spread its core programming to any device and network Lu's phone touched.

The hard part was going to be getting Lu's phone, but that was Clark's area, not mine.

Waiters mingled among the guests, offering trays of hors d'oeuvres. Absently, I took one from a tray and popped it in my mouth. Chewing, I asked Clark, "What is this? It's really good."

He glanced at the bite, saying, "Pâté on a crostino," before eating it.

I choked. "Pâté? As in duck liver?" The bite turned to playdough in my mouth and I couldn't swallow.

Clark looked at me. "If you puke, I swear to God, I will *not* hold your hair."

I looked at him helplessly, holding the mushy food in my mouth.

"I've never had to ask this particular question before," he said, "but can't you swallow?"

I shook my head, then did a little dry heave. Oh God . . .

He cursed, then handed me his pocket square. Turning away, I spit the bite into the fabric and wrapped it up. Gross. Spotting a potted plant, I glanced around before poking it in among the dirt and leaves.

"Thank you," I breathed, relieved to have that over with.

"You are *so* high class," Clark said. "Let's hope they don't serve caviar." He took my elbow. "Next time, ask before you put something in your mouth." He frowned. "That didn't come out quite right."

The next waiter walked by and I asked very specifically what he was serving and when I found out it was just flank steak on bruschetta, I took one.

"No mushrooms, right?" I asked. He shook his head. "Nothing weird?" I persisted.

"No, ma'am."

Clark rolled his eyes, stuffing the food in his mouth and chewing. He snagged another glass of champagne and took a long drink.

We wandered Lu's direction, mingling along the way. I didn't have to do very much except smile and sip my champagne. Everything was going fine until we were about halfway there.

"Don't I know you?"

A woman stopped me with a hand on my arm. She looked midtwenties and very pretty.

"I don't think we've met, no," I said, giving her a polite smile. Shrugging off her hand, I took another step, only to be stopped again.

"No. You look familiar. I swear I know you," she persisted.

And it struck me. My newfound Internet fame. She probably had seen me on Twitter or TMZ or something. Her outing me would be very, very bad.

Clark appeared to come to the same conclusion I did because he stepped between her and me, forcing her to let me go. "Excuse us," he said. His hand rested possessively on my lower back, propelling me forward with him and away from the girl.

"That was close," I muttered, half to him and half to myself.

"Not nearly as close as this is going to be," he replied.

I glanced up at him, a question on my lips, then saw where he was looking and followed his gaze. The man who'd been speaking with Lu who had looked familiar to me had turned and was facing us now. It turned out that I actually did know him. I knew him very well.

"Jackson," I murmured in surprise. "What's he doing here?"

"He looks like he's thinking the same thing about us," Clark replied.

It was true. Jackson's eyebrows had climbed when he spotted us and now he was frowning. He headed in our direction, meeting us in the middle of the room.

"What the hell are you two doing here?" he asked.

"I could ask you the same," I replied, thinking fast. If Jackson outed us, we'd lose our chance at Lu. "But it'll have to wait. We're here for work, and I'd really appreciate it if you wouldn't blow our cover."

"Your cover?" He looked confused, not that I blamed him.

"Mark Dale," Clark said, giving his alias and holding out his hand. Jackson shook it automatically. "And this is my date, Suzi."

Suzi? Really? Ugh. "Nice to meet you," I said.

Jackson's expression cleared as understanding dawned, then his jaw tightened. "The pleasure's all mine," he said with a forced smile. Leaning forward, his lips grazed my cheek. "I think you and I are going to be having a long conversation, my darling."

His whispered words and the leashed anger in them made me wince, but I forced my fake smile. "That sounds lovely."

"Jackson, will you get me another drink?" A woman had come up behind him and was glancing curiously at Clark and me. Statuesque with long, red hair, her black dress sparkled and had a slit up the side, exposing a perfectly shaped leg.

I gritted my teeth. "And who is this?" I asked him.

"This is Rebecca," Jackson replied. "My companion for the evening. Rebecca, this is Mark and . . . Suzi."

She smiled in a blandly polite way, her crimson lips curving and showing off Angelina Jolie–worthy cheekbones. "How do you do?"

It wasn't a question that she was interested in hearing an answer to because she immediately dismissed us, turning her attention back to Jackson and winding one bare arm through his. "Do get me another drink, Jack. The champagne is simply divine."

Jack? Exactly how well did this chick know him?

I opened my mouth to ask just that question when Clark suddenly pushed us past them, his arm tight around my waist.

"Save it," he said. "Now's not the time for a lovers' spat."

I bit back a retort, because he was right. I pasted a smile on my face as Clark gazed adoringly down at me . . . and ran right into Lu.

"Hey, my apologies," Clark said, helping him right himself. "I wasn't looking where I was going."

"Obviously." Lu's curt reply was laced with his accent, undisguised irritation on his face as he straightened his cuffs. He gave me a cursory glance, then moved on.

"Did you get it?" I asked Clark.

"Of course." He slipped the phone into my palm. "Now go. I'll be waiting for you."

I hurried away to find the ladies' room and locked myself into a stall. Pulling out my new toy, I cloned Lu's SIM and inserted the new one. I was nervous and trying to hurry and I nearly dropped the phone. Doing something like this in theory and doing it in reality and under pressure were two very different things.

"Oh God, that would've been bad," I whispered to myself, picturing trying to explain a shattered phone screen to Clark. He'd never let me live it down, if he didn't kill me, that was.

My heart was racing and I felt light-headed as I packed up my things inside my purse. Luckily, no one else was in the bathroom when I came out. I paused for a moment to take a deep breath before opening the door.

Clark was waiting at the end of the hallway. "Here," I said, passing the phone back.

We walked together back into the dining room. I spotted Lu patting his pockets and looking around. He'd already missed his phone. Damn.

"You're going to have to do it," Clark said, pressing the phone back into my hand.

"What? Why?" I asked, alarmed.

"Because he got a good look at me, but barely glanced at you. He'll know something's up if I give it back to him."

I frowned and prepared to argue more when Clark cut me off.

"Trust me on this," he said.

His eyes were serious, his dark brows drawn together . . . and I believed him.

"Okay," I said with a nod. "What do I do?"

"Go to the security guard on his left," Clark said, motioning with his chin. "Tell them you found the phone and wanted to return it to whomever lost it. Don't let on that you know it's Lu's."

"Got it."

I pushed my glasses up my nose and straightened my shoulders. I could do this. Easy as pie. I'd just found a phone, that's all. And the security guard was obviously not a guest, not with the earpiece, so it was natural I'd give it to him.

"Excuse me," I said, not bothering to use my bad fake smile on him. "I found this on the floor over there. I'm sure whoever lost it would like it back."

He took the phone from me, looking me over carefully. "Yes, I'm sure. I'll see to it."

"Thank you." I turned away, stopping short at the woman who'd accosted me earlier and was there again.

"I *knew* you looked familiar! You're that girl—what's her name?—Oh yeah. China. You kicked Jackson Cooper to the curb, right? This is so cool! I didn't know they'd have celebrities here tonight." She gushed at me, her voice way too loud.

I stared at her, aghast. Reflex made me turn to see if Lu had heard. He was staring at me. While Clark had said he hadn't paid me any mind before, he certainly was now.

I had no idea what to do. If Lu's security guards found out I wasn't the name on the invitation, would they throw me out? Call the cops? Or would they bypass the American justice system in favor of their own type of interrogation?

"You followed me here? Really?" Jackson had taken my arm and pulled me forward while speaking loudly. "That's quite an extreme. We broke up, remember? The paparazzi are going to be all over this. Come on, let's get you home."

I was too shocked and scared to do anything but let him lead me back down the stairs and outside. Wait, what about Clark? Had he made it out, too?

"Nice one," Clark said to Jackson, stepping out of the shadows. "Thought for sure that chick had blown it."

Lance pulled up, driving a limo this time. Jackson yanked open the back door. "Both of you, get in."

I didn't argue or wait around to see what Clark decided to do. I wanted to put as much distance between Lu and myself as I could, so I scrambled inside the limo. They must've had a battle of wills because it took a few moments before Clark got in, then Jackson, who shut the door.

"Hold here," he ordered Lance, then pressed the button to raise the divider between the front and back.

"I'm not into threesomes, if that's what you're thinking," Clark deadpanned.

Spotting a decanter of scotch, I reached for it and splashed some into a glass, which I downed in one swallow. It burned going down. Now that the ordeal was over, I was shaking. The aftereffects of adrenaline.

"What is going on?" Jackson asked, his voice like steel. "And don't give me some shit about it's a secret and you can tell me but then you'll have to kill me."

"Nothing gives you the right to know," Clark retorted. "Not even that you're the great Jackson Cooper."

"Me getting her out of there is what gives me the right to know. I don't know how you coerced her into helping you, but Lu isn't someone you should fuck with. He's worth literally billions and he didn't get there by being a nice guy."

"No shit. You think we were there on a whim? And trust me, if you hadn't gotten her out, I would've."

"Stop," I interrupted. "Being around you two is like being with two children. You bicker like teenage girls." Dialing my cell, I waited until Roscoe answered. "Are you getting the signal?"

Regardless of what was going on with Jackson, I wanted to make sure the job was done. After all, I'd been through having a duck's mushy organ in my mouth tonight. I had to rephrase that inside my head right after I'd thought it. *Damn Grandma's romance novels and euphemisms for male genitalia.*

"Yeah, the signal is coming through loud and clear. We're uploading software now. We should have everything on that phone along with eyes and ears going forward."

I let out a sigh of relief. "Fabulous. Have a report ready by morning." After Roscoe's affirmative, I ended the call. Jackson and Clark were still arguing.

"I think you mean *thank you*," Jackson said, his voice dry. I reached for the decanter again, but he took it from me. "Tell me the truth, China. Why were you there?"

I sighed. I didn't see a way out of telling him *something*. And it wasn't as though Clark would rat me out to Gammin. "I told you I work for the government," I said. Jackson nodded. "It's a top-secret organization. Tonight, we needed to hack Lu's phone and I was the only one who could do it. Clark handles operations, I handle tech." In a nutshell.

"A secret organization?" Jackson asked with a frown. "That does what exactly?"

Use the software you helped create and thought you destroyed to monitor domestic and international communications.

Nope. Couldn't say that. I was saved by Clark.

"The whole purpose of it being a secret organization is that no one knows about it," he said. "The very fact that she's told you of its existence is against the law. Are you going to put her in even more danger by making her divulge information that you don't need to know?"

"I'm not the one putting her in danger," Jackson snapped. "You are."

"She was doing her job."

"What about you?" I interrupted. "Why were you there tonight? What were you discussing with Lu? And who was Rebecca?" Of all those questions, I wanted the answer to the last one first.

"Rebecca is a friend," he replied. "She accompanies me to events sometimes."

"What kind of friend?"

"We've dated a few times, if that's what you're asking, but now we're just friends."

"Do I really need to be here for this conversation?" Clark asked, sounding bored.

"No, you don't." Jackson opened the door. "Get out."

Clark climbed out of the limo and Jackson followed him. Wondering if I should go, too, I scooted forward but stopped when I overheard Jackson speaking.

". . . second time I've had to pry my girlfriend away from you," he was saying. "You don't want there to be a third."

"Is that a threat? Seriously?" Clark scoffed. "First, a guy like you threatening me is laughable. That's really all that has to be said, but since I'm sensing a recurring theme here, I'm going to address that, too."

I couldn't see what happened next, but suddenly Jackson was slammed against the side of the limo and Clark's voice changed to a low rasp I had to strain to hear.

"I'm only going to say this once, so listen carefully. Mack and I work together. That is all. Work partners is all we are or will ever be. So you can set your inner caveman aside. Not to mention that treating Mack like a piece of your property is insulting. She may trust you, but I don't. You don't want to piss me off by jerking her around."

"You're a liar and you're dangerous," Jackson hissed. "I don't like you being around China. Tonight's a prime example of why. She may be disposable to you, but she's not to me."

There was a slight scuffling sound, then Jackson was back inside the limo and slammed the door. He toggled a button and barked, "Drive." The car began moving.

"What was all that about?" I asked.

"He's an asshole."

Tell me something I don't know. "Yes, but we were working tonight. It was my job to go, not because of any decision Clark made. You shouldn't blame him."

"He knows what he's getting into. You don't."

Anger flashed through me. "Actually, I do. I may be young, but I'm far from stupid. And I don't need you to fight my battles for me. Clark works for *me*, not the other way around. So if anyone's going to yell at him, it's going to be me."

The limo had stopped and I impulsively hopped out. We were downtown, sitting at a stoplight. I'd catch an Uber home.

"China, wait . . ." Jackson called.

Forget waiting for an Uber. A taxi worked just as well.

"We're on a break, remember?" I said to Jackson, flagging down a cab. "Go back to *Rebecca*. Give the tabloids someone else to talk about." Hmm. That came out with a bitterness I hadn't expected.

I got inside the taxi and left Jackson standing on the sidewalk, staring after me.

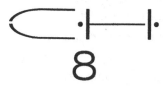

8

I was up late—way past my bedtime—reprogramming my firewall for my home network. And because I couldn't sleep. I didn't know what to do about me and Jackson. He'd made me angry tonight. Though I'd spent a lot of time exceeding others' preconceived low expectations, it had been jarring to hear Jackson second-guess my decisions. On the one hand, it had been sweet, him going all Jealous Boyfriend on Clark. But on the other hand, his reasoning was that basically I was dumb.

My smarts was the one thing I had that was irrefutable, so pretty much the quickest and most surefire way to piss me off was to imply that my intelligence was questionable. This was the first time Jackson had ever done that, and I didn't like it. Not one little bit.

"He can just go back to Rebecca," I muttered to myself, giving her name a nice little bitchy sneer. "They won't have anything they can talk about . . . though I doubt talking is what occupies their time." My self-delivered pep talk ended on a sour note as I remembered how pretty Rebecca was and how long her legs were.

A message popped up on my computer screen, catching my eye.

Talking to yourself . . . it's the first sign you're going crazy.

I froze. More words appeared.

Of course, you're pretty strange anyway.

So my firewall hadn't helped. He was already in my network. And wanted to make sure I knew so I could admire his mad hacking skills.

"I'm not the one eavesdropping on strangers," I said. I wasn't surprised that he'd activated my computer's webcam.

You can learn a lot of things, eavesdropping on strangers.

"Like what?"

Like how you're violating about half a dozen laws with the surveillance you do.

Technically not true, since we were operating under a Presidential Directive, but I couldn't tell him that. By nature, those were secret.

"How do you know what we do?"

A little birdy at another alphabet agency told me.

My heart rate kicked up even more at that. If someone else did know about Vigilance, it could very well be the mole Gammin suspected.

"Really?" I asked. "Which agency is that?"

Why should I tell you? You're all as bad as each other.

Not a lot to disagree with there. "Some things are necessary to keep people safe."

You try to predict terrorists. No one can do that.

"We can, and have," I said. Which was true. One of the first people Vigilance had flagged was a Syrian refugee who'd been planning a car bomb at a sporting event in Texas. The federal agents had captured him before he'd managed to carry out his plans.

The ends don't justify the means.

"In your opinion. But why are you hiding? You know who I am. At least do me the same courtesy."

So you can have me arrested and sent to some secret government prison, never to be heard from again? I don't think so.

"Then at least tell me who your source was."

Nope. Sorry. Can't do that either.

"So what's the point of this conversation then?" I asked. "To brag? I did not appreciate you messing with my Iron Man, by the way. It's very expensive."

That was totally sweet.

Whatever. I was growing tired of the conversation. "I'm pulling the plug if you don't give me a reason why I should bother continuing to talk to you."

Okay, here's one. You're in danger.

As far as reasons went, it was a pretty darn good one.

"And you know this how?"

Can't say.

Figured. "Being 'in danger' is pretty vague," I said. "Can you be more specific? Technically, I'm in danger every time I drive my car."

I just know you're a threat to someone important.

A shiver trickled down my spine. "I think you're lying," I said. "I'm going to bed now." Reaching over, I unplugged my network again. Then grabbed my phone and called Roscoe.

"You got it?" I asked when he answered.

"Yep. Good job, boss. We're monitoring now."

The hacker had taken the bait—as I'd known he would. No hacker could resist bragging. Now he'd carry the little bot I'd hitched onto him from my firewall right back to where he came from. By morning, I should know everything there was to know about him.

"Thanks. I'll see you in the a.m."

I put a piece of electrical tape over my webcam before changing into my pajamas, just because it freaked me out a little. I was making progress on the hacker problem, I'd done a good job tonight with Lu (making me feel like a combination of Black Widow and James Bond), and Clark and I hadn't killed each other. Work was going very well . . . so why did I feel so unsettled?

I stared at the ceiling way too long, thinking. I realized that my vague discomfort was all about the people around me. Jackson and I on a break. Mia at her parents and not sure she was going to return. As upset as I was about Jackson, one thing kept ricocheting through my head, and that was Clark's declaration that we were only and would always be just work colleagues.

Should I just forget it? Absolutely. And yet . . .

Clark and I had once shared kisses that I still couldn't forget. I wished more than anything that I could. My life would be much easier if I did. He'd made it very clear to Jackson that there was nothing between us and never would be. And I should be fine with that. I should be.

I should be.

The next morning, I tried to get back into my routine, but with Mia gone it felt all wrong. I'd finally taught her the difference between a heaping teaspoon of coffee grounds and a rounded teaspoon, but it mattered little if it was just me.

Emotions were uncomfortable for me. I preferred the language of binary and code. Understanding how I was feeling left me frustrated and confused. I didn't like feeling . . . sad. Which was how I felt. It made me unsettled and unbalanced. And I didn't know what to do about it. How could I fix relationship problems when it wasn't just up to me? Last I checked, it took two people to form a relationship.

Roscoe was in my office first thing. "His name is Lai Kuan-Yu. He's Taiwanese, a student at MIT, and seventeen," he said, placing a tablet on my desk with a photo of a young Asian man. His hair was longer in the front than it was in the back and he had a lip piercing. "Been in trouble a few times with the FBI, but they could never prove anything. Too smart for that, though he likes to see how far he can push it."

"Any ties to terrorist groups?"

"Not that I've been able to find so far."

"What about the Chinese?"

"First thing I checked," Roscoe said. "There's no love lost there. He was part of Anonymous when they launched the DDoS attacks on the Chinese back in 2014."

I remembered that. Over thirty Chinese government websites had gone down in that Denial of Service attack. The hacker group Anonymous had claimed responsibility, citing support for several Hong Kong "hacktivists" who had been arrested by the Chinese.

"So just your usual don't-trust-authority, I'm-smarter-than-the-next-guy type of personality?" I asked.

"Pretty much. Keeps to himself. Lives alone in an apartment outside Boston." His phone dinged an alarm. Switching it off, he dug a baggie from his pocket that looked like it contained some kind of seeds. He popped a few in his mouth and chewed.

"What's that?" I couldn't help asking.

"Pumpkin seeds."

"What happened to the pork-and-protein-shake diet?"

He grimaced. "Made me constipated. I'm trying a seed-and-wheat-germ combination now, alternating every other day with citrus. It's supposed to increase my energy levels. So far, it's really working. Can't you tell?"

Roscoe's trademark monotone hadn't changed in the slightest, his droopy eyes and mouth reminding more of Eeyore than ever.

"Yeah, of course," I said, adding in my forced smile.

He gave me a nod and chewed a few more seeds.

"What about Lu?" I asked. "Intelligence coming in on him?"

"Yeah, Lu's been very active, speaking to several administration contacts," Roscoe said, updating me on the state of our project. "And Jackson Cooper."

That got my attention. "What did they discuss?" It hadn't occurred to me until later that he hadn't answered my question last night about why he'd been speaking with Lu.

"Jackson accused Lu of attacking Cysnet's networks and citing them in that investigation with the State Department. Tong Enterprises is on defense, playing at being outraged at accusations of hacking and theft when, dollars to donuts, they're guilty of the very thing they're accusing Cysnet of doing."

War of the hackers. Not gripping reality TV, but a deadly game all the same. With lives around the world affected intrinsically in every way by technology at risk—disruption to key services such as gas or water, Internet outages, military technological espionage—hackers were on the cyber frontlines. China, Korea, and Russia in particular attempted to hack the Pentagon and military contractors on a regular basis. Not to mention the terrorist groups always on the watch for vulnerable systems where they could create havoc.

"Is Cysnet under a black budget contract to hack Lu?" I asked.

"If they are, I haven't seen evidence of it," Roscoe replied.

"Let's monitor traffic into Cysnet's network. Let me know if it looks like Lu's people are attacking." I paused. "Anything else interesting?"

Roscoe hesitated, then handed over a sheaf of papers. "This conversation."

I glanced through the transcript, my eyes getting wider. "This isn't good."

"That's what I thought."

"Any idea who he was speaking to?" I asked.

"It was scrambled and encrypted on the other end. Government issue, or maybe military."

Better and better. "Is Clark in yet?"

"I think I saw him earlier, yeah."

"Can you ask him to come to my office on your way out? He needs to see this, too." And help me figure out what we were going to do about it.

"Will do, boss."

Roscoe left and a few minutes later, Clark gave a perfunctory knock on the glass door before strolling in. He settled into a chair opposite my desk, knees spread and reclining more than the chair's lines should have allowed.

"You owe me a pocket square," he said, folding his hands across his abdomen. He'd actually dressed nicer for work today—still in dark jeans, but paired with a button-down chambray shirt. The cuffs were turned back, exposing his wrists.

I grimaced. "Sorry about that. I'll get you one." Did they sell pocket squares on Amazon? They must. They sold everything from four pounds of caviar at eighteen grand a pop, to a body pillow in the shape of half a torso including an arm, for crying out loud.

He snorted, his lips curved in the ghost of a smile. "I'm joking, Mack."

"Oh," I said, thrown off slightly. Recognizing jokes wasn't in my list of skill sets. I shook my head to refocus. "Okay, well, here's what I wanted you to see." I handed him the transcript. He read it quickly, his expression sobering.

"I take it we don't know who he was talking to," he said.

I shook my head. "Roscoe thinks they were using a government or military-grade scrambler on the other end, to prevent any kind of tracking."

"There isn't a long list of who'd have that kind of device."

"And it should be an even shorter list of people who know about that weapon." The weapon I was talking about was a groundbreaking type of gun that could fire a twenty-five-pound projectile at over a mile a second. It sounded more like a cannon than what I thought of typically as a "gun." And someone was telling Lu all about it.

"Looks as though Lu is also working as a spy for his government, acting as intermediary between them and the American source," Clark said.

"We have to tell someone," I said. "They're talking about meeting to exchange plans for the gun in return for money. We can't let that fall into Chinese hands."

"Who will we tell? We don't know who the source is, if it's NSA, CIA, DoD . . . the list goes on and on."

True, but . . . "What do you propose we do?"

"It says here they're supposed to meet tonight for the exchange. I'd like to move it to later."

"We can call Lu," I suggested, "impersonate the unknown caller, and tell him it has to be later."

"Sounds good. Let's do that," he said.

"And what'll you do?"

"I'll take care of nabbing the spy red-handed before he meets with Lu."

It sounded like a good plan to me. "Okay. I'll have Sam get on the phone call."

"You're not going to have Sam do the talking, are you?" Clark asked.

"Of course not. But Sam's our telephony expert and the best one to spoof the call to Lu's cell." Sam was short for Samarth, who was Indian. His accent was quite pronounced. "I'll have Derrick do it. We'll modulate his voice so it's a match, and we won't say much."

"Good."

"Who are you taking with you?" These things were always dangerous and I didn't want Clark to go without backup.

"I hadn't planned on taking anyone," he replied.

"You need to take backup," I said firmly. "Someone from your team."

"I said I don't need it," he argued. "I like to work alone."

"You're too valuable of an asset to risk by not taking along someone for backup," I said. Our gazes clashed in a battle of wills. "It's not an option, Clark."

His lips pressed into a thin line and I wondered if he'd openly defy me . . . and what I would do if he did. But after a moment, he gave me a curt nod and rose to his feet.

"Let me know once the meet time has been changed," he said, heading out of my office. The door swung shut behind him.

It took about two hours to get everything just right and the call made. I was on pins and needles as I listened, but Derrick was spot-on, having listened to the actual recording Roscoe had made of the spy's voice.

"I have to change the time," he said, sounding anxious.

"Are you having second thoughts?" Lu asked.

"No . . . but I have to work and can't get away. Can we do it later?"

"Of course. Eleven p.m. Same place."

"Got it." Derrick ended the call and I could breathe again.

"Excellent work," I told him and Sam. "Any chance he suspected anything?"

"Well, I am not a mind whisperer," Sam said, his accent thick, "but he seemed to accept the change of plan without a surprise."

"Mind reader," Derrick automatically corrected. "And I agree. I think we're safe."

I nodded. "I'll let Clark know." Getting up, I left the soundproof room where we'd made the call, leaving them to put away the equipment, and headed for Clark's office.

On a different corridor than mine, his office was smaller, but not by much. He had a computer that I thought he only used for company email and when I walked in, I was momentarily taken aback by the dismembered handgun on his desk.

"What are you doing?" I asked.

He looked at me as though I'd asked him what color the sky was.

"Cleaning my weapon." The *Obvs* was implied in his tone.

"You have to do that?" I'd never thought about it, but I supposed a gun needed cleaning just like anything else.

"If I want it to work when I need it to, yeah."

Okay then. "Lu thinks the meet's been changed, per your request. Eleven o'clock."

"Perfect."

An idea struck me. "I think I should be issued a weapon." I didn't know why I hadn't thought of it before.

Clark snorted. "Please tell me you're joking."

I replayed my words, looking for something amusing in them, came up empty. "Why would that be a joke?"

"Because you're a techie who'd probably only get yourself shot in the foot if someone actually gave you a weapon."

He began reassembling the handgun. I stepped forward and held out my hand.

"What?" he asked.

"Give it to me."

"I haven't put it back together yet, in case you hadn't noticed." The dripping condescension in his tone set my teeth on edge. But still I stood there, hand outstretched. Finally, one eyebrow raised, he set the weapon in my hand.

Closing my eyes, I reversed the image of the parts on his desk that I'd seen, turning it into a map inside my head. Reaching down, I unerringly picked up the first part. Twenty seconds later, I set the gun down on the desk—fully assembled—and opened my eyes.

Clark was staring at me, his gaze unreadable. "Nice party trick. How'd you learn that?"

"Jackson taught me how to shoot. I wanted to know how the gun worked. So I took it apart."

He didn't say anything for a moment, his brows drawn together. "Is that how you do it, then?"

"What do you mean?"

"You find something you don't know about or don't know how to do, so you just decide to learn?"

"Well . . . yeah." Now it was my turn to imply the *Obvs*.

He shook his head. "That's pretty amazing."

"No, it's not. Anyone can learn anything, if they put their mind to it." Something I wholeheartedly believed.

"You're wrong."

"Excuse me?"

"I said," he paused to eject the magazine, check it, and slam it home again. "You're wrong."

"How am I wrong?"

"Anyone can't learn just anything. Joe Blow off the street may not comprehend theoretical physics any more than Mary Jane can learn how to run a bulldozer."

"I don't believe that. You just have to have the will to learn—"

"Bullshit. You're trivializing how exceptional you are."

That creeping embarrassment I felt at compliments struck me and I glanced away, nervously pushing my glasses up my nose. If it wouldn't be so obvious I was uncomfortable, I would've tightened my ponytail.

"Well, will you check on me getting issued a weapon?" I asked again.

He stood, tucking the gun into the holster at his side. "I will."

"Thank you. So who's going with you tonight?"

"Genna."

My eyebrows lifted. "A woman?"

Clark's lips twisted. "Don't tell me you of all people are sexist."

"Of course not. I just thought you'd want someone more . . . capable." Genna was Clark's hire. A six-foot German brunette with a short, sleek haircut that set off her sharp cheekbones and full lips. She'd been the German version of a Navy SEAL, the official name being one I couldn't pronounce. I'd felt every inch the cliché dowdy, geeky girl when I'd met her.

"She could bench-press *you*," he retorted. "I think she can be my backup."

"Of course. I wasn't trying to second-guess you." I changed the subject. "I'll let Gammin know what we've found so far."

"Did you find out what Lu and Coop were talking about last night?"

"Jackson says Lu's company has been cyber-attacking his."

"Why? Have they been doing any government contracts?"

I shook my head. "No, but they're a very prominent tech company. They're always on the cutting edge. It's not a surprise that they're a target for Chinese hackers. My larger concern is actual weaponry being given to the Chinese by people in our own government." The very idea was offensive to me.

"Sounds like the quicker we get our hands on this spy and debrief him, the better," Clark said.

"Good luck then. And let me know when you have him in custody."

"Will do."

I thought again of the gun in Clark's holster as I left his office, and the nagging worry at the back of my mind. *He is more than capable of apprehending one man, especially with backup*, or so I told myself. I didn't know which was harder . . . being out on a job as I'd been last night, or sitting in an office waiting.

Gammin was less than thrilled about our plan.

"You should've run it by me first," he said.

I bristled. "You gave me autonomy to handle situations and inform the correct authorities as I see fit, not hold my every decision up for your scrutiny and approval."

"Terrorism is one thing. Espionage is another."

"Until we find out exactly who this person is and where they work, I thought it best to take the lead. It would benefit Vigilance to be able to debrief them first. Clark agreed."

"What else have you found with Lu?" he asked.

"You'll be receiving an encrypted file with his communications," I said. "We're also following up on the people he's contacted. Some are US citizens who work in various government occupations." A worrying bit of information, if the unknown spy was any indicator.

"The Chinese never send anyone over here without them having a specific task. Given Lu's high profile and wealth, I'm sure his tasks are more comprehensive than most."

"We'll keep you posted," I said, ending the call shortly after.

I was on my second Red Bull when Roscoe came into my office without even bothering to knock.

"We have a problem."

The dread in the pit of my stomach I'd been trying to ignore gained ten pounds.

"Tell me."

He handed me a typed transcript. "Lu knows something's up. He started using code. Zack picked up on it first." Zack was our needle-in-a-haystack guy. He could find the one line of code that broke the whole thing, and he was a genius at puzzles. His previous job had been encryption analysis for the CIA.

"So what is he saying?" The transcript looked like an ordinary conversation to me, which was the best kind of code to have.

"He's still working on it, but I think we should warn Clark."

I glanced at my watch. It was thirty minutes until the meet. Lu and the guy had arranged to meet in Nash Square, which was smack in the middle of downtown, only a block or two from the capitol building.

"Yes. Contact Clark and Genna. Tell them to proceed with extreme caution, that we don't know what Lu may be doing."

"You got it."

He was on his phone immediately, and I watched, chewing my nails while I waited. A bad, nasty habit I should really stop doing. Roscoe frowned, looked at his cell, then put it to his ear again.

"What's wrong?" I couldn't help myself from asking.

"He's not answering. It's going straight to voice mail."

"Try Genna."

I waited, moving on to the next nail on my right hand.

"Same thing." He glanced at me. "Something's not right. I think someone is jamming the signal where they are."

It took a moment for those words to process. "That's impossible. Who'd be operating a jammer strong enough? That we wouldn't already know about?"

Getting out my own cell, I tried calling Clark, too. It went straight to voice mail.

"I don't know, but if we don't figure it out, we're not going to be able to warn Clark."

I was already on my feet and grabbing my keys. "Pinpoint the jammer and disable it. I'm going to warn Clark."

"You're not in Ops, boss," Roscoe warned. "You should call someone else in to do it."

"By the time I do that, it'll be too late," I said. "Clark and Genna are my responsibility and I'm not going to let them walk into a trap. Not if I can help it." I brushed by him and rushed out the door, bypassing the elevator in favor of the stairs. In thirty seconds flat, I was running through the garage to my car.

Nash Square was fifteen minutes from Vigilance and I drove as fast as I dared. Being pulled over by a cop would slow me down even more. I told myself that we were probably worrying over nothing, that Clark could handle himself even when something unexpected happened. That was what he was paid very well to do. And Genna was capable, hand-picked by Clark to have his back, so the weakest link here wasn't them so much as it was probably me.

But my job responsibility wasn't to sit in the safety of the office when I knew my people were headed into a fluid situation where the danger level could have just increased exponentially.

I parked a block away from the square, made sure my phone was on vibrate and shoved the keys in my pocket. As an experiment, I tried to make a call. I had no bars on my phone and all it showed was that it was searching. Definitely within the bubble of the jammer, then, which meant Roscoe had been right.

Secret spy agent I was not, though I supposed at least I had the fact that I was wearing tennis shoes so my steps were silent on the pavement. Traffic was nearly nonexistent in this area at this time of night on a weekday, and as I crossed the street toward the square, I realized I had no idea how to find Clark.

The square was surrounded by streetlights, but the park itself was full of trees still in their fall foliage glory. Concrete paths crisscrossed through the grass and trees, and I skirted a small war memorial. The view of the streets was diminished the farther I ventured into the center of the park. Sound seemed muffled as well, though maybe that was just my imagination.

My eyes were slowly adjusting to the darkness, but every shadow seemed to hide something more, and I cursed watching too many episodes of *Supernatural*. I stopped for a moment to listen.

Cars passing by. The whisper of wind through the dry leaves overhead. Sirens in the distance. But nothing that would make me think anyone besides myself was in the park. Had I gotten the time wrong? The place?

Tentatively, I ventured farther, my steps slower and more deliberate. A cold gust of wind sent a shiver through me and I tugged my flannel shirt tighter around my torso. Up ahead, I saw the faint outline of a bench. As I grew closer, I squinted, then pushed my glasses up my nose.

A man was sitting on the bench, a dog on a leash at his side. Was it Clark? I couldn't tell from where I was standing.

I moved forward, trying to see without giving away that I was staring. And it would've been fine . . . if I hadn't tripped over my own feet and nearly done a face-plant.

The man turned then, but it wasn't Clark. It was Lu.

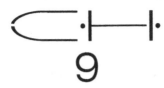

9

I was frozen with surprise and a dawning horror at just how badly this had gone. Where was Clark?

"You," Lu said, rising from the bench. "I must say, I am surprised. Though perhaps not as much so since I found out who you really are."

"What are you talking about?"

"China, the girl genius prodigy who used to work for Cysnet and Jackson Cooper."

I was unnerved. He knew my real name. "I was just working late, thought I'd get some air," I said, making it up on the spot. "Good to see you again." I turned to go, but was halted by two men who'd melted from the shadows to block my path.

"Don't be so quick to leave. We should talk."

I turned back toward Lu, swallowing hard. "What do you want?"

"Have a seat." He motioned to the seat on the bench next to him.

"People know where I am. I'll be missed." It was as much a warning as it was an attempt for a way out.

"I won't keep you long. Sit." This time it wasn't a request. I sat. "I was told some very interesting information from a . . . former contact," he began. "And I think you and I could come to a mutually beneficial agreement."

"I'm a computer programmer," I insisted. "I don't know what we'd have to talk about."

"Please give me some credit," he scoffed. "I know you're much more than a computer programmer. And you're involved in a secret government surveillance project."

I swore inside my head, but said nothing.

"My government . . . deeply appreciates those willing to share technology. After all, technology helps bring countries out of the dark ages and betters the lives of its people."

I had a sick feeling in my stomach.

"However, I know that the American people are the kind who wouldn't take well to knowing exactly how much of their activities and communications are tracked by their government."

"What are you saying?"

"I'm saying that if you would agree to . . . share . . . your latest technology with us, then we can agree to keep its existence secret."

That sick feeling increased. "And if I don't?"

Lu gave a shrug of his shoulders, gazing off into the shadows. "Your press is easily manipulated. Your people pathetically easy to whip into a fury of righteous indignation. I imagine congressional hearings and investigations would begin immediately." He turned to look at me, his eyes glittering in the darkness. "Your short life would be over before it's even begun. You could run, but you couldn't hide. Snowden quickly realized that."

I decided to stick with the playing-dumb card. "Listen, I still don't know what you're talking about, but even if I did, I wouldn't do anything that would betray my country."

"That's laudable," Lu said with a nod. "High ideals. Typical of Americans." Suddenly, he leaned toward me, taking me by surprise, and my breath caught in my chest. "Just remember that in the business of global politics, you mean nothing. And you will be chewed up and spit out if you cannot justify your existence. Either by my country . . . or your own."

My heart was hammering in my chest at the menace in his words. The dog growled and Lu stood.

"I'll be in touch," he said. In another moment, he was gone, the men with him until I knew I was alone.

My knees were too weak to stand, so I sat there on the bench, replaying the conversation inside my head. Lu's insinuations and threats echoing in my ears.

"What the fuck do you think you're doing?"

I nearly jumped out of my skin at the outrage in Clark's voice, which came from right behind me, accusing me from the shadows. Terror gave way to relief, then anger.

"Where were you?" I jumped to my feet, whirling around.

"Doing my job. I didn't know you were such a control freak as to jump into something you don't understand and fuck things up so badly." His tone was scathing.

"I came here to warn you," I gritted out. "Lu started communicating in code, but there's a jammer here and we couldn't call."

"Then you should've just left it to me," he retorted. "Not rush headlong into a situation you know nothing about."

His criticism struck a chord, but I buried it, instead lashing out. "I was worried for your welfare. And Genna's. Where is she?"

"She followed Lu, of course. Leaving me to deal with you."

The anger and menace in his tone sent a shiver down my spine, and I wished there was more light in the park. Clad all in black, Clark blended in to the writhing shadows, and I felt smaller and younger than usual.

"So you didn't capture anyone?" I asked, ignoring his anger.

"I didn't say that."

"I'm not playing Twenty Questions," I snapped. "Spit it out. Where is he?"

"He's dead. Found him with his throat slit. Over here." He turned and I followed him across the park to an area enclosed with pines. The scent of the needles drenched the night air, incongruous with the sprawl of the dead body on the ground. An inky black pool of what could only be blood stained the bed of needles.

That I wasn't expecting, and it robbed me of my bravado. The unnervingly close encounter with Lu and the two guys—probably the same ones who'd killed this man just minutes before—started to hit me. It could've been me with my throat slit. My hands began to shake and I didn't know if it was from fear, shock, adrenaline, or all three. To hide that from Clark, I shoved my hands in my jeans pockets.

I cleared my throat so my voice would be steady. "Did you identify him?" It was so dark, and I didn't want to get any closer.

"Working on that. We need to get out of here. The cops will be here soon and I don't want to have to answer difficult questions."

I nodded, not trusting myself to say any more.

"Where'd you park? I'll catch a ride back with you."

Leading the way, I kept my hands in my pockets and my eyes on the ground, telling myself to get a grip. I was supposed to be the boss. I could handle dead bodies and threats—had handled them before. If anyone suspected I *couldn't* handle it, I'd lose their respect. Respect was all I had, especially with Clark. Hell, if he knew how much I was rattled, he'd laugh at me.

The pine-needle scent seemed to cling to me as I got in the car, only it was tainted now, with the sweet metallic scent of blood. I fumbled with my seat belt as Clark got in the passenger side, my fingers strangely numb.

"Did you forget how to work it?"

I barely processed his sarcastic comment. All I could think about was that damn smell. It seemed like it was everywhere inside the car, stifling me. I sucked in more air, trying to breathe.

"Hey, you okay?"

I tried to nod, but I couldn't focus. God, what was wrong with me? I couldn't drive like this. I turned to Clark, to ask him to drive, but Clark wasn't there.

Freyda sat in my passenger seat.

I stared, stunned, the smell of pine itching inside my nose. She was saying something to me, her lips moving, but I couldn't hear her. I had to warn her, had to tell her what was going to happen. Light from the streetlamps filtered into the car. Somewhere out there, there was a man with a rifle.

"Freyda—"

I had no more than gasped her name when there was a shot, and her head exploded the same way it had before.

I screamed.

Blood and brain matter was everywhere, and still I screamed. I sucked air into my lungs to scream more and heard a voice.

"China. It's Clark. You're okay. Freyda's not here. It's Clark."

I stopped screaming, my mind scrambling to process the words I heard with what I was seeing. Confused, I blinked hard, squeezing my eyes shut. When I opened them, Freyda was gone and Clark was there. He was watching me and talking, repeating the same thing over and over.

"It's Clark. You're okay. Can you hear me, China? It's Clark—"

"Oh God, Clark . . ." I was so relieved to have the image of Freyda gone that I nearly burst into tears. That's when I realized it wouldn't matter—my cheeks were wet already. My hands were clutching the steering wheel as though holding on for dear life.

"Do you know where you are?"

I nodded. "My car. Wyndemere." The parking lot that had been so dark, just like this one, and surrounded by pine trees.

"No, Mack. You're not at Wyndemere. You're in downtown Raleigh. Just you and me. You're safe, I promise. No one's going to hurt you. I won't let them."

Yes . . . yes, he was right. I was by the Square. Lu had spoken to me. Then I'd seen the body and smelled the blood and the pines . . .

A shudder wracked me at the memory. "Downtown. Right." My voice was little more than a broken whisper as reality reasserted itself.

"I'd better drive."

I didn't argue as Clark got out of the car and rounded it. My fingers were numb and unable to work the seat belt clasp, which I could hardly see since I was still trying to stop my eyes from overflowing.

My door opened and Clark's hands gently brushed mine away, undoing the seat belt clasp with ease. I scrambled out of the car, relieved to no longer smell the pine trees.

"Hey, look at me," he said, closing his hand around my elbow.

He was standing right in front of me, so it wasn't as though I had an option to look elsewhere. I took a shaky breath and raised my watery gaze to his, expecting to see impatience or perhaps even derision on his face. Instead, his expression was serious, his dark brows drawn in a frown.

Slowly, he lifted a hand toward me until the backs of his knuckles barely grazed my damp cheek.

The touch undid the fragile hold I had on my control and the tears flowed even faster. In a flash, my glasses were gone and Clark had pulled me into his arms.

I wasn't pretty when I cried—the single crystal tear hovering on eyelashes was for television and movies—which was one of the many reasons I tried *never* to cry. Besides me being an ugly crier, it was a pointless emotional response. It didn't solve anything. It just gave me a headache and stuffy nose. And it was such a girl thing to do. As a woman in a field who was constantly surrounded by (usually older) men, crying just didn't happen. Like Tom Hanks had said, "There's no crying in baseball."

But Freyda had looked so *real*. The smell had been the same, with identical dim streetlights and the familiar confines of my beloved Mustang. If I'd just been more aware that night, maybe she wouldn't have died.

"It wasn't your fault," Clark said, his hand running soothingly down my back. "There wasn't anything you could have done to save Freyda."

He'd wrapped me tightly in his arms and for once my small size wasn't a detriment. His body enveloped mine, shielding me from everything around us. I fought to control my breathing and stem the tears. Clark was right. Logically, I knew there was nothing I could've done to save Freyda that night. But knowing it, and really *knowing* it, were two different things.

We stood there for a long time, Clark uncharacteristically patient as he held me and waited for my heart to stop racing and my sobs to subside. Embarrassment crept over me as I finally got my raging emotions under control. I'd completely lost my mind—hallucinated, even—then broke down in hysterics. All in front of Clark. He'd never respect me again after this, a fact that bizarrely made me want to start crying again.

"I-I'm sorry," I managed to say, my voice still thick. "I don't know what happened." I knew I should probably step back, but then I'd have to look at him. My pride couldn't handle that yet.

"You had a flashback, that's what happened."

I frowned. "Post-traumatic stress?"

"Yeah."

My nose was running so I eased back, trying to wipe it with my sleeve as inconspicuously as possible. I had to look a mess and I was glad for the darkness.

"Do you know what triggered it?" Clark asked, handing me my glasses. Gratefully, I slipped them on.

"No idea. Seeing the body maybe?" That had been traumatizing in and of itself.

"You've seen dead bodies before without this happening." He paused. "Or is this not the first time?"

I shook my head. "No. I've never done this before." I.e., made a complete fool out of myself in front of a direct report. I tried to slip between him and the car so I could round to the other side. Home had never sounded so good.

"Let's get one thing straight," he said, pulling me to a halt with a hand on my arm. "*You* didn't *do* anything. It happened *to* you. It's not a choice, and not something you can predict or prevent."

I was taken aback at the vehemence of his tone. "I, ah, appreciate the sentiment. But it doesn't change the fact that I was unable to do my job for several minutes. I might still be a bawling mess if not for you helping me." I swallowed hard. "Which I have to apologize for. You shouldn't have been put in that situation. It was unprofessional of me."

Again, I tried to turn away, but he spun me around and my back hit the side of the car, startling a gasp from me.

"Are you fucking kidding me right now?" His eyes fairly shot sparks, his jaw so tightly clenched it was a wonder he'd gotten the words out.

"What are you—?"

"You just belittled yourself and every other person who's had a PTSD episode," he spat. "*Unprofessional.* Please. And you're damn lucky I *was* here because obviously the night Freyda was shot bothered you a hell of a lot more than you let on."

"I couldn't help her!" My shout surprised me more than it did him. I lowered my voice. "I couldn't help her and then it wasn't even a person anymore . . . just awful, disgusting blood a-and brain all over. And I could smell it, for miles as I drove. The wind tore through the broken windows and all I could smell was the pine trees and the blood—"

And I realized.

"That was it." I raised a shaking hand to rub my forehead. "Tonight. The pine trees. The smell. That must've been what triggered it. I remember getting in my car and the smell was all I could think about. It was like I couldn't breathe."

"Smells are a common trigger," Clark replied. He stepped back, crossed his arms over his chest, and tugged off his shirt.

My jaw dropped and I stared. "Have you lost your mind?" Not that I didn't appreciate the view. As a way of getting my mind off dead bodies, the sight of Clark's naked chest was right up in the Top Ten. Okay, Top Five.

"Not yet. Here." He handed me his shirt.

I looked from him, to the shirt, and back to him, completely lost. "And?"

"Put it on. Different smell. No pine. Then we can get back in the car, which I'd really appreciate. I'm not saying it's cold out here, because it's unmanly to be cold, but it is a bit nippy." He crossed his considerable arms over his chest. *Oh. Oh wow.*

I shook my head and looked away because frankly, it was hard to think clearly with his naked skin twelve inches from me. Too befuddled and shocked to argue, I slipped off my flannel and pulled his shirt on over my *Save the Clock Tower* T-shirt.

I was immediately engulfed in his scent. Clark didn't wear a lot of cologne, but it was familiar, the memory of the one time I'd been lucky enough to smell it on his skin up close and personal playing through my mind like an R-rated highlight reel. He'd been right. Scents were strongly linked to memories, and I'd much rather remember our one ill-fated encounter on his sofa than Freyda's remains in my car.

"Better?" he asked. I nodded. "Good. Let's get out of here."

We got in the car and he started driving. I didn't notice that we weren't headed back toward Vigilance until we'd turned onto the highway going the opposite direction.

"Where are we going?"

"You shouldn't be alone anymore. Not with Lu knowing exactly who you are and some psycho stalking your network."

"Lai Kuan-Yu," I said.

Clark frowned. "What?"

"The hacker. He's an MIT student, from Taiwan. Here on a student visa. We don't think he presents an actual physical threat and we're monitoring him now."

"The hacker got hacked?"

I nodded. "No honor among thieves, right?"

Clark huffed in agreement. "I'm glad he's not a threat, but Lu is still too risky to chance it."

"To chance what?"

Clark looked at me like I was an idiot. "Did you not hear what he said? Lu knows about Vigilance. And he knows you have direct knowledge of it. Why should he wait for you to decide to sell? Not when he can just grab you and haul you off to China."

I couldn't wrap my head around that. "He couldn't just . . . take me away," I argued. "I'm a US citizen on American soil."

"You think the Chinese give a damn?"

I didn't know what to say. My knowledge of international spies and the machinations of foreign governments was limited to fiction. But I trusted Clark. If he said I was in danger, then I believed him.

Which brought to mind Kuan-Yu. He'd known I was in danger, too. But how had he known about Lu? Or was there someone else out there gunning for me?

My head was hurting from trying to unravel all the lies and subterfuges. I briefly longed for the time when it was just me, my earbuds playing eighties hair bands, and my computer. I wasn't cut out for this job, but had no idea how to remove myself from it without also fearing for my life.

"Do you think . . . Gammin would ever let me quit?" I asked. The miles were speeding by and the darkness outside my window was briefly broken by the full moon appearing from behind some clouds.

Clark glanced at me, then back at the road. "That would have to be done very carefully."

Yeah. No kidding. I let out a sigh and rubbed my forehead again. A headache pounded in the back of my skull.

"Why do you want to quit?" he asked.

His question startled a humorless laugh from me. "You're joking, right?"

"Am I laughing?"

Well, no. No, he wasn't. He seemed perfectly serious. "I'm a computer programmer, not some kind of intelligence specialist. I should be behind a monitor, not overseeing a project like this. I have no training. I'm going to get myself killed or worse, someone else."

"That's easily rectified."

"Which part?" I groused. "Because unless you know how to make a Horcrux, when someone's dead, there's really no coming back from that."

Clark laughed and I looked at him. As usual, I must've said something funny without meaning to. When I actually *tried* to be funny, no one got it but me.

"My magic wand is in for repairs," he deadpanned, "but I meant the training part. If you want to be trained in spycraft, I can train you. As well as give you some other pointers."

He wanted to help? Help *me*? "Why?" I blurted. Clark wasn't exactly altruistic.

"Because first, if something else happens like tonight, which it shouldn't," he gave me a look, "you will know enough to hopefully not get you or anyone else hurt."

I could live with that.

"And second, if you quit, they'll have to find someone to replace you and, well, the devil you know, right?"

Gee, that made me feel all better. Such a charmer.

"Okay then. I accept."

We drove for a few more miles in silence until he turned off the main road. I'd lost track of what direction we'd been traveling—north, south, east, west were just points on a compass to me—and gazed out the window. We were going deeper into the Carolina woods, which made me apprehensive considering the prevalence of pines. But then I remembered Clark's shirt.

Trying to be as surreptitious as possible, I ducked my head, pulling at the fabric until it was at my nose, and inhaled deeply. The scent was comforting and my nerves settled.

In another ten minutes, we pulled onto a dirt road, prompting me to finally speak. "Where in the world are we going?"

Clark answered promptly. "My place."

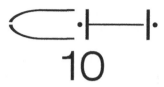

10

"Oh." Clark was taking me to his "place." That was . . . unexpected.

"Were you expecting a safe house or something?"

"I don't know. I guess so. I hadn't really thought about it." I'd been too busy smelling his shirt.

"It'll do for now."

As we rolled into a clearing and the car slowed, I realized it would more than "do." Jackson also owned a cabin in the woods, but it was definitely a cozy log cabin. This—apparently what Clark called his "place"—was akin to a log mansion in the woods.

I'd seen plenty of nice homes before, but this one . . . this was incredible.

A sprawling A-frame log home, the entire front made of huge windows. A deep deck wrapped around the front and I imagined the back as well, at about the level of what must be the second floor.

"This is your house?" I asked as he pulled up and turned off the engine.

"When I'm here, yeah."

He got out and I followed. There were some lights outside that shone on the house, but mainly it was lit inside, showcasing the wall of glass. When we stepped up onto the porch, I was stunned. The wooden door was ornately carved and set amid more glass, with an iron chandelier above us.

"Clark . . . I . . . it's beautiful," I stammered. "I've never seen anything like it."

He smiled, a real, nonsarcastic smile that reminded me of when I'd first met him and he'd seemed so open and natural. "Wait till you see inside."

He opened the door and held it for me, which meant I had to step by him. Usually, no big deal. But at the moment, he was still bare from the waist up. Make that from the hips up.

His jeans hugged that sweet spot on his hips that, if a man worked out like Clark did, showed the definition of his obliques (I'd looked it up once—in the name of science—to find the name of that particular muscle). It was a spot my fingers itched to touch, just to see how hard it was. However, I didn't think he'd appreciate that. And I really didn't need to add sexual harassment to my list of failures tonight.

Averting my eyes and being careful not to let any part of me touch him, I scooted past him over the threshold. A beeping told me he had an alarm system and I waited for him to punch in the code. When he did, he flipped on the lights and I was amazed all over again.

A beautiful, curved staircase led to the second floor, which had an atrium so you could still see out the windows. A huge stone fireplace dominated the great room, with rich mahogany leather sofas placed around it. There was a matching chaise in the corner. To the far left, I could see a doorway, which led to the kitchen.

"This is amazing. Truly." It looked as though I'd stepped into one of those architectural magazines. I stopped gaping and turned to Clark. "Thank you for showing me."

Perhaps it was because I was a private person who had difficulty putting my emotions into words, but I knew that Clark bringing me here wasn't just for convenience. A hotel would've worked for the night.

This place was too unique, too lovingly cared for, for me to believe it was just a house. I'd rank it along the same way I felt about my "office"—where I kept all my collectibles and anything that meant something to me. It was personal, and viewing it was akin to peeking inside someone's diary. To me, the house had the same feel. It was his *home*.

Perhaps it was the way I'd spoken, or maybe he saw something in my eyes that said I'd seen too much, but he didn't reply. He just nodded and asked, "You want a drink? I know I could use one."

"Yes, please." I needed a shot of something to calm me, not only from the flashback, but now also an unsettled nervousness from being in Clark's house.

He flipped on a lamp and I saw a well-stocked minibar in the corner on a sideboard. Taking out two glasses from the cabinet, he asked, "What's your poison?"

My experience in varieties of liquor was minimal. I'd only just recently begun appreciating alcohol, so I shrugged. "I'll have what you're having."

"Sapphire and tonic."

I had no idea what that was, so when he handed me a glass filled with ice and a clear liquid, I didn't know what to expect. Jackson always drank bourbon or scotch. I took a tentative sip.

"Well?" he asked.

"I like it. Kind of bitter, but it also tastes . . . clean."

"Clean?"

"Yeah, like bourbon has all these undercurrents of flavor but this tastes . . . clean." It was the best way I could describe it. I drank some more and decided it was pretty darn good. When we finished, he refilled both our glasses and handed me mine.

"I feel better already," he said. "You're probably hungry. I'm starving," and headed toward the kitchen.

I followed, more slowly since I was still trying to take everything in, and the kitchen was no less impressive than the rest of the house. Granite counters, top-of-the-line appliances, gas stove with hood . . . it was a gourmet chef's dream.

"Make yourself at home," Clark said. "I'll be right back."

He disappeared up a little staircase in the corner that I hadn't seen. I marveled at how the stairs didn't creak. I didn't think I'd ever been in a house where the stairs hadn't creaked.

My stomach growled. I'd been so nervous tonight, I'd skipped dinner, so my stomach felt as though it was eating me from the inside out. Opening the fridge, I glanced inside.

Considering the way Clark had hogged down that burger and fries right along with me last week, he stocked a lot of healthful foods.

Since when had "healthy" fallen out of favor and been replaced with "healthful" anyway? "Healthful" sounded like someone had just made up a new word when they couldn't think of "healthy."

My wayward thoughts on the English language aside, I pulled out a carton of eggs. I found some deli ham, Swiss cheese, and butter. While I was no chef—or even a chef-wannabe like my friend Bonnie—I could make an omelet.

A bit more snooping and I found a pan, spatula, and bowl. Before Clark reappeared, I had the pan preheating and was whisking the eggs in a bowl.

"I see you took my advice," he said, sitting down on a bar stool on the opposite side of the counter. He'd put on a smoky gray pullover sweater with a half zip in front. It wasn't zipped up very much and I could see skin underneath.

I paused in whisking. Had I misunderstood him? Had he just been being polite with an often-used societal welcome? "Was I . . . *not* supposed to make myself at home?"

Suddenly horrified that I'd yet again misinterpreted and unintentionally offended, I abruptly stepped back. "I-I'm so sorry. I didn't mean to—"

He was up and around the island in a blink. "Relax, Mack," he said, resting a hand on my shoulder. "I'm not upset. It's fine."

I looked up at him. In the back of my mind, I noticed that color of the shirt made his eyes seem more gray than blue. But I was still trying to puzzle out what I was supposed to do or not do. I was in his home, after all, which was nice of him to bring me here. The last thing I wanted was to behave in a way he'd find insulting or offensive.

"People don't always mean what they say," I said at last, trying to figure out how to put into words something I always struggled with. "Sometimes, they even mean the opposite."

Clark studied me. "I bet that's hard for you."

"It's *exhausting*." And took more brainpower than I was willing to sacrifice.

His lips twitched in an almost-smile at my vehemence. "Okay, then I'll make you this promise," he said. "And pay attention, because I rarely make promises."

Intrigued, I waited to hear what he'd say.

"I promise that if I say something to you, I will always mean it. No guessing, no double-speak, no subterfuge, no lies. I'll tell you the truth and mean what I say. Okay?"

That was one heck of a promise. "You'll always tell me the truth?" That part seemed a little more farfetched than the rest of it.

"I didn't say that I'd be able to tell you anything and everything," he said. "But if I do tell you something, it'll be true. Agreed?" He held out a hand.

I didn't know if I should trust him to keep his word or not, but if he was being sincere, I'd be an idiot to pass this up. But still, rarely was something offered for nothing.

"What do I have to do in return?" I asked, wary.

He dropped his hand. "What do you mean?"

"Quid pro quo, right?"

Shrugging, he said, "Fine. Then you agree to do the same."

I was a crappy liar so it wasn't a difficult promise to make. "Deal." Now it was my turn to hold out my hand and we shook on it.

"You get the plates, I'll make the eggs," he said.

It was his kitchen, so I didn't object. Soon, the aroma of cooked ham and eggs filled the kitchen and my stomach growled again. I remembered where the plates and utensils were stored and set them out. Then wandered to find a bathroom to wash up.

Given the lateness of the hour and the stress of the day, I was feeling the wear of exhaustion. Setting my glasses aside, I splashed some water on my face to wake up a little. Tugging the elastic band from my hair, I ran my fingers through it, sighing as I rubbed my scalp. My hair was heavy and long, but a ponytail grew tiresome after so many hours.

I still wore Clark's shirt and I hesitated before tugging it over my head. It had been exceedingly kind—and intuitive—for him to give it to me, which made me start wondering . . .

"Food's ready," Clark said when I returned to the kitchen. He set the two plates, now filled with a steaming omelet each, on the bar. Glancing at me, he paused for a moment, and I wasn't sure what he was looking at. I pushed my glasses up my nose and hopped up on one of the bar stools, a bit of a production given my height.

"Need a booster seat?"

I shot Clark a look at his wisecrack and he snickered, taking the seat beside me. Digging into the eggs, I wolfed down the food in minutes.

"'s really good," I mumbled, my mouth full. "Thanks."

"No problem."

I finished my second "sapphire and tonic" and sighed. I was feeling much more relaxed now, and sleepy. But still, I was the guest, so I slid off the stool and rinsed our plates, taking the lead in cleaning up. He had done the cooking, after all. As I was loading the dishwasher, I asked, "How did you know I was having a flashback? Or how to help me?"

"Lots of people have them. And it wasn't like I needed you to do an interpretive dance to figure out what was going on."

I turned, confused. "I don't know how I could've—" Then I saw his face. "Ah. Sarcasm."

He touched his finger to his nose. "Now you're catching on."

I smiled, because in retrospect his joke had been amusing, and wished I had that innate ability to immediately know if someone was joking or being literal.

"Have *you* ever had a flashback?" I asked.

For a moment, I didn't think he'd answer. "We're going to need another drink for that conversation."

That sounded good to me, so I picked up my empty glass and followed him back out into the great room. He made us more of the "clean" drink, then flipped a switch on the side of the fireplace, causing flames to suddenly appear.

"Oooh, fancy," I teased, settling onto the leather sofa. I frowned. Had I just *teased* Clark? The sapphire elixir was magic. I suddenly felt like Raj on *The Big Bang Theory*—alcohol made me normal.

"I don't like getting ash on my clothes," he said, settling on the couch as well. "Are you cold?"

"A little."

Reaching to the side, he produced a fluffy blanket and handed it to me. Pulling my knees to my chest, I cuddled into the softness, tucking the fabric around me. The leather was cold, but the blanket helped.

"Well?" I prodded him once I was settled.

"It's not a nice story," he warned.

"If you've had flashbacks about it, I didn't really think it would be."

He still hesitated, taking another drink, and I suddenly felt bad for making him tell me. "It's okay," I said. "If you don't want to talk about it, you don't have to." But he shook his head.

"It's nice to know you're not alone when these things happen, so I'll tell you." He took a deep breath. "It was years ago and I'd just started in human intel. I was new to the job and to Iraq, and not as cautious as I am now. I recruited someone, my very first. A woman. Her name was Sayeeda."

Clark was staring into the fire as he spoke, his voice low enough that I had to listen closely to hear. He still held his drink in his hand, but seemed to have forgotten it.

"Her grandfather was the head of the Iraqi police. And he was nuts. Her father was even worse. She was terrified of them, but she was twenty and naively thought she could help her country. The Iraqi police were prone to bribes, and they were just as likely to help you as shoot you in the back. Her father liked to play both sides of the fence—supposedly working with us while also keeping alive his ties to the insurgents—so when he'd meet with the Iranians, she'd take photos and names and bring them to us.

"She was . . . incredibly brave. But back then, everyone was suspicious of everyone else. I guess they still are. One night we met and used the intel she gave us to blow up two depots where the insurgents were storing stolen arms. They went crazy on her father, believing that he'd been the one to betray them."

He paused and I saw the Adam's apple move in his throat as he swallowed heavily. I didn't speak, just waited.

"He figured it out, knew it had to be his daughter."

A feeling of dread filled my chest, and when he didn't continue, I almost didn't want to ask. "What happened?" My voice was barely above a whisper.

"He gave her to them to save face. I won't tell you what they did to her. They dropped off her body in front of the base, left her just enough alive so we'd see her die. So *I* would see her die." The bitterness and self-loathing in his voice was hard to miss.

There was a rancid taste in my mouth and I took a long drink to get rid of it. I could well imagine what they'd done to her. It horrified me and I hadn't even seen it, unlike Clark.

Reaching out, I rested a hand on his arm. "I'm really sorry."

My touch seemed to startle him from his reverie and he turned to look at me. The firelight was reflected in his eyes, mesmerizing me. I could feel his muscles beneath my fingers and my mind drew in the picture of what Clark looked like underneath his shirt.

The moment seemed to stretch, turning from poignant into . . . something else. Something heavy and holding its breath.

Clark abruptly stood and took my glass from me. "I think that's enough sharing for one night." He headed for the kitchen without another word.

Suddenly, I was embarrassed. Had he thought I was coming on to him? That would be mortifying. But how do you ask that? *So, if you thought I was making a pass at you, I just want you to know that I totally wasn't.* No, that wouldn't be awkward at all.

Exhaustion swept over me, physical and mental. I wanted to sleep so badly, I could just curl up here on the couch. Come to think of it, that was probably the plan. It wasn't as though I was going to kick Clark out of his bed.

Scooting down the couch, I readjusted the blanket and closed my eyes. Counting backward was the scientifically proven best way to go to sleep so I started at one hundred.

99 . . . 98 . . . 97 . . . 96 . . . 95 . . . 94 . . . 9 . . . 3 . . .

I woke and didn't know where I was. It was that strange sense of dis-placement where it took a good five seconds or more before memory returned.

No longer was I on the sofa, but alone in a bed. Trying to remem-ber how I'd gotten there, I had faint recollection of being carried. Clark must have carried me from the sofa to a bed. How . . . thought-ful of him.

It wasn't yet light outside and I wasn't sure what had woken me. I lay there for a minute or two, then I heard something.

Flashes of the Iron Man attack went through my head, but I wasn't at home and it would be a very slim coincidence if Clark also owned a life-size replica.

The noise was a moaning sound . . . Clark?

Jumping out of bed, I immediately stubbed my toe. I started muttering fiercely under my breath as I rubbed the bruised dig-its. "Fucking shit. Shit fuck." My repertoire of curses wasn't very creative.

The room was really dark with barely any ambient light, but I man-aged to feel my way to the door. It opened without a sound and I stood in the hallway, listening.

The moans came again from my right. I followed the sounds to a room two doors down, but hesitated before opening the door. What if Clark wasn't having a nightmare? What if he was having a good dream? Like one of *those* dreams? Interrupting that kind of dream wouldn't be awkward *at all*.

Cautiously, I eased open the door. There was a bit more light in here and I could see Clark lying in the middle of a king-size bed.

He was thrashing in the covers that were twisted around his legs and torso. Sweat glistened on his skin and his chest was heaving. The expression on his face was one twisted with pain and anguish.

So not one of *those* dreams.

I knew I wasn't supposed to touch him—as he'd made sure not to touch me during my flashback—so I hurried to sit on the side of the bed, calling his name.

"Clark, it's okay. Wake up, Clark. It's just a nightmare. Wake up." I repeated the litany over and over, as loud as I could without shouting.

He kept writhing for a few minutes, but I kept it up, until he finally calmed. I thought maybe he'd settled back into sleep, then gasped when he sat straight up and grabbed my shoulders in a viselike grip.

"Sayeeda . . ."

His voice was steel on gravel, his fingers biting into my flesh.

"Clark, please, it's me. China. I mean, Mack." I was desperate for him to wake up. "You're hurting me!"

Those words were the right ones because he suddenly snapped out of it. I could see awareness return to his eyes.

"What the hell are you doing?"

"I-I heard you," I stammered. "I-I was worried—"

"You shouldn't be in here."

The way he said it, the way he still gripped my shoulders, scared me. If someone asked me to describe a man—a dangerous man—on the edge of losing control, it would be Clark in that moment. A chill washed over me.

"Clark, please . . ." My voice broke.

He suddenly released me and I sprang to my feet, putting some distance between us. My heart was hammering in my chest and my palms were sweaty. The wall was at my back, but I was still hesitant to leave. The kernel of worry for Clark kept me rooted to the spot.

Shoving his fingers through his hair, he released a pent-up breath. He was bare-chested and his legs were bare as well. Sweat glistened on his skin, but I was more worried about his state of mind.

"Are you all right?" I whispered into the darkness.

Instead of answering, Clark threw aside the covers and stood. That's when I saw he slept nude.

Oh. Oh my.

I hastily looked away, my face burning, as Clark grabbed a pair of jeans and tugged them on. He didn't bother fastening them, just took my hand.

"C'mon," he said. "Let's get you back to bed."

I didn't protest—didn't know what in the world to say—and let him lead me back down the hall to the room I'd just come from.

He readjusted the sheets for me and stepped aside, but it was weird. Something was off. As usual, I was clueless as to what it was and I fumbled for the right thing to say.

"Clark, I can't just go to sleep, not knowing if you'll be all right."

"I'm always all right. Get in."

But I didn't. I stayed where I was. "I'm not. Not until you tell me."

"Tell you what?"

His eyes glittered in the darkness and he loomed over me. A shiver ran down my spine, but I still didn't move. At this point, I didn't know if it was because I was trying to help, or because I was too frightened.

"Why did you call me Sayeeda?"

It felt as though there was a bubble around us. Nothing else existed. And I waited to see if he'd answer me. Finally, he did.

"You look like her."

My heart skipped a beat.

"Your hair. Your eyes. Talking about it tonight . . . it brought it all back."

"I-I'm sorry." I didn't know what else to say.

"It's not your fault. Go. Get back in bed, Mack."

I finally got my feet to move and I climbed into bed. Clark pulled the covers up, tucking them under my arms. My head was full of questions without answers, and an overwhelming feeling of empathy for Clark.

Impulsively, I reached up, resting a hand along his cheek before he moved away. The shadow of whiskers on his jaw scraped softly against my palm.

"It wasn't your fault."

He froze. I wasn't sure if that was a good thing or a bad thing, but I thought it bore repeating.

"What happened to Sayeeda wasn't your fault, Clark."

"You don't know that, but thank you for the sentiment." And he was gone.

It was a long time before I fell back to sleep.

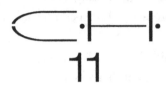

11

My cell phone woke me up and I fumbled for it. I didn't recognize the number, but I answered anyway.

"Hello, is this China . . ." a man's voice said, before massacring my last name. Fifteen letters long and unpronounceable by anyone I'd ever encountered. I stopped him midattempt.

"Speaking. Who is this?"

"John Dunlap, Department of Justice."

I sat up in bed, now fully awake. I certainly hadn't been expecting that. "Mr. Dunlap, what can I do for you?"

"We'd like to question you regarding your work at Cysnet under the direction of Jackson Cooper."

I squeezed my eyes shut. *Damn.* "I see. And is this a request or a demand?"

"At the moment, it's a request. But we can make it a demand, if you prefer."

Threats from the government. How strange and unusual. I rolled my eyes. "I understand. When and where will this questioning take place?"

He gave me an address downtown and I memorized it. "Does today at ten o'clock work in your schedule?"

I'd rather it be sooner than later, so I agreed.

"Thank you," he said, not bothering to try my last name again. "We look forward to speaking with you."

I needed a shower and coffee and my own home, in exactly the reverse order.

It was early even by my standards and I searched near my bedroom, finding a bathroom that had enough spare toiletries under the sink for me to wash my face and brush my teeth. I had no brush or comb so had to use my fingers to smooth my hair well enough to pull it back into my ponytail. Finally, I slipped my glasses on.

They were an older pair that the optometrist assistant had convinced me were fashionable at the time—black horn-rimmed with tiny rhinestones in the corner—but I'd never gotten used to them and had gotten a new pair from a different shop. Now I was forced to wear them until I got a chance to replace the ones that had been broken Saturday night.

The house was even more stunning and breathtaking by daylight. The view out the back looked over trees and a river, the fog of early morning still clinging to the grass. A seating area in front of the windows beckoned and I couldn't help creeping closer for a better look. I had no idea if Clark was awake or not, and part of me hoped he wasn't. Last night had been . . . strange, even by my standards.

I sank down into a cozy, overstuffed chair just as I smelled coffee. I glanced up as Clark came around the corner carrying two large mugs.

"Thought I heard you up," he said, handing me one.

"Had a phone call this morning," I said, taking a sip of the steaming brew. Clark raised his eyebrows in question, settling into the matching chair opposite me. "The DoJ. They want to question me today about Cysnet."

"That's not good. Are you taking a lawyer?"

I hadn't thought of that. "Do you think I need one?"

He shrugged. "That depends. It's a protection for you, but they haven't accused you of anything. You might wait and see where the questioning goes. I imagine they're wanting you as a witness, not as someone to prosecute."

"Witness against Jackson, you mean."

"They're looking for more information. I think you can tell them enough to satisfy them without compromising Jackson. Or yourself. Cysnet did nothing wrong, though that may not stop them. Just be circumspect."

I looked at him. "Circumspect. Have you met me?"

He snorted his coffee and choked on a laugh. After coughing a couple of times, he said, "It'll be okay. You can do it. You just have to think a few steps ahead, that's all. Give them enough, but no more. As smart as you are, it'll be a piece of cake."

Clark's words were a welcome surprise and I sipped my coffee. Last night ran through my head, but I decided not to say anything. The adage *let sleeping dogs lie* came to mind, one that my grandma'd had to explain to me when I was fifteen.

"Thanks for letting me come here last night," I said. "But I'd better get home. I need to change and head downtown for this meeting."

"You can't just go home," he said. "Lu still knows about you, and he killed someone last night."

I ignored the first part of what he said. "Did Genna check in with you? Did she follow him? Did they find out who the guy was?"

"Lu just went back to his hotel. And the police ran an ID check on the dead guy. His name was Fred Dwyer. He worked for the DoD."

"Why would Lu kill him?" I asked. "He had to have known a lot of information."

"I don't know. Maybe he had a change of heart. People do sometimes. That weapon he's after could be just the tip of the iceberg. Or maybe it was a warning to a bigger fish."

"Like who?"

"Like you."

That struck the nerve I'd been trying to ignore. "I've got to go," I said, jumping to my feet so quickly, I nearly knocked over my coffee. "I know you're worried, and I appreciate that, but I'll be fine. I work almost directly for the president of the United States. I'm incredibly important and would be very difficult to replace. I'll be okay."

I needed my normal routine. Nothing bad would happen to me if I could just get back to routine and schedule. If I said that, I knew I'd sound crazy and I knew it wasn't logical to think like that. But routine made me comfortable and in control—two things I hadn't felt for too many days in a row.

Clark had stood, too, and he looked unconvinced, but there wasn't anything else he could do—short of forcibly restraining me—and he knew it. He gave a curt nod.

"Fine. I'll see you at the office afterward."

"Okay." I passed by him, glancing one more time out the window at the beautiful view, then paused. "Clark?" He turned, his dark brows frowning slightly. "Thank you for showing me this place. And for helping me last night."

His face smoothed and I had the fleeting impression that he was relieved. Maybe he was glad I hadn't brought up what had happened in the middle of the night?

"No problem."

I hurried downstairs, grabbed my keys from the table in the hallway, and was out the door.

The building where I was supposed to meet Mr. Dunlap was one of those nondescript office buildings that housed a dozen or more businesses.

I took a deep breath before going inside. I didn't want to do this, but also didn't have a choice.

I adjusted my jacket when I got in the elevator. I'd worn a dark pair of jeans, my *Not All Who Wander Are Lost* T-shirt, and a black suit jacket my grandma had made me buy years ago. It was the one business-attire garment I owned.

Pushing my horn-rimmed glasses up my nose, I tightened my ponytail and stepped off on the twenty-first floor. The corridor was quiet and I navigated to the suite number Dunlap had specified, hesitating before pushing open the door.

A welcoming reception area lay beyond, with a few sofas and chairs, akin to the waiting room of a psychiatrist's office rather than a government agency. It was empty save for myself and a woman sitting behind a desk. She glanced up when I walked in.

"I'm here to see—"

"Yes, welcome," she interrupted me with a polite smile. "Right this way."

I followed her down a hallway past several closed doors. We entered an open room that looked like your average generic conference room.

"Can I get you something to drink? Coffee? Water?"

"Do you have Red Bull?"

She looked at me for a moment, then smiled the perfect, polite smile that I never could quite master. "I'm sorry, but we don't."

"It was worth a shot. Thanks."

She left and I considered the seating before choosing a chair. Back to the windows so a glare wouldn't be in my eyes, and somewhere in the middle, not the end.

I was nervous, the urge to tighten my ponytail nearly overwhelming. The last thing I wanted to do was implicate Jackson in any wrongdoing and jeopardize not only his company, but his freedom as well.

They had me wait nearly seven minutes before entering, three men, all in suits. I stood when they walked in the door.

"Good morning," the first to enter said, and I noticed he didn't attempt my last name again. "I'm John Dunlap. Thank you for coming. These are my associates." He didn't introduce them, just gave a generic hand wave their way after shaking my hand. All three took side-by-side seats opposite me. Fabulous. I felt as though I was facing the Inquisition.

"Nice to meet you," I said. Completely false, but societal convention and all.

"We won't be taking up much of your time," he said, opening a legal pad and brandishing a pen. One of the "associates" pulled out a voice recorder and set it on the table. I eyed it. "We just want you to answer a few questions and you can be on your way."

I nodded stiffly, waiting for the "few" questions.

"You worked at Cysnet for a total of how long?"

"Four years."

"And you worked on a variety of different projects, correct?"

Duh. "Of course."

"Any of these government projects?"

Trick question. The Vigilance project had been government, but through a third party: Wyndemere. "Maybe. I don't remember."

"You don't remember if you worked on a government project?" he persisted.

"Some could have been," I said. "I was there four years. That's a lot of projects, some of which I may only have worked a little on." Which was perfectly true.

"Do you recall working for a company called Wyndemere?"

"Yes."

"And what sort of work was it?"

"Project management." Also true.

"And what was the purpose of the project? What was it to be used for?"

Ah. Dicey territory. "I can't speak to the purpose of the project. Cysnet was hired to complete it. That's all."

Dunlap gave me a sardonic smile. "I find it hard to believe that you wouldn't know the purpose of a project costing over fifty million dollars."

Holy shit. Had that been how much they'd spent? Wow. "I wasn't privy to the start of the project. A contractor's death was what brought Cysnet in, as the project was on a deadline."

"You're talking about Tom Lindemann," he said. "Who committed suicide."

Tom hadn't actually committed suicide, he'd been murdered, but I went with the "official" story. "Yes."

"And there were several other Wyndemere employees who suffered fatal . . . accidents . . . while working on the same project as you, correct?"

"Yes."

He glanced up from his notepad, eyebrows raised. "Yet you and Mr. Cooper were unscathed."

Was I supposed to apologize for that? It sounded bad when he put it like that, as though our being alive was proof of guilt. I didn't know what to say at first, then my logic kicked in. "Do you have a question? Because that was a statement, not a question."

"I'm just wondering what the project's purpose was that left so many people dead in the wake of its completion."

"Again, that's a statement."

"Let me rephrase. What would you conjecture would be the purpose of the project on which you worked for Wyndemere?"

"I don't feel comfortable speculating."

The sardonic smile again. "Come now. A woman as obviously intelligent as you—a genius, in fact—would surely have a few theories as to the purpose of a project you'd been brought in to complete?"

"Anything I say would be a guess," I said. "And I'm not in the business of guessing. If you want to know the purpose of the software written, I suggest you go to the source."

"And who would that be?"

"Whoever paid, obviously."

Dunlap leaned forward. "Well you see, that's the thing. We can't seem to find who exactly authorized such an expenditure. All trails lead to a dead end."

I wasn't surprised. The NSA had been the first to commission Vigilance, then abandoned the project once the whole Snowden story broke, fearing more press about government surveillance on its citizens would make things even worse. Vigilance had been resurrected and finished under a secret presidential directive. And I seriously doubted Gammin had left anything to chance in protecting the secrecy of the president's involvement.

It was my turn for a sardonic smile and raised eyebrows. "You mean to tell me that the government of the United States can spend over fifty million dollars, and the Department of Justice can't trace where the money came from?" I laughed a little. "It sounds like you may have your own problems."

That must have struck a nerve because his expression turned from knowing to a stiff sort of embarrassment.

"If you don't have anything further," I said while I had him at a disadvantage, "I need to get back to work. I trust you know how to reach me, should you have any more . . . questions." I got to my feet before he could respond.

"Of course. Thank you for your time," Dunlap said, also rising, but I was already through the door. I didn't breathe properly until I hit the street.

I needed to get to work so I started walking, but my attention was caught by something else.

Lance was standing on the sidewalk beside a car. When he caught my eye, he discreetly beckoned.

I was mindful of anyone who might be watching as I walked over. "What are you doing here?" I asked.

"Mr. Cooper is waiting in the car," he replied, opening the back door.

I hesitated for a moment, glancing around first, then hurriedly slid inside. Lance closed the door behind me. Jackson was sitting in the backseat.

"What in the world?" I asked. "How did you know I'd be here?"

"I have my sources." He paused. "So what did you tell them?"

"Nothing. I said nothing at all. Their questions were more insinuations and subtle accusations than anything concrete. I don't think they have any hard evidence at all. Just conjecture and supposition."

"Why did you agree to come?"

The look on Jackson's face was blank, which I knew was a bad sign. I tried to think of what I'd done wrong, and came up empty. "I had to go," I said. "They threated to subpoena me otherwise. It was better this way. I gave them nothing, but still appeared to cooperate. Did you think I'd throw you under the bus?"

"I didn't say that. It's just . . . I know you have a hard time with . . . communicating. I was afraid perhaps they'd tricked you into saying something you shouldn't."

My lips pressed together in a thin line. "It's gratifying to know you think so highly of my abilities," I snapped. "Or my loyalty. Speaking of loyalty, why isn't the president backing you up? Protecting you? Everything you did was at his bidding, his demand. Why should you or your company pay the price?"

"He has to distance himself. Politically speaking, he has an election to win in eighteen months."

"He'll toss you to the wolves just so he wins reelection?"

Jackson shrugged. "He's a politician. It's nothing new."

I was about to tell him what I thought of that when my cell phone buzzed. Taking it from my pocket, I saw it was an unknown number from Florida. Normally, I wouldn't answer an unknown number, but Grandma lived in Florida so it might be her.

"Hello?"

"Hello, is this China?"

"Yes. Who's this?"

"This is Serenity Escape," the woman said, naming the retirement community where my grandma lived. "I'm Phyllis. We're calling about your grandma."

My heart skipped a beat. Grandma was the closest thing I had to a mother since my real mom had passed away when I was eight. If something had happened to her . . .

"What's wrong? Is she okay?"

"She's fine," the woman soothed me, "but she's had an . . . episode."

"What do you mean? What kind of episode?"

"A minor cardiac infarction."

Doctor-speak for a heart attack. "Oh my God! Is she all right? Where is she? Can I speak to her?"

"Please, please, calm down," the woman hastened to assure me. "She's all right. We needed to inform you of her status, though."

"What's her status?"

"She had the episode last night. But she's doing fine today and is anxious to return to her own place. For now, we're keeping her under observation."

"I want to see her. I'll be on the first plane down."

"Of course. We thought you might want to. I'll let her know you're on your way."

"Thank you." I hung up.

"What's wrong?" Jackson asked.

"It's Grandma. She's h-had a heart a-attack," I managed. It rocked me. My granny was my rock. She didn't change, even when everything else did. *What would I do if something happened to her?* Then I immediately felt guilty for the selfish thought.

"Is she all right?"

I nodded, my thoughts too overwhelming to speak.

"You'll take my private jet down," he said, his tone firm. "Right away."

"I can't do that," I argued. "Not when things are so . . ." My voice trailed away. I had no word to describe how unsettled things were between us.

Jackson toggled a button on the console. "Lance, get Vince to fire up the jet for immediate departure to Pensacola."

"I can fly commercial." And not owe him anything.

"What's the point of having a rich boyfriend if you can't take advantage of all his toys?"

Yes, that was certainly a plus. Impulsively, I asked, "Will you come with me?"

"To Florida?"

I nodded. "I'd like for you to meet my grandma. She's the most important person in the world to me. Except probably for Mia."

Jackson studied me, then smiled. "If that's what you want, then yes, I'll come."

Which is how we found ourselves in Pensacola, Florida, four hours later.

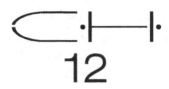

12

I heard my granny before I saw her.

"I'm fine, I tell you. You're wasting your time and money keeping me here, and don't think I don't know that it's a racket. Where's that male nurse I had earlier? Julio, I think was his name. Send him back around, would you? He had a really nice rear on him, that one does."

Oh God. Yep, that was my granny. I heard Jackson snort next to me, then try to cover it up with a cough.

Pasting on a smile, I tapped on the open door. "Grandma? You decent?" I stepped around the corner and spied her lying propped up in bed, a mound of pillows supporting her. She glanced over, saw me, and her face broke into a wide grin that lit up her eyes.

"China girl! What in the blazes are you doing here?"

I rushed toward her, hugging her carefully. My chest had been tight but now it relaxed, my relief at seeing Grandma overwhelming me.

"Thank God you're all right," I said.

"Of course I am," she shot back. "It'll take more than a little ol' heart attack to knock me out of the game." Her keen eyes looked past me. "And who have we here? A hot new doctor for me? Why, you shouldn't have."

I snuffed a laugh through my tear-clogged throat, blinking my eyes. "This is my . . . boyfriend. Jackson. Jackson, this is Granny."

He stepped forward, looking ever so dapper in his shirt and jacket. I'd convinced him to relax a bit and leave the tie behind, but he'd refused to meet my grandmother in just shirt sleeves.

"So very pleased to meet you, Cybil," he said, gently squeezing her frail hand.

"Oh, call me Granny," she said, her pale cheeks pinking like a young girl's. "Everyone does."

"Thank you for the privilege," Jackson said, bowing slightly over her hand. "I'd be honored."

If Granny was fifteen, she'd have fluttered her eyelashes. As it was, she looked decidedly pleased with herself.

"Isn't he a charmer," she said in an undertone to me. Jackson and I both smiled, giving each other mirrored looks of amusement.

"He certainly is," I agreed, turning back to her. "Now tell me what happened. They were very vague on the phone."

"Sweetie, it's not pretty." She glanced at Jackson. "And I'm not sure it's appropriate for mixed company."

"Don't be silly," I said. "Jackson is very pragmatic and sophisticated about the world. I'm sure nothing you say can shock him."

Granny gave a heavy sigh. "I suppose you're right. And after all, at my age, what's the point of being embarrassed?"

That should have given me pause, but she launched into her story.

"You know I've been seeing Larry since Viagra Wednesday three weeks ago," she began. I nodded, almost able to feel Jackson's question in the air, unspoken. *Viagra Wednesday?* "Well, we saw each other a few more times, and then last night, we had dinner, and then we . . ." She trailed off, giving me a meaningful look, eyebrows raised.

Ah. "Got it," I said. "So what happened? Did it not . . . go well?" How did one ask one's granny if the sex was good?

"Oh no, it was good," she said. "Very, very good. I must say, China, that man could do things with his—"

"I'm sure he could," I interrupted, somewhat shrilly. I really didn't need the images, thank you very much. "So what happened?"

"Well, during . . . you know . . ."

"Yes, I know," I said, hurrying her along.

"He just . . . stopped. All of a sudden like. And I tapped his shoulder and said, 'Larry, are you all right?' But he didn't do anything. He just lay there, like a beached whale on top of me."

Oh God, I so didn't need the details . . .

". . . and after a minute or two, I realized he hadn't fallen asleep, like I'd thought at first. But he'd *died*. While we were having sex, China, can you *imagine*?"

I couldn't and didn't want to.

"And it must've just been the shock of it because before I knew it, I had trouble breathing. So I managed to roll him off and get to a phone. And it was a good thing, too, because my chest was feeling much too tight when the paramedics arrived. It was too late for Larry, the poor man, but in time to help me."

I struggled to wrap my head around the fact that my granny'd had a man die while having sex with her and blurted out the first thing that came to mind. "The odds of dying from a heart attack during sex are about one in ten thousand," I said. "There's a higher likelihood of suffering a cardiac event during road rage, shoveling snow, or being the guest of honor at a surprise party."

"What she meant to say is that must've been awful," Jackson said, giving me a sideways glance.

"Well, it certainly was at the time, I'm not gonna lie," she said. "But now, I must admit, it's given me quite the reputation among the single gentlemen here."

"What?"

"Oh yes," she nodded sagely, "I'm now quite the catch. So good in bed, you might die from the pleasure of it."

Jackson was attacked by a suspiciously convenient coughing fit, and I gave him the side eye, catching the grin he couldn't conceal.

"How long do you have to stay?" I asked, wanting to distract Granny from telling any more of her story as a geriatric man-eater.

"Oh, just another day," she said. "I can leave tomorrow. I'm trying to get them to send Julio in for my sponge bath." She gave me a wicked grin, her eyes gleaming. "He's twenty-two and has biceps as big as my thigh."

I rubbed a tired hand over my eyes. While relieved that Granny seemed okay, the worry and stress had taken a toll on me, not to mention the revelations about her sexcapades. I could've gone my whole life without knowing that information.

"You look like you're about to drop," she said, taking my hand in hers. "I can't believe you came down so quick, honey. They shouldn't have bothered you. I told your brothers that I'm fine and not to worry."

"Don't be ridiculous," I said. "And you're not a bother. I don't want to hear any talk like that." I kissed her cheek.

"Go and get some rest," she said, squeezing my hand. "I don't need you hovering over me tonight. They have people here for that."

"Okay. We'll go, but I'll be back to take you home tomorrow," I said, giving her another hug. "Do you need anything?"

"Just a sponge bath," she countered, glancing at Jackson. "I don't suppose your man friend has any nursing experience."

It was my turn to suffer a coughing fit as Jackson paled underneath his tan. "Um, I don't think so, Granny. But I'll ask them to find Julio for you as I leave."

She smiled, leaning back against the pillows. "Perfect. Thank you for coming, China girl."

"You don't have to thank me," I said. "It's what family does. Now I'll see you tomorrow." I pointed a finger at her. "Don't make trouble."

"Who? Me?"

"Your innocent act is fooling no one," I retorted. "Least of all, me."

"Aw, now don't be like that."

I harrumphed at her, giving her a look that she wholly ignored as I headed out the door, followed by Jackson.

"Your granny," he said, "she's quite a character."

I snorted. "That's a nice way of putting it." My granny was a firecracker and always had been. At least, that's what the legends said.

"I think you take after her," he said, surprising me.

"Really? How? She and I are nothing alike. Granny leaps into circumstances without considering the consequences. She has no consideration for propriety or societal convention. She's pretty much a force unto herself. How in the world are she and I alike?"

Jackson shook his head and just smiled, leaving me to wonder what he was thinking, and headed for the exit. After a few steps, he put his arm around my shoulders, and I let him. We stayed like that all the way to his car, parked in the hospital garage. He opened the passenger door for me, and I gratefully slid in. I was exhausted. Even though it was early evening, I felt as though it were midnight.

I closed my eyes as he drove, not knowing or caring where we went. Usually, I was a control freak and needed to know exactly what the plan was: where I was staying, how far away, what were we doing once we got there, etc. But with Jackson, I innately trusted him to take care of things. He was supremely competent in that aspect, at least. So I could relax, and I dozed.

I woke when we stopped, the car's engine turned off, and I looked around. "Where are we?"

"I have a friend who lives here. Said I could use his place for a few days."

Jackson got out and rounded the car before I'd had much time to process this. He opened my door and I got out, the smell of the sea and salt assailing me. I could hear the ocean very close by.

"Where are we?" I asked as he took my hand.

"Not too far from your granny, if you're worried," he replied. "We could be there in thirty minutes, if necessary."

By now we were at the door to a house that loomed large above me. Jackson punched a code into a lock and opened the door, pulling me inside after him.

Marble flooring and granite countertops. Chandeliers and white leather sofas. It was a beautiful place, elegant with clean lines and simple sophistication. Out the back I saw sunlight and followed it to a terrace that spanned the length of the house.

"Wow," I breathed, leaning against the railing. The sun was setting, turning the sky into a kaleidoscope of pinks and oranges and purple. Only about a hundred yards away was the water's edge, the waves gently lapping at the white sand. The terrace was filled with luxurious furnishings—sofas and chairs with cushions meant to embrace you as you took in the gorgeous view.

"Hungry?" Jackson asked, leaning against the railing next to me.

I closed my eyes, the breeze caressing my face. "A little." It had been a while since breakfast and I'd skipped lunch. Now that I'd seen Granny and reassured myself she was okay, I could eat again. "I probably need to call work, let them know where I am."

"Why? You're entitled to a family emergency."

There was a tone in Jackson's voice. Anger, maybe? An irrational response, so I debated my reply. "True, but you wouldn't just disappear without telling anyone, right?"

He didn't look much happier, but seemed to accept that. Sliding his arms around my waist, he pulled me into him.

"I'm sorry. I'm not trying to be an ass. It's just that I . . . don't want to share you."

He was right on the being an ass part. But I didn't understand what he meant. My dating life was a flatline with the occasional spike from a blind date or setup that went nowhere. "You don't share me."

"Don't I?"

I was confused. "What are you talking about? Granny?"

"Clark."

Oh. "I don't get it," I said, exasperated. "Why are you stuck on this? Your reaction to him and me working together has been all out of proportion. He's not an ex-boyfriend or something. We just work together."

The wind took my hair, loosening tendrils from my ponytail that blew into my face. Jackson caught them, tucking them behind my ear in a sweet, gentle gesture that made me feel like one of *those* girls. The ones so pretty and feminine, who you saw on perfume commercials with the sexy guy looking utterly dumbstruck by their beauty.

"It's hard to explain," he said. "And it'll probably make me sound like I'm thirteen again."

"You have to tell me something," I said, unbending. "Because obviously it bothers you and I need to understand why."

He loosened his hold and let me go, turning his gaze out to sea and resting his arms against the railing. He'd discarded his jacket inside and the breeze made his hair ruffle as though invisible fingers ran through it.

"I know you were bullied as a kid," he said. "I was, too. I've mentioned it before."

"I remember." Hard to believe the gorgeous billionaire genius hadn't been popular in school, but that was kids for you.

"It makes an impact on you," he continued. "I'm sure you know that. Affects you and molds you into a different person. More cautious, more wary, more fearful."

I certainly understood that. I'd been a friendly, outgoing kid until after I'd been bullied a few times. Then I realized it was better to be quiet and unnoticed. Difficult, given my educational path, but it had never been my goal to be the one who stood out.

But I wasn't following how this related to Clark. "I do understand that," I said. "Both of us went through bullying in school. But how is Clark a part of that?"

He glanced at me. "Clark is a woman's wet dream. Big guy, built, good-looking. Plus the whole military thing." He shrugged. "When I think of him, I'm back to being that scrawny, nerdy kid stripped naked and duct-taped to the school flagpole. Why would you want me when you could have him?"

Even if he'd said he was a serial killer, nothing would have shocked me more. Jackson was beautiful, with warm brown eyes and a killer smile. Thick, chestnut hair, over six feet tall, lean but muscular. He was one of the smartest men on the planet—literally—and was rich enough to buy his own island if he wanted. The fact that he'd just confessed to me his insecurities was sobering. Men like him didn't make themselves look weak for just anyone. Yet he'd done so . . . for me. So I would understand.

"Jackson . . . I don't know what to say. I guess I thought you were aware of . . . your own appeal. You're gorgeous, smart, wealthy, funny. Women fawn over you."

"Thank you, but that's not how it feels sometimes. And with the money comes doubt. Is a woman paying attention to me because she likes me for me? Or does she just see the money?" Our eyes met. "I think that's why I've been holding back from us. I've been burned too many times by women I thought loved me, when really, they just loved my money. I was stupid and naive for so long. Then I met you, and you're nothing like them. I want to trust you, but old habits and fears are hard to let go."

My heart hurt for him, that last barrier I'd erected to protect myself crumbling into dust. I reached up, cradling his cheek. His eyes closed and he tilted his head into my hand, turning slightly so he could kiss my palm. I moved closer, sliding my arm around his waist.

"I am not lying to you. I'm not using you. And I'm not going to be fickle and flake out on you just because my coworker is an attractive guy."

He opened his eyes, his expression grave. His eyes were like windows to his soul, so expressive I could see the decades-old hurt in them. Impulsively, I stood on my toes, pressing my lips to his.

"I believe you," he whispered.

He took me in his arms and my mouth opened beneath his, my arms winding around his neck. The scent of the ocean mingled with his cologne as his tongue stroked mine. His lips were soft, leading me and drawing me with him to where nothing mattered but his touch.

Breaking off the kiss, Jackson looked at me and what I saw now in his eyes made my heart beat faster. He took my hand and led me inside. I barely noticed where we were going, unable as I was to look away from his eyes.

Down a hall and through a door, then he was undressing me. First the button-up, then the T-shirt, dragged over my head. The jeans and shoes followed. The glasses were gently set aside and I was left in a pale-pink-with-white-polka-dots matching bra and panty set (demi bra with adjustable straps). I reached up to take my ponytail down and he stopped me.

"Don't. I like that part."

The slow slide of the elastic band was like foreplay. He dropped it and used both hands to run his fingers through my hair. I closed my eyes and moaned in appreciation, my nipples tightening in response. I reached for the buttons on his shirt, but he stopped me.

"Not yet."

My bra was undone with a flick of his fingers. I shrugged off the straps and let it fall to the floor. His gaze on my breasts was like a caress.

169

I didn't move as he cupped each breast, lifting them as he bent his head. The touch of his tongue on my nipple sent a bolt of heat through me and my eyes fluttered shut; I slid my fingers through his hair as his mouth closed over me and he sucked, first one breast, then the other, paying due homage to them both.

Knees weak, I clutched his shoulders as his hand slid down inside my panties. His fingers slipped between my folds to the core of me. He pressed kisses to my neck as he touched me. I tried to remember to breathe.

"I want to taste you." His words whispered against my skin, and a brief touch of his tongue to the pulse throbbing in my neck.

He walked me back until my knees hit the edge of the bed and I sank down. Tugging at my panties, he pulled them down and off my legs. Then he dropped to the floor, pushed my knees apart, and buried his head between my thighs.

It was heaven. Pure bliss. I moaned again, not wanting to close my eyes against the sight of him doing this to me. His hands spread me further, baring the most intimate part of me to him. His tongue was heat and torment, bringing me to the edge. Faster he'd kiss me, until I was almost there, then he'd slow down and tease me with featherlike strokes.

"Oh God . . . oh please . . . Jackson . . ."

My whole body was covered in a sheen of sweat, my legs splayed as I clutched his head to me. All I could focus on was what he was doing to me. Nothing else existed but the orgasm hovering close, but just beyond my reach.

He slid a finger inside me and I gasped. He added another, pumping his fingers as he licked my clit, his tongue mimicking his fingers. It was a move he'd done before that he knew I loved. Jackson fucking me with his fingers and tongue, still fully dressed, was an incredible turn-on.

"Oh yes, oh yes . . . please . . . don't stop . . ." My entreaties became moans, then cries as a powerful orgasm crashed into me. Jackson laved my clit in long sweeps of his tongue, prolonging the pleasure until even that gentle touch became too much and I had to push him away.

I was panting, my eyes nearly glued shut, and limp from the bone-wringing orgasm. Jackson looked both satisfied . . . and ravenous. Without a word, he stripped while I watched, my libido perking up with each newly revealed patch of skin. His cock was straining against his pants and I waited eagerly for its appearance.

"You are so beautiful," I murmured when he was fully naked.

The waning sunset painted his skin a light bronze and his hair a deeper shade of mahogany. The muscles his suits camouflaged were on full display and my eyes followed the carved indentations of his abdomen down to his thighs.

"Mr. Happy looks pleased to see me," I said, grinning. My pet name for his "member" made him chuckle, then he picked me up from the edge of the bed. I took the opportunity to kiss his neck and shoulder, the muscles there tight as he carried me around the bed and put me down smack-dab in the middle.

When he crawled in after me, I pushed at his shoulder until he lay on his back, then scooted down between his legs. I had Mr. Happy in my mouth before Jackson could say a word. He was thick and hard—I grasped his shaft as my tongue circled the sensitive tip.

Opening my eyes, I glanced up to see Jackson watching me, his eyes burning with want. The heat inside me spread and I took him deep in my mouth, his answering groan making me smile. Cupping his balls, I gently massaged them as I slid my tongue along his length.

"Holy shit, China," he gasped. His hands clutched at the sheet as I took him deeper, provoking another groan.

His hips jerked upward into my mouth and I let him control our movements. His fingers tangled in my hair as he pumped his cock. I was pretty good at this but even so, I had to stop to breathe after a few minutes. I'd barely brushed all my hair back from my face before Jackson had tossed me onto my back and was kissing me.

It was a long, deep kiss of need and desire. He was kneeling between my spread legs and when he ended the kiss, he sat back to position Mr. Happy in the right spot.

I didn't know why, but this was one of my favorite things to watch. Something was so erotic about seeing him readying himself to take me. An ancient and primeval part of me recognized the ownership in that moment, that I belonged to him and this was when we sealed that pact.

The feel of his cock stretching me, filling me, made both of us sigh in pleasure. It felt so good, so right. I circled my legs around him, holding him close to me as he began to move. We didn't kiss. He was watching me, his gaze on mine, which felt even more intimate than kissing while we made love.

He grew harder inside me, moving faster. I couldn't keep my eyes open as another orgasm crept up on me.

I cried out, this one even more intense than the last, and he paused, still buried inside me.

"Oh, God, that was amazing," I breathed as he started to move again, slow at first, then harder and faster. My body was so sensitive, the pleasure became more intense at each stroke of his cock against me. I clutched his sweat-slicked shoulders, tears leaking from my eyes at the overwhelming sensation.

"China . . . China . . . I'm coming . . . oh God!" He thrust harder, shouting wordlessly as his body convulsed. I held him close, memorizing the feel of him on top of me, inside me. I was still having aftershocks and the feel of his cock pulsing sent another ripple of pleasure through me.

Afterward, we lay there. He was panting and I stroked his back, my legs holding him close. If there was a spiritual plane to making love, I felt as though we'd just touched it.

"I must be crushing you," he said, pushing himself up on his arms. He brushed a kiss to the tip of my nose.

I smiled. "It's fine. I love the weight of you on top of me."

"Ditto," he said, flipping over onto his back and taking me with him so I ended up lying on his chest. I rested my chin on my folded arm so I could look up at him. He used both hands to brush my hair back from my face and looked deeply into my eyes.

"I love you."

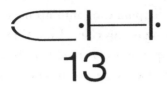

13

My heart skipped a beat and my smile faded. I blinked. Had I really heard what I thought I had? "What did you say?"

Jackson's eyes twinkled. "I said that I love you. I didn't want to say it during. Didn't want you to get the wrong idea."

"Are you sure you're not just feeling the postcoital euphoria associated with the release of oxytocin, most commonly referred to as the *afterglow*?"

"I'm sure," he said, his smile widening.

Oh. Well, that put a whole other spin on it. Jackson said he loved me. It was a really big deal. Even I, experience-devoid as I was, knew that. I also knew the socially acceptable reply was "I love you, too," but I hesitated.

Jackson's smile faded as he ran his fingers through my hair. "You don't have to say it back. I understand."

I couldn't bear the thought that I was hurting him. "I'm sorry," I said. "It's just that . . . I don't know. Not yet. It feels so soon."

"I didn't realize that there was a time requirement on loving someone." There was a slight bitterness to his voice, but I didn't know if I was imagining it or if it was really there.

"Love is a powerful emotion and declaring its presence to someone is a major step in a relationship," I said. "It sets expectations for the other person, whether intentionally or not."

Now his face was impossible to read. "So you'd rather I *not* tell you that I love you," he said, making it a dry statement rather than a question.

"I didn't say that. I just don't want to go too fast. Only a few days ago, you were on a date with another woman." Which still rankled. "And you never did tell me why you were there or what you were speaking to Lu about."

"Then we're even because you won't tell me what you're doing that requires you to work with Clark," he retorted.

That postcoital bliss had all but evaporated and with a sigh, I scooted off him. I had the feeling I'd ruined the moment, but was at a loss as to how I could've reacted differently. Falling in love with Jackson felt like a slippery slope. The past few days had made me aware of how very much the landing could hurt, regardless of how euphoric the fall was.

Saying those three words wasn't just a declaration, but also a commitment. At least it was from my point of view, and maybe that was the crux of it. I didn't trust that Jackson and I both viewed it the same way.

Without a word, he got up and disappeared into the bathroom, the door closing behind him.

I cleared my throat several times, wanting to keep my composure. Getting out of bed, I dressed and headed for the kitchen.

The sun had set and the sky outside was dark, but I opened the doors to the terrace so I could hear the ocean waves against the sand. Next, I searched the refrigerator. My stomach was gnawing my insides and anything sounded good.

I found enough lettuce and veggies to make a decent salad, so I started putting that together. It helped, having something to do, and

I heard the water start running from the bedroom. Jackson must be taking a shower.

After making two salads, I checked my phone. Two missed calls—number unknown—with no voice mails. Hmm. Plus text messages from Mia and Clark. I checked Mia's first.

Did you hear about Granny??

I hastened to reassure her. *Yes, and I came to see her. She's doing really well. Tell your dad for me. Going home tomorrow. Don't worry. XOXO*

Then Clark's.

Everything okay?

I'd told him about my grandma and having to leave for Pensacola. In my absence at Vigilance, he was the next one in charge, with Derrick's help on the tech side, of course.

She's okay. Taking her home from the hospital tomorrow. How's work? Anything more on the package left in the park?

Influx of funds right before. Gambling debts.

Ah. So Mr. Dwyer'd had a gambling problem. An obvious thing to look for, if you're a foreign agency looking to recruit—or blackmail. It was something Gammin had warned me about. I didn't have a lot of sympathy, though perhaps I should've. I'm sure he hadn't considered he'd end up dead rather than merely a debt-free traitor.

Noted. Anything on our common friend?

Yes. He's left for parts unknown. Working on locating. G wants to take a closer look at business negotiations.

Gammin wanted more information on what Lu had been up to while he was here.

Find anything?

F Comm chair had backdoor. Working on staff now.

Not surprising. The Senate Finance Committee had the power to modify trade deals and put them up for a senate vote. If the chairman of the committee had secretly met with Lu via backdoor channels, the president would want to know what was discussed. So Gammin was having Vigilance run surveillance on the staffers, to find out if anyone knew what had been said.

Ok. Keep me in the loop. I went to put down my phone, but it buzzed again with another message from Clark.

Be careful.

Not exactly an outpouring of worry, but coming from Clark, it was nearly the equivalent. I was surprised he bothered to even send that. Clark seemed to be a me-first-everyone-else-a-distant-second kind of guy. I couldn't blame him. If I'd lived through what he had, I might feel the same. It was much easier not to care.

I had to check my email so I opened my laptop and connected to Wi-Fi, then my VPN to the office. Thirty-five new emails. Ugh.

Going through them quickly, I flagged some for priority and sent off a few quick replies to others. I was nearly done and about to sign off when I had a thought. Opening another window, I began typing, running software in the background until I found what I wanted. The bot I'd piggybacked onto Kuan's system. A moment later, I'd activated his webcam and pulled up another screen. I couldn't see him, but could hear him tapping the keys of his keyboard. I'd thought maybe he wouldn't have covered his camera, but that had been too much to hope for. Oh well. At least I could hear him through its mic.

Payback's a bitch, I thought as I started typing.

Doing your homework? I asked. The keyboard tapping stopped. I could hear some kind of music in the background. *Maroon 5 fan?*

"Who is this?" he asked.

Not really fun to be hacked now, is it, I typed on the screen.

I heard a low laugh. "It's you. It's China. Right?"

Bingo.

"Pretty sweet," he said. I heard a squeak, as though he'd shifted in his chair. "Color me impressed."

That wasn't my goal, but considering your skills, I'll take that as a compliment.

Kuan laughed. "So what do I owe this visit? Just a demonstration of your mad skills?"

Not exactly. Sometimes we need people like you who can . . . work off the radar. Since hacking into a government agency is a federal offense, I'll overlook your transgression in a quid pro quo agreement.

"Oh really. What kind of quid pro quo?"

There's a Chinese businessman named Simon Lu, I typed. *He's currently off the radar. We need to know where he is and what he's doing.*

"Lu?" he asked. "I know him. He's a Chinese spy. I've tracked him before."

Even better. I figured with Kuan's Taiwan background, he'd harbor plenty of animosity toward the Chinese. *Great. So you agree?*

"Yeah. No problem."

Excellent. I'll be in touch.

I signed off the VPN and shut down the computer just as I heard Jackson coming back.

"Everything all right?" he asked.

I turned around to see him fresh from the shower, his hair damp, and he wore an unbuttoned shirt with shorts and bare feet. My gaze caught on his chest and I suppressed a little sigh.

"Yeah, I'll tell you while we eat. I made a couple salads if you're hungry."

It didn't take us long to eat, famished as I was, and I filled him in on Lai Kuan-Yu and how he'd hacked my home network. "But now he's working for me," I said. "He's really good—scary good. Heck, you might want to give him a job when he graduates."

Jackson didn't say much to this and I didn't know if that meant he was in agreement or just considering.

After we were done cleaning up, Jackson caught me gazing out at the moonlight on the ocean. "Want to go for a walk?" he asked, handing me one of the glasses of white wine he'd poured.

I glanced down at my feet. "I'll get sand on my feet and jeans."

"Take off the jeans."

My eyebrows shot up, but he just laughed. "There's no one around, it's the off-season. Besides, your T-shirt is long enough to cover you."

He had a point, so I slipped off my jeans and followed him outside and down the stairs from the deck. I sipped my wine as we strolled toward the water, and he took my hand so I could keep my balance on the shifting sand beneath my feet. It was cold, which took me by surprise as I'd expected the sand to be warm.

Walking hand in hand on the beach while a full moon shone overhead was arguably the most romantic thing I'd ever done, yet I could feel the tension between us like a living thing, and I regretted not saying *I love you* back. It wasn't as though I could tell him now, though, not just out of the blue. He'd know it was a result of guilt.

But there was something else I could do to let him know how I felt.

"I work with Clark because I have to," I said. The waves crashed onto the shore as the tide was receding, rougher than they had been earlier. "The software you wrote—what Wyndemere wrote—wasn't destroyed. It's been put to use . . . by the US government."

Jackson stopped in his tracks, pulling me around to face him. Reluctantly, I looked up, wincing at the anger and disbelief on his face.

"Please tell me you know this secondhand," he said, "and not from personal hands-on knowledge."

Slowly, I shook my head. "I'm sorry, Jackson. But I wasn't given much choice. Vigilance is up and running . . . and I'm overseeing its implementation."

He looked as if I'd slapped him, and he didn't reply. Instead, he turned and paced away a few steps, then stopped. Downing the rest of his wine, he suddenly hurled the empty glass into the waves, then stood there with his hands braced on his hips.

Cautiously, I approached him, leaving a few feet between us. "Jackson, I'm sorry," I repeated. "I couldn't tell you. They threatened me. Even now, I can't leave. I know too much. I stay to try and do as much good with the software as I can and keep the wrong people from finding out about it and using it for their own purposes."

The wind whipped his shirttails behind him and I took a few more cautious steps until I could rest a hand on his arm. I took it as a good sign that he didn't push me away.

"That software was never supposed to see the light of day," he said. "They promised me."

"Who promised you?"

"Gammin. He said they'd keep it as a last resort, that only in a state of impending attack would they call it into play."

I wasn't at all surprised Gammin had lied. He'd rob his own mother to save his skin. "Do you think Gammin could be using the DoJ to get rid of you? You're no longer useful and you have information that could be damaging." What a horrible thought that was. The last thing someone wanted to think as a private citizen was that the government was out to get you.

"I don't know," he said with a sigh.

"Jackson," I said, waiting until he glanced down at me. "You can't tell anyone about Vigilance. If it gets out, there will be a huge scandal and Snowden-like media coverage all over again. For sure Gammin will know I told you, which would put both of us in danger."

His jaw tightened and he shoved his fingers through his hair in wordless frustration. I dropped my hand to my side.

"Why didn't you tell me before?" he asked. "When maybe I could have helped you?"

"It wasn't your decision to make," I said. "And the less you knew, I thought the safer you'd be. After everyone that died at Wyndemere, I think the only thing protecting you is your high profile. And the only thing protecting me is that I know best how the software works. But neither condition is a permanent deterrent, not if we pose a threat."

"How does Clark figure into all this?"

"I handle gathering intelligence and reporting red flags. Clark handles . . . operations. I guess you could say I'm the brains and he's the muscle."

"You mean to tell me that Vigilance has the power to act without any government oversight at all? No one to report to and no one has to justify the legality of your actions?"

Well, when he put it like that, it sounded really bad. And he looked pissed, his lips pressed into a thin line and his brows drawn together in a frown like a thundercloud. I felt the need to defend what we were doing, though I didn't 100 percent agree with it myself.

"The president of the United States is our authority," I said stiffly. "We operate under his orders and knowledge. Since he's the commander in chief, I didn't see a reason to refuse."

"Do you have that in writing? A *Get Out of Jail Free* card?"

I'd signed a contract, but the verbiage hadn't been crystal clear on authority and protection in case the worst happened. At the time, I didn't see that I had a choice, and I still didn't.

"What do you expect me to do?" I asked, throwing my hands up. "I made the best out of a bad situation." I hesitated, then decided to come clean. "Though Lu found out about me."

"What do you mean?"

"He threatened me. I think he wants me to be an informant and work for them."

"Jesus, China." He shoved his fingers through his hair again, which I always liked because that left it just a little messy.

"I'm not going to," I said. "There's nothing he can say or do that would make me turn traitor. But it's as if he's working with people in our government whose agendas aren't in the country's interest. It's all cloak-and-dagger, and being responsible for something like Vigilance was never something I wanted to sign up for."

"The potential for abuse is massive," he said. "Not to mention if other countries got ahold of it. I'd hate for the Chinese and North

Koreans to get their hands on this, not only for our sake, but for their own populations."

"If you distrust the Chinese so much, then why are you cozying up to Lu?"

"There's an executive order in the works," he explained, "that would give the treasury the ability to impose sanctions on any company, individual, or entity that harms national economic policy or national security by benefitting from stolen secrets and property."

"How do you know this?"

"I have close ties to some congressmen," he said. "I've been lobbying them to bring this issue up and give some teeth to the penalties. Now that it may finally be happening, the Chinese aren't happy. Lu in particular."

"Why Lu?"

"Because his company would be the first one sanctioned."

Oh. Well then yes, I could see why he'd be upset. "So why is he talking to you?" I asked.

"Cysnet is actively being attacked by the Chinese. And we found out last week that they were in the process of recruiting Wei Sun to steal from Cysnet."

My jaw dropped. "You're kidding me?" Wei Sun was vice president of engineering at Cysnet. He'd worked there since Jackson had started the company. I'd personally worked with him on several projects and come away with a healthy dose of respect for his intellect and professionalism. "He was going to betray you? Betray Cysnet?"

"Everyone has a weak spot."

"How'd you find out?"

Jackson looked away. "We always monitor any employees with Chinese ancestry."

It was my second time to be stunned. "Seriously? That's . . . that's crazy. And illegal, right?"

"It's my company. I can monitor whomever I choose. Everyone's monitored to some extent, but to ignore the aggressive recruitment of naturalized Chinese-Americans by the Chinese would be naive as well as dangerous. To the company, its employees . . ."

"Yes, you're right," I said. "I was just . . . surprised. So you're trying to work a deal with Lu?"

Jackson nodded. "He ceases and desists his attempts on Cysnet, I use my connections to make sure his company isn't one of those that are sanctioned."

"Not exactly fair," I observed.

"Fair is an illusion when it comes to money and politics."

We stood, side by side, staring into the waves. A quid pro quo of information between us, which I felt meant more than declarations of emotional attachment.

"Jackson, how many women have you said that to before?" I wasn't sure I wanted to know the answer, but it was too late to take the question back now.

He didn't answer at first and my heart sank. I shoved my bare foot into the sand, watching the silicon dioxide particles shift between and over my toes. They needed painting.

"Is that what you think?"

My attention was torn from contemplating the sand and my need for a pedicure as Jackson pulled me toward him.

"You think I've said that to, what, a dozen other women?"

He looked angry again, and . . . hurt.

"I didn't mean—" I began, but he interrupted.

"Yes, you did. I know I may have dated a lot, been in the papers, but I don't say those words to just anyone. The last time was years ago and she left me for an actor."

I winced at the bitterness in his voice. "Jackson, I'm so sorry. I didn't know."

"You couldn't, obviously. I'd just hoped you'd know that I wouldn't tell you I loved you, China, if I didn't mean it."

He turned away and I had the sudden panic that I was going to lose something I'd just found and hadn't yet realized its full potential.

"Wait!"

Jackson stopped. His back was to me, looking stiff and forbidding. Still, I approached him and placed my hands lightly on his arms.

"I didn't mean to hurt you," I said, resting my head against his back. "This is all new to me. I'm as afraid of making the wrong move and getting hurt as you are."

He turned and I held my breath, hoping I hadn't completely ruined everything. Finding our way through this relationship felt as uncertain as the shifting sand underneath my feet.

"I do care about you," I said, reaching up a hand to cradle his cheek. "So much. It feels like falling in love . . . at least, that's what it seems. I don't know. I've never been in love before."

Lightly grasping my wrist, he turned his face into my palm and pressed a kiss there, then drew me into his arms. He rested his chin on top of my head.

"I shouldn't have pressured you," he said.

We stood like that for a few minutes, the breeze a balm as much as the sound of the waves were.

"You know, if you're marking off sexual positions," he said, "maybe we should add a different list, too."

"What kind of list?" I liked lists. Checking things off them felt momentous and gave me a warm feeling of accomplishment inside.

"Places. Such as on the beach. It's on a lot of bucket lists."

I looked up at him, checking to see if he was serious. I couldn't tell. "Coitus in the sand would be extremely uncomfortable, as well as unsanitary. And there is wildlife, too, sand fleas, spiders, crabs—"

"Wow, talk about killing the mood," he interrupted with a laugh. "I bet I can take your mind off all that."

"I seriously doubt it. I guarantee you that my vagina does not need exfoliating."

"Then you can be on top."

He lifted me up, making me squeal, and I wrapped my legs around his waist. I was tired of being tantalized with his unbuttoned shirt, so I pushed it off his shoulders and down his arms. He juggled me from one arm to the other so he could let it fall to the ground.

His chest was bare and warm, the skin smooth underneath my fingers. I took my time touching his shoulders and arms.

"You going to kiss me, or what?" he asked, his lips twisted in a half smile.

As though I needed to be asked twice. I wrapped my arms around his neck and pressed my lips to his, to the man who'd been the first to tell me he loved me. Nonrelation, that is.

Our tongues tangled, the heat between us making the cool breeze seem nonexistent. His lips were soft, his arms holding me hard and strong. His hand slipped down the back of my panties to between my legs and he slid a finger inside me.

I moaned against his mouth, something about the way he was touching me—and in a public place—made my libido go from Zero to Take-Me-Now. I had an exhibitionist streak, apparently. Huh. Who knew?

Jackson knelt down and I tore my lips from his. "Don't you dare put me in the sand."

"Have some faith."

He lay back on the beach and maneuvered for a moment. Sitting back on his thighs, I watched him undo the buttons on his shorts, freeing a very aroused Mr. Happy. The moonlight played on his skin, turning it silver and accentuating the definition of his rectus abdominus—more akin to an eight-pack than the much-renowned six-pack. He looked like some kind of pagan god, splayed on the beach to be worshipped and adored.

"Take your shirt off."

The sight of what awaited me if I did had me hurrying to comply. If I was on top, there was a much smaller chance of sand getting places it shouldn't.

I took him in hand and his eyes slid shut. Mr. Happy was pleased at my touch, getting harder in my grip. I settled over him, positioning him at my entrance before sliding down. Jackson hissed between his teeth, his hands squeezing my hips.

The squats I did to try to stay in shape proved very beneficial to this position, and the only place I got sand was on my knees.

Granny was waiting for us when we got to the hospital the next morning.

"They never did send in that Jose," she said, looking disgruntled. "They tried to foist some old woman on me. I sent her on her way right quick." Since Granny was over seventy, her calling someone an "old woman" was like the pot and the kettle. But she never saw herself as old. *Age is just a number*, she'd tell me.

I wasn't quite sure how to respond to that, so I changed the subject. "Ready to go home?"

"As if you have to ask. This place smells and the food is bad." She was decidedly grumpy as she picked up her purse and we headed out the door.

She insisted on stopping at a Cracker Barrel on the way home, putting away a heaping plate of biscuits and gravy.

"Granny, you probably need to dial back on the gravy," I said. "You did just have a heart attack, you know."

She motioned away my concern with a flick of her hand as she sipped her coffee. "That was an incident brought on by the shock of a dead man in my bed," she said. "Not my diet."

I wasn't so sure about that, but trying to argue with her was like blowing wind at a brick wall. So I ate my blueberry pancakes and let it go. Jackson had already finished his Old Timer's Breakfast and drank his black coffee without comment.

"So tell me about you two," she said. "Jackson, what do you do for a living?"

I'd told her about Jackson and me weeks ago. Actually, Mia had let that particular cat out of the bag. She'd been thrilled and regularly quizzed me on how things were going. Now that she had him in her clutches, I realized he was about to be grilled—Granny Style.

"I own a software company," Jackson replied. "That's how China and I met."

"Well, I'm usually one to say you don't sleep with the boss," she said with a wink at me, "but in this case, I think China breaking the rules turned out for the best, don't you?"

Jackson smiled at me. "I would have to agree."

"So have y'all talked wedding?"

Pancake went down the wrong way and I choked, grabbing my water to try to get it down. I coughed and spluttered while Granny slapped me heartily on the back.

"Granny," I managed to croak once I'd stopped coughing. "We're not getting married." Talk about hitting a sore spot.

She frowned. "Not ever? You know I don't approve of living in sin."

"We don't live together," I said, skirting the "sin" part. "So you don't have to worry. We just started seeing each other a couple of months ago. There's no rush." It felt incredibly awkward to be having this conversation after what Jackson and I had just gone through. Was it normal for everyone to think of marriage after only two months of dating?

Jackson was watching this exchange with interest and now she fixed her beady gaze on him. "You do right by my girl," she said sternly. "Or you and I are gonna have words."

Seeing my five foot four granny chastise a billionaire tech giant in the middle of the morning rush at Cracker Barrel was surreal. I inwardly cringed, since he'd already wanted to "do right" by me and I'd nixed the idea. For now.

"Yes, ma'am," Jackson replied, his expression sober. "I will do my best."

She gave him a curt nod, as if it was all settled. "Let's go out to the store," she said. "I'd like to shop a little." She burped delicately into her napkin.

It was another forty-five minutes of shopping, oohing and aahing over the "cutest little things" she saw. Jackson had to step outside a few times for phone calls, dutifully carrying the things she picked up to buy.

"Isn't this just adorable?" she asked me, picking up a pillow that said *This Ain't My First Rodeo*. I mumbled something agreeable as I followed her around the store. The only thing I liked shopping in an actual store for was bras, and Cracker Barrel didn't have a lingerie department.

When we finally checked out, Jackson insisted on paying, despite my objections.

"Honey," Granny said to me, taking me by the arm and leading me away from the register, "let the man pay. They like to do that. Makes them feel like they're the provider. You'll make him feel less manly if you keep wanting to pay."

I didn't bother arguing with her, just followed her out to the car and waited for Jackson. Twenty minutes later, we were pulling into the Serenity Escape entrance. The drive was blocked by a gate and I gave Jackson the code to punch in the keypad. Granny's place was in the farthest duplex, the second to last on the block.

They were ranch-style duplexes—stairs were out of the question in a retirement community—with two or three bedrooms, a full kitchen, living room, storage area, and patio. Each had a privacy fence for their lawn and between the duplexes. Flowers bloomed in pots in front of doors all up and down the street, giving it a homey feel.

When she'd first moved down here, we'd gone to a store that sold furniture by the room. All the pieces you'd need to decorate a living room, or a bedroom. Just pick the colors you want and choose from several options. Granny had decided on a tropical palette reminiscent of 1974, but she'd insisted that since she was moving to Florida, she needed to "not stand out like a country bumpkin."

We settled her inside, Jackson not even flinching at the chartreuse sofa and flamingo-print bedspread, though he did give a sideways glance to the fake palm tree. I fussed over her, getting her pillows just right and making sure she had the remote close at hand for the television.

"Now, I've spoken to the staff," I said, "and they're going to send someone over to check on you tonight and for the next several days. I signed up for the in-home meal service too, for at least a month."

"I want to see that menu," Granny said, reaching for the papers I held. I moved them out of her reach.

"Forget it. You're eating healthier, at least for a little while. Chicken, fish, high fiber, lots of fresh veggies."

She grimaced. "Lord, that sounds awful. Add fried chicken, and fried okra. And strawberry rhubarb pie. Jackson, talk some sense into her."

"I'm not getting in the middle of this one," he said good-naturedly.

The doorbell rang and I got up to answer it.

"Sit down here and keep me company," Granny said to him, patting the bed beside her. "I want to hear about how wonderful you think my granddaughter is."

I nearly doubled back, but the doorbell rang again and I had to hurry to the front.

An older gentleman stood on the steps, clad in a brown suit that had to be at least thirty years out of date, a straw Panama-style hat, and clutching an elaborate bouquet of bright yellow sunflowers. He smiled when I opened the door.

"May I help you?"

He gave a little bow and lifted his hat to me. "Good afternoon. I am Harold Williams and I live just across the way there." He motioned with the sunflowers to a set of duplexes down the street. He spoke in an old-world-style Carolina Southern accent that made me think of magnolias and mint juleps. Granny had a Southern accent, too, but it was more frog legs and Mason jar glasses.

"I heard dear Cybil was feeling poorly, so I thought I'd bring her something to cheer her up. There's nothing quite like a sunflower to brighten a cloudy day."

Humph. Yeah, I just bet. Granny had a new rep, she'd said. Neighborhood temptress. Suddenly, I felt like a dad guarding his teenage daughter.

"How long have you and my granny been friends?" I asked, crossing my arms over my chest.

Harold's smile remained. "Oh Lord, we've known each other for nearly a year now, ever since I moved in." Seeing my hesitation, he glanced around, then added in a stage whisper, "And we play in the poker game together."

All right then. She probably did know him. I stepped back, still not smiling, as Harold let out a breath and scooted past me into the living room.

"I'll just let Granny know you're here," I said. "You can have a seat."

Harold perched on the edge of the sofa and removed his hat, taking a moment to smooth the thinning hair on his head and straighten his tie. I rolled my eyes and headed back into the bedroom.

". . . so much smarter than those other kids, and was never vindictive when they were mean to her. Just like Jesus."

Oh my God. Had Granny just likened me to . . . Jesus?

"You have a visitor," I blurted before she could go any further with that analogy. I sank when put in water. "Harold Williams. Do you know him?"

Her eyes lit up. "Oh! Oh my, Harold came by to visit little ol' me?" She patted her hair, the silver curls bouncing at her shoulders. "Do get me my bed jacket from the closet. And my compact to powder my nose."

"I'll just go say hello to Harold, shall I?" Jackson asked.

"Oh yes, and offer him some tea or coffee. Or a shot of whiskey. It's in the cabinet by the television."

"Drinking at this hour?" I chastised her.

She pooh-poohed me. "Honey, none of us worry about things like that anymore. Drink it while you can still enjoy it, I say."

I couldn't argue with that.

There was a pink silk bed jacket in her closet, embroidered with tiny white roses. "Very pretty," I said, helping her into it. I retrieved her compact and watched in some amusement as she added makeup to her cheeks and nose.

Granny had amazing skin, which was why she could get away with looking a decade younger than she really was. She maintained staying out of the sun was her secret, and constantly was on me to stay out of the sun, even though I'd told her many times that my job and hobbies lent themselves to a year-round pasty white complexion.

"Okay, I'm ready. Show him in."

Granny looked like a queen in her bed jacket, sitting among a throne of pillows, awaiting her courtier. But when I returned to the living room to fetch Harold, I was in for a surprise.

"Who are you?" I blurted.

Two more aged men holding bouquets of flowers sat on the sofa next to Harold, like a geriatric version of *The Dating Game*.

"This is Rodney," Jackson said, appearing at my elbow and carrying three glasses all filled with a measure of amber liquid. He handed one to Rodney. "And this is Tom." Another glass. "And you met Harold." Last glass.

"Um, okay, then," I said, at a loss as to what to do . . . other than take them in to where my granny was receiving her callers. "Follow me."

I felt like a mother duck as they fell in line behind me, the paper wrapping their bouquets crackling as they walked. We filed into Granny's room and I saw a grown, elderly woman transform into a young coquette again.

"Why Tom . . . and Rodney . . . and Harold . . . why, I'm tickled pink! And you've come bearing gifts. How sweet! China, do get a couple more chairs so these gentlemen can set a spell."

I did her bidding then left her to it, not really seeing that I was adding anything to the conversation as they discussed her "ordeal" in the most genteel terms and oblique references I'd ever heard.

"I think I need a drink now," I muttered to Jackson. "Can you believe this?"

"Your grandma is popular."

"You could say that."

There was another knock on the door.

"You've *got* to be kidding me. More men?"

I opened the door in a huff, but it wasn't another elderly gentleman. It was two men in suits and wearing mirrored sunglasses. One of them flipped open a badge and ID.

"Special Agent Brooke, FBI."

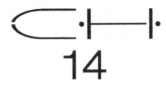

14

I stared dumbfounded at the men and the badge, then noticed photographers and several people with seriously heavy-looking television cameras. I couldn't see any of their faces, just the electronic eyes watching. Jackson suddenly appeared beside me.

"What's going on?" he asked.

"Mr. Cooper," the agent said, spotting him. "We're here for you."

"What does that mean, you're 'here for me?'"

"Please step outside, sir."

My stomach flipped over and I watched in dawning horror as Jackson moved past me and the other agent took out a pair of handcuffs.

"Jackson Cooper, we're placing you under arrest by the United States government," he said, loud enough to easily record. It infuriated me, his obvious playing to the cameras.

Jackson didn't say a word and I knew he didn't want to give the cameras anything more for their evening news. But I couldn't just let him be taken away like this. I ran outside.

"Wait!"

The men all turned and I pushed past the agents to Jackson. "What's going on? What should I do?" I asked, keeping my voice as low as possible.

"Call Lance," he said. "He'll know what to do."

I nodded. "Okay." Having a task—a plan—helped immeasurably. I realized I was still nodding and stopped.

"Put my sunglasses on for me, your worship."

Your worship? Oh. Oh, yeah. Jackson's sunglasses were hooked to the front of his shirt and I was sure he'd like them on before they marched him to the car in handcuffs.

That thought made my eyes sting and my fingers fumbled with the wire frames, sliding them on him. When they were on, he suddenly leaned down and pressed his lips to mine. It wasn't just a dry peck, either, but a full-on-with-tongue-heat-searing-toe-curling kiss as though there weren't a dozen people watching us. I had to grip his biceps to keep my balance.

"Really?" An agent snorted.

Jackson lifted his head and gave me a wicked half smile. I heard the clicking whir of cameras capturing the moment.

"I love you," I blurted.

"I know."

The agents pushed Jackson through the press and were putting him in the backseat of a nondescript government-issue gray sedan. The crowd followed, filming. I stared after the car, feeling as though I'd swallowed a chunk of lead that was making little lead babies in the pit of my stomach. The car turned the corner and was out of sight.

As one, the crowd turned and made a beeline for me, shouting questions. For a second, I was a deer frozen in headlights. Turning, I ran for the duplex, slamming the door just in time.

Okay, I had to think. I had to call Lance. Then I had to figure out how to escape my granny's house with the press outside.

Lance sounded a lot calmer than I felt.

"Don't worry," he said. "I'll contact the attorneys immediately."

"Will they be able to help?" I fretted.

"Of course. That's what they're paid to do. And as for you, don't speak to the press, please."

"I won't."

"I'll call you back shortly with your travel itinerary back to Raleigh."

"Okay."

And that was the extent of my To Do list, and it didn't feel good at all to check that off.

Laughter erupted from Granny's bedroom, reminding me that some people were blissfully unaware of what had just transpired outside. I was at loose ends, feeling something close to panic nibbling at my mind.

I was out of my home, out of my routine, and with no more tasks to fix the problem at hand. Granny was okay and occupied. I'd dealt with work last night and everything was routine and quiet at the moment. Lu was off the radar and maybe had decided to just go home. Unlikely, but I could always hope. Kuan could hopefully tell me more soon.

Opening Granny's fridge, I stared at the contents. I wasn't hungry, but I could see it had been a long time since she'd cleaned it out. Grabbing a random jar, I checked the expiration date. It was out of date by six months. The next jar was out of date by over a year. I started making a stack.

Twenty minutes later, the entire contents of the refrigerator were on the kitchen table and counters. I had a bucket of warm water and was on my hands and knees, scrubbing down the inside of the refrigerator. My head was completely inside the box when I heard Granny exclaim.

"What in heaven's name?"

I scrambled backward and promptly caught my ponytail on a shelf. "Ow. Owowowow." It took a second to detangle myself, then I was sitting on the linoleum with four sets of eyes staring down at me.

"I was just cleaning out the fridge," I said.

"I can see that," she said, scrutinizing my face. Her lips set in a line as she studied me. "Gentlemen, I must say I'm feeling a bit tuckered out. If you wouldn't mind—"

She didn't even have to finish that sentence before they were falling all over each other with apologies and good-byes and get-well-soons. Graciously seeing them out, she was back within moments.

"Should I ask why there's a posse of reporters on my porch?" she asked.

"It's Jackson," I said. "He's been arrested." It felt weird saying it, as though I was hearing someone else say those words.

"I see." Granny glanced around the kitchen and grimaced. "Let's get these things back in the fridge before they spoil."

"Food left at room temperature is usually safe for up to two hours," I said absently, grabbing a trash bag and loading it with everything that was expired. "After that, it's best to throw it away, even if it doesn't smell bad."

"Why don't you tell me what happened?" Granny asked, putting the eggs back in the fridge.

"They just . . . came for him," I said. "The FBI. I don't know what's going to happen now, but it's serious." I tied the garbage bag closed and began helping put stuff back.

"They won't come for you then?"

I shook my head. "No, I don't think so. Jackson's the one with the multimillion-dollar company." Now, the Chinese might be a different matter.

My cell phone buzzed and I answered. Lance told me that Jackson's plane would be ready to take me back to Raleigh by the time I arrived at the airport. I thanked him and hung up after making him promise to let me know if he heard anything more.

Gathering my things, I took Jackson's car keys from the counter. "I've got to go," I told Granny. "Will you be all right?"

"I'm as right as rain," she said. "It's you I'm worried about."

The last thing she needed was me stressing her out. "I'm really fine," I assured her. "I promise."

"Honey, why would you think you can lie to me? I know you're not fine." She gestured to the fridge. The expression on her face was one of pained sympathy. "You didn't even arrange things according to food group, bless your heart."

Oh no. I'd gotten a *bless your heart*. That was about as pathetic as you got in the South, except maybe if she'd added on an *I'll say a prayer for you*.

"I'm just worried," I confessed. "But it'll be okay. Jackson can afford a platoon of lawyers. I'm sure he'll be released by tonight. I need to get back, though, so long as you'll be okay. The nurse will stop by in a couple of hours and dinner will be brought by shortly after that."

Granny gave me a hug. "You take good care of me, China girl. Now go on and be there for your man. And be safe."

Running the gauntlet of press was interesting and I nearly backed over a couple of them, trying to get out of the driveway. I didn't know what was so riveting about watching me get into a car and drive away, but they filmed and photographed it, all while shouting questions at me. I'd taken a page from Jackson's book and worn my sunglasses.

The plane was waiting, which I had to admit was awesome. I could get used to a private plane at my disposal. I was starving, too, so after takeoff, I raided the galley for food. There was some fruit, little bags of pistachios, pretzels, and some kind of trail mix. With a shrug, I grabbed some of everything, plus a minibottle of wine.

When we landed, it was after six and evening had fallen. I was taken aback to see Lance waiting for me with the car. I crossed the tarmac toward him.

"That was really nice of you to come," I said, "but you didn't have to do that. I could have caught a cab or an Uber."

"Actually, I did have to come," he replied grimly. At my questioning look, he just opened the back door.

"Welcome back!" Clark said, peering out from the backseat. "Hop in."

Now I understood the pained look on Lance's face. I'd look like that, too, if Clark was in the backseat of my car.

I slid in and Lance closed the door behind me. "What's going on? Why are you here?" I asked.

"Heard about Coop's problem," he replied, resting back against the leather seat, his arm stretched across the top. "The DoJ is looking for reasons to seize Cysnet, which would give them access to all the software they've ever written."

"They wouldn't find any ties to terrorists or enemy states," I said, glancing toward the front as Lance began driving.

He raised an eyebrow. "Oh, wouldn't they? You wanna bet your boyfriend's life on it?"

"They're not going to kill him," I said.

Clark released a put-upon sigh. "Let me explain how this works, O Naive One. The government finds its airtight, smoking-gun case against the poor slob they've targeted. In this case, Coop. They railroad him through the justice system, turn public opinion against him, and destroy his life."

"Jackson has the best lawyers on the planet," I interrupted. "They'll be able to help him."

"Even if by some miracle he's not convicted," Clark continued, ignoring me, "his stock will tank and turn his company into a worthless pile of paper. He'll have to sell cheap, probably to a government contractor and competitor of his, conveniently giving them access to everything. After that, you'll wake up one morning to find that your dear Coop killed himself over the disgrace and crush of his broken dreams."

I stared, open-mouthed. "That—that's ridiculous. Jackson would never commit suicide."

Clark closed his eyes and rubbed his forehead, as though it took all he had to deal with the inanity of my comments. "Of course he wouldn't. Didn't Wyndemere teach you anything?"

The "accidents" that had taken the lives of two programmers, and the apparent suicide of the project manager that had started it all. I swallowed hard. I'd told Jackson that his high profile was keeping him safe, but it looked as though I'd spoken too soon.

"So what do we do?"

"Coop's too smart to not have something to cover his ass," Clark said. "Did he tell you anything?"

"Um . . ." I went through our conversation last night. I certainly didn't want to divulge to Clark that I'd told Jackson about Vigilance, but he had said something he hadn't elaborated on. "He mentioned something about a *Get Out of Jail Free* card," I said. It had been in reference to me, but if he asked if I had one, surely he'd made sure of his own security.

"Perfect. Did he tell you what it was or where?"

I shook my head. "No. We didn't really discuss it further." We'd been too busy having sex on the beach, the memory of which must've shown on my face because Clark rolled his eyes.

"TMI," he said. "What about today? I saw the footage of his arrest. He said something to you. What was it?"

"They're playing the footage?" I asked, dismayed.

"On a constant loop, yeah," he said. "So what did he say?"

"Um, nothing important. He said to put his sunglasses on for him. And . . . he called me *your worship*." Which was definitely new, but perhaps he'd been trying to lighten the moment.

"Really? You guys have some weird endearments. Then what?"

This was embarrassing. "I-I told him I loved him," I said, my cheeks burning. I hadn't said it last night and I couldn't let him go without him hearing those words from me.

"Good for you. Did he say it back?"

"What are you, Dear Abby?" I snapped.

"Stop acting like a lovesick teenager," he retorted. "Did he say it back?"

"He said it last night," I replied, wanting to defend my declaration to Jackson.

"And so he said it today."

I thought about it, frowning. "Actually, no. He said, 'I know.'" Which was weird. Had it been because of the cameras? He didn't want such a private thing to be recorded and splashed all over the Internet?

Clark snorted. "It figures. Only you two would reenact *The Empire Strikes Back* in a moment of crisis."

Perplexed, I asked, "What do you mean—oh. *Oh* . . ." My eyes widened. "*That's* what he meant."

Now it was Clark's turn to look confused. "What?"

"He meant Han and Leia," I said, my mind moving faster than my mouth could keep up. "That's why he called me *your worship*. Han calls Leia that. It has to be the outfit, the one he likes." Why he'd want to call to mind that outfit in particular was strange. Could he have left a message for me or something?

"The outfit?"

Now my mouth caught up and I winced. "I like to cosplay," I said with a shrug.

"Cosplay?"

"You know, dress up like fictional characters." It wasn't uncommon for those who had never heard of cosplay to give me the exact same look that Clark was giving me at the moment. "It's fun," I muttered, looking away.

"Okay, let me get this straight. You like to . . . dress up. And Coop knows this, thinks it's great, and has a favorite costume?" I nodded. "And he meant a *Star Wars* costume?" Another nod.

The confusion in his expression cleared, a smirk slowly spreading on his face. "Coop, that dawg," he snorted. "There's only one *Star Wars* costume that every man fantasizes about. And you have one? Princess Leia's metal bikini?" He looked as though he couldn't decide whether to be impressed or laugh.

"It cost a fortune," I said, defensive. "I wanted it to be as authentic as possible. And for the record, it's from *Return of the Jedi*, not *Star Wars*, which refers to the franchise but I think you're confusing it with *A New Hope*."

"Whatever. How often do you wear it?"

My face was burning again. "I don't."

His eyebrows flew up. "You *don't*? Why the hell not? It's Coop's favorite, apparently."

"It chafes," I muttered. He'd talked me into trying it on for him, but thankfully it hadn't been on for very long.

Now Clark did burst into laughter and I gave him a dirty look, which he ignored.

Thank God we pulled into my driveway then and I didn't have to continue the conversation. I was up and out of the car the moment it was safe to do so, hearing Clark follow me as I went into the house.

I stopped short. "Oh no," I moaned.

Clark jerked me back, moving me behind him, and his gun was in his hand. "What?" he asked, glancing around the living room. "Did you hear something?"

"No, not that," I said quickly, alarmed. I hadn't thought of what Clark's reaction would be. "It's The Doctor."

"The fish?"

I pushed past him to my fish tank. "I wasn't here to feed him last night." The tank was pristine and clear, but The Doctor was floating on top. Clark appeared next to me.

"Missing one feeding shouldn't have killed him," he said.

I scratched the bridge of my nose. "I might've missed more than one."

"How many is this now?" he asked. Clark knew of my difficulty in keeping my goldfish alive. It was why I'd named him The Doctor, so I could just keep the same name no matter how many iterations of fish occupied the tank.

"This is number seven."

"Wow."

"Don't judge."

With a sigh, I fished (ha!) The Doctor's body from the tank and consigned him to his final resting place in the North Carolina sewer system.

My Leia outfit was in a special box underneath my bed. Pulling it out, I lifted the lid up on its hinges. The bikini lay on a bed of purple satin. Clark crouched down next to me.

"Any chance you'd try it on?" he asked. I shot him a look and he shrugged. "Worth a shot."

Searching the metal cups, I found nothing. There was nothing extra inside the box either. Pulling out the bikini bottoms, I glanced inside them.

"Found it."

There was a small metal box with a magnet on the back, stuck right in the crotch.

"Hate to say it, but I like his style."

I ignored Clark's commentary, pulling the box off. I handed it to Clark as I carefully replaced my precious costume and pushed the box back underneath the bed. Clark had opened the box and held up a thumb drive.

"Looks like we found his *Get Out of Jail Free* card."

"Damn it!"

I wanted to throw something in frustration. We'd found the thumb drive all right, and Jackson had encrypted it so well, I still couldn't break into it and I'd been at it for hours.

"I thought you could hack into anything," Clark said. He was lounging on my couch, booted feet up on my coffee table, arms locked behind his head. The television was playing some action movie.

"I never said that," I snapped. "And I've never tried to hack something of Jackson's."

"So what now?"

"I think I'm going to have to take it into Vigilance." I had about half a dozen people on staff who could probably hack into it.

"You can't do that," Clark said, unfolding his arms and dropping his feet to the floor. "If something on that drive implicates Gammin or the president, the last thing we want to do is expose it to a network they have access to."

"No one would give them information I haven't cleared," I said.

"Bullshit. Everyone has a weakness and I don't believe for a second that Gammin doesn't have someone on the inside of Vigilance who's loyal to him and him alone."

It was depressing how much I *wasn't* surprised at that information. I really hated working for the government, especially a part of the government that was as secretive and clandestine as Vigilance.

"Okay," I said with a sigh, taking off my glasses and rubbing my eyes. It was a good thing I didn't wear mascara or I'd look like a raccoon. "What do you suggest?"

"Don't you know anybody?" he asked. "Hackers all kind of know each other, right? Isn't there somebody else you could ask for help? Somebody off the grid?"

I thought of Kuan. "Yeah, there is." He wasn't local, but he still might be able to help. Unfortunately, despite repeated attempts to reach him, he wasn't online. He would've been my hacker of choice, but there was nothing I could do if he was out in meatspace.

An hour later, I was still typing furiously on my laptop. I had multiple chat windows open and was hitting dead end after dead end.

"Hackers are so paranoid," I muttered as yet another contact told me to commit an anatomically impossible act.

"With good reason," Clark replied. "Or do you not recall what you do for a living?"

That made me feel even worse. I liked to think I was the Good Guy, but if these hackers knew what I did, they'd label me a sellout, a traitor, or worse.

I hadn't heard anything from Lance, which also worried me. If the lawyers had succeeded in getting anywhere with the DoJ, he'd have called to tell me. The only person I *had* heard from was Mia, who'd texted me two gifs that were circulating through social media: one of me putting Jackson's sunglasses on, and another of him kissing me. I didn't bother checking my Twitter feed, afraid of what it would say. Apparently the trending hashtags were #CuffsAreHot and #GottaWearShades.

"Who are we looking for again?" Clark asked.

"His name is Bulldog," I said. "He's an elite black hat who's as paranoid as they come. I thought he was just a myth until a few years ago."

"Why? What happened then?"

"I was at DefCon in Vegas and there was a contest. They always have them. Try to hack into this, find vulnerabilities for that, and a lot of times there's money involved for whoever wins and how fast they can do it.

"Anyway, the biggest and baddest contest was hacking into Microsoft's latest and greatest server operating system. They offered a million dollars to anyone who could hack it in under thirty minutes."

"Did you?"

I shook my head. "It took me forty-five. But it didn't matter. It was hacked in seven minutes and twenty-three seconds by a hacker calling himself Bulldog."

Clark let out a low whistle. "I bet that really pissed them off."

"You could say that. There was a lot of egg on their face and I heard over a dozen people got fired from Microsoft the next week."

"Damn. So this is the guy you think can help us? And he lives around here?"

"Yeah. Rumor was he used to work in Silicon Valley but left a few years ago for the East Coast. Yash said he heard he'd set up shop here."

"Who's Yash?"

"A friend of mine. His specialty is cell phones, though." And never leaving his apartment if he could help it, or letting anyone inside. But no need for Clark to know that my friends were . . . eccentric.

A line popped up on one of my chat screens. I scanned it, hope flaring inside, and typed a response. After ten seconds of anxious waiting, another line popped up.

"Yes!" I typed back. "We've got something."

"Is it him?"

"I think so. I'm trying to convince him to meet us."

"Why would he meet us if he's that paranoid?"

"I have something he wants."

"What?"

Pulling out the flash drive from my computer, I stuffed it into my pocket and shut the lid on my laptop. I grabbed my keys and tossed them to Clark. "C'mon. We have to take a drive. I call shotgun."

"Are you sure you want to do this?" Clark asked as we parked and got out of the car. "That had to have cost a mint."

"You have no idea." I glanced around the deserted street. Cars were parked, but their owners were nowhere nearby. It was the middle of the night and broken streetlamps punctuated the darkness; only a few remained lit, their feeble light barely penetrating the shadows.

Houses built over half a century ago lined the street. Dilapidated and unkempt, but still occupied by the looks of many of them. The souls inside seeming to ooze hopelessness and despair. I shivered as though a living thing had stepped across my grave.

"He said he'd meet us at the empty Singer warehouse on the corner," I said, nodding toward a three-story brick building.

"Yeah, that doesn't look creepy at all," Clark muttered, taking out his weapon and checking the magazine before shoving it into the front of his jeans.

"*Creepy* is just a societal image that's been impressed upon you since you were old enough to understand fear," I said. "In reality, we fear the darkness because it conceals the unknown."

"It's creepy, Mack," he retorted. "An abandoned warehouse in the no-go district of Raleigh, in the middle of the night? Check, check, and check."

I shook my head at his superstitions and headed across the street. Clark fell into step behind me. The shadows were thick and I told myself there was only my imagination to fear as we approached. Nothing was as scary as what the human mind could conjure.

The door was hanging slightly off its hinges and Clark helped me prop it open. Darkness even deeper than outside loomed beyond the opening. Taking out my phone, I turned on the flashlight and took the first step.

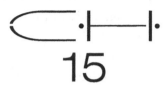

15

Clark followed Mack inside, watching the shadows carefully. Her trust in the hacker—whatever his name—was disconcerting. As was her persistence in wanting to help Cooper. He'd brought her nothing but trouble, but she was oblivious to it. He could only assume that her lack of experience allowed her to still feel that ridiculous optimism of a new relationship.

She walked into the warehouse, pushing the glasses up her nose in that gesture she made whenever she was nervous. Not that he could blame her. He'd been on plenty of missions before and regardless of what she said, this place *was* fucking creepy.

His weapon was in his hand and he longed for night-vision goggles. At least then he could see. As it was, he had to rely on his other senses: hearing and that sixth sense of being able to feel someone's presence.

"He said to go to the third floor," she said in something close to a whisper.

"So we're just supposed to do what he says?"

She shrugged, aiming her phone around to light up the room. It was as bad as he'd feared, with dust and cobwebs, piles of unknown detritus, and little pellets of what could only be rat turds.

"There's the stairs," she said, and headed toward them.

Clark had serious doubts as to the integrity of the wooden staircase, so he stuck close behind Mack. As usual, she was oblivious to physical danger. On the second floor, a stair creaked and his arm shot out, grabbing her around the waist. And not a second too soon. The stair cracked and gave as he yanked her back.

"Oh! Oh wow. That could've been really bad."

"No shit," he grumbled, sounding calmer than he felt. Protecting Mack sometimes felt as though he was one step behind in a game with rules only she knew. She was tiny and if she'd have let him, he'd have just kept her tucked under his arm the whole time they were in there. But even as he thought it, she was squirming to be released.

"Thanks," she said as he reluctantly put her back down.

"Be careful," he admonished. She started up the stairs again, moving more slowly than before.

The creaking of the aged wood did nothing to soothe his nerves, and he didn't like it at all that she was taking point.

Another flight and they'd reached the top floor. If possible, it was even creepier up here. Dusky moonlight filtered through the dust-encrusted windows, lighting up a more dismal scene than the floors below.

"He lives here?" he asked her.

"I doubt it," she replied. "This is like a demilitarized zone where he can meet clients."

"There isn't even any electricity," he said. "How can he possibly do anything?"

She searched the floor. "Appearances aren't always what they seem."

Just as Clark was about to ask her what that cryptic statement meant, she stopped and crouched down. Her thick ponytail swung over her shoulder as she examined something on the floor. She turned, looking in the opposite direction. In a flash, she was on her feet and moving. Clark hurried to catch up just as she reached a panel on the wall. Swinging open the cover, she flipped something, and the lights came on.

"How the hell did you do that?" he asked, scanning the room for any threats as well as ways of escape.

"It's an old trick," she said. "Not a big deal if you know what to look for."

Which, obviously, she did. As usual, she acted as if it were no big deal that she was the smartest person in the room . . . by far. Clark wasn't fooled into thinking he ranked anywhere close. Not that she seemed to notice or ever mention it.

He moved closer to her, not liking the exposure the space provided or how they were easy targets through the dark windows. "So where is he? This master hacker?"

"Who's the tool?"

Clark swung around, shoving Mack behind him. He trained his weapon on the man who'd just stepped out of the shadows.

Five foot nine, two hundred pounds, with hair that was in need of some kind of style, the hacker looked every inch the disgruntled high school grad who'd never gotten his due.

"Bulldog, I'm guessing," Clark said.

"Duh. My shoe size is higher than your IQ. Where's the girl? She said she had it. I'm not doing anything until I see it."

"I'm here," Mack said, stepping out from behind him. "And yes, I have it."

Sticking her hand in her pocket, she pulled something out and opened her palm. The gold ring glinted in the light.

Bulldog inched closer, his mouth falling open slightly as he stared. "One ring to rule them all," he whispered in an awestruck voice.

Mack abruptly closed her hand, hiding the ring. "Only four rings were made for use in the film. Two were given to Elijah Wood and Andy

Serkis. One is on display at the shop of the goldsmith in New Zealand who crafted them. The last one—the one used for scenes with Sauron—that one was stolen by a crew member and lost, reappearing for sale on clandestine parts of the Internet." She paused. "I'm its third owner."

Bulldog swallowed, reminding Clark of an addict in need of a fix. "All right. So what do you want for it?"

Mack held up the thumb drive. "I need this decrypted."

He snorted. "That's all? No problem." Unzipping the backpack he carried, he pulled out a laptop and rubber keyboard. After booting it up, he plugged in the thumb drive and opened a black command-prompt screen. He typed a few things and responses came back. "Looks like he's encrypted a volume within a volume," he mused, typing a bit more.

"I know that," Mack said. "But brute force wasn't working and there was no foothold for guesswork."

"The thing is," Bulldog replied, "it's like being a fortune-teller at a fair, where you have to read your customer to know whether you've hit the right phrases. Hacking isn't guesswork, it's knowing your target and how a computer works. Nothing is random, so even though the encryption thinks it's all just ones and zeroes, in reality there's always a pattern."

Clark rolled his eyes. That's what they needed right now: a lecture on the creative genius that was hacking.

Mack didn't say anything, she just watched, and Clark wondered if she could understand what Bulldog was typing into the screen. He assumed she could. The text reflected off her glasses as she bent over his shoulder, watching. It all looked like Greek to Clark, but he wasn't paid to do her job. He was paid to do his, which was why he started exploring while they dealt with the files.

The deserted warehouse was nearly a full city block long and had been built in the early part of the last century to make sewing machines, first the manual kind, then electric. What it lacked in height with only three stories, it made up for in raw square footage. The hallway outside the room they were in seemed to go on forever, a gaping maw of darkness just beyond the reach of Clark's flashlight.

The hair on the back of his neck prickled and he abruptly switched off his flashlight. It took roughly twenty minutes for the human eye to fully adjust to seeing in the dark. He instinctively knew they didn't have that much time. He double-timed it back to Mack.

"You done?" he asked. It looked like they were. She was busy reading the screen while Bulldog was examining the gold ring. Why anyone would get so enthralled over a movie prop, Clark had no idea, and he *really* didn't want to know how much Mack had paid for it.

"Yes," she said slowly, still looking at the screen. Reaching around Bulldog, she typed something and the window closed. "We can go." She yanked the thumb drive from his computer.

Her phone buzzed and she looked at the screen and frowned.

"Who is it?"

"Derrick."

Before he could tell her to ignore it, that they needed to go, she answered.

"Hello?"

Clark couldn't hear the other end of the conversation, but he did see Mack go about three shades paler, which was quite a feat given her already sun-deprived skin.

"How many?" she asked. "Okay. Thanks." She ended the call.

"What's going on?" Clark asked.

"This place has been under surveillance and Derrick tapped into the satellite feed. We have company. At least a dozen of them, converging on us. Armed."

Clark could see the pulse underneath her jaw was beating triple-time and her hands were in fists. The last thing he wanted her to do was panic. She was glancing all around the room, as if waiting for someone to jump out at them and yell "Boo!"

"Look at me," he said. She didn't respond. He gripped her arms and repeated it. "Mack, look at me." She jumped a little, her wild eyes meeting his. "It'll be okay. I'll get you out of here. Trust me." She gave him a hesitant nod.

"Okay. I trust you."

"What do you mean a dozen armed men are here?" Bulldog piped up. "Are you kidding me?" He started cursing under his breath as he stuffed his equipment into his backpack. The gold ring glinted on his finger. "You're on your own. I'm out of here. Don't follow me. I don't want your trouble on my heels." He took off down the hallway and disappeared into the darkness.

It would've been helpful to follow Bulldog since he knew the layout of the building, but then again, Clark would rather take his chances on their own.

The first thing they had to do was get out of this location. "Can you pull up the schematic on this place?" he asked her.

She gave a curt nod and pulled out her phone. "I'll have Derrick send it to me," she said as she texted. "It should only take a minute or two."

Clark hoped they had that long. Her phone buzzed and she handed it to him. It took Clark all of twenty seconds to memorize the map.

"Okay." He took her hand and latched her fingers onto the back of his jeans. "Hold on and don't let go." If he had to shoot, he'd prefer to use both hands. There were seventeen rounds in his Glock and an extra magazine in his back pocket. *Never leave home without it* wasn't just for his American Express card.

"Don't you need the map?" Mack asked in a hushed whisper. "Maybe we should follow Bulldog?"

"I memorized it," he said. As for Bulldog, with as much noise as he had been making, Clark doubted he'd made it very far, but he decided not to tell her that.

He went to the door, her fingers tightly gripping his jeans as she crept behind him. There was darkness no matter where he looked as they left the pool of light behind. Stepping through the entry would make them the perfect target to anyone hiding out there, but staying in one spot made them sitting ducks. If there was someone waiting, they'd find out quick enough.

Taking a breath, he stepped forward and waited. When no bullets came flying out to meet him, he released his breath and turned right, his eyes adjusting to the darkness.

"Derrick just texted me," China whispered. "He can see their heat signatures. He says there are three men coming opposite us."

Nice. So going forward wasn't an option. "What about down the hall?"

She relayed the question. "He says there's some kind of opening to the first floor that's impassable, and the stairs have two men positioned at the third and second floors. Four more are also patrolling the factory floor."

It appeared either way, they were screwed.

"Tell him thanks but you need both hands now."

He felt more than heard her shove the phone into her pocket, then she was holding onto his jeans with both hands, pressing close against his back.

Two was better than three, so Clark bypassed the first option. They were cornering them, expecting them to try to go down. But the building was big. Big enough to get lost in.

The floor was a maze of interconnecting rooms. He painstakingly headed south through them, stepping silently and avoiding anything that looked unstable. Mack followed close behind, saying nothing, though he could feel her fear like a living thing.

Rats ran across their path, squeaking and scurrying. Clark whirled, hauling Mack close and slapping his hand over her mouth just as she let out a little involuntary scream. Women and rodents. It was always the same.

"Screaming would be a bad idea," he whispered in her ear. It was odd. She didn't wear perfume, but she always smelled sweet.

She nodded and he took his hand away from her mouth.

Gunshots rang out and Clark reacted instantly, taking her down to the floor and covering her body with his. He'd seen where the shots came from and returned fire, snapping off three rounds. There was a crash and clatter as the target fell, then nothing.

Scrambling up, Clark hesitantly approached, his ears alert for any movement, but there was none. Reaching down, he yanked the night goggles from the man's head and put them on.

Much better.

Hurrying back to Mack, he saw she was still lying on the floor. She was probably in shock and terrified. He crouched down next to her and took her arm.

"Mack, get up, let's go. We need to keep moving."

She didn't say anything, but let him help her up. He latched her onto his jeans again and started moving. He was positive that the shots had echoed through the building and they'd all be converging on this spot.

He headed south again, moving much faster now that he could see. Mack kept up, though she stumbled a couple of times. They heard shouting behind them. Guess they'd found their buddy.

"Not much further," he said. By his calculations, they should be close to the end of the block and another exit.

She stumbled again and Clark had to catch her before she fell. He got a good look at her face and felt a stab of panic in his gut. Her pupils were dilated and her lashes fluttering, as though she were trying to stay awake. She was breathing too fast and her lips were pressed tightly closed.

"What's wrong?" Was she going to pass out? He shifted her slightly and the shirt she always wore over her T-shirts moved. That's when he saw the blood.

"God damn it, Mack! Why didn't you tell me you'd been hit?" His horror mutated into anger as he hissed at her, and he bit back more words. *Nice job, dickhead. Yell at your partner that you let get shot.*

"'m sorry," she murmured. "Just wanted to keep moving. Want to go home."

Home was out of the question. She needed a hospital, but he didn't say that. The urgency to get out of here was now even more pronounced. The place was a death trap.

As if to prove his point, shots ripped past him and he ducked. A room was up ahead and he had no idea where it led, but anywhere was better than an open hallway.

"C'mon, Mack," he said, hoisting her up over his shoulder in a fireman's carry. She was dead weight and it was a good thing she was little.

He ran through the doorway into another of the endless maze of rooms, then grabbed the doorframe because there was no more flooring. Teetering unbalanced on the edge, he had a sickening lurch in his stomach as he saw the twenty-foot gap below.

"That would've left a mark," he muttered.

Backing up, he fired shot after shot, giving himself time to reassess, and saw the stairway at the end of the hallway. He bolted for it, making the corner just as more gunfire struck the wall.

Yeah, it was probably best that Mack was passed out for this.

He took the stairs fast, firing point-blank when he rounded the landing to the first floor and someone stood in his way. They fell back down the stairs. Clark kicked their gun away and kept moving. Mack was light, but she was getting heavier with each step.

A body at the bottom of the stairs nearly tripped him and he recognized Bulldog. Guess he hadn't made it out after all. Reaching down, Clark checked for a pulse. There was none.

He took a couple of steps, then stopped and doubled back. "I'd better not go to hell for doing this," he said as he pried the ring off Bulldog's finger and shoved it in his pocket.

Bursting through an exit, they were expelled onto the street. He didn't wait around to see if they'd realized he and Mack had slipped through their fingers. Sprinting down the street to the lot where they'd parked, he unlocked her car and maneuvered her into the passenger seat. He tucked his gun into the holster at his back and reclined her seat.

Blood was on her shirt and her jeans. Pulling up her T-shirt, he let out a breath of relief to see there was just a nasty graze on her side. The wound in her thigh was what concerned him. There was an entrance wound, but not an exit, and blood oozed from the hole. Of course, that was when she chose to wake up.

"Clark," she murmured, blinking at him. "What's going on?"

"You're hurt," he said. "I have to get you to the hospital."

"Nnnnoo," she half said, half moaned. "Don't. People get sick in hospitals."

"I'm not a doctor, Mack, and you've got a bullet lodged in your thigh."

"It hurts," she whispered, her voice breaking. "Please." Her blue eyes shone behind her glasses as she tried valiantly not to cry.

And that was that. He could no more defy her wishes than if she'd asked him to please dive off the nearest bridge.

"I'll take care of it," he promised, laying a hand along her cheek. God help him.

The speed limit was a suggestion and stoplights were optional as he drove Mack's car. If he had time, he'd appreciate what a fine machine it was. It had surprised him, the first time he'd seen a little nerdy thing like her climb out of it. Not many women owned muscle cars, and given her usual predilection for shying away from the spotlight, it was an unusual choice.

That was Mack, though, a walking contradiction. So smart it was scary, yet too trusting to understand how easily she could be used. Completely unaware of her own beauty and appeal, she dressed herself like a geek, which somehow only seemed to enhance her femininity.

And now she was hurt and it was all his fault. She was the brains, he was the gun. He should be the one lying there with a bullet in him.

She whimpered and his foot dropped on the accelerator.

"Clark?"

"Yeah, I'm here." He reached over, feeling for her hand. It was too small, too cold, and too fragile in his grip.

She didn't say anything else and he hoped that she was unconscious again. He'd seen plenty of wounds in his time. Men with arms half blown off and their guts more outside their body than in, but his palms were sweaty and there was a sick feeling in his stomach that hadn't been there since Sayeeda had been delivered to him.

Clark pulled into the driveway of PFG Security, screeching to a halt outside the gate. He punched the button on the intercom and waited impatiently.

The screen flashed and a man's visage appeared. "State your . . . oh, it's you. A little late for a visit, Clark, don't you think?"

"I'm calling in a favor," Clark snapped. "Dr. Jay owes me."

The screen went dark and the gates slowly opened. As soon as it was clear, Clark rocketed through.

The building in front of him was a cross between a business and a home. Three stories and made of stone, it sported a formidable façade of two-story Dorian columns and windows that sparkled from the lights inside. Even the front door was imposing, twelve feet tall, six feet wide, and made of wood four inches thick.

Not that Clark was noticing any of that right now. He lifted Mack in his arms, carrying her to the front door, which was already swinging open on its heavy hinges.

A man and woman rushed out, both dressed in medical white jackets, and pushing a stretcher. The man went to take Mack from him.

"I'll carry her," Clark insisted, holding her closer. He marched past them into the foyer where another man was waiting. His skin was the color of espresso and he wore slacks and a dress shirt.

"Calling in your favor?" Dr. Jay asked. "It's been a while."

"We'll catch up later," Clark said. "She needs help. Gunshot wound to the thigh."

"Bring her this way." He led Clark past the winding marble staircase, light from the chandelier gleaming from its polished steps. An archway behind the stairs led to a set of double doors with frosted glass. He held the door, then motioned into the next room. "In there."

Clark carried Mack inside and gently laid her on the examining table. The two assistants were there in seconds, scurrying with equipment, an IV, and things he didn't even have a name for. Clark was quickly pushed out of the way as one began cutting her jeans to remove them and another got the IV started.

"Any idea of allergies?" Dr. Jay asked him. Clark shook his head. "Medical history? Anything I should know about?"

"I have no idea." Now that he'd gotten her here, he felt helpless watching as everyone else knew what to do to fix her.

Her eyes suddenly popped open and her whole body stiffened.

"It's okay, miss," Dr. Jay said. "We're going to help you."

"Where am I? What are you doing?" The panic in her voice was heartbreaking.

Clark maneuvered his way between the assistants. "I'm here, Mack. It's okay." He took the hand of the arm that didn't have an IV in it. "You're going to be fine. I promise. It'll be okay."

"Clark? What happened? I can't see anything."

He'd taken her glasses and stuffed them in his shirt pocket. She must be blind as a bat without them. Clark leaned closer to her. Hopefully, she was nearsighted.

"I'm here. Can you see me?"

Her blue eyes focused on his face and she relaxed ever so slightly. Everyone else was moving fast and with purpose around them, but she and he were caught in still life inside a bubble.

"You're hurt, but my buddy the doc here is going to take care of you," Clark reassured her.

"We're giving her something for the pain now," one of the assistants said. He was injecting something into Mack's IV. "She's going to start to get a little woozy."

Clark rubbed her hand in both of his, leaning on the bed with his elbows so she could see him. Her eyelids grew heavy but she still fought the medication. The death grip she'd had on his hand went lax.

"Feel s'much better," she said with a sigh. "Is this a bad dream?"

"I wish it was, Mack."

She grimaced. "Don' call me that. Don' like it."

Clark frowned. "You don't?"

"'s a boy's name," she mumbled, her eyes closing. They took longer to open than before. "'m a girl."

"I'm all too aware that you're a girl," Clark said. He didn't know if she'd heard him or not. "What do you want me to call you?"

She didn't answer for a long time and he thought perhaps she'd finally succumbed. But she spoke. "Baby. Never been called baby by a man before. Think it'd be kinda nice . . ." Her voice trailed away.

"Time to take her into the OR," the doctor said. "You can wait outside. We shouldn't be long."

There was a flurry of movement as they wheeled her out, and she looked much too small and pale on the gurney. Then they were through another set of doors and gone.

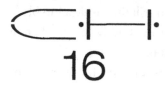

16

Waking up wasn't usually something that was difficult for me to do. My alarm went off, I popped out of bed. I started the coffeepot. I showered. I did my morning routine.

Today it felt as though I'd been run over by a truck.

I pried open my eyes, expecting to see my bedroom. But it wasn't my bedroom. It was somewhere strange. And everything was blurry. I reached out for my glasses on the nightstand, but there was no nightstand.

Panic clawed at me and I tried to see. Glowing green lights were nearby, and something was stuck in my arm. It was like something from a nightmare.

"Easy there," a familiar voice said.

"Clark?"

He leaned over me. "Yep," he said, rubbing his eyes and smothering a massive yawn. He was sitting in a chair by the bed—the hospital bed—I was lying in.

"Am I in the hospital?" I asked, alarmed. Those places were death traps.

"Nope. You made your feelings about hospitals quite clear," he said. "We're someplace else. But very sanitary, I assure you."

"What happened?"

He frowned. "You don't remember?"

I searched my mind, but came up empty after a certain point. "We cracked the encryption. Then I got the phone call. People were in the building. We had to get out." I shook my head. "After that . . . nothing."

Something crossed his face, but it was an expression I couldn't read. I just knew it wasn't normal for him. Regret, maybe? Relief? It was impossible to tell.

"What happened?"

"The short story is you got shot," he said. "I wanted to take you to a hospital, but that freaked you out, so I brought you here."

"Where's here?" It looked very hospital-like, which made me nervous.

"Some old . . . colleagues of mine run a security firm outside of Raleigh. They keep a doctor on staff and state-of-the-art medical facilities. They took care of you."

Took care of me. Okay, time to take stock of my body. Did I have all my limbs? Check. Could I move my toes? Check. Fingers? Check. There was a dull throbbing coming from my thigh and a soreness on my side. Feeling around a little, my fingers touched thick gauze on my thigh.

"There was a bullet lodged in you," Clark said. "You were really lucky. They got it out without any problems and it hadn't hit the bone, so no fragments. You needed some blood, but should make a full recovery."

I'd been shot. It was hard to wrap my head around that. Getting shot was something only seen in the movies or on the news. I, China Mack, wasn't supposed to get shot. I was supposed to sit safely behind a computer, drink my Red Bull, and listen to eighties hair bands on my earbuds.

"I don't even recognize my life," I said, feeling lost. Everything that used to anchor me—from Granny to my daily routine—was all in flux. There was nothing I could count on, nothing steady.

"Hey, it's all right," Clark soothed. It was even harder to see him in the dark, plus I didn't have my glasses. But he was near and he held my hand, which should've been weird, but wasn't. "It's been a rough week, but it'll get better. The point is, you're going to be okay."

"Am I?" I sounded pretty pathetic and Poor Pitiful Me. Which I thought I was allowed. After all, I *had* been shot, for crying out loud. Wait until I told Buddy. He'd probably call me some kind of superhero and let me have a 10 percent discount.

"Hey," Clark said, making me look at him. I could see his eyes now, he was close enough. They were red for some reason and I thought he'd probably had a hard night, too. "You're tough. You'll get through and be better for it."

Something occurred to me then. "Clark, how'd I get out of there if I got shot in the leg?"

He shrugged. "I carried you, obviously. Pain tolerance and blood loss isn't your thing, not that you've got a lot of blood in you to lose. You were out like a light."

My eyes widened. "You . . . carried me?" Clark. Notorious for only caring about himself and barely able to tolerate me, had actually *carried* me from that building.

"Yeah and, oh, by the way," he dug into his pocket, "Bulldog didn't make it, but I got this back for you." Taking my hand, he slipped a gold ring on my finger. The One Ring. "Thought you'd want it back."

I stared at it dumbfounded. "Bulldog . . . didn't make it?"

"Sorry, Ma—I mean, China."

My throat grew thick, but I swallowed it down, closing my hand into a fist. The ring felt cold on my finger. "It was my fault."

"What was? Bulldog?"

I nodded, unable to speak.

"Oh, did *you* call in the assassin squad?" he asked with heavy sarcasm.

"Of course not," I managed. "But—"

"And did you tell him to run off when he should've stuck with us?"

"No, but—"

"And did you pull the trigger on the weapon that killed him?"

"He would never have been hurt if I hadn't got him to meet us and help me."

"I doubt hacking is a safe profession," Clark said. "Especially late at night in a deserted warehouse. He knew what he was risking."

It felt wrong to be somewhat comforted by the logic in his words, but I couldn't deny it.

There was a hiss from one of the machines and I stiffened. "What was that?"

"Just the next dose of your pain meds," Clark said. "It's okay."

"When can we leave?" I wanted my own home, my own bed, and my *Star Wars* pajamas. "This pillow is really thin." And I wasn't wearing underwear, which felt *really* weird. I squirmed a little.

"Here," Clark said, adding another pillow underneath my head. "Better?"

"'s okay." My eyes were heavy again, but I wasn't ready to sleep. "Need underwear."

"Excuse me?"

I pried my lids open to see Clark looking confused. "They took my underwear. I can't sleep without underwear." Obviously.

He got a strange look on his face. "How about a drink of water instead?"

Oooh. That sounded good. "Yes, please."

Clark stood and stepped away into the blurry part of my vision. I grew anxious. Had he left? Was I here alone in the dark? In a strange place?

"Clark?" I called. "Did you leave?"

"Shh, no, I'm here."

He was back and I let out a breath. "I thought you'd gone. You're not going to, are you?" I didn't want to be alone in a strange place.

"Just getting you some water," he said, sliding an arm behind my head and helping me sit up. The water was barely cool but it tasted like heaven.

"Thank you," I sighed once I'd drunk my fill. He gently lowered me back to the bed.

"I'll stay with you. Don't worry."

I was floating in a pleasant cloud of painless lethargy, the medication doing its work. It took a few minutes for me to realize that Clark was planning on sleeping on a very uncomfortable-looking chair. Guilt hit me and I struggled through the cobwebs in my mind.

"Don't stay here," I murmured. "You can't sleep there."

He was up and by the bed in an instant. "It's fine. Don't worry. Get some rest."

"No . . . here." I squirmed, moving to the side of the bed. "There's room."

"China, I can't—"

"Shh," I slurred. "Lo's of room. Please." I couldn't bear at the moment to think that the man who'd carried me from danger should be made to sleep in a chair.

I was too tired to keep my eyes open and felt rather than saw him climb into bed beside me. He was stiff and unrelaxing, which made me unable to sleep. Reaching over, I felt for his arm and pulled it over to rest on my abdomen.

"Clark?"

"Yes?"

"Thank you . . . for saving me."

"You're welcome."

"Clark?"

"Yeah?"

"Why?"

"Why what?"

"Why did you bother?" It was a puzzle to me. We weren't even friends, really. Were we?

The arm that was merely resting on me suddenly tightened, pulling me closer. "Why the hell wouldn't I? We're partners, you and me."

His arm was warm and the solid presence of his body beside me made up for the hodgepodge of my current existence. I relaxed, and his breath brushing my hair was the last thing I remembered.

Two days passed and I was itching to get out. I'd pestered the doctor nonstop until he'd stopped coming by when I was awake.

Clark had made regular appearances, even bringing by Chinese food for me. And not just any Chinese food. Takeout from the only place in town I used.

"I don't get why you only eat Chinese from this one restaurant when there are about half a dozen better ones within a five-mile radius," he said, cracking open his fortune cookie. "You will die alone and poorly dressed," he read. He rolled his eyes. "Nice." He crumpled up the slip of paper and popped the cookie in his mouth.

"That wasn't chicken," I read from my fortune. I stopped, looking up at Clark with wide eyes. "You don't think—"

He burst out laughing. "Now I know why you like this place. That was priceless."

He refused to let me have my laptop, saying that he didn't trust the network where we were staying, which meant I was left to watch television all afternoon. At least I found reruns of *Supernatural*.

"So I have news," he said the next afternoon as he unwrapped a sub sandwich for me. I'd been scouring the channels for any updates on Jackson, but once he'd been arrested, they'd lost interest in the story. "But I don't want you to get all worked up."

"What happened? Is Jackson all right?"

"He's still in custody," he said, "They're not allowing him to see his lawyers."

"They have to let him see his lawyers," I argued, opening the sub and removing the lettuce. "It's a constitutional right."

"If he'd been charged, but he hasn't been charged with anything. They took him into custody, but are requiring him to cooperate based on FISA."

"FISA?" I paused in dissecting my sandwich.

"Foreign Intelligence Surveillance Act," he clarified. "It's basically a web of laws that's trapped him into complying with what they tell him to do, most specifically in the area of surveillance."

"And if he doesn't cooperate, they'll accuse him of aiding terrorists and seize Cysnet." Something else to worry about.

"Looks like it." He watched me resume putting my sandwich back together. "What are you doing?"

"They never assemble it correctly," I said. "The cheese should go first, then the meat, then the tomato and the lettuce should be last. They put the tomato on top, which lets the bread become soggy. If they'd just put the lettuce on top of the tomato, it would be a barrier to the juice from the tomato and the bread would stay nice and dry."

He just looked at me, slowly chewing a bite from his own sandwich.

"I don't like soggy bread." Duh. I mean, who did? Ick. "So what do we do now?"

"Are you going to tell me what was on that thumb drive?" he asked.

I hesitated. "I would, Clark, I really would . . ."

"But?"

"But, it's dangerous." And I wasn't exactly appreciative that *I* even knew what was on it.

"Don't you know?" Clark said, his lips twisting in a half smile. "I laugh in the face of danger. Bwahahaha!"

I laughed in spite of myself and his smile widened. "Yes, so I've heard." My smiled faded. "But in all seriousness, I'd rather wait. I don't want to tell you unless I absolutely have no other choice." It was hard to say that. Part of me wanted to share what I'd found, just so I wasn't the only one carrying the knowledge. But Clark had risked his life to save me when he'd been outnumbered and outgunned. Which reminded me . . .

"Did you get anywhere on finding out who you killed the other night?"

He shook his head and took another bite of his sandwich. "The place was clean when I went back. Even Bulldog's body was gone."

I winced, that wound still fresh, and a flicker of regret crossed Clark's expression.

"How's your leg?" he asked, in an obvious attempt to change the subject. "Your first war wound. It's a badge of honor."

"It's better than yesterday," I said, deciding not to go into the facts that a) I hadn't been in a war when I was shot and b) that it was hardly honorable to get shot, pass out, and have to have your partner carry you to safety. "So can we leave today? Please?"

"Yeah, I think so. The doc says as long as you take it easy, you should be past the danger zone of infection."

I breathed a sigh of relief. "Good. Any news on Lu?"

"Nope. He appears to have disappeared. The State Department thinks he's gone back to China."

"That's a relief. Though it's a little odd he'd leave without pursuing that whole thing with me." He said he'd "be in touch." I was more than grateful he'd moved on, hopefully thinking I knew nothing after all.

"Yeah. It is." Clark didn't say anything more and we finished our sandwiches before he left to see about getting me clothes to go home in. The ones I'd worn were blood-spattered and shredded.

"How's this?" he asked when he returned, holding up a cotton dress in a floral print.

"It looks like something out of the 1989 Laura Ashley catalogue," I said, wrinkling my nose.

"Beggars can't be choosers. This is all they had in your size. You can change when you get home."

Gingerly, I took it. "Is it new? Has someone already worn it? Did they wash it afterwards?"

"Again, let your OCD kick in when you get home. You *do* want to get home, don't you?"

He had a point and turned his back while I maneuvered the dress over my head, but then I had problems trying to pull it the rest of the way down. I was unable to stand on my own, so the dress was caught at my waist.

"Are you done yet?"

"I . . . almost. I just . . . can't . . ." Trying to wiggle from one hip to the other, the fabric moved by fractions of inches over my rear.

Clark turned around and I squealed, trying to cover the parts of me that *still* didn't have underwear. "Don't look!" I reprimanded him. "Turn around."

"Please. To quote one of the best lines ever, 'If you've got something I haven't seen before, I'll throw a dollar at it.'"

As I was trying to puzzle out what that quote was from, he'd lifted me and tugged the dress into place down my thighs to my knees.

"Thank you," I said grudgingly. "Though you could've been more of a gentleman and closed your eyes."

Clark stopped and our gazes caught. His eyes had a wicked gleam in them. "I never said I was a gentleman."

The huskiness in his voice and the way he held me against him made my breath hitch and my heart skip a beat. His hand was still on my thigh and the heat from his touch seared through the fabric to imprint itself on my skin.

Time bubbled and expanded, freezing everything . . . then it suddenly snapped back into focus. Heat flooded my neck and I pushed his hand off my leg and looked away. I was absolutely clueless as to what to say, or to even understand what had just happened. My hands fluttered at my hair, wanting to tighten a nonexistent ponytail. I settled for shoving my glasses up my nose instead.

"I'll get the crutches," he said, then he was gone, the door swinging shut behind him.

I took the next few minutes to get my bearings. It had to be the medication, playing tricks on my perception. Clark was being helpful and sweet—something I should be grateful for, considering how I'd seen him behave before. He was my partner and . . . my friend. Yes, if I were being honest, he was my friend, too. I shouldn't read too much into something I didn't even understand.

Clark returned after a few minutes and it was as though nothing had happened. He adjusted the crutches for my height and helped me onto them, then grabbed my plastic bag of stuff and my phone.

He opened the door and waited. I just looked at him.

"Are you coming?" he asked. "They're not self-propelled, you know."

"I, ah, I've never had crutches before," I confessed. "How do you work them?"

"Seriously. You've never had crutches before?"

"No. Crutches would imply that I'd broken or sprained something doing an athletic activity. The closest time I've come to needing crutches was when I twisted an ankle falling down the stairs."

"How did you fall down the stairs?" he asked.

"Well, I was carrying a laptop at the time, which I did a lot. But this time Oslo had left out a baseball bat at the top of the stairs and I didn't see it." I'd escaped with only a twisted ankle. The laptop hadn't been so lucky. I'd been really angry at Oslo after that.

"You're lucky that was your worst injury," Clark said. "People die falling down stairs."

"Yeah, well, that's what I told Oslo, who just sneered and told me to watch where I was walking. But I got him back."

"How?"

"I waited until the night before he had a big paper due, then switched his keyboard format to DVORAK rather than QWERTY. It typed gibberish and he had no idea why. He spent hours trying to figure it out and refused to ask me. Finally, he had to go to an all-night computer lab to type his paper. He got home about six in the morning and had to turn around and go right to school."

Clark chuckled. "Not bad for a . . . how old were you?"

"Eight."

He shook his head and took the crutches from me, making sure I was supported against the bed before moving away. "Okay, here's the general idea."

The next ten minutes were spent learning the finer points of how to move about without falling down. I would've wiped out—twice—if Clark hadn't caught me.

"I'm not very . . . coordinated," I said after the second near mishap.

"No kidding."

Finally, I had enough of a hang of it to feel somewhat confident enough to leave the room. Clark stuck close by me as we made our slow and painful way to the front door. Dr. Jay met us at the door and wished me well. When I passed him, I heard him speak in an undertone to Clark.

"We're even now. My debt is paid. Don't come back."

"You need to work on your bedside manner, doc," Clark shot back.

I pretended not to hear and kept slowly moving forward. Clark appeared at my elbow, watching to make sure none of the cracks in the pavement tripped me up.

It was a relief to get into the car and I settled back, closing my eyes. That had been more exhausting than I thought it would be. Clark got in the driver's seat and I dozed while he drove me home.

I had to repeat the process when we pulled into my driveway; the awkwardness of getting the crutches in place and trying to maneuver to the front door made me feel about as natural as a giraffe riding a bike. Clark had made it look so easy.

"Surprise!"

I slipped and fell back, my heart lodging in my throat as I braced for my fall. But Clark was there yet again, catching me.

Mia stared in shock, a hand over her mouth. "Oh my God! Aunt Chi! What happened? Oh no!" She ran toward me, helping Clark get me inside and onto the sofa.

"I think you about gave me a heart attack," I said, breathless. My heart was pounding like I'd just run the Kentucky Derby. "What are you doing here? I thought you were staying home?"

"I was worried about you," she fretted, her pretty face creased in a frown as she sat cross-legged next to me. "I hadn't heard from you and social media was quiet, so I told Dad I wanted to come back. He took me to the airport and I flew in last night." She glanced at Clark. "What are you doing here, asshat?"

"Mia!" I admonished as Clark raised a dark eyebrow, but he interrupted me.

"It's okay. I've been called worse."

Still, it embarrassed me and I shot Mia a look. To her credit, she looked abashed. "What happened, Aunt Chi? What did you do to your leg?"

Should I tell her I'd been shot? As if he could read my thoughts, Clark caught my eye and said, "It was my fault. Was practicing throwing knives and didn't mind the perimeter well enough. Your aunt got nicked."

"Oh my God, you *stabbed* her?" She sounded more outraged than when she'd gotten a 99.9 percent on her calculus exam. "Are you out of your mind?"

"It was an accident," I said, grateful that Clark had been more quick thinking than I had been. "I was in the wrong place. My own stupid fault."

Mia fussed over me, keeping her eyes averted from Clark, and I realized she didn't know how to treat him. She didn't know much about our relationship other than he'd treated me poorly once upon a time.

"I'll check in on you tomorrow," Clark said, watching Mia tuck a blanket over my legs as though I were paralyzed rather than just temporarily ambulatory-impaired.

"Thank you," I said to Clark as he headed for the door. He paused and glanced around. "For everything."

He nodded, the shadow of a smile flitting across his face, then he was gone.

"What can I get you? Are you hungry? Do you need anything?" Mia seemed very upset about the whole thing, which upset me.

"I'm fine, I swear," I told her. "I just would love a bath. And my hair hasn't been washed in four days." Which was totally eww. "There's enough grease in my hair to lube my Mustang."

"I can help with that," she said, jumping to her feet.

Ten minutes later, she'd run a bath and was helping me into the bathroom. It was a little uncomfortable, undressing in front of my niece, but she was as professional as a nurse and soon I was soaking in steaming hot water, my injured leg propped on the edge of the tub.

"So what's going on with you and Clark?" she asked, folding my Laura-Ashley-esque dress.

"What do you mean?" I hedged.

"Well, you used to hate him," she said, "and now you're all BFFs. I just don't know where I'm supposed to land on this. Is he off my shit list?"

"He's a work colleague," I said. "And . . . he's been extremely helpful in getting me medical attention and making sure I could recover. So . . . you should probably be nice."

"But he totally treated you bad, Aunt Chi," she protested. "He was mean to you."

I took a deep breath. "I know. But sometimes it takes a while before two people learn enough about each other to get along. We didn't start out well, but we're much better now. I don't think he'll be . . . mean to me . . . again."

She locked eyes with me and after a moment, she nodded.

"Okay. Holler if you need me."

I sat in the tub until the water turned cool, mulling over all the things that were wreaking havoc on my life at the moment. From Lu and his mysterious disappearance, to the DoJ effectively holding Jackson hostage. It was enough to make a girl want a bottle of wine.

Mia reappeared after a bit. "Are you ready to get out?"

"Yeah. Though I still couldn't wash my hair." The maneuverings proved too complex and arduous for me and I'd given up.

"We can take care of that. Turn around."

Glancing questioningly at her, I nonetheless obeyed. Turning around, I positioned my leg on the opposite side and leaned back.

Mia had started the water again, testing it for the right temperature. I leaned back, closing my eyes, and felt her hands gently direct the water through my hair.

"Why are you doing this?" I asked. It was a thankless task, though I appreciated it immensely, barely suppressing a moan as the hot water flowed over my scalp.

"Because I love you, obviously."

The room was quiet save for the splashes of water as she shampooed and conditioned my hair. I felt pampered and . . . loved. I didn't let my hairdresser wash my hair because the idea of using the same sink as countless other strangers made my OCD alarm go off. Therefore, no one had washed my hair for me since before my mom had died.

That thought brought back memories of her humming as she poured carafes of warm water over my head, suds slipping down my back. Time supposedly healed, but I never thought of my mom without the sharp pang of loss in my chest. I'd made my way without her, but she'd been the one person who'd understood and accepted me unconditionally.

It dawned on me that, in Mia, I'd found someone else who didn't require me to change before they loved me. She, too, knew who I was and loved me anyway. It was a poignant revelation and I was even more grateful she'd decided to return rather than stay home.

Mia helped me dry off and get into my beloved *Star Wars* pajamas. We didn't say much and I thought she could probably tell that my emotional state was fragile. Now that I was home, I could finally relax. The trauma of my injury and not hearing from Jackson for so long was hitting me hard. I felt the way you do when you're on the verge of tears, but you're able to hold them back just fine. Until someone looks at you—really looks at you—and asks, "Are you okay?" Then you burst into sobs. That was how I felt. That any moment something would push me over the edge into a blubbering mess, and I was afraid if Mia was any nicer to me, that's just what I would do.

"Get some sleep," she said, putting her arms around me. "Text me if you need anything."

I nodded, hugging her hard and trying to convey what I couldn't put into words. I kissed her cheek and gave her one last squeeze before she turned out the light and softly shut the door.

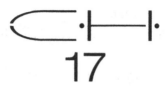

17

Mia was a godsend over the next few days, helping me with my crutches and waiting on me to the point that I had to tell her to go sit down and stop hovering. I made her promise not to tell her dad because if she did, then he would tell my other brother, and *my* dad, and I didn't want them to start a family intervention about my job and have to explain how I got shot while programming computers. I'd been pretty vague about my new job, but my family hadn't pressed for details. To them, I did "something with computers," which was enough information.

I called Gammin after a week of not hearing anything from Jackson, and I didn't waste time with social niceties.

"Why is the DoJ still holding Jackson?" I asked. "He's done nothing wrong."

"No, but he's picked a fight with Lu, who has powerful people protecting him."

"Why? The Chinese aren't exactly our friends."

"No, but his company is expanding underwater infrastructure to carry more bandwidth that he can sell. It'll cost well over a billion dollars. Only three companies in the world can do that kind of job, and one is a US-based corporation."

I rubbed my forehead. "And let me guess, they're big donors to the president's reelection campaign."

"Politics is one big game of you-scratch-my-back-and-I'll-scratch-yours," he said.

"Jackson already did what you wanted. He finished Vigilance for you," I argued. "Isn't it time for you to scratch his back?"

"Jackson's a big boy. He knew what he was getting into. He's just on the losing side of this one."

"But the DoJ could trump up charges against him, indict him for collaborating with enemies of the state. He could lose Cysnet."

"Then he should consider his next move carefully, perhaps negotiate a truce with Lu."

"We don't even know where Lu is," I said. "And it's wrong to let Jackson pay the price just because of some underground cabling project."

"I need to go," Gammin said, his voice cold. "I'm glad to hear you're doing better. I trust you'll be back at work soon?"

I was furious. "Listen to me, Gammin. If you don't do something and get Jackson out of trouble, I'm going to make sure your boss never gets reelected."

Silence.

"What do you mean?"

"I mean that I know what he did twelve years ago, and I have the evidence to prove it. The president won't have a snowball's chance in hell at reelection once I get through." I knew I was taking a big chance, threatening Gammin like this. But I also felt I had no choice.

"I'll . . . consider your offer," he said.

"You have until morning." I ended the call. Now I just had to wait and hope Gammin came through because I really didn't want to follow through on my threat. Wearing sweats, glasses, and my hair in a pony-tail, I didn't exactly look like a master blackmailer.

My leg was well enough to stand and walk on it by now. The doctor had said I was very lucky, that the bullet was likely a ricochet. If it had been a direct hit, the damage would've been much worse.

Yeah, that's how I felt. Lucky.

"Lucky, my ass," I grumbled to myself as I foraged in the fridge for dinner. Bonnie had brought by two casseroles when she found out I'd been hurt. Only one had been edible. Not even the stray dog I some-times fed out back would touch the other one.

Tonight wasn't Monday, but I had a craving for pizza. I deliberated for a while, even dialing twice before hanging up both times. Routines were routine for a reason and technically tonight was breakfast-for-dinner Thursday, but I didn't feel like cooking. With a sigh, I picked up my cell again.

It took repeating my name three times before they believed it was actually me. Then when Reggie arrived with my pizza, he asked me twice if I was all right and if there was anything wrong.

"Just felt like pizza," I said with a forced smile. Was it really so bizarre for me to order pizza on another night of the week? I asked Mia as we were stuffing our faces and she rolled her eyes.

"You're joking, right?" She plucked a piece of pepperoni from her slice and ate it. "If I put the milk back in the refrigerator with the handle on the wrong side, you get all twitchy."

"But why would you put it on the right? You open the door with your right and reach in with your left. It just makes sense you'd turn it so the handle is on the left." A logical and obvious choice.

"I get it. It's just that some things are really important to you that aren't important to other people. And your routine is one of them."

"Routine is good," I said, defending myself. "Our bodies and minds like routine. Then we know what to expect and can be prepared for surprises." Not that I liked surprises. Though lately, they seemed to like me a *lot.*

She winked at me. "I don't mind. I think your OCD is one of your endearing qualities."

"I've been more flexible lately," I said, and maybe it sounded a little pouty.

"Don't get me wrong, Aunt Chi, I don't think there's anything bad about you being the way you are. Truly. You don't have to apologize or change." She gave me a fierce hug. "I love you just the way you are."

"I love you, too," I blurted, surprising both her and myself. Her smile was blinding.

"I know you do," she said. "But it's nice to hear."

We settled back, chewing our pizza and queuing up the episode of *Supernatural* that I'd missed. It felt good not to be alone.

By the next morning, I'd still heard nothing from Gammin. I knew I had to play my last card.

You couldn't just ring up the president of the United States, even if you had the number. To bypass all the layers of security and bureaucrats around him, you had to have the number *and* know how to enter it. Some numbers were pressed longer than others, and there were pauses at different times. Lucky for me, this was one of those handy pieces of information that was on Jackson's thumb drive.

I counted to three before pressing the next number and holding it for two beats. Three numbers in rapid succession, then held down the last number for another two beats. I put the phone to my ear and waited.

There was a clicking sound on the line, then it began to ring. I held my breath and waited, my palms sweaty at what I was about to do. Only the thought of Jackson losing everything kept me from hanging up.

"Hello?"

It was a voice I'd heard countless times on television, and my breath let out in a whoosh.

"Mr. President," I said, my mind suddenly going blank.

"Who is this? How did you get this number?" He sounded irritated. I'd irritated the leader of the free world.

"That's not important," I said, getting my head back in the game. "I have something I think you'll want very much."

"Really?" he asked, his sarcasm thick. "You haven't even identified yourself and now I'm supposed to believe you have something I want?"

I took a deep breath and told him what I had. There was silence on the other end of the line.

"I see," he said at last. His voice no longer held sarcasm or irritation, but was deathly serious. "I won't ask how you came to be in possession of that."

"I wouldn't tell you anyway," I replied. "But I'll give it to you, if you give me something in return."

"Please don't let it be money. That would be incredibly boring and predictable."

"No, sir. I don't want money. I want a pardon."

It took me over two hours to drive to the Air Force base in Norfolk, Virginia. I was nervous about getting through the gate, but the guard looked at my ID, then waved me through. A man standing next to a Jeep was waiting on the other side and he approached my window.

"Please follow me," he said once I'd lowered the glass. "And don't deviate."

I nodded, but he was already heading back to his vehicle. The headlights swung around, illuminating the darkness, and I followed in his wake.

The base was massive and busy. While I was driving, I saw several planes take off and land. We were headed toward one of the runways and the huge hangars that flanked them, when he slowed to a stop.

Sticking his arm out the window, he motioned me toward a parking lot. I understood and drove into it, finding a relatively close space, then joined him in his Jeep. We didn't speak and once I'd shut the door, he was off again.

As we neared the hangars, I saw a huge plane waiting, lit up. The airstairs were down and were guarded by two men in uniform. On the side of the plane were written the words *United States of America*. Air Force One, in colloquial terms. My heart rate doubled.

The airman driving me took me within twenty feet of the stairs, then stopped. I figured it was showtime and got out, though I wasn't moving very fast. My leg ached and I was trying to compose myself. My nerves were strung so tight it felt as though I might snap at any moment.

The guards didn't look at me or say a word as I passed them and began climbing the stairs. I felt very small next to the massive plane. There was no door and no one to greet me, so I gingerly poked my head inside.

Another airman, this one in a different uniform, glanced up from where he was tidying up. He smiled politely. "China?"

"Yes."

"This way, please."

He led me straight through two doors, past a lounge area with plush, leather seating, then up a set of stairs. I'd never been in a plane with stairs inside before and it felt claustrophobic.

At the top of the stairs, he turned right and rapped on a closed door. A voice called to come in and he opened it.

"Your guest is here, sir."

"Show her in."

The voice was one of command and I instinctively cringed before I caught myself. Straightening my spine, I moved past the crew member and stepped into the room.

It was a conference room and the president was seated in the head chair at an oval table. The door closed softly behind me and I was left in indecision. Should I sit down? Should I wait for him to tell me to sit down? He wasn't royalty, so I shouldn't bow or anything, but was there some kind of protocol for this?

He got to his feet and extended a hand. "Pleased to meet you, China."

I shook his hand. "Thank you, Mr. President. Likewise." That seemed right. At least, he didn't look appalled at any breach of etiquette.

"Please, have a seat."

Deciding to forego overthinking it, I sat on his right with one chair separating us. I felt underdressed in my jeans, tennis shoes, and black T-shirt with the silhouette of a doe and the word *Always* printed underneath. The president was wearing a suit and tie that oozed expensive elegance. His hair was a dirty blonde carefully cut and smoothed back from his forehead. His eyes were a dusky gray-green that seemed to see right through me. He was taller and bigger than I thought he'd be, at least six foot two and his shoulders were as wide as Clark's.

"Thank you for seeing me, sir," I said, my nerves getting to my tongue. "I know you must be really busy." *Duh. He was the president of the United States, China. Yeah, he probably had a To Do list.*

"You didn't exactly leave me a choice, now, did you?" he asked. Even I could recognize that as a rhetorical question, so I didn't reply. "It's not often I'm threatened by a private citizen," he continued.

"Sir, I'm not threatening you," I hastened to say. "I swear. I'm just hoping we might . . . reach a mutually beneficial compromise."

"You say you have evidence of me committing murder," he said dryly. "That's quite a statement. And you knew my private line. Those two pieces of information make you a very dangerous person, China. And dangerous people tend to *be* in danger."

I swallowed. "Now it sounds like *you're* threatening *me*."

"I'm not a threat to you," he said. "I just want us both to know where we stand. You say you have incredibly damaging evidence of a felony I allegedly committed. Why don't we discuss that?"

First, I glanced around the room, wondering who was listening. As if he read my thoughts, the president said, "This room is soundproof and cannot be penetrated by any device to eavesdrop. It's the communications room and I assure you, our conversation will remain private."

I had no choice but to trust him, so I gave a curt nod. "Very well. I have in my possession a report made by the FBI on the suicide of a senator twelve years ago. I believe you knew that senator."

"He was my great-uncle, yes." No other emotion. Just a statement of fact.

"One member of the forensics team disagreed with the findings and wrote a counter report, arguing that the death could not have been suicide. Not with the trajectory of the bullet or the wound. He argued that the senator had been murdered."

He said nothing, so I continued. "Only you and two other people were in that room, Mr. President. A woman and another man. All of you told the exact same story, which was accepted as fact, despite the ludicrousness of the idea that a seventy-year-old senator could've committed suicide in front of three people without anyone being able to stop him." This time I waited out his silence.

"How could you possibly prove the authenticity of that report?" he asked. "The man who wrote it died six years ago."

He'd just acknowledged that he knew of the report, which meant there was some truth to this, and if there was fire where there was smoke, I could get burned. I chose my words carefully.

"Sir, I wouldn't need to. The mere suggestion that the leader of the free world had direct knowledge of and possibly committed or assisted in covering up the murder of a sitting US senator would be grounds enough for investigation. And once they start investigating, who knows where it could lead? There is no statute of limitations on murder. Even if you didn't do it, one of the two others with you must have, in which case they'll be dragged into it as well. I believe they're related to you? A half brother and sister-in-law?"

Finally, a reaction. His gaze darkened and a chill went down my spine. Fight-or-flight adrenaline kicked in and I had to quell the overwhelming urge to turn tail and run. Though he'd said nothing, his body had tightened and his jaw was set. The look in his eyes had me wanting to cringe back into my chair.

"It's one thing to threaten me," he said, his tone glacial, "but I take threats to the ones I love very seriously. Don't underestimate me."

My palms were sweaty and my mouth dry. I couldn't blink as I stared into his eyes, now a stormy gray. "I need your help, sir. I don't want to use this information, but if you can't or won't help me, I'll have no choice."

There was a pause. "What is it you want from me?"

I took a deep breath. "Jackson Cooper," I said. "He's being held by the DoJ. They want Cysnet, and want him to quit pursuing sanctions against Simon Lu's company. I want you to issue a preemptive pardon for him."

"That's quite a favor. What will I get in return?"

I held up the thumb drive. "This has the only copy of that report. The original was destroyed. I checked. We both know the man who wrote it is dead. I give this to you and you'll never hear about it again."

"How can I be sure of that?"

Now I was stumped. "Because I say so. I give you my word."

For the first time, his expression softened and his lips relaxed from the thin line they'd been pressed in. "It's been a while since I was asked to rely on someone's honor," he said. "That mentality went away a long time ago."

"I keep my word," I said. "I know it's an antiquated notion, but I don't break my promises."

The president shifted in his seat and I was again reminded of his size. He could crush me if he wanted, and the Secret Service would probably help him hide the body.

"It took a lot of courage—or stupidity, depending on your point of view—for you to do this," he said. "You must care about Mr. Cooper a great deal."

"Yes, sir. I used to work for him." A true statement, though it left out a lot. I thought he must've known all I wasn't saying too, since he raised an eyebrow. But he didn't comment on it.

"Do we have a deal, sir?" I asked. This was the one and only card I had to play. He could take my thumb drive and have me thrown into a dark room that no one knew existed and not have to do a thing for me. But the president used to be a Navy SEAL and I was counting on him having the kind of honor I associated with members of the military.

He looked at me, really looked at me, and I resisted the temptation to look away from his penetrating gaze. I thought he was a good man, regardless of the report I'd read. The senator who'd died had been a Class A Shit, in my opinion, and I had no idea what had really happened in that office, nor did I care. All I cared about was making sure Jackson was saved.

"Yes," he said at last. "We have a deal." He held out his hand for the thumb drive. I hesitated, then dropped it into his palm. At some point, one of us had to trust the other. I was in a bad position to try to wait him out.

Just then, the door burst open, making me jump about a foot. A little towheaded, pajama-clad boy came rushing in and flung himself at the president.

"Daddy!"

The president caught him up in his arms and lifted him onto his lap. He was smiling now, looking completely different from how he'd looked just moments before.

"What are you doing in here?" he asked the boy. I knew immediately who he was. *Christopher.* "Where's your mom?"

"I'm here," a woman said, her voice a bit breathless as she stepped into the room. It was the First Lady and my nerves came back with a rush. "Sorry, sweetheart. He got away from me." She had a girl on her hip who had the same blonde hair as the boy. They were twins—the boy and girl—about three years old, though the girl was smaller than the boy.

"It's fine," the president said.

The little girl—Cate was her name—had blonde curls and was resting her head against her mom's shoulder. Her blue eyes watched and she was quiet, taking in everything around her. She wore a little pink nightgown with matching fuzzy socks.

"We should be taking off soon," the president said. "And we'll be in London by morning. It'll be easier to get the kids down once we're airborne."

"How soon is soon?"

The president glanced at me. "We're finishing up here."

I took that as my cue and scrambled to my feet. "Yeah, I was just going."

The First Lady looked at me and smiled. "Please don't let us rush you."

Now I wasn't someone who read the tabloids and such, but I'd followed the president and First Lady's romance, charmed by watching them interact. I'd been captivated by news footage of them in public, watching as he'd say something in her ear and she'd smile. Or she'd rest her hand on his arm and he'd immediately turn his attention to her.

The First Lady had long, dark hair and cornflower blue eyes. She was tall and slender without being rail thin. Her face was beautiful in the classic way of amazing bone structure—her nose and cheekbones and arched brows—but it was her smile that turned her from an intimidating figure into your best friend, your neighbor, the girl next door, your sister. Warm and broad, her smile lit up her eyes and made you feel as though you and she were sharing the same joke.

To be in her presence now—them together and their children—was overwhelming and I went from calm deal-maker who'd just tacitly threatened the Commander in Chief to a bumbling fangirl who desperately wanted to hold the sleepy Cate.

"No, it's fine, really," I said. "It's getting late and I should be going."

Christopher was busy studying the shiny gold bar he'd removed from his dad's tie. The president shifted the boy on his lap. "I'm sure we'll be talking again soon, China," he said. "I'd like a report directly from you on how the project is going. Say in about four weeks?"

I swallowed. Prepare a report and present it directly to him? "Um, yes, sir. Of course."

"Excellent. I'll have Gammin put it on my schedule."

"Mr. President, you're being rude," the First Lady chastised. She turned to me. "I'm Ann."

"I'm China," I said. "It's such a huge honor to meet you. I've been a big fan of yours for a long time and think you're so pretty and nice. And I love your clothes. You always look good in everything. Even when you were *so* pregnant with the twins, you looked amazing. But your inaugural gown was the most beautiful thing I'd ever seen." I shoved my glasses up my nose, realized that I was babbling, and shut my trap.

"It's nice to meet you, China," she said, still smiling that magic smile. "That dress was beautiful, wasn't it? It was given to the Smithsonian for their First Lady exhibit. You can see it there sometime if you're in DC."

Cate squirmed a bit, twisting around, and held her arms out to me. I stared, dumbfounded.

Ann laughed. "It seems she likes you. Want to hold her?"

Before I could answer, the warm little monkey was handed over to me. I hadn't held a kid in years, not since Mia was little, and I was awkward. Cate didn't seem to mind though. She studied me with her serious eyes and reached up to touch my glasses.

Now, I had coasters at home with images of the First Twins (as the press had nicknamed them) and a pristine copy of three magazines that had done full-spread photos of the First Family. To actually be holding Cate was surreal. Nearly as surreal as standing on Air Force One watching Christopher blink sleepily in his dad's lap.

"She's . . . so sweet," I said at last. "It must be hard to raise a family and do this job."

"It is, but we make it work," Ann said. "What about you? Do you have children?"

I shook my head. "Not yet." The answer popped out, surprising me. I hadn't really thought about having kids before, had never gotten further than even finding someone to date, much less marry and have a family with. But my subconscious must've been doing the planning for me because the little girl in my arms felt good and she smelled of bedtime stories and teddy bears, pigtails and tea parties.

A uniformed officer tapped on the open door and popped his head in. "We should start boarding, sir," he said.

The president nodded. "Absolutely." He stood, shifting Christopher in his arms, and I took that as my hint.

"Thank you for meeting with me," I said to him, handing Cate back to her mother. "And for letting me meet your family."

"Of course," he said. "The pleasure was all mine." There was a sardonic undercurrent to his words that wasn't lost on me. Ann seemed to have caught it as well. She glanced from him to me, then grabbed something from a table nearby.

"Here," she said, handing me a small box. "A memento."

I inspected the box. It was the limited-edition presidential M&Ms. Only served aboard Air Force One, one side had the presidential seal, the other had his signature. As far as mementos went, this one was pretty darn cool.

"Thank you," I said. The officer was politely waiting for me and I followed him through the plane to the back stairs, where I exited to the tarmac.

The officer who'd driven me in was waiting and he took me without a word back to my car. After the tension and nerves of the past few hours and meeting the president, it was all I could do not to slump behind the wheel. But people were watching and I drove back the way I'd come, not breathing easy until I was past the front gate and hit the open highway.

I was approximately five miles from the airbase when flashing lights appeared behind me. Reflexively, I glanced at my speedometer. No, I wasn't speeding. A sick feeling roiled my stomach and I slowed down and pulled to the side, hoping beyond hope that the car would pass me by. But it didn't.

I stopped on the shoulder and rolled down my window, watching in my rearview mirror. The lights were still flashing but now that we'd stopped, I saw it wasn't a patrol car but a sedan with lights on the dash. A door opened on each side and two men stepped out.

I debated for an instant stepping on the gas and hightailing it out of there. But car chases never ended well, and I dismissed the idea as soon as I had it. But I was still terrified as they approached, one on each side of the car. I felt as though I was being cornered, like a mouse in a cage.

"Is there something wrong?" I asked when he bent down to my window. "I wasn't speeding."

"Step out of the car, please."

He was wearing sunglasses and it was the middle of the night. A chill went down my spine. I didn't move, my fingers inching toward the gear shift.

"I wouldn't do that." The metal barrel of a gun was suddenly leveled at my temple. "Step out of the car."

The president. He'd betrayed me. It had to be him. How else would they have known to find me here, on this road, at this time of night?

I wanted to cry and scream in rage and frustration. He'd seemed so genuine. So sincere. So . . . nice. It just goes to show how very bad I was at reading people. Though to be fair, the president was an expert politician whose career depended on his ability to make people believe him.

Getting out of the car slowly, I reviewed my options, which weren't many. They both had weapons and surely wouldn't hesitate to use them. I was in the middle of nowhere with no place to run. The traffic hurtling by at seventy miles an hour wouldn't stop for me, not with police lights still flashing. But I couldn't erase the dread in my gut that told me if I went with them, I might not again see the light of day.

I shut my car door and waited. Sure enough, the man went to take my arm. Quick as I could, I shoved his gun hand up and away from me. He fired and the shot went wide. I tackled him as another shot shattered the glass window of my car. *Dammit.*

We wrestled on the ground and the gravel dug into my cheek and hands. He was much stronger than me, manhandling me facedown. I saw an opportunity. His arm by my face. I grabbed his wrist and bit down hard. I tasted blood—eww—and he yowled. The gun dropped from his hand and I snatched it up. Squirming onto my back, my hand got wedged between us. He gripped my wrist and twisted. There was a snap and I screamed just as a gunshot sounded.

Everything stopped. His body collapsed onto mine, pushing the air from my lungs until I couldn't breathe for his weight on top of me.

Suddenly, I was free and could breathe, but was staring into the barrel of yet another weapon.

"Aren't you a dangerous bitch?" the other man snarled. With one hand, he yanked me to my feet, jostling my wrist and making pain arc through me. "Lights out," he said, swinging his arm. There was a sharp, blinding pain in the side of my head, then nothing.

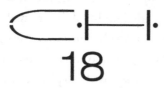

18

Jackson Cooper paced his room, or as he preferred to call it, his cell. Appointed to somewhat resemble a hotel, it still lacked the thing he needed the most: an unlocked door. It had been more than a week with no word and no contact with the outside world. The only person he'd been allowed to see was the man who was determined to break him.

The door opened in the middle of step two thousand and five. Jackson spun on his heel, bracing himself for another interrogation session. He wasn't disappointed.

"Ratched," he said by way of greeting. He'd nicknamed the asshole after Nurse Ratched from *One Flew Over the Cuckoo's Nest*. "Come to waste some more time?"

Ratched was as tall as Jackson, but was underweight by a good twenty pounds. He made up for it with a mean streak that reminded Jackson of the kid in school who wasn't good at anything except being a bully.

"You think you're really going to hold out forever?" Ratched asked.

"I don't have to hold out forever," Jackson replied. "I just have to hold out longer than you. And I have no worries that I'll be able to do that."

Ratched smirked, an oily curving of his lips like that of a shark about to bite. "Things are about to change, Jack. We're going on a little trip."

With that, two other men entered the room, each taking hold of Jackson's arms. They hustled him out the door.

To get out of that room was blessing enough and Jackson inhaled deeply. The air was a little fresher in the hallway, but it was more the fact that he had more space around him than ten-foot square.

"Where we going, guys?" he asked, his tone nonchalant as he scoped out the hallway that looked like a typical government facility. All concrete and drab paint. They didn't answer him, not that he thought they would, and dragged him into an elevator and down three floors to the basement level.

Jackson was a computer geek. He had been since he was old enough to understand electricity, which was four years old. He'd had his share of being bullied and tormented as a child, until he'd gotten older and discovered what pumping iron and boxing could do. A couple of altercations later and the bullies gave him a wide berth.

But hardcore interrogation, the likes of which the CIA would employ, was something beyond his experience. He'd heard about it, of course. Who hadn't? And his gut twisted in knots as they led him farther and farther in the dark depths of the underground.

His father had always told him that courage wasn't the absence of fear. It was doing what had to be done *despite* your fear. And that's what he felt now. Fear. It angered him. Made him want to hurt someone, like a tiger fighting its chains until it was too exhausted to resist. He had to curb his rage. Be smart. He was smarter than all these goons put together. He could outwit and outsmart them, if he was patient and didn't give in to the fear.

The room they took him to was something out of a nightmare. A slanted, metal slab was the focus, with a concrete floor and walls. There were no windows. It smelled, too. Of mold and mildew and . . . Jackson sniffed. Human waste.

The realization made bile rise in his throat but he swallowed it down. They wrestled him onto the table, but he didn't make it easy. He broke one guy's nose and the other one's finger before they managed to strap him down. They even tightened a strap across his forehead, making it so he couldn't move his head. That's when he knew what was coming, and an ice-cold fear swept his veins.

"Well, don't you look pretty," Ratched sneered, looming above him. "I think leather straps suit you, Jack."

"Does that turn you on, Ratched? Gotta strap 'em down first?"

His face turned red. "You're going to regret every nasty word you ever said to me, *Jack*. In case you haven't noticed, you're at my mercy here. No one knows where you are." He leaned down and put his lips by Jackson's ear. "And no one cares."

"You should really have a mint," Jackson said, wincing. "I mean, I'm just saying. But truly. My grandma always said, if someone offers you a mint, you should always take it. Granted, I don't have one on me at the moment, but if I did—"

Ratched's fist slammed into his jaw, silencing Jackson as pain ricocheted through his head. He squeezed his eyes shut to focus and clear his vision, then reopened them. He looked ready to pop a blood vessel. Jackson smiled.

"Do you know how over your career's going to be when I'm through with you?" Jackson asked. "You won't be able to find work hunting dog shit thieves in Tijuana."

"You're the dog shit," Ratched retorted. "And I'm through playing nice with you." He stepped back from the table and a cold dread gripped Jackson.

"So melodramatic," Jackson taunted. "Are you sure you're not really a teenage girl underneath those effeminate trousers? I hear black is slimming."

This time, Ratched ignored him, taking a step backward as one of the men who'd wrestled him down stepped into his line of sight. It was the one whose nose he'd broken. Blood had pooled and been soaked up by his shirt, a gray long-sleeved thing that fit like a second skin over muscles that could only have been accentuated by steroids.

"You should use some stain stick," Jackson said. "I hear blood is a bitch to get out of polyester."

"Shut the fuck up," the man growled.

"I thought you wanted me to talk," Jackson said, slanting his eyes toward Ratched. "Now this monkey is telling me to shut up. Make up your mind."

In response, the man threw a towel over Jackson's face, using his hand to hold it down. Jackson felt the icy hand of fear curdle his gut. This was make-or-break time. But even as he steeled himself against what he knew was coming, he was unprepared when the icy water hit his face.

It was unlike anything he'd ever experienced. Once, when he was little, he'd gone to the city pool with his grandma. Three local boys had decided to pick on the scrawny white kid, tormenting him and ultimately holding him underwater until his lungs had burned for air. He'd fought for his life then, fought like he never had before. He'd finally emerged, choking and coughing up chlorine-tinted water, panic clawing his gut. The feeling of almost drowning was something he'd never forgotten.

It was the same feeling, only worse, because he couldn't move, couldn't see, couldn't do anything to save himself. The water was endless, filling his mouth and nose, the slant of the table accentuating it even more. He strained at his bonds, the leather cutting into his wrists, as he fought with no avail to take a clear breath, but all that entered his lungs was water.

It felt like an eternity before it stopped. Jackson coughed and retched, blinking in the sudden light as the sodden towel was removed.

"Now do you want to tell me who's running that software?"

The answer was China, and there wasn't a chance in hell that Jackson was going to give up her name to this fucking asshole. He'd fucking drown on his own vomit first.

"I'm really looking forward to that new J.J. Abrams movie," Jackson panted. "I bought tickets ages ago. I hear it's really good."

It was almost worth the burning in his throat to see Ratched's face get all mottled with rage. He motioned to the man and dread consumed Jackson. Before, it had been the fear of the unknown. Now, he knew exactly what was coming and somehow, it was worse.

He tried not to take a breath to keep his nose and throat from filling up with water, but he couldn't help it. The unending water seemed to trigger an almost primeval survival response, forcing him to take a breath, even though logically he knew he'd only get water in his lungs.

Time ceased to have meaning. After the fourth time, he couldn't keep up with the smartass responses and just remained quiet, concentrating on breathing.

He'd have given anything to stop the water . . . anything but China. He kept her image firmly fixed in his mind. Her dark hair—long, thick waves tousled from making love and spread on the white pillow in his bed. Her smile, bright and clear when she found something amusing. Her eyes, so blue and trusting as she looked up at him. Intelligence shining from their depths. The confusion in them when there was something she didn't quite get. Her literal take on *everything*, though she was getting better at recognizing hyperbole or a joke.

He loved her. It had been a surprise to realize, but he did. Why else would he let himself go through this otherwise? She was innocent and naive, despite her genius. She was young and didn't deserve what he'd dragged her into. Because when it came down to it, Jackson had been the one to set her life on its current path.

But at the moment, he had the first serious doubt that he'd ever see her again.

His breath hitched and he coughed, spoiling the small break he'd been given. It was then he decided that even if he didn't make it out of this, he wouldn't regret his loyalty to China. And he *would* be loyal. He would not break.

Exhaustion consumed him after more water, until he wanted to beg for mercy, beg for death, beg for anything that would stop it. It was only by the thinnest thread that he clung to his resolve. And now the terror wasn't of the waterboarding, but that he'd betray China.

He couldn't tell if it was the water or if he was crying when they finally removed the towel. Everything was mixed up in his head and he could only hold tight to the image of China. Unending tremors shook his body and his throat was raw and burning. He was beyond the ability to joke or be sarcastic, his only thought was getting to the next minute without breaking, then the next after that, then the next after that.

"You're a tough son of a bitch," Ratched said. "I must say. I'm impressed. But now that you know what awaits you, I think a little time to dwell on it will do you good."

Hands undid his straps and hauled him to his feet. To his mortification, his knees immediately gave out and they had to hold him up so he didn't collapse on the floor. His clothes were soaked and the room was dank and cold.

With little ceremony, they dragged him down the hall to a room that was most definitely a cell, complete with a dingy cot and steel toilet in the corner. They dropped him right inside the door, his knees hitting the hard concrete. The metal door clanged shut and he was alone.

Jackson took a minute to catch his breath and get his bearings before climbing to his feet. The room was even smaller than the last and he sat heavily on the squeaky cot. Even as he was taking stock of his physical condition, another part of his mind was turning facts over in his head.

Ratched was taking one hell of a risk, treating him like this. The only reason Jackson could even fathom that he'd be so reckless was because he thought Jackson wasn't going to get out and have an opportunity to strike back. Or that public opinion would be such that even if he *did* get out, he'd be unable to press charges.

He hoped that China had been able to find that thumb drive and taken it to Lance. But if that had been the case, he would've been out of here by now. Lance had strict instructions to plug that thumb drive into Jackson's workstation and execute one line of code Jackson had made him memorize. If that failed . . . Jackson didn't want to finish that thought. He didn't know how long he could hold up against the waterboarding. If he was honest with himself, he might not even last another round of it.

The thought of being dragged out of the cell for another session of it made him want to retch. Nothing had prepared him for that. Nothing *could've* prepared him for that.

The door flew open, startling him, and he jumped to his feet despite his aching body. It seemed too soon for more, but it wasn't the goons from earlier at the door. It was his lawyer, flanked by two men in Air Force uniforms. Ratched stood behind them.

Relief swept him, so overwhelming that he had to tighten his hands into fists to keep them from shaking.

"It's about time, Conrad," he said, his voice a grating rasp. "Did you get lost or something?"

Conrad looked horrified, then furious. "Is this where you've been keeping my client?" he asked, rounding on Ratched. "Are you out of your mind?"

"Your client is accused of collaborating with enemies of the Unites States," Ratched replied, game-faced. "We were hardly going to handle him with kid gloves."

Conrad hurried to Jackson. "We're leaving. Immediately. Come on."

Mustering what reserves of strength he had left, Jackson straightened his shoulders and walked out. When he got to Ratched, he paused and leaned down.

"My condolences on losing your 401k, your savings, and defaulting on your mortgage," he said so only Ratched could hear him. "That's too bad."

Ratched got all mottled in the face again. "I'll keep the bed reserved for you," he retorted.

"Payback's a bitch."

With that, Jackson and Conrad followed the two uniformed men down the hallway and up the elevator until finally, warm sunlight bathed his skin and fresh air teased his nostrils. It wasn't until they were in the backseat of Conrad's car and the driver had pulled away that Jackson spoke.

"What the hell took so long?"

Conrad was rummaging in a duffel bag and handed him a shirt. "Here, this is dry," he said. "We have a press conference to do."

"Fabulous. I have some things I want to say." He discarded the still-sodden shirt and pulled on the fresh polo.

"I have a statement prepared and you're going to have to stick with it."

"What kind of statement?"

"This one." He handed Jackson a single sheet of paper along with an electric razor.

Jackson read it through once, then again. "Are you kidding me? A pardon? How?"

"You tell me," Conrad said grimly. "I knew you said I'd be getting information that would get you out, but nothing came. I've been working through back channels, trying to find out where you were being held, then the paperwork came this morning. A preemptive pardon. I thought you donate to the other party?"

"I do, or I did," Jackson said. "I have no love lost for the current administration."

"Then why in the world would he do this?"

"I have no i—" He stopped. It couldn't be. That thumb drive had his private encryption key. No one could've broken it. Not even China. Right? Even as he thought it, he doubted. That was the only explanation, but the idea that she'd blackmailed the president with what was on that drive made his blood run cold. "We have to make a detour first."

"What? Where to? Do you need to go to the hospital?"

"No. I need to see China." What had she offered in return for his pardon? Had she really thought she could blackmail someone with that kind of power and remain unscathed?

"We don't have time, Jackson. I called the press conference—"

"Damn the press. Where the hell have they been the past few days? Clamoring for my release? Of course not. I'm surprised they haven't already tried and convicted me. How much did Cysnet's stock drop?"

Conrad hesitated. "Thirty-five percent."

Jackson cursed under his breath. "I'll worry about that later. Release the statement if you want, but I don't have time for a press conference. Take me to the airport." Conrad handed him his cell and with one phone call, he'd arranged for his jet to be fueled up and waiting for the trip back to Raleigh.

It was dark by the time Jackson parked his car in China's driveway. He'd tried calling her cell, but it went right to voice mail. He'd tried texting as well, but got nothing. By the time he got to her door, he was fighting panic. Rapping hard on the door, he called out, "China! Are you in there?"

The door flew open, but his relief was short-lived. Mia stood there instead of China.

"Is she here?" But he knew already that she wasn't. Mia had been crying, her face pinched and white.

"I can't find her," she said. "And she's not answering her phone."

"When was the last time you saw her?"

"Yesterday morning. She said she had some things she needed to do, then she left."

"She didn't say where she was going?"

Mia shook her head. Tears overflowed her eyes and she flung herself at Jackson. "I'm so worried! I'm afraid something's h-happened to h-her!"

"Shh, it's okay," Jackson said, awkwardly patting the teen on her back. "Let's go inside."

She sniffed and stepped back, swiping at her wet cheeks. Jackson followed her in and shut the door behind him.

Nothing looked different or out of place, he noticed as he walked through. He knew where China kept her computer and that's where he headed. Upstairs and into her office; he noticed Iron Man was not in his usual spot.

Strange. She hated anything moved from its designated location. And that thing wasn't light. He should know. He'd had to move it before.

Settling in front of her computer, he switched it on. It booted in less than ten seconds, but a network error popped up. Frowning, Jackson followed the network cable and saw the router was unplugged. An overabundance of caution while she wasn't home? Or something more?

The log-in screen came up and he typed in the log-in she'd created just for him. A big relationship milestone, that—log-ins for each other's computers. Akin to exchanging apartment keys for normal people. But neither of them fit the definition of "normal."

Now to find out what she'd been up to while he'd been off the grid . . .

Jackson went through the normal suspects—web history, recently accessed programs and files—and saw she had tried to get into his thumb drive. It didn't look as though she'd been successful, though, which made it even more mysterious as to how he'd gotten the pardon. If indeed it had been she who'd done it.

In the middle of what he was doing, a window suddenly popped up and text appeared.

It's about time. China's been taken. You need to go get her.

Jackson stared at the screen. "Who the hell are you?" he muttered. To his surprise, more text answered him.

A friend.

Nice. Only China would have a virtual friend who could pop in and out of her network at will. Then he remembered.

"Kuan, right? China told me about you. Said I should hire you when you graduate."

I wouldn't mind that.

"So you should be able to tell me who took her and when. Where is she?"

Lu has her. They flew from Virginia to LA, then west from there. I couldn't tell where. I'm working on getting the flight plan.

Lu. How had he gotten to her? Or taken her out of the country without anyone finding out he was smuggling her on board? China's reminder about a possible NSA mole was looking more certain by the moment.

"And how do you suggest I 'go get her?'" Jackson asked.

Money can buy anything. And you have a lot of it.

True. "Okay . . . Kuan. I'll be in touch. Let me know if you find out anything else."

Roger roger.

A *Star Wars* reference. Birds of a feather . . .

Mia was waiting for him when he came downstairs. "Did you find anything?"

"Yes. She's currently . . ." How much to say? ". . . out of the country. But she may need some help, so I'm going to go help her. You stay here, and don't leave. Understand?"

Another jerky nod.

A harsh knock on the door sounded and Jackson automatically reached for the nonexistent weapon at his waist. They'd confiscated that.

"That's probably Clark," Mia said, rushing past him to the door.

"Clark?"

"Yeah. I called him earlier. He's Aunt Chi's partner. She said to call him if I couldn't reach her." She swung the door open and sure enough, the son of a bitch himself stood there. "Thank God you're here," she exclaimed.

Hold the phone, what the heck was he? Chopped liver?

Clark came striding in, all Charles Bronson swagger and shit, his black jeans and black leather jacket completing the cliché uniform of Man of Mystery.

"What are you doing here?" he asked Jackson. "Aren't you under house arrest, or something like that?"

"I got a hall pass," Jackson replied. "Where's China?"

"I don't know. I found her car, abandoned, outside of Virginia Beach. One window was shattered."

"There's no way she'd leave that car voluntarily."

"I know."

"What are we going to do?" Mia wailed, then burst into tears again.

"Mia," Clark said, his voice hard. "*Mia.*" She looked at him. "Get ahold of yourself. This isn't doing anyone any good, especially Ma—China."

"You're right," she sniffed. "I'm just so scared for her."

"It'll be okay," Clark assured her. "I promise."

"Are you going to help Jackson get her back?"

Clark glanced at Mia. "What do you mean?"

"He said she was in another country and he was going to get her back."

And there went Jackson's plans for working alone.

"You know where she is?" Clark asked, his voice sharp and accusing.

"Maybe. It's a slim lead, but better than nothing."

"Then why are we still here?" He was out the door without another word and Jackson followed, giving Mia a glance on the way out. She was chewing her nails and looked on the verge of tears again. "Feed the fish," he told her.

He confronted Clark outside in the form of a hard right to the jaw.

"What the fuck was that for?" Clark snapped, rubbing his face. "You want to do this *now*?"

"All I know is that you're supposed to be her partner, the one who looks after her. And she's *gone*. Lu has her. Where the *fuck* were you while she was being run off the road and taken?"

Clark's face turned a shade paler and Jackson knew he'd hit his mark. Figuratively more than physically. He doubted he could do anything to hurt Clark more than whatever thoughts were running through his head.

"Blame can wait until later," Clark rasped. "If we don't find her in one piece, I promise, you get the first shot at me."

"I'll hold you to it."

Jackson followed Clark to his car and got in the passenger side. "Do you have any sources that can help find her and get her out?"

Clark nodded. "Yeah. But it's going to take capital. The liquid kind."

"That's not a problem."

Clark snorted. "I didn't think it would be." He shoved the car into gear and tore off down the road.

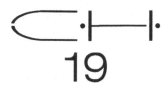

19

Nausea clawed at my stomach, wrenching me from a fitful doze. I grabbed for the little tin bowl they'd given me and retched. I'd eaten nothing, which meant throwing up was even more miserable on an empty stomach.

The ship rolled and I moaned. If I could have killed myself, I happily would have. I didn't think I'd been more miserable in my entire life. I didn't know how long I'd been on this transport from hell, but it felt like an eternity. I hadn't realized I was prone to seasickness, and I could have gone my whole life blissfully in ignorance.

The door to my cabin opened and the woman who'd been the only face I'd seen walked in. Petite and Asian, she either didn't understand English, or pretended she didn't. All my attempts at conversation had been met with a smile and silence. This time she held a tray with water and a little bowl of something.

Setting the tray down, she brought the bowl to me. She said something I didn't understand, and motioned for me to eat.

"Oh, God, no, I can't possibly eat anything." The very thought made my stomach clench.

She was insistent, motioning again to the tin bowl I was using to be sick in, then back to the bowl of pinkish stuff. Finally, I got it.

"Oh, this will help me feel better?" Now that was a different story. I took a little bit of the cold stuff, put it on my tongue, and chewed. Ginger. Pickled ginger, by the taste of it. "That's right," I said, even though I knew she wouldn't understand me. "Ginger was used by Chinese sailors to alleviate the symptoms of seasickness."

I managed to get a few mouthfuls of it down and only by focusing hard, kept it down. The woman smiled and nodded, saying a few more things I couldn't understand. My stomach did feel a little better. Not normal, but the ginger had taken the edge off so I could at least function.

"Thank you," I told her. She probably didn't understand the words, but my sincerity seemed to get my message through. She nodded again and left the room.

I got up from the small bed and tried the door again—which I had after every time she'd left—and it was locked, just as it had been every other time.

My body was weak, and even just that small trip across the room made me lightheaded. I knew I was dehydrated so I started sipping some of the water, alternating it with more ginger, until I'd drunk the entire glass. When I was finished, I felt better—not could-run-a-marathon better, but could-stand-up-without-falling-over better.

I had no way to tell what time of day or even what day it was. They'd taken my phone from me and I didn't have a watch. The only thing in the room was a bed, an overhead light, and a tiny cubicle bathroom that made a plane's lavatory seem spacious.

There was a small porthole above the bed and I'd avoided looking out since it had only made me sicker to see alternate views of the water and sky, depending on the waves. Now I felt I could glance out for a moment, at least to see whether it was night or day.

Standing, I poked my head up. I saw water, and sky, and guessed the time to be about midday. I could distinguish nothing else, so sank down onto the bed again.

If I let them, panic and terror were just there waiting at the edge of my mind. I had very vague memories of what had happened after I'd been ambushed in my car. I must've been drugged because there were needle marks on my arm and only hazy images of people and dark places and being moved.

That the president had betrayed me nearly made me ill all over again. That he'd be so cold as to have me kidnapped and thrown onto some kind of transport was nearly incomprehensible, so incongruous was it with the man I'd met with on Air Force One. The man who'd held his son and kissed his wife and shook my hand. I was at his mercy now and I could only pray that even if he didn't keep his word with me, that perhaps he had for Jackson's sake.

Now that I wasn't throwing up my left lung, I was exhausted. I could do nothing to help myself at the moment, so I might as well get some rest so when the time came, I *would* be able to escape.

Pulling the blanket up over me, I closed my eyes and tried not to think about Jackson, or Clark, or Mia, or Granny, or anyone I loved, or how lost and alone I felt. Sleep and blissful unawareness came quickly.

When I woke, the first thing I realized was that we were no longer moving. The second was that I heard voices outside my door.

I sat straight up, blinking away the sleep from my eyes. The panic I'd been trying not to think about earlier smashed its way to the front of my brain and set up a tent.

The door opened and I jumped to my feet to be ready. Ready for what . . . I had no idea. It was instinctual. What I didn't expect was who walked in.

"Lu."

He smiled. "I did say that you would hear from me soon," he said. "I must admit, I favored air transport here rather than this." He glanced around the room, his lip curled slightly in disdain. "But I hoped you would use the time to think about your situation."

I swallowed, my throat as dry as sandpaper. "And what exactly is that?"

"We'll discuss it. But first, let's go somewhere more comfortable, shall we?"

He walked out the door and I took it I was to follow, which was fine with me. I never wanted to see that room of misery again.

Two men fell in behind me as I followed Lu. They both towered over me and were wider than two of me. I doubted Lu had hired them for their brainpower.

It seemed to take forever to get off the boat and I had to walk slower than I wanted to because my leg started to ache. When I finally reached open air, I sucked in a deep breath. Fresh air had never tasted so good.

The "boat" was really a cargo ship and its size made my jaw drop. I'd never been on anything like it, though now that I had, I wasn't anxious to repeat the experience. Cranes were already lifting containers that were stacked ten high on the deck.

Lu paid none of this any mind as we walked the gangplank to the docks. A limousine was waiting, but Lu stopped outside it and turned. "Take her in the next car," he told the men behind me. "She . . . smells." He slipped inside the limo.

I clenched my hands into fists, feeling my face flush. Washing facilities in my "room" had been limited to just a sink, so it wasn't as though I'd been able to bathe properly, which was entirely Lu's fault. If he'd wanted to embarrass me and make me feel uncivilized, he'd accomplished it.

I was acutely aware of being dirty when they shoved me into the back seat of a sedan and crowded in front. My clothes were grungy and I'd scrubbed a couple of vomit stains out of my shirt the best I could. My hair was lank and greasy and I'd pay a fortune for a stick of deodorant.

We drove and I was able to see where we were. Sort of. At first, I thought it was mainland, but then I realized it was an island. And not a very large one at that. After about a fifteen-minute drive, we entered a gated tunnel and began heading down.

I quickly realized this was an advanced military establishment. Guards with weapons were everywhere, as were technicians in red jumpsuits and wearing hats. We stopped when the limousine did and I got out without being asked. The guards glanced at me, but didn't try to stop me. After all, if I ran, where the hell would I go?

That thought sent another stab of fear and panic through me and my knees weakened. I grabbed on to the car to steady myself. Everyone around me was Chinese and speaking what I assumed was Chinese or Mandarin or whatever dialect they spoke. Which meant there was about a 99 percent likelihood that I was no longer on US soil.

Lu stepped up next to me. "What do you think?" he asked, gesturing to the cavernous space in front of us. Metal stairs went up at least four levels from where we were, and the tunnel kept going so far, I couldn't see the end of it.

"What is it?"

"It's Vigilance, of course. *Our* version. All it needs . . . is you."

I was shown to a much better room than on the ship, that had a real shower and even a change of clothes, though I didn't appreciate the new wardrobe. It was all dresses, and not even typical dresses, but the silk Oriental kind with the high neck, tight cap sleeves, fitted bodice to either a flared skirt or fitted skirt with a slit up the leg. The embroidery was gorgeous, though, and after the longest shower of my life, I finally chose a blue one.

My still-damp hair went up into its usual ponytail, and my glasses didn't do the dress justice, but I didn't particularly care. I'd been told to dress for dinner and found some comfortable satin slippers with a low heel to wear. Everything was in my size, even with my lack of stature. The dress was the perfect length and didn't touch the floor.

The door was locked, of course, so I took the opportunity to go over every inch of the room. There was nothing remotely electronic, not even a digital clock. MacGyver couldn't have fashioned a communication device out of what I had. Lu wasn't stupid. Without anything better to do, I arranged the dresses in the closet by color, which made me miss Mia. Would I ever see her again?

I was so hungry, I thought I could eat anything. But when I was finally led to where Lu was already seated at a table inside a room decorated much more lavishly than the rest of the compound, I found I was mistaken.

"What's this?" I asked, eyeing the small bowl of soup in front of me.

"Bird's nest soup," he said, taking a sip from his spoon.

I picked up my spoon. "Like egg drop soup?" I liked that, and it kinda looked the same.

"No, it's the nest of swiftlets. A bird that builds its nest with its own saliva. The saliva hardens, forming the nest. It's a delicacy, and a wonderful source of iron, potassium, calcium, and magnesium."

So were Flintstones Vitamins. I dropped my spoon. "Bird spit? No, thanks. And here I didn't think I could get sick again so soon." I didn't feel the need to be polite. Lu had already taken me away from my home, my country. Though he was being nice now, when he found out I wasn't going to cooperate, I fully expected that nice guy to turn. "Is there a cheeseburger somewhere around? Maybe a McDonald's? I could really go for a Big Mac."

Lu raised his eyebrows, but didn't comment, merely raising his hand slightly. Instantly, a woman was there in a formal Chinese dress even more traditional than mine. She took away my bowl, then Lu's. I waited, taking in our surroundings.

The lack of technology in my room didn't apply to this one. Everything was run by computer and there were touchpads on the walls, automatic sliding doors, and sensor lighting. I had no doubt voice control was enabled as well and that I was probably being watched and recorded.

A domed plate was put in front of me simultaneously with one in front of Lu. The women lifted the domes and the familiar smell of grilled beef hit my nostrils. A burger dripping in cheese and piled high with bacon and tomatoes sat on my plate, complete with a mountain of shoestring fries.

Lu had some kind of fish on his plate, but I didn't pay much attention, attacking the burger as if it might jump up and run away at any moment. Half of it was gone before Lu spoke.

"Are you enjoying your meal?" he asked.

I nodded, still chewing.

"You know, you're not what I expected," he said. "A genius intellect in the body of a tiny female. Who would have thought?"

"Since when did sex or size have anything to do with intellect?" I asked. *Judge me by my size, do you?* Yoda asked inside my head.

"My point is that not everything is what it seems. Such as that burger you're devouring." He nodded toward my plate. I stopped chewing. "Almost anything can be dressed up in a pretty package and presented as one thing, when in reality, it's another entirely."

"What do you mean?" I had a bad feeling about this.

"Why it's rat, of course. Have you never eaten rodent before?"

Oh. My. God. My stomach rebelled almost immediately and I turned to the side to see that apparently my reaction wasn't unexpected. One of the women was there with a trash can and yet again I emptied the contents of my stomach. Horror tinged my mind and the tears stinging my eyes weren't just from vomiting. I'd just been fed *rat meat.* I'd blindly eaten it without question.

I wiped my mouth with my napkin, my hands shaking like a leaf. I didn't look at my plate, couldn't think any more about what was on it or what I'd eaten or I'd get sick again.

"What do you want?"

"Your life is very simple from now on," Lu said. "As I've just shown you, I can make your life pleasant . . . or unpleasant. All you have to do is enter the coding for the Vigilance algorithm into our system and customize it for our needs."

"And what are those needs exactly?"

"We have built a database consisting of every government employee in the United States. Every soldier, secretary, bureaucrat, and politician. With the help of Vigilance, we'll be able to most accurately predict those who are in positions of power, those who possess intelligence access, and those who are close to those same individuals. Vigilance will tell us their weaknesses and secrets. Those who can be exploited."

It was exactly as Jackson and I had feared when creating Vigilance. A tool used to keep the population "safe" largely depended on that government's definition of the word, and China's definition was much different than America's.

"We also want to expand to include other nation states, hence the size of the facility."

"Such as?"

"Japan would be extremely helpful. As would Russia." He smiled benignly. "We spend a great deal of time and resources on recruiting foreign assets. This will make it ever so much easier."

Every secret anyone was trying to hide would be vulnerable to blackmail. I could already see inside my head how to tweak Vigilance to give people a score on their likelihood of being susceptible to threat or enticement from China. Someone needs money and they also are a congressional aide to the Speaker of the House? And that was just one example.

"And you expect me to help put this in place for you?"

"You sound as though my expectations are unreasonable."

"They are. There is no way I'm going to do that. You want to kill me, fine, go ahead. My life isn't worth putting the security of my country at risk. Chinese cyber-espionage is bad enough without making it easier for you. Social engineering hacking augmented with cyber-espionage would put China number one on the nation-state power structure."

"We already own much of your software," he said. "So many lax businessmen come to this country, using our networks, and are surprised when we infiltrate their companies and take from them. This is just one more way we can and will take from you."

"You steal because you can't create it on your own," I retorted. "If you want Vigilance so badly, write the code yourself."

"Why wait for that when it's sitting right here in front of me?" His smile was chilling. "You seem eager to embrace the role of martyr, the curse of your age and idealism. Fortunately, I had foreseen such a response." He patted his mouth with his napkin and rose from his chair. "Come with me."

Refusing would be pointless so I stood on unsteady legs and followed him out of the room.

We were in the part of the facility that reminded me of a luxury hotel. On the ground floor, we passed an ornate fountain adorned with fresh flowers, their scent perfuming the air. Various seating alcoves were placed strategically and the lighting was warm and muted. Music floated from hidden speakers, calm and soothing.

Stepping into an elevator, I saw there were three floors above and an additional four beneath us. He pressed the button for the second sublevel. When we stepped out, I stumbled to a halt, my mouth falling open.

Stretched out in front of me were racks and racks of servers, more than I'd ever seen in my life. Lu hadn't been exaggerating. They were indeed set up and prepared to house billions of terabytes of data. There had to be thousands of servers and data drives—hundreds of thousands. It was cold, too, obviously, because the kind of heat all those machines were putting out had to be incredible. Their cooling system was up to the task, which also explained why it was underground.

"As you can see, we've been preparing for some time," he said. "On this island, we are far enough from the mainland to avoid interference or prying eyes. And we're underground, which hides us from satellites. Not to mention that thousands of tons of rock stand between us and any missiles launched our way."

"Island? What island?"

"An artificial one we built," he said. "We're in the South China Sea, near the Spratly Islands." At my blank look, he sighed. "I take it geopolitics isn't part of your genius?"

"No one's an expert on everything."

"The South China Sea is very important. More than a third of the entire world's maritime traffic goes through it. More than sixty percent of Japan and Taiwan's oil imports travel these waters, and eighty percent of China's. In short, whoever controls the South China Sea has a stranglehold on those nations and can affect the entire world economy."

I was quickly following where he was leading. "So by making your own islands, you're creating a footprint and presence. You get to spread your military here and it's left to the treaties Taiwan and the Philippines made with the US to stop you, which would draw China and the US into direct conflict. Essentially . . . World War Three."

"I knew you'd catch on," he said. "As you can imagine, this facility cost a great deal of money and the PRC is most interested in its preservation. They will throw the might of their military to defend it, should it come to that."

"If the US finds out what you have here, we *will* destroy it."

"They are welcome to try. America's military is spread thin and focused on religious jihadists whose fondest desire is to blow themselves up." He rolled his eyes. "They've been a convenient distraction while we've been building up and expanding our military capabilities."

"Why are you involved?" I asked. "You're a businessman, not a politician or military."

"Yes, but I had access to what was needed. Foreign intellectual property. The networks I built and control handle eighty percent of the Internet traffic going into and out of China. Not much gets by me."

We'd been walking down the nearest aisle and I glanced up to see the miles of cable going into the ceiling. Air brushed my face, a constant current, and the chill in the air made the hairs stand up on my arms.

Lu finally turned into another hallway that led to a room that was so reminiscent of the Vigilance control center, it was eerie.

"Surprised?" Lu asked with a smile. He leaned closer. "I have extremely good sources."

I felt too small in the cavernous room, and I was the only female. All the workers—and there were about a dozen of them—were clad identically in white jumpsuits. Several eyes glanced my way, but no one approached at first. Then I saw a man who was dressed differently catch Lu's eye and begin walking toward us. He wore black slacks and a white button-down shirt.

When he reached us, he executed a smart bow at Lu and greeted him in Chinese. Lu's reply was genial, though his bow wasn't as crisp or as deep.

"China, may I introduce Zhang? He'll be hosting my next . . . demonstration."

"This way, please," Zhang said. His face showed zero interest or emotion, just an automaton doing as he was told.

We followed him into an office similar to my own, with eight screens lining one wall. I glanced at them with interest . . . and felt my stomach drop to my feet.

Granny was on all of them. She was in her duplex, puttering around the kitchen. In the senior center, chatting with a group of friends. Watching television with her feet up and holding a bottle of her favorite beer. Laughing while holding a hand of cards. Reading one of the hundreds of Harlequins I'd sent her.

Tears sprang to my eyes as realization set in. I swallowed hard, but my throat was dry.

"What are you doing?" I managed to ask, my voice only just above a whisper.

"Surely a woman of your intellect doesn't need an answer to that question," Lu said. He clasped his hands behind his back and managed to look both disdainful and sympathetic. "I know how very important your . . . Granny . . . is to you. Didn't you just rush to her aid when she had a mild heart attack? I must say, I was very impressed with your devotion."

Oh God. I'd led Lu right to her. The blood left my head in a rush and I stumbled. Lu grabbed my arm, keeping me upright, but I jerked away as my vision cleared.

"Don't touch me," I gritted out.

"I understand the feminine temperament is fragile," he said. "Do let me know if you need to sit down. I'm sure we can accommodate you."

His false sincerity was insulting, and meant to be such, I had no doubt.

"I'm fine. What do you want with my grandmother?"

"It's very simple, but I've found simple is really the most effective. So long as you work for us, do as I say, your beloved Granny is free to live her life to the fullest. However, you refuse to do what's requested of you, Granny will be the one to suffer.

"Of course we'll have to take it easy at first," he continued. "We wouldn't want her frail heart to give out too soon. You'll have a front-row seat, of course. Perhaps even get to speak to her, so you can tell her

274

exactly how you are the one responsible for putting her through pain and misery."

"She's an old lady who's never hurt a soul. Why would you do such a thing? You can hurt me, not her." I couldn't even begin to imagine my grandma being put through any kind of pain at the hands of this bastard.

"Quite easily. You see, *you* are much more valuable to me than she is, and she is valuable to *you*. It's all a matter of leverage, a concept I'm sure you're familiar with, I have no doubt."

I decided to try a different tack. "You realize my disappearance isn't going to just go unnoticed. I'm pretty damn important. They're going to look for me and eventually they'll tie you to me. Your bank accounts will be frozen, your assets seized, you may even lose your company."

He laughed—actually laughed—at me.

"Americans are such idealists. Truly, if it wasn't so much to my benefit, I'd feel sorry for you." He stepped closer until he was in my space. I fought the urge to step back. "How do you think I found out about you in the first place?"

My mind didn't want to put that two and two together, but I had no choice. "The mole," I said. "The mole in the NSA. They work for you."

"The NSA, you say? Hmm. I'm glad that's what you think. But to get to my point . . . no one is coming to look for you, China. You've been sold out. Even someone as valuable to your government as you is ultimately expendable."

If my lungs weren't automatically made to inflate, receiving signals from my brain stem so that I kept breathing, the shock I felt would've stopped everything. I was amazed it didn't. What Lu said couldn't possibly be true. He was lying. He had to be. It was the oldest trick in the book. Take away my hope. Without hope, what point was there in not cooperating and making things as easy on myself as possible?

I had to buy time. Surely that was it. Gammin would be calling in the cavalry any day.

And they'd attack China to save me?

The truth was plain to see, but I didn't want to.

"I need some time," I said. "And giving me something I can actually eat would be nice. Starving me to death isn't part of your plan, is it? Because I really don't work well on an empty stomach."

"Of course. Some food and rest will no doubt help you see things more clearly."

I cast one last look at my granny, who had no idea she had been spied on or was being spied on. All because of me. Just like when Mia had been threatened. I was toxic to those I loved. How long before I was responsible for someone's death?

Lu didn't take me back; he summoned two other guys to do it, one in front and one behind me. They were both just as big as the earlier guards. I had no chance of overpowering them or getting away. The place was a labyrinth and I knew I'd only seen a fraction of it.

What I *did* notice was the badges they scanned to open all the locked doors. They wore them attached to their chests and they had fractal codes imprinted on the front.

They deposited me in my room without a fuss and left, but I wasn't about to go to sleep.

I searched the room again, now with different goals in mind. And this time, I didn't come up empty-handed.

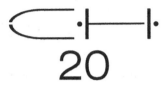

20

"This is taking too long," Jackson complained. "It's been four days, and we're nowhere near closer to finding her than we were before."

"We've narrowed it down to the South China Sea," Clark replied. "There are hundreds of islands and man-made islands there. It takes time, even with satellites."

"I've given you over five million dollars to get information, and you've got it narrowed down to three and a half million square miles. Awesome job."

Clark bit back the sharp reply. Jackson was used to getting results fast, and if he couldn't get results from someone else, he'd do it himself. But in this situation, he was powerless, which was why he was currently pacing Clark's office in Vigilance.

Clark hadn't wanted to let him in, but there was no reason not to anymore. He was the one who'd written the algorithm that was the heart of Vigilance. He knew of the program's existence. He might as well plant his ass in a chair and help find China, which was currently what everyone there was doing.

"How are Granny and Mia?" Clark asked.

"They're enjoying an unexpected vacation to my chalet in Vail. With an abundance of security."

At least that was one less thing to worry about, Clark thought. Money had its uses.

Roscoe suddenly burst into the office. "I've got a lead," he blurted, breathless. The man looked like he hadn't slept in days, which was how he usually looked, but today he had an added manic gleam in his eye that bespoke sleepless nights and a fervent obsession. "Here." He slapped a satellite image down on Clark's desk. Jackson was there in an instant, looking over his shoulder.

"What is it?"

"It's a man-made island near the Spratly Islands," Roscoe said. "But rather than an airstrip, they built a port. Two days ago, a cargo ship docked there. It unloaded minimal cargo, then left."

"Why do you think that's where she is?" Jackson asked.

"Because we've been tracing this ship through the webs of ownership ties. It goes through a shitload of government agencies and finally ends with Wang Heu, second cousin to the president of the PRC."

"And?"

"And his brother-in-law is Lu."

Jackpot.

"Good work," Clark said. "I take it you've got coordinates and intel for me?"

"Already uploaded." Roscoe shifted from one foot to another. "So . . . are you going to go get her?"

Clark glanced up from the photo. "You bet your ass, I am."

Roscoe grinned, relief crossing his face. "Good luck," he said, and left the office.

"I'm coming, too," Jackson said.

Clark sighed. He should've known lover boy wasn't going to be left behind. A pang of something too close to jealousy twinged in the center of his chest, but he ignored it.

"Fine. But bring your checkbook. What the Chinese lack in loyalty, they make up for in their love for the almighty dollar."

It took another six excruciating hours to gather more satellite photos of the island and get the equipment and people Clark needed to do what shouldn't be done. Gammin had made that abundantly clear via teleconference when he'd been told China's location.

"We cannot jeopardize relations with the Chinese right now," Gammin argued. "The trade deal is still on the table and the Treasury Department is pushing hard to be able to sanction companies engaged in theft of intellectual property. We cannot accuse them of *abducting* an American citizen."

"But that's exactly what they did," Clark retorted. "Your leak that we *still* haven't found despite months of trying told him all about her, including how to find her. We owe it to her not to leave her hanging."

"She understood the risks when she took the job."

"Did she?" Clark asked, struggling to keep a grip on his anger. "Did she know she'd become a target for hostile foreign governments? Because I bet she just thought she was doing a service to her country, a job no one else wanted or was qualified to do."

Gammin said nothing.

Clark moved closer to the screen on his office wall where Gammin was doing his best impression of a poker face.

"Do you have any idea what could happen to her? If she doesn't cooperate? Or if she does cooperate, but then outlives her usefulness? Have you ever seen a Chinese labor camp? Or one of their prisons? She wouldn't last a week. This is what you're consigning her to."

"The US Consulate will be able to help her—"

"The US Consulate doesn't know of her existence!" His anger and frustration was near to boiling over and Clark was bitterly reminded of why he'd gone freelance in the first place. Fucking politicians. They wanted you to put your life on the line for them, but when the chips were down, they'd sell you out in a second to save their own worthless skin.

"You do not have authorization to conduct any operation on Chinese soil," Gammin said. "Is that clear?"

They glared at each other in an unspoken war of wills.

"Yes. Perfectly clear," Clark bit out.

The transmission cut off with nothing further from Gammin. Not that it was a big loss. Spineless political hack.

Of course, that hadn't stopped Clark from putting together a team and plan to rescue his partner. The ramifications if he didn't succeed wouldn't be pretty, and probably were also grim if he did. Not that he cared—he could take care of himself. But he felt he had to be up front with Coop.

"Listen, this is not going to be a sanctioned op," he said to Jackson as he checked his weapons and ammunition. "The guys going with me are all ex-military and trained for this sort of thing. They still do it for a number of reasons, money being the primary one—they have to make a living somehow. Some also do it for the adrenaline, others because it's just who they are. They're warriors, soldiers, and that's all they know how to be."

"So what are you saying?" Jackson asked, watching him strap a pistol to his ankle.

"I'm saying, if we get caught, no one's coming to rescue the rescuers."

"What about the people in charge of this place? They don't want to get China back?"

"Gammin says no."

Clark's phone buzzed and he glanced at the screen. "Time to go, Coop. Last chance to sit this one out. I can't promise your safe return."

"I didn't ask you to."

Jackson felt like a fish out of water as he sat on the speeding boat among eight other men, all dressed in fatigues and armed to the teeth. All he'd been able to do was provide the money to hire the transport to get them this far. Clark's contacts had provided the equipment and the boat. They'd given him a Kevlar vest and a set of fatigues, as well as a pistol.

"Just don't point it at any of us," Clark had said. Jackson had bit back a smartass retort. He didn't want to piss off the man who was risking his life to rescue China.

But what he *could* do was get into Lu's system and help the team find China. Hopefully.

He checked his satellite uplink and toggled the screen. *Kuan. You there?*

The reply was quick. *Yep. Their network security perimeter is a rip-off of Cisco's latest. And not ripped off very well. That's the problem with these bloodsuckers. They don't understand the shit they steal.*

Preach to the choir later. What did you find?

An image appeared on the screen and with a toggle of a switch, Jackson sent it to the tablets each of the men in the boat was holding.

"Building schematic," he called out so they all could hear him.

Did you find where China's being held? he typed.

Working on it.

Patch me in. Two's better than one. He waited for the link, then connected through Kuan.

Done.

Clark was busy talking to the men and drawing on the screen, which appeared simultaneously on all the other tablets. It was a bunch of military-speak, assignments, and planning. Jackson listened with half an ear as he worked. Clark had been less than forthcoming about their exit strategy, especially if they were detected. His actual words had been, "If they chase us in the middle of the South China Sea, we're totally fucked." So Jackson thought he'd better have a backup plan. Just in case.

When they were two miles out, the boat slowed and stopped. Nerves attacked Jackson's gut, but he steeled himself. Considering what China was going through, this was nothing. By now, she probably believed no help was coming.

"This is where we part ways, Coop," Clark said. "We need you and the hacker buddy controlling the tech. That diversion needs to happen so their quick response force is occupied. That'll give us the opportunity to get in."

"Got it."

"And don't forget the doors."

"I said I got it."

Clark hesitated, then added, "We'll get her, Coop. I promise."

Their gazes met and held. Jackson gave a slight nod. He'd harbored suspicions that Clark wasn't as indifferent to China as he pretended. But whether those were ties of loyalty to a colleague and partner . . . or something more . . . he didn't know. And right now, he didn't give a damn. Just so he cared enough to get China back.

"We'll radio when we're in position."

Jackson watched as the men piled into two black rubber boats. They were silent, no further talking among themselves. They had enough weaponry and ammunition on them to take down a small town. In this case, he just hoped it was enough to rescue the woman he loved.

The island was built on a natural reef in the sea, and as they drew closer, they heard an alarm sound. Clark stiffened, waiting. The waves slapped against the side of the boat. The men watched him, waiting for the word to either continue . . . or abort.

Lights went on at the port and there was a flurry of activity. As Coop had promised, the fake alarm drew away the security force in the opposite direction. There would still be some left, but they could be handled.

Normally, an op like this would require weeks of planning, training, and rehearsal. They didn't have that kind of time. Luckily, they'd worked together a lot, knew each other's moods and body language. And their training was impeccable. But even with all of that, it might not be enough. Clark hoped luck would be on their side.

They were abnormally silent as they disembarked and stowed the boats. The schematic Coop had given them said there was an entrance on the southwest side of the compound, though "compound" seemed inadequate to describe the size and complexity of the facility. It was a behemoth, with most of it underground.

Clark took point, deliberately setting aside his worry for China and his trepidation about doing an op with no rehearsal. Emotions didn't help at this point, they only hindered. Achieve the objective, neutralize any threats, retrieve the package, extract safely—all without alerting the whole facility to their presence. Piece of cake.

Right.

Coop and his buddy were as good as their word because the door was unlocked when they got there. From the schematic, they were entering the part of the facility most likely to have living quarters. It made sense. This far out from the mainland, it wasn't as though the employees could commute.

There was a bit of static in Clark's ear, then he heard Coop's voice. "The tech inside is state of the art, which worked in our favor. They keep track of their employees via facial recognition. There's only one person there listed as Unknown."

China.

Clark sent back one click of his mic. *Message received.*

"Third sublevel, sixth corridor on the right, fourth room on the left."

He sent another click and Coop went silent.

Two men peeled off to watch their exit route, leaving six. The corridor was deserted . . . and hot. At least eighty-five degrees. Fifty more feet with no interference. Clark hoped their luck held.

They reached the corner and he took a breath, letting it out as he peered around, his rifle held at the ready. He kept his eyes straight ahead and waited for the pressure of a palm on his back, signaling that his six was clear and they could keep going.

He moved quickly. There was an elevator, but stairs were preferable. They were also clear of threats. Two more men peeled off for a safe retreat, leaving four for the hostage team.

Clark's heart rate was beating double-time, the adrenaline in his veins giving him the heightened awareness he needed. Especially when he emerged from the stairwell to see a guard. The guard looked shocked to see him, which worked to Clark's advantage. Before he could bring his weapon up, Clark had plugged three rounds into his center mass. He went down.

Time to move before more arrived.

"Presence is announced," Clark said in his mic. "Gloves are off."

They made it down the corridor and took the sixth one on the right. Two more guards went down in a flurry of bullets. Fourth room on the left. The pressure on Clark's back gave him the go-ahead . . . and he kicked in the door.

He'd been expecting to find China, and he wasn't disappointed. But what he saw horrified him.

"Holy shit," he breathed.

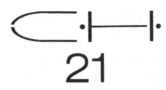

21

It took me thirty minutes to find what I needed in the room. Once I had my supplies, I got to work. Of course, it took hours, and even then, I wasn't finished. Plus, I had to keep stopping when people came, hiding my stuff underneath the mattress.

Food—normal food—arrived. At least, I hoped it was normal. It appeared to be a turkey sandwich, but I didn't eat the turkey—just the bread, lettuce, and tomato. No way was I eating any more meat they brought.

I worked until I couldn't keep my eyes open. I had to start over four times. I didn't even bother changing out of my dress, just hiked it up so I could sit cross-legged on the floor. I slept for a few hours, then woke up and went back to work.

There was a knock at the door and breakfast was delivered. A bagel and a banana. Not exactly a buffet of options. I worked faster because I fully expected my stay of execution to be coming to an end. And I was right.

I slid the piece of laminate into the cleavage of my dress as another knock sounded. I pushed my glasses up my nose and got to my feet as the door opened. My limbs were stiff and I winced as feeling started coming back into my right foot.

It was the same two men who'd escorted me back to my room. I followed them to the same place I'd been last night. Lu was waiting, wearing a freshly pressed suit, sitting behind a modern glass desk, and drinking tea from a fragile, porcelain cup.

"Good morning," he said. "Have a seat. I was just checking up on a few things."

I sat down, glancing to where he gestured. It was Granny again, but this time I was prepared for the sight of her. I steeled myself, looking at all the screens and feeling my chest tighten. Then one of the screens caught my eye. I looked closer, then let out a slow breath, relief flooding through me.

"I take it you have made your decision," Lu continued.

I nodded. "Yes, I did."

He smiled. "Excellent. I thought you might see it my way."

"Then you're going to be disappointed," I said. "I'm not going to enable this facility to position itself as Big Brother of the entire planet, nor am I going to ignore the fact that doing so would also likely instigate a series of domino-like events that would result in World War Three."

The smile had long since fled from his face. "So you are going to consign your beloved grandmother to pain and agony rather than do my bidding."

"My Granny is safe and sound," I said, praying I was right. "And I'm betting you have no idea where she is. These videos are old." I gestured to the screens. "From before I even went to see her. So threatening me with hurting her isn't going to work."

Lu's expression was hard, his eyes cold as he watched me. "You are very astute," he said. "I had hoped it would not come to this."

I lifted my chin despite the chill that went through me. "One person's life isn't worth what you're asking me to do."

"Well. I suppose we will see exactly how far you're willing to go for that belief."

Not exactly comforting words, but I'd expected nothing less.

He nodded at the guards. "Take her to Garrison Six. Encourage her to see my point of view."

I sprang up from my seat, yanking the piece of laminate from my dress, and ran to the nearest door. They all had the same scanner next to them. I slammed my palm on it, the laminate in my hand. The blue lasers scanned my palm, highlighting the marks I prayed I'd made correctly. I waited, holding my breath, and it was just as I was hauled away from the scanner that it turned green.

I let out my breath and turned to see Lu on his feet.

"What did you do?" he asked. I smiled. "Tell me! What is that? Bring that here, whatever she has."

The guard pried the piece from my hand and dragged me with him like a rag doll as he took it to Lu. Lu looked at it, turning it over in his hand, then held it up to the light.

"What is this?" he asked me.

"That's for me to know and you to, well, I'm sure you can fill in the blank."

His lips thinned. "Get her out of my sight."

The guards were none too gentle this time, and I wasn't taken back to my room. I was taken to a frigid, moldy cell with concrete walls and floor, and nothing in it but a hole in the ground. I didn't want to think about what I was supposed to do in that little hole.

The guy holding me gave me a shove and I stumbled, falling to the floor. It was damp and dirty and I cringed in disgust.

"The boss said we should persuade you," Guard A said. It was the first time I'd heard him speak.

"I think leaving me here to consider my options would be an excellent start," I quickly replied. "It's quite uncomfortable and unsanitary."

I didn't want to consider the germs I was sure were currently crawling all over me.

The guard grinned. "I think we can do a little better."

The blow hit before I could prepare, a hard kick in my side that hurt so badly, I couldn't draw breath to scream. It burned inside, like a fire that wanted to consume me.

I was yanked up by my ponytail, my feet scrambling to try to stand. My glasses fell off, clattering to the floor. One arm I wrapped around my middle, the other instinctively raised to try to free my hair. I caught sight of the fist flying toward my face too late to do anything but suck in a breath.

It hit my cheek with the force of a two-by-four, pain exploding in my face and radiating through my head. My eye felt as though it was going to pop from its socket. Darkness clouded my vision and I fought to remain conscious as my head sagged. He held my arms behind me, pain enveloping my shoulders as my weight dragged down.

There was a punch to my stomach, then another, until I was retching, my head hurting so badly it felt as though it was going to fall off my neck. I tasted blood.

"P-please," I stammered, feeling blood and saliva trickle from my mouth. "Please s-s-stop."

The guard holding me spoke. "Enough. She's little. It won't take much to damage her. He'll kill us if we do that."

I was abruptly dropped to the floor, hitting my knees and head on the concrete. Hair covered my face, my ponytail long gone. I heard the door open, then close with a clang of finality.

My entire body hurt and my face was bleeding and beginning to swell. I could feel it. I didn't know how I was going to go another round of that. There was a sharp pain in my chest every time I drew a breath. I'd never been in such agonizing pain in my life.

◆ ◆ ◆

I was jerked from unconsciousness by the slam of the door against the wall. Instinct took over and I curled into as tight a ball as I could, tears leaking from my eyes. They were back. They were going to beat me again. I wasn't some kind of badass. I would cry and beg and probably pee myself.

"Holy shit."

I heard the words, but didn't process them. Hands touched me and I whimpered, cringing away.

"Please don't beat me again," I begged, hating myself even as I said the words. I should be stronger, hold out longer, but I hurt so badly . . .

"Shh, it's okay. I've got you. You're going to be okay."

Tentatively, I looked up. In the dark, with only one good eye and no glasses, all I could see was a black shape. A man. He leaned closer and I could see. His face was painted in black grease but his eyes . . . his eyes were the pure blue of the summer sky.

"Clark?" I was afraid to hope, afraid I was just hallucinating.

"Yeah, baby, it's me. Now let's get you out of here."

He was exceedingly gentle as he lifted me in his arms and I heard him saying things about a "package" and "non-ambulatory," but I was in too much pain to make sense of it.

I clung to Clark, terrified he'd leave me. I could taste blood mixed with tears and saliva as I rambled nearly incoherently through swollen lips, begging him not to put me down.

"Shh, I'm not going to leave you. Trust me. I'd never leave you."

There was something really loud and Clark turned fast. Gunfire. It had to be. Then it was all around. I was shaking with fear, burying my head in Clark's neck. His hold on me was tight enough to hurt, but I didn't make a sound.

Men were shouting, then we were moving again. More gunfire, then shouting. "Clear!" I prayed and held on, gritting my teeth as each step Clark took sent stabs of pain through me.

Fresh air hit my nostrils and we were moving fast. Gunfire came after us as Clark ran. I finally chanced a look up and saw as he climbed into a rubber boat.

"Go go go!"

The boat's engine revved and water sprayed. Clark crouched down, covering me with his body as gunfire pinged around us.

"They're in pursuit," someone yelled out.

Dread consumed me. They were going to catch us. Kill us. The rescue would be short-lived.

Clark was talking, but into a mic by his mouth. Then he yelled something about a secondary extract. I didn't understand what was going on. Everything was noise and chaos, water and the rip of the wind as we raced through the waves.

Suddenly, the gunfire stopped and the wind was coming from above, tearing at my hair. The noise was overwhelming. The boat gave a burst of speed and we shot upward, then stopped so abruptly that Clark nearly lost his balance. The wind was gone and so was the water, then the noise level suddenly dropped. A light came on.

"China, can you hear me? Talk to me."

I couldn't move, not yet. I was wet and shaking and couldn't think straight. Had I been rescued? Or was this some elaborate hallucination?

"You're safe. Talk to me. Say something." He pulled back and his words penetrated the fog in my brain.

I tipped my head back, trying to see him. When I could finally see him, I heard him suck in a breath. "I'm okay," I said, my voice a hoarse rasp.

"You are not fucking okay," he said, brushing my wet hair back from my face. His fingers softly brushed my swollen cheek. "I'm going to kill him."

"My chest hurts," I managed to say.

That got his attention. "Okay, baby, I'll take care of it. Just hold on." He stood, lifting me up, and pain rocked me again. I whimpered, my eyes squeezed shut and pressing my lips closed so I wouldn't scream.

We were moving again, then I heard a man speak.

"Thank God. You got her."

The relief was unmistakable, as was the voice.

"Jackson?"

"Give her to me," he said.

"Don't be an ass," Clark retorted. "She's hurt and in shock. She needs a medic. Transferring her to you will only increase her pain."

"She's hurt? What's wrong with her?"

I could hear the worry and I wanted to reassure Jackson that I was okay, but it was all I could do not to make oh-God-I'm-hurting-so-much noises.

We were moving again, then I was being carefully laid down on a stretcher. I looked around with my one good eye. The other was swollen shut. I saw Clark on one side of me and Jackson on the other. They looked so good, tears began leaking from the corners of my eyes.

"I can't believe you came for me," I managed. "I hoped, but it just seemed . . . impossible."

"Shh, don't try to talk," Jackson said, taking my hand in his. His face was pale and drawn with worry.

A man with a stethoscope around his neck appeared in my line of vision. "Step back," he ordered. "I need space to work."

Both Clark and Jackson reluctantly moved away. The man above me smiled kindly. "It's going to be all right. I know you're in pain. Can you tell me where?"

I haltingly told him where I hurt and how I'd gotten that way. His face looked grave.

"Okay, I'm going to give you some medication for the pain, and I don't want you to worry. Try to relax."

Medicine sounded wonderful and I didn't utter a peep when he put the IV in. It barely registered on my pain scale. Perspective, I suppose.

Things grew even fuzzier and I saw Clark and Jackson, still hovering. I managed a smile, or what I attempted to be a smile, and held out a hand to them. Jackson took it while Clark hung back.

"I want to go home," I said, blinking lids that seemed much heavier than usual.

"You bet. You're going home. And you'll be better soon."

"Did it blow up?" I asked. Jackson just looked confused. "The data center," I said, struggling to form the words through numb lips. "I uploaded fractal code to change the cooling system from Celsius to Fahrenheit. The cooling systems should've turned off."

"I don't know—"

"Yeah," Clark interrupted. "It blew as we were bugging out."

"Good." I swallowed and blinked again. "Where are we?"

"On a *Chinook*," Clark said. "Heading to the Philippines."

Philippines. That was good. Anything not Chinese was good.

It took longer to open my eyes this time. The doctor was still working on me but I didn't pay attention to him. I watched Clark and Jackson, who were both watching me. Except I felt happy and they both looked very intense.

I was about to ask them what the problem was, but then there was nothing.

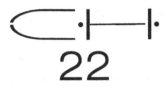

22

I had two cracked ribs, a fractured cheekbone, multiple bruises that made my torso black and blue, broken blood vessels that had turned the white of my eye red, and a swollen and bruised face that made it impossible for me to look in the mirror. Not that I could see very well. I'd lost my backup glasses in that cell.

The doctor kept saying how "lucky" I was. I'd suffered no internal injuries to my organs or bleeding, which surprised him, given my size. If I had, it was likely I would've died before I'd been rescued.

I tried to feel grateful, but all I felt was pain.

Jackson hadn't left my side since they'd brought me into the hospital. He'd insisted on being there for the X-rays and helping me get cleaned up, washing my face with warm water and a cloth.

"How long has it been since you slept?" I asked him as he rearranged the pillows underneath my head. The words came out slurred, my lips partially swollen and split.

"It doesn't matter," he replied, picking up a plastic cup of water with a straw and holding it to my lips. "Drink. You need water."

I obediently drank. "When can we go home?"

"You shouldn't be moved yet," he said. "You need time to rest."

Tears filled my eyes. "Please," I said. "Please take me home. I want to go home."

His gaze searched my face, then he nodded. "Absolutely. I'll make it happen."

Jackson was as good as his word. In a few hours, I was being loaded onto a private jet, stretcher and all, and though I kept telling him I could walk, he refused to let me.

"If I'm taking you home, then you're going under my rules," he said.

A doctor and nurse came along, which I thought was overkill, not to mention an imposition on them.

"They can stay overnight in a hotel and I'll send them back tomorrow," Jackson assured me. "Your health is the most important thing right now."

I didn't remember much after that. The doctor kept me in a foggy state with pain medication and sedatives. Jackson sat in a leather chair next to me and the few times I woke, he had fallen asleep. His eyes had dark circles under them and he had several days' growth of beard on his jaw. I reached out and took his hand in mine, then fell back asleep.

Jackson insisted on taking me to his place and I didn't put up too much of a fight, especially when he explained that Granny and Mia were enjoying his French chalet in Vail, complete with housekeeper, butler, and chef . . . and a dozen armed security guards.

I finally got to walk as I refused to let him carry me up the stairs like some kind of pathetic attempt to recreate the scene from *Gone with the Wind*. Lance was ahead of us, wringing his hands and fussing like a mother hen over me as Jackson steered me toward his bedroom. He'd looked stricken with shock when he'd first set eyes on me.

"Are you hungry? You must be hungry. What would you like? Soup? Yes, I bet soup would be best. Nice and warm, hearty and healthy. I'll be back with soup." And off Lance went.

I chuckled a bit as I shucked my shoes and climbed into bed. "I must really look like hell if he's running off to cook soup for me. Just tell him not to put kale in it, please."

"Got it," Jackson said with a smile. "No kale." He tucked me in, brushed a kiss to my forehead, and followed Lance downstairs.

It felt so good to be in a real bed again, and not just any bed, but with Jackson. And to have normal clothes. He'd given me one of his shirts, which I was loath to change out of. So we laid in bed, ate soup and crunchy bread, then I made him take off his shirt and curled up against his chest, resting my uninjured cheek on his warm skin.

"Tell me what happened," I said. "How'd you find me, rescue me, get away?" It was all a foggy memory to me, feeling more as if it had happened to someone else than to me.

"Maybe you should start," he said, his fingers combing slowly through my hair. "You got into my thumb drive."

I twisted to look up at him. "Was I not supposed to?"

"You were supposed to take it to Lance."

"Well, it wasn't as though you left detailed instructions," I groused. "And what the heck were you doing with that kind of information anyway? It could've gotten you killed."

"Says the woman who blackmailed the most powerful man in the world," he gently retorted. "That wasn't what I'd intended to do with the information."

"Then what was your plan?"

"What was important, was *how* I got that information on the senator's supposed suicide," he said. "But it's all right now. I bartered that for those helicopters that got us out of the South China Sea."

"Bartered with . . . ?"

He winked. "The same man you blackmailed."

"I didn't realize you were on such close terms with the president."

"He and I have a business relationship. In this case, I was more than happy to let him know how I came by that information."

"Which was?"

"Gammin," he said.

My jaw dropped. "You're kidding me."

Jackson shook his head. "He had it on his home system that I hacked into. The president has known for a while that those files were out there somewhere. Gammin told him he was trying to find them, so he could destroy them and protect the president. He was grateful to hear of Gammin's duplicity."

"Grateful enough to send American helicopters into disputed Chinese waters?" I asked.

"Yep."

"I guess it helps to have friends in very high places."

His response was to kiss my forehead again. "Anything for you."

"I thought the president had betrayed me. That he'd sent those men after me."

"No. Gammin did that. But I don't think we'll need to worry about him anymore."

I cuddled closer, inhaling the scent of him. I'd been afraid I'd never be in his arms like this again. "Hold me tighter," I whispered.

"I don't want to hurt you."

"You won't."

His arms pressed me closer to him. It was quiet, save for the low volume of the television playing a rerun of *Castle*. I could hear his heart beating underneath my ear, the slow, steady sound as reassuring as the sun rising in the east.

"Kuan helped, too," he said. "Told us Lu had taken you. Your crew at Vigilance found the island. Clark put together the strike team. Kuan and I took care of the technical details to help them get in and out." He paused. "It was a team effort."

Tears stung my eyes. All those people had gone to such trouble and effort just to get me back? It was illogical for them to put themselves at such risk for me alone, yet the effect on my emotions was . . . overwhelming.

"You have a lot of friends, China," Jackson said. "They all care about you."

I swallowed the lump in my throat, but it still took a few minutes before I could trust my voice to speak.

"Did your lawyers clear up everything with the DoJ?" I asked.

"The preemptive pardon pretty much took care of it," he said. "The press had a feeding frenzy and the president will definitely pay a political price. But it took care of the problem. The stock has stopped its freefall. The DoJ has closed its investigation."

I had a surge of satisfaction. It wasn't often that the good guys won the day and the bad guys got what was coming to them.

"I love you," I said, looking up into his eyes. It was suddenly imperative that I tell him. This time, there was no threat of imminent arrest or separation, but if anything, the past few weeks had shown me that you had to seize the moment . . . or the moment would pass you by and might never come again. And regretting something I *didn't* do seemed much worse than regretting something I *had* done.

"I love you, too," he said, his lips curving into a soft smile. "And as soon as you're all better, I look forward to showing you how much."

We were as close as it was possible to be, which was exactly what I needed. And I fell asleep with Jackson's arms holding me, his breath stirring my hair, and his scent all around.

It took another two weeks before I went back to work. I wore jeans and my *Sunnydale Blood Drive* T-shirt. I was still sore and the catalogue of my injuries—from the gunshot wound to the cracked ribs—was putting a big dent in my pretax health cafeteria plan. But I was alive, so I didn't complain.

"Welcome back, boss," Roscoe said, bursting into my office, looking like a somewhat-cheerful Eeyore. Derrick, Mazie, and the whole gang trailed after him. One person was carrying cake, another had several bottles of champagne. They set the cake on my desk. "We're glad you're not dead."

"Thank you for that, Roscoe," I said. "As am I."

"We're breaking the no-alcohol-at-work rule," Mazie said. "But I thought this deserved champagne." Several people opened bottles, their corks making a festive *pop!*

"Chocolate cake, cream cheese icing, with fudge sauce on the side, and vanilla ice cream," Derrick said. "Did we miss anything?"

My smile was so wide, it hurt. "That's . . . incredible. Thank you all so much. I wouldn't be here if not for your work to find me. I don't have the right words to tell you how very grateful I am." Indeed, even those words felt so inadequate. But I didn't know what else to say.

"Raises speak for themselves," Roscoe said with a shrug. There were chuckles around the room.

"A toast," Mazie said. "To the best boss ever. Clever, smart, beautiful, and the instigator of Casual Every Day."

"Hear hear!" the crowd responded, raising glasses all around.

My face flushed at the effusive compliments and I pushed my new glasses up my nose. "Wow, you guys must really want that raise," I said when it had gone quiet again.

More laughter, though I didn't see what I'd said that was funny.

"Time for cake," Roscoe said, brandishing a knife. Soon everyone was chatting, happily munching on cake and drinking champagne, spilling out of my office into the hallway outside.

I scanned the crowd, noticing one face very conspicuously absent. Clark.

"He's not here," Mazie said in an undertone, sidling up to me.

"I don't know what you're talking about," I said, taking a bite of my cake.

She looked at me, a smile playing about her mouth. "Of course not."

Being the boss, I did have to wrap up the party and tell everyone to get back to work, but I stood at the door and thanked everyone as they left. I was surprised at the warm smiles and even the hugs I received in return. I wasn't that thrilled about the hugs, but thought it would be rude not to accept the embraces.

I had so much work to catch up on that I was there long after I should've left to go home. My cell rang at about eight o'clock.

"I'm sorry," I said by way of greeting Jackson. "I'm just swamped."

"I know you are, but you don't want to overdo it," he said. "There will be plenty of time tomorrow."

"Okay, okay, I know. I'll be home soon." It was slightly odd that that popped out of my mouth. Technically, my home was where I paid the rent. Yet, I'd just said it in reference to Jackson's house. Hmm.

I had to promise two more times before he'd let me go and when I finally hung up, there was a warm feeling inside. *Someone who loved me was waiting for me to come home.*

I logged off my computer and turned out the lights. The skeleton crew was down on the floor but it was deserted up by my office. I locked my door and turned to head down the darkened corridor to the elevator . . . and nearly jumped out of my skin.

"Clark!" My hand flew to my throat, the shock and surprise—as well as a bloom of pleasure inside—made my heart race. "You startled me."

He moved closer, well within my eighteen inches of personal space. "Sorry I missed your party today."

I swallowed, suddenly nervous. I hadn't seen him since he'd carried me out of that cell. My memories were vague, but I'd had dreams about it since then. Dreams of him touching me and calling me "baby." I'd chalked it up to too many meds. The idea of Clark calling me "baby" was laughable.

"It's okay," I said, releasing a breath. "I know you're busy. Though we should probably schedule a time to debrief, for the record." I realized I was pleased to see him, to talk to him. My smile wasn't even my fake one.

"Sure."

There was an awkward pause. I couldn't see his face in the dark, whereas mine was illuminated in a shard of light. I pushed my glasses up again.

"Thank you," I said at last. "I haven't had a chance to say that, to you or to the other men who rescued me. You put your lives on the line and . . . I'm exceedingly grateful."

"Your face is still bruised," he said, ignoring my thanks. He lifted a hand toward me. I stopped breathing for a moment, but he dropped his arm before his skin could touch mine.

"I'm actually much better," I said into what felt like an uncomfortable silence. "The ribs aren't causing me pain anymore, and the hardware the doctor put inside my mouth to stabilize my cheekbone has done its job. I expect I'll make a full recovery without any lingering issues." The nightmares were another story.

"You shouldn't have been hurt in the first place," he said, his voice laced with bitterness. "I should've been there. Shouldn't have let you leave my house."

I frowned. "I fail to see how you could have forced me to stay," I said. "Not only am I your boss, the abduction of an American citizen by a Chinese businessman on US soil is . . . unprecedented. No one is to blame. It was just an . . . unfortunate incident."

"An unfortunate incident?" he echoed. I nodded. He stepped closer and I had to tip my head to look up at him, but now I could see his face. The stark pain in his eyes made my breath catch.

"Clark . . . I'm not Sayeeda."

The name made him flinch and I instantly regretted saying it.

"You easily could have been," he said. "Nearly were. They weren't gentle with you. Another beating, you would've been dead." His voice was low and filled with emotions I couldn't name. "I can't do this, China," he continued. "Not again. Do you know why I've worked alone for so long?"

I shook my head, words failing me. I couldn't blink, the intent light in his eyes holding my gaze captive.

"Because I don't want to *care*. Caring brings nothing but pain, and guilt, and sadness."

"What are you saying?" Did he mean he cared . . . about *me*? Not just the job?

"I'm resigning," he said. "But I wanted to say good-bye before I left."

My stomach dropped and for a moment, I was speechless. I certainly hadn't expected . . . this.

"Clark . . . I . . . I can understand how you'd be upset—"

"I'm more than fucking upset," he ground out. "I was lazy, and complacent, and you paid the price."

"I have to disagree," I argued, frantically trying to think of how to convince him not to leave. "On the contrary, I think your work at Vigilance has been outstanding. Aside from some possible anger management issues which can easily be addressed with the staff psychiatrist, and perhaps some team-building exercises—"

"Stop," he interrupted. "I've made up my mind."

My throat grew thick and I looked away, blinking rapidly, and gave him a curt nod. "Obviously, it's up to you," I managed. "If you choose to make a decision based on emotions rather than logic—"

"I'm not doing this based on emotion," he interrupted.

"Of course you are. You're afraid."

He stepped closer, my back being pushed to the wall.

"What am I afraid of, China?"

I swallowed hard, tipping my chin to look up at him. I could smell his cologne, the scent bringing back a flood of memory and feelings.

Me in his arms. Hurting. Terrified. My face buried in his neck, smelling the scent of his skin and sweat. The sound of bullets and the taste of my own blood on my tongue. His voice in my ear. "I'm not going to leave you."

"You're afraid of failure," I blurted. "Afraid that a wrong move will put someone else in jeopardy. And while that's laudable—"

He kissed me.

Clark and I had kissed before, back when it had been him playing a role, and it had been good. But that had been all about seduction and lust. This wasn't.

Need. Longing. Fear. Those were what I felt now, but I didn't know if those were his emotions, or mine.

Time stopped, the world faded, and it was just Clark, his lips on mine, his body pressed against me. His tongue swept inside my mouth, caressing and tasting me like he'd never get enough. His kiss felt urgent, desperate, as though he teetered on the edge of something deep and dark.

His hand cupped my jaw, the roughness of his palm gentle against my cheek. When he finally drew back, he trailed his lips up my injured cheekbone, pressing a kiss to the still-tender skin.

I stared at him, my eyes wide. My thoughts were frozen as I struggled to process what had just happened. Speech was impossible, even if I had an inkling as to what was appropriate to say.

He spoke, his voice a low growl. "If I stay, I will fuck up your life. Guaranteed. You don't want that."

But Vigilance will be losing a very valuable asset. I fought for logic through the morass of emotions clogging my brain. "You—" My voice cracked and I had to clear my throat. "You will be missed."

He looked at me and I couldn't make myself break his gaze. He reached out, grasping the long strands of my ponytail and draping it over my shoulder. "You're special, China, and not just because you're smart. Remember that."

I had that frustration of not having the right words to say what I was feeling, and then my chance was gone. *He* was gone.

I couldn't move for a moment, reality taking too long to sink in. Clark had left, and I'd never get to see him again.

My chest ached, and it wasn't because of my injured ribs.

My cell rang and I glanced at it. Jackson. The man who loved me—who I loved—was waiting for me. At home. I pressed the button.

"Yeah, I was just on my way to the car . . ."

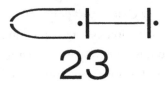

23

President Blane Kirk loosened his tie, sliding it from underneath the collar of his shirt and tossing it on the nearby sofa. The jacket had already been discarded. It was easier here at Camp David. Not quite so formal. Not quite so strict. And not quite so scrutinized. The last reason was why he'd come.

"It's about time."

Blane turned to see his half brother walk in the room. He already had a drink in his hand.

"Thought you were going to make me wait all night," he groused, sprawling on the sofa and propping his booted feet on the walnut coffee table. "Leader of the free world and all."

"It's good to see you too, Kade," Blane said, pouring himself a measure of scotch. He sat in the leather armchair across from his brother. "Sorry I kept you waiting." His dry sarcasm made no impact on Kade though, who just shrugged.

"'s okay. Luckily, you've got pretty damn good booze, brother." Kade raised his glass and winked one clear blue eye, the black brow above curved in a wicked arch. "Thought I deserved to sneak a little. I've been a . . . very . . . good . . . boy."

Blane sighed. His brother's self-assured arrogance wasn't news to him. But then again, he'd earned it. Kade's skills had proven to be very useful over the years. Especially now. In politics there were few who could be trusted absolutely. Blane could count on one hand those who fell into that category.

Trust had proven even more fragile—and valuable—given his ex–chief of staff.

"Did you get the files from Gammin's computer?" he asked.

"Of course," Kade said. "You always ask, as though you doubt my mad skills." He took another drink of his scotch. "Just sorry I couldn't pinpoint the son of a bitch sooner."

"It's my fault. I trusted him. I should've seen that he'd changed. He'd become . . . obsessed with reelection, power . . . the whole nine yards." Blane shook his head. He'd not wanted to see the man Gammin had become. He'd been with Blane for such a long time. A trusted confidante.

"Shame about him selling that chick to the Chinese," Kade said. "Total dick move."

Blane agreed. "I'm glad Cooper came to me. She didn't deserve that."

"Yeah, blackmailing the president takes some major fucking balls."

Blane grimaced. "No kidding." He took another swallow. "You're sure no one knows it was you?"

"Please," Kade snorted. "They think I'm some Taiwanese kid going to MIT. Kuan something or other. She's smart though, gotta hand it to her. If I hadn't caught that bot she hijacked on me, things could've gone way different."

"What bot?"

"Oh, she tracked me, thinking she's all smarter and shit. Had to find a stand-in super quick. Sell it, you know? And she bought it."

"Just so long as nothing leads back to you. The press gives me a hard enough time as it is, having my brother as an adviser. I don't need to give them more ammunition."

"Relax. Think of us as the Kennedy brothers." He tipped his head and made a face. "With*out* the bullet wounds."

Blane's cell rang and he glanced at the screen. Ann. "Hey, babe," he answered.

"Cate won't go to sleep until you sing the song," she sighed. "I've been trying to placate her for fifteen minutes. Do you have time?"

He laughed softly, pleased despite the inconvenience to his wife. "Of course I can sing to her. Put her on." He glanced at Kade.

"Aw, c'mon," Kade said. "I wanna hear a lullaby, too."

Blane flipped a finger his way and Kade grumbled as he pried himself off the couch.

"Fine, but I'm holding the bottle hostage. You have to come beat me at pool if you want it back."

Blane nodded, distracted now that he heard a small voice on the end of the line.

"Daddy?"

As he sang her their bedtime song, he was reminded of why he did what he did. To keep her safe, and all the others like her and Christopher. To give them a better world. And he looked forward to hearing from China Mack on the best way to do that. It seemed his trust in her *hadn't* been misplaced.

ACKNOWLEDGMENTS

Thank you to Melody Guy for your incredible patience and willingness to wade through this manuscript multiple times, positive in your belief that I could make it better. Even when I get my nose out of joint, you love me anyway.

Thank you to my amazing editor, Maria Gomez. You've been an absolute pleasure to work with and your joy is infectious. Always personable, always professional—you're the standard by which all editors should be measured.

My agent, Kevan Lyon, who is always in my corner and has a memory surpassed by none. I have no idea how you do it.

Thank you to my wonderful family, always so patient with my moods—swinging up or down depending on how my manuscript is going. Your love and support mean everything to me.

To the friends who have helped make my life a better and happier place—Leslie Thompson, Marina Adair, Nancy Naigle, Tracy Brogan, Rebecca Zanetti, Jill Sanders, and Catherine Bybee.

To my amazing publishing team at Montlake Romance—"thank you" seems too inadequate for how thankful I am to be a part of Montlake and APub. Anh, Jessica, Susan, Kim . . . and all those behind the scenes that do the cover, the copy, the editing, the proofing, the marketing. You're all stars to me!

ABOUT THE AUTHOR

Tiffany Snow has been reading romance novels since she was too young to be reading romance novels. Born and raised in St. Louis, she attended the University of Missouri in Columbia, earning degrees in history and social studies. Later she worked as an information-technology instructor and consultant. At last, she now has her dream job: writing novels full-time. Married with two wonderful daughters, Tiffany makes her home in Kansas City, Missouri. Visit her website, www.tiffany-snow.com, to keep up with her latest projects.